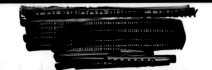

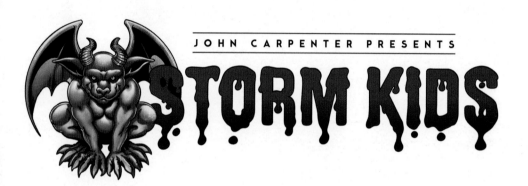

JOHN CARPENTER PRESENTS

STORM KIDS

Series created by
JOHN CARPENTER and **SANDY KING**

STORM KING
COMICS

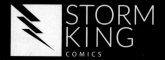

JOHN CARPENTER PRESENTS

STORM KIDS

MONICA BLEUE: A WEREWOLF STORY

Written by STEVE NILES
Art by DAMIEN WORM
Color Assistant ALYZIA ZHERNO
Lettering by JANICE CHIANG
Edited by SANDY KING
Cover art by DAMIEN WORM

Book Design by SEAN SOBCZAK
Title Treatment by JOHN GALATI

Publishers: John Carpenter & Sandy King
Managing Editor: Sean Sobczak
Storm King Office Coordinator: Antwan Johnson
Publicity by Sphinx PR - Elysabeth Galati

John Carpenter Presents Storm Kids: MONICA BLEUE: A WEREWOLF STORY TPB, August 2020.
Published by Storm King Comics, a division of Storm King Productions, Inc.

AGES 12 AND UP

STORMKINGCOMICS.COM

 DOWNLOAD THE FREE STORM KING APP!
Available now, for iOS and Android!
Get all the news from Storm King and John Carpenter in the palm of your hand.

 STORMKINGCOMICS @STORMKINGCOMICS STORMKINGCOMICS JOHNCARPENTEROFF

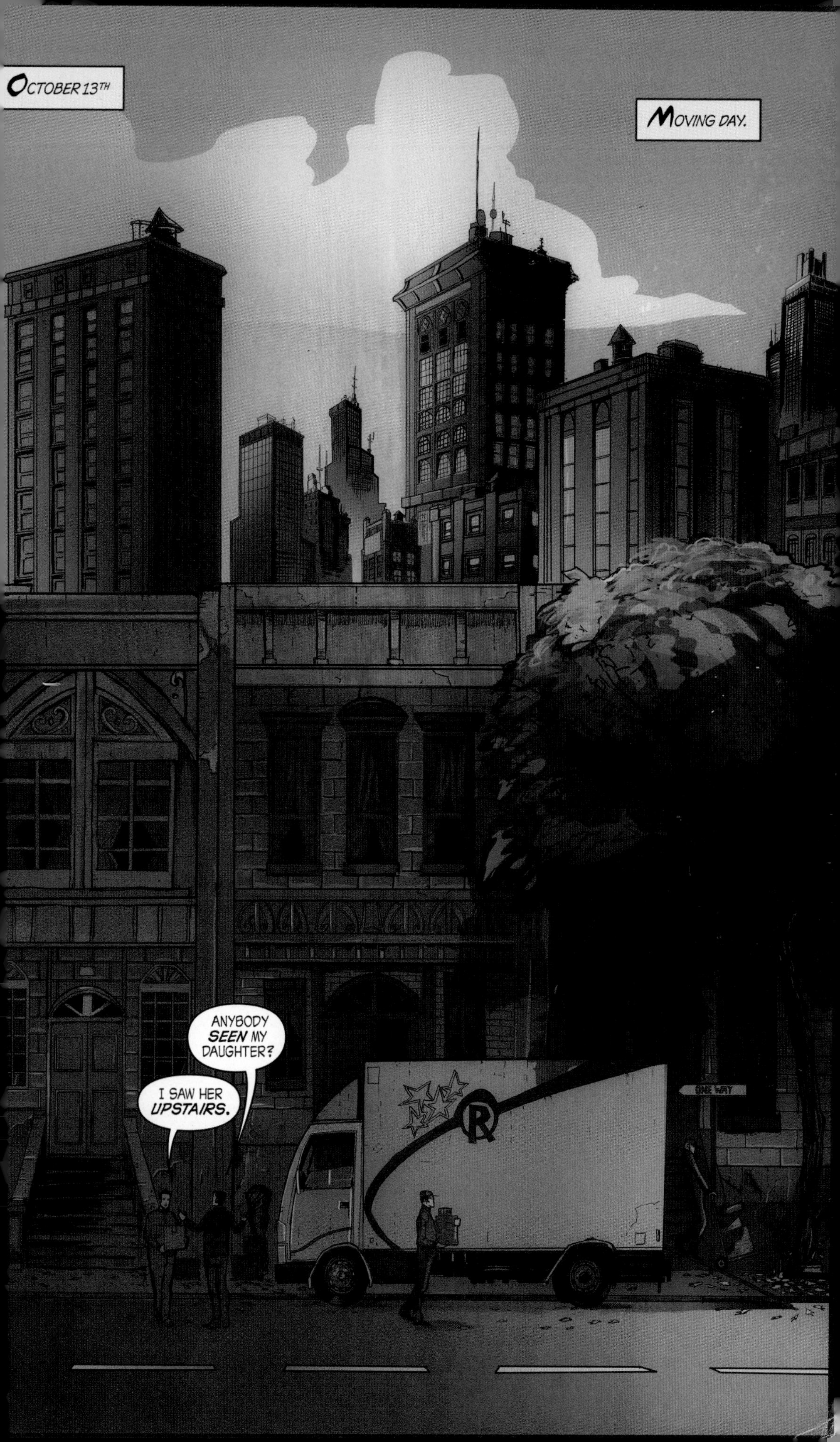
October 13th
Moving day.
ANYBODY SEEN MY DAUGHTER?
I SAW HER UPSTAIRS.
ONE WAY

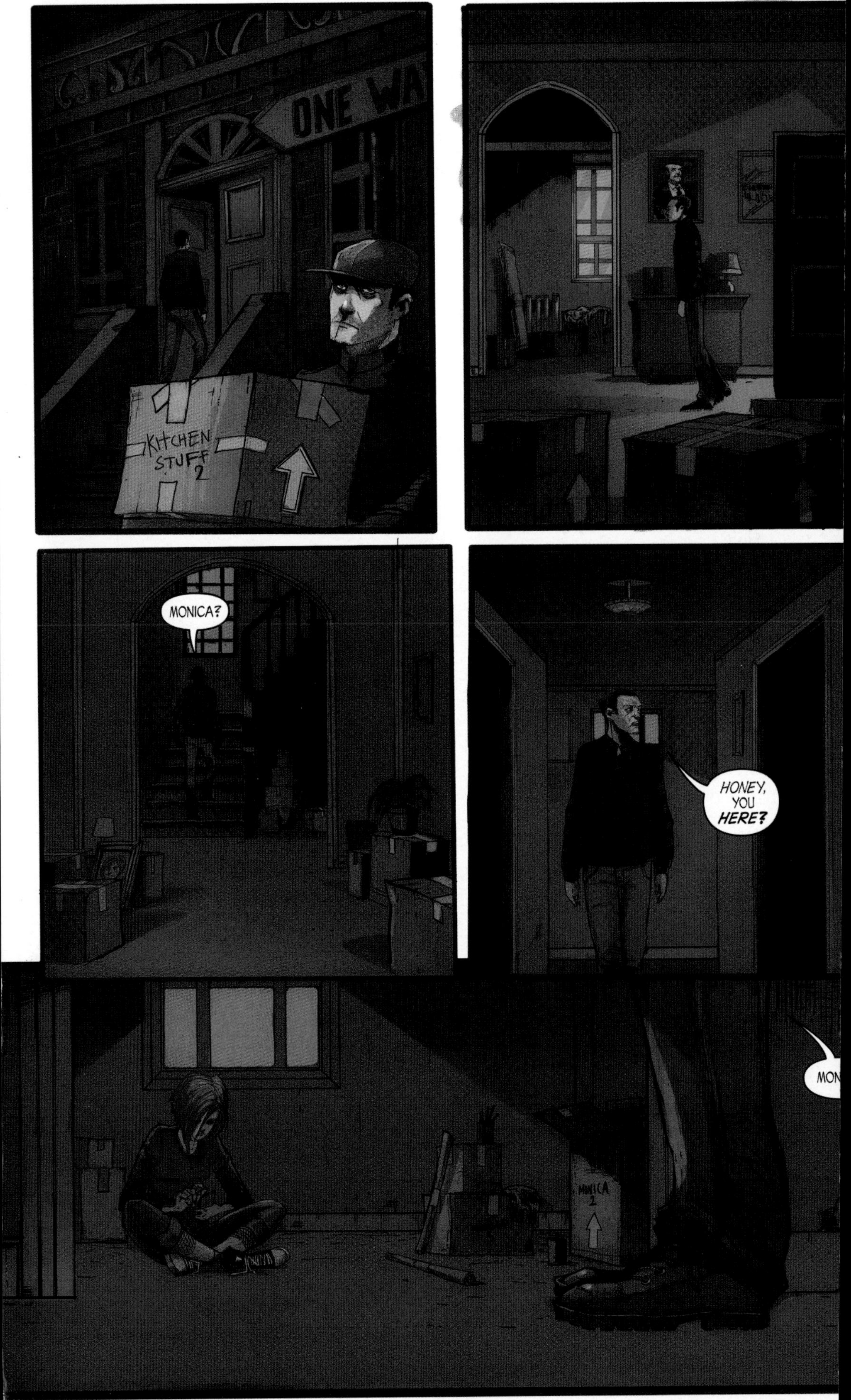
ONE WA
KITCHEN STUFF 2
MONICA?
HONEY, YOU HERE?
MONICA 2
MON

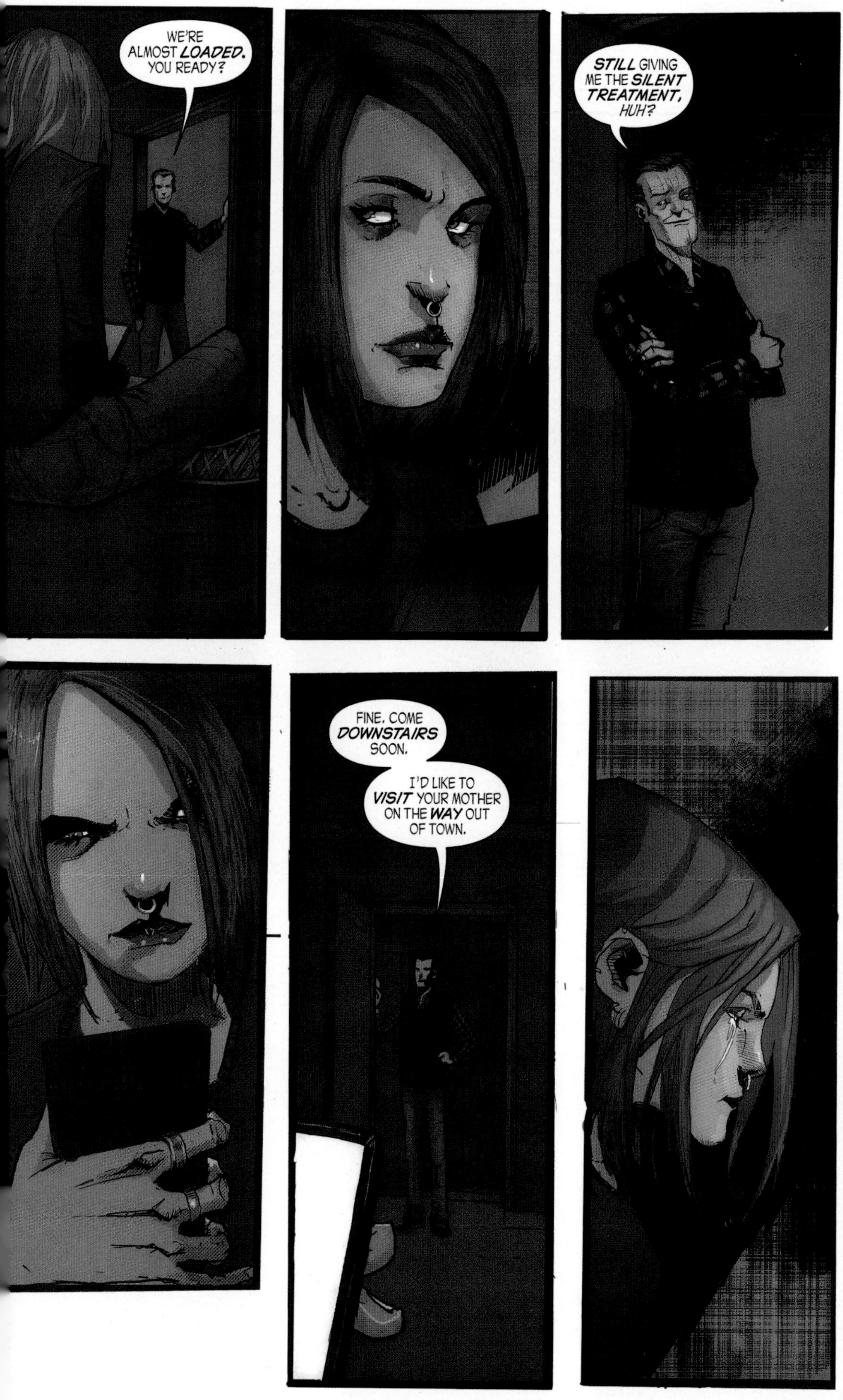
WE'RE ALMOST LOADED. YOU READY?
STILL GIVING ME THE SILENT TREATMENT, HUH?
FINE. COME DOWNSTAIRS SOON.
I'D LIKE TO VISIT YOUR MOTHER ON THE WAY OUT OF TOWN.

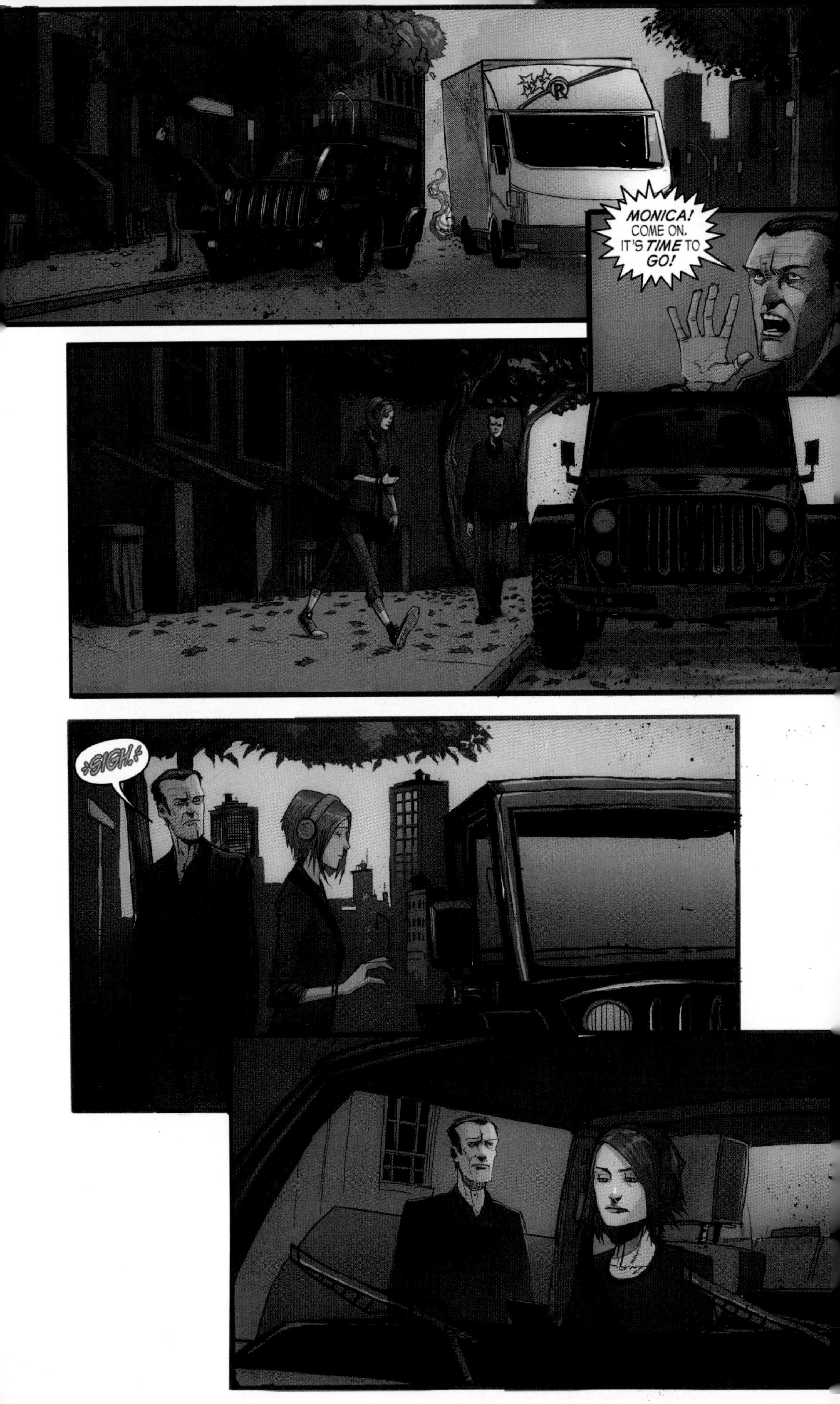
MONICA! COME ON, IT'S TIME TO GO!
SIGH.

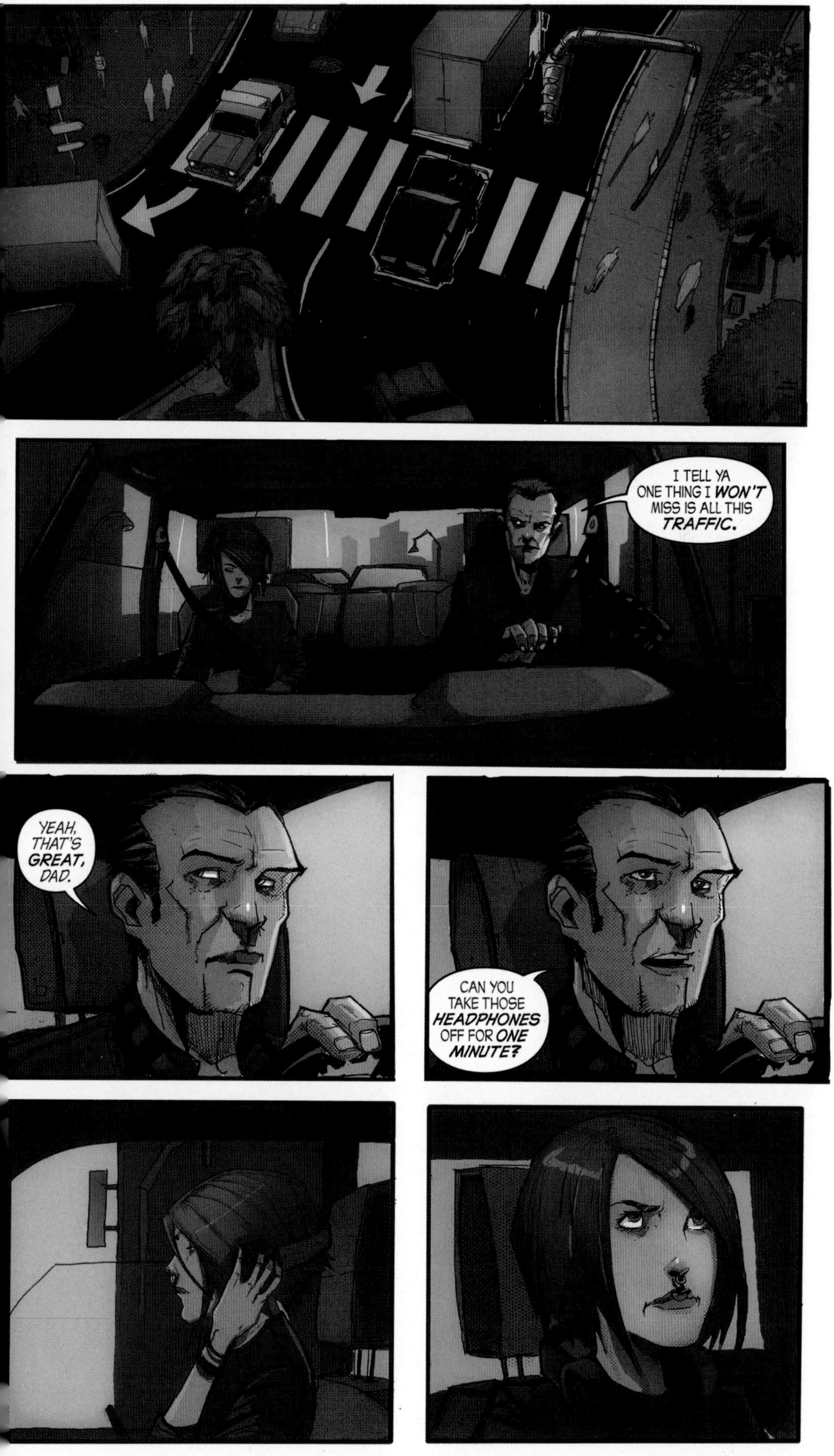
I TELL YA ONE THING I *WON'T* MISS IS ALL THIS *TRAFFIC.*
YEAH, THAT'S **GREAT,** DAD.
CAN YOU TAKE THOSE *HEADPHONES* OFF FOR *ONE MINUTE?*

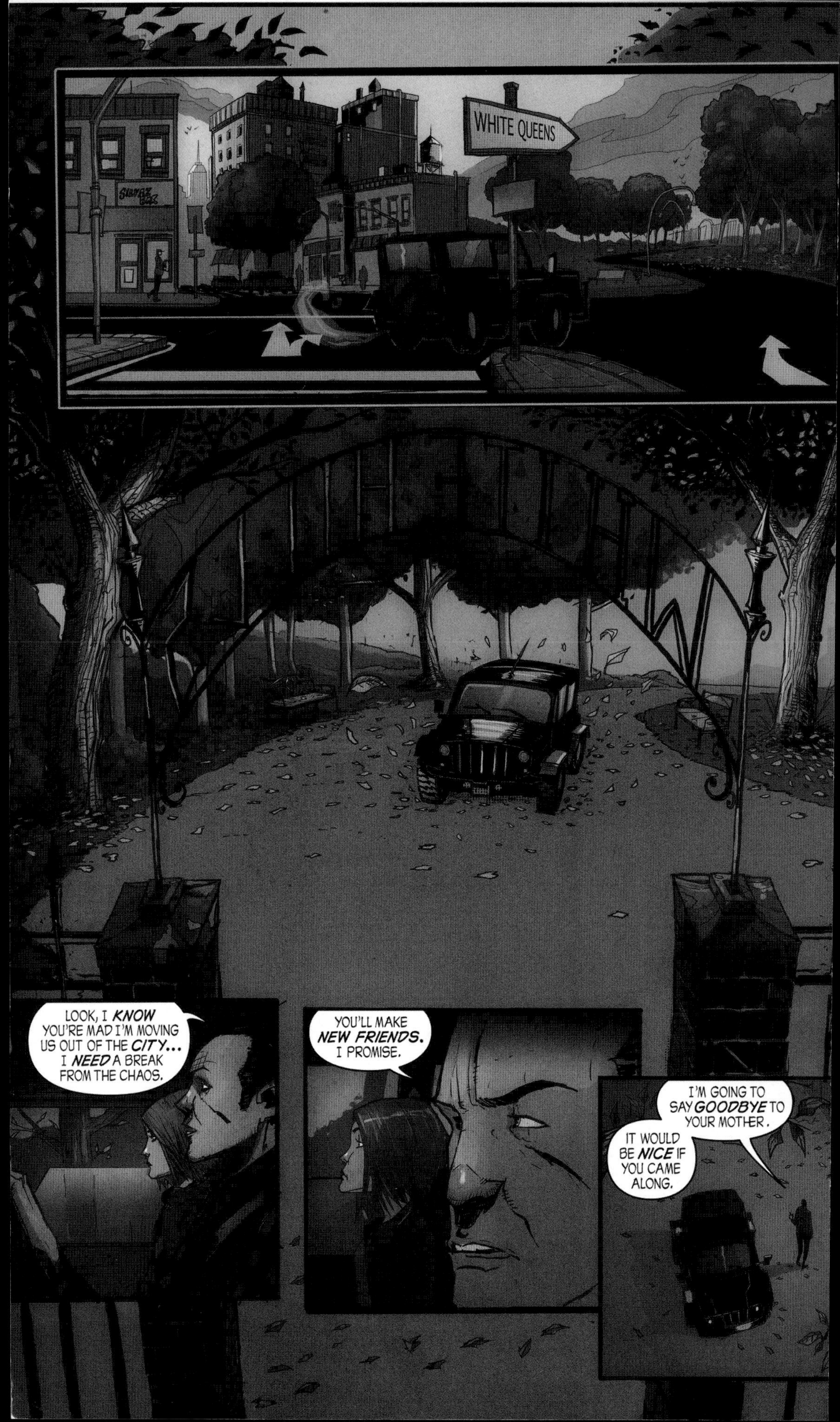
WHITE QUEENS
LOOK, I KNOW YOU'RE MAD I'M MOVING US OUT OF THE CITY... I NEED A BREAK FROM THE CHAOS.
YOU'LL MAKE NEW FRIENDS. I PROMISE.
I'M GOING TO SAY GOODBYE TO YOUR MOTHER.
IT WOULD BE NICE IF YOU CAME ALONG.

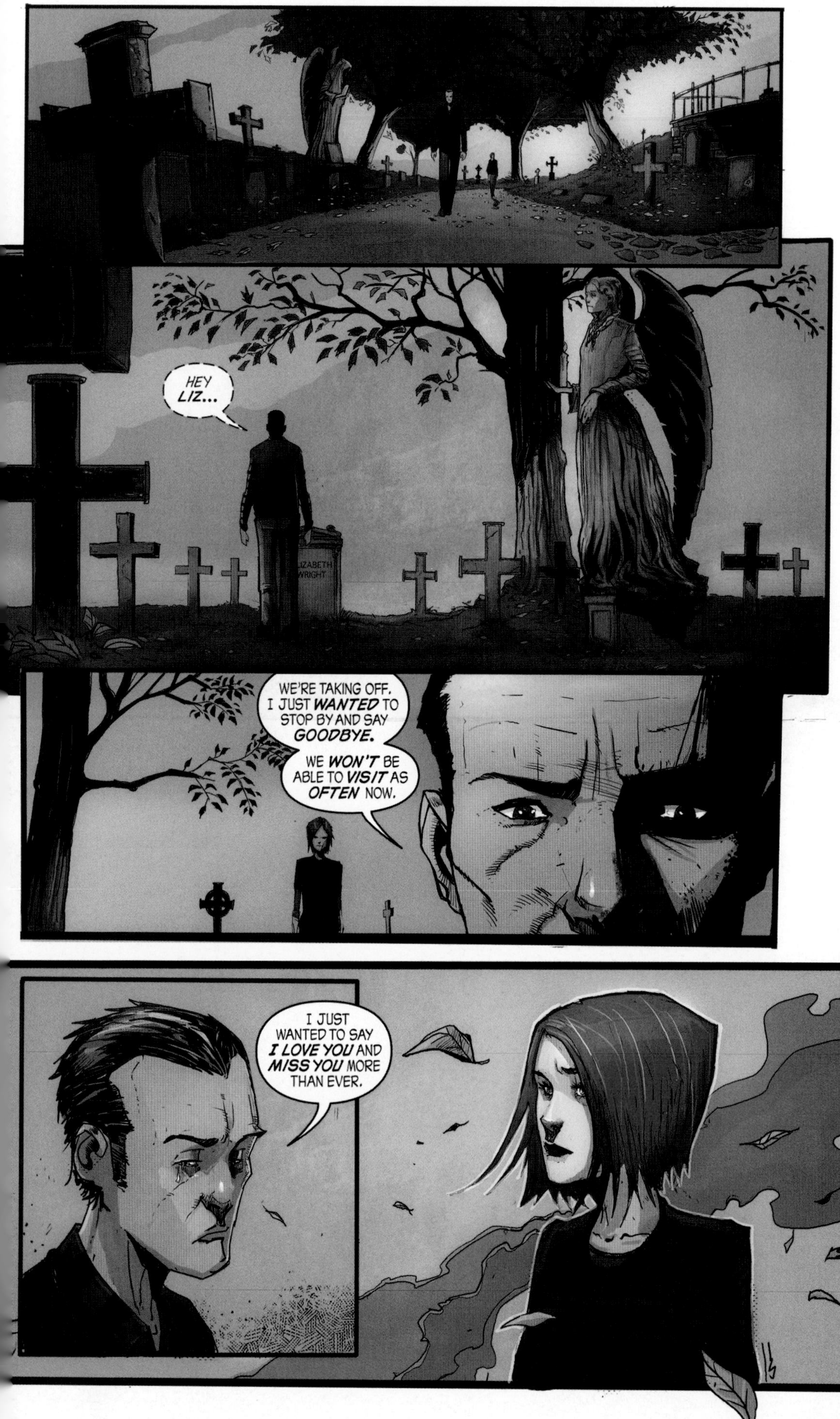
HEY LIZ...
ELIZABETH WRIGHT
WE'RE TAKING OFF. I JUST WANTED TO STOP BY AND SAY GOODBYE.
WE WON'T BE ABLE TO VISIT AS OFTEN NOW.
I JUST WANTED TO SAY I LOVE YOU AND MISS YOU MORE THAN EVER.

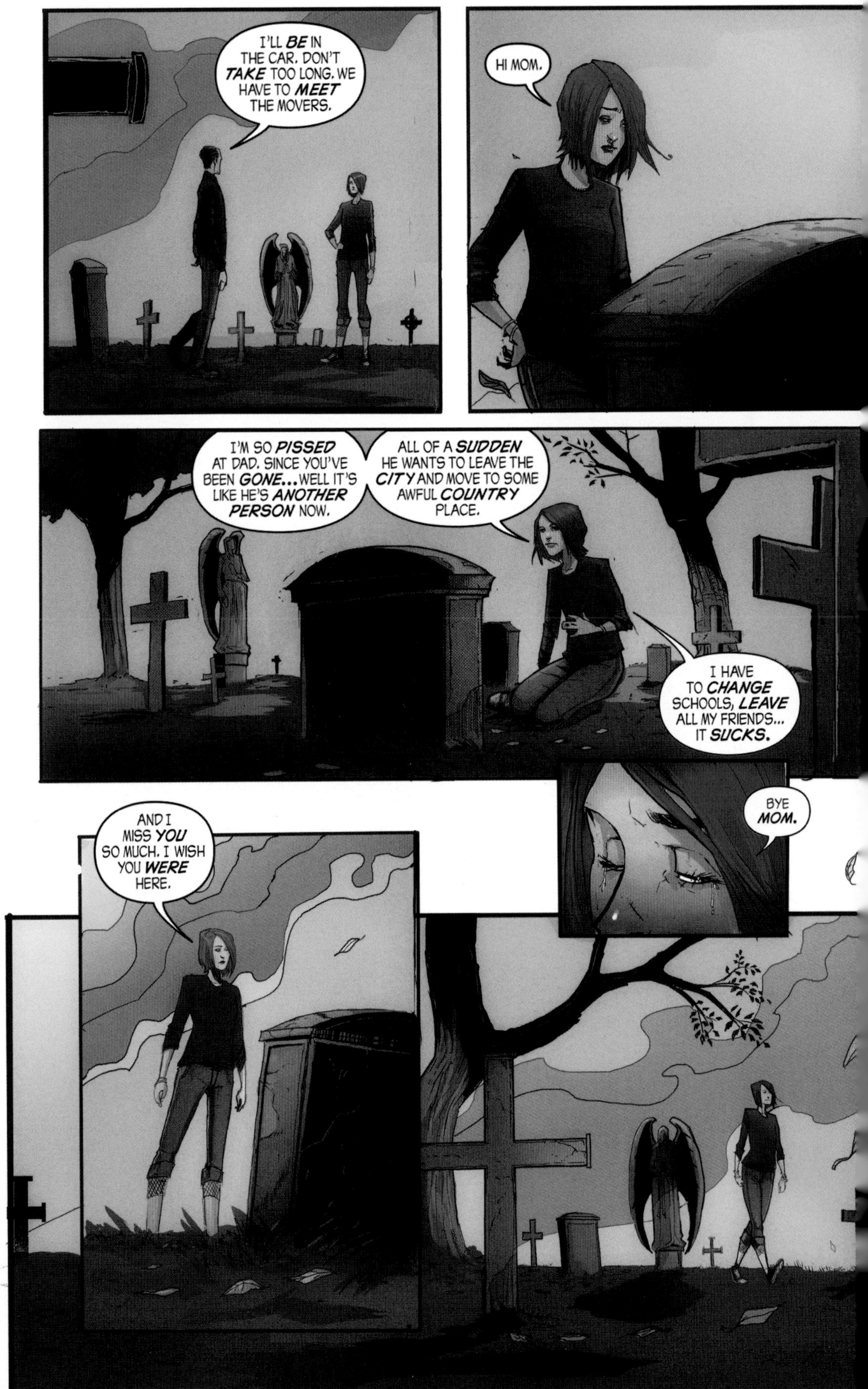
I'LL BE IN THE CAR. DON'T TAKE TOO LONG. WE HAVE TO MEET THE MOVERS.
HI MOM.
I'M SO PISSED AT DAD. SINCE YOU'VE BEEN GONE... WELL IT'S LIKE HE'S ANOTHER PERSON NOW.
ALL OF A SUDDEN HE WANTS TO LEAVE THE CITY AND MOVE TO SOME AWFUL COUNTRY PLACE.
I HAVE TO CHANGE SCHOOLS, LEAVE ALL MY FRIENDS... IT SUCKS.
AND I MISS YOU SO MUCH. I WISH YOU WERE HERE.
BYE MOM.

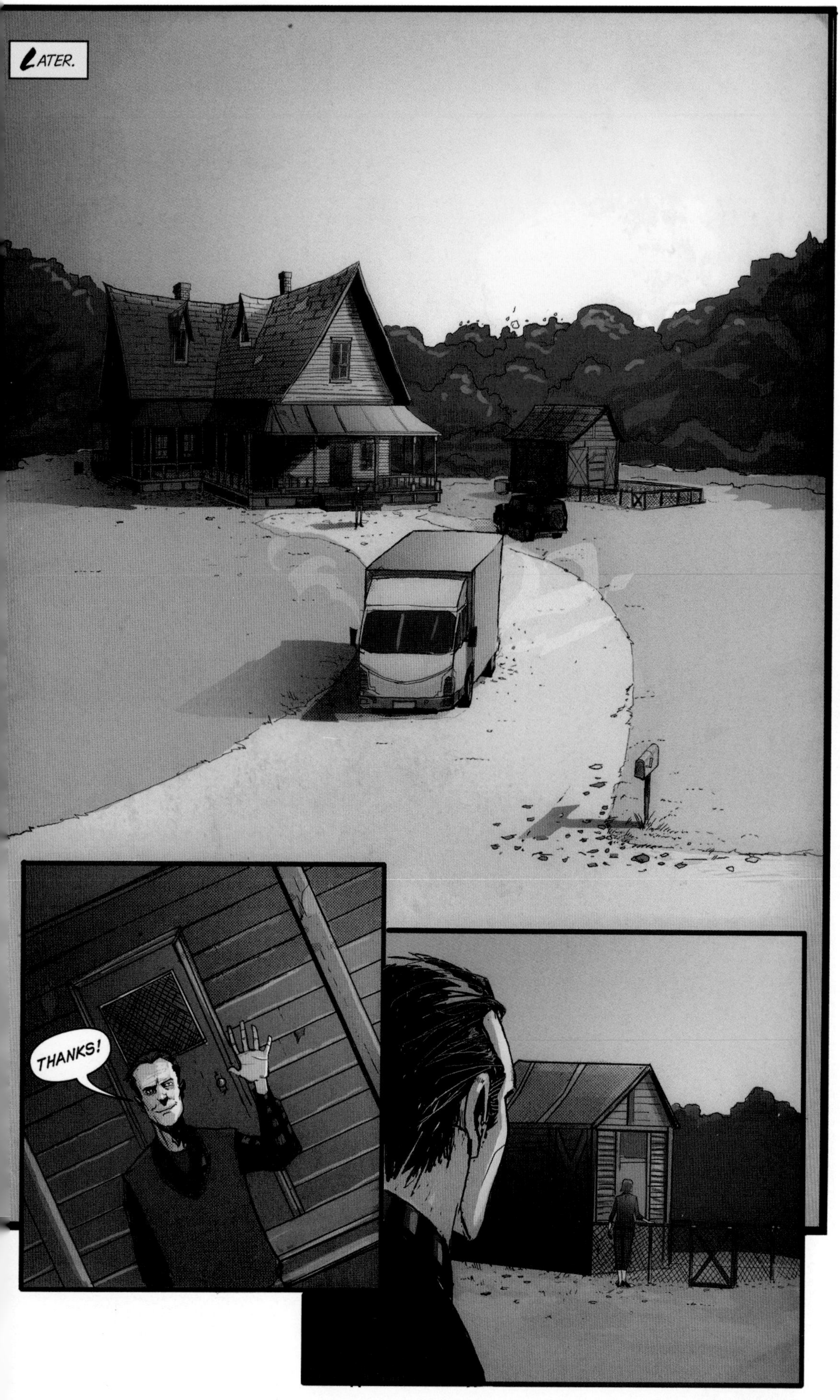
LATER.
THANKS!

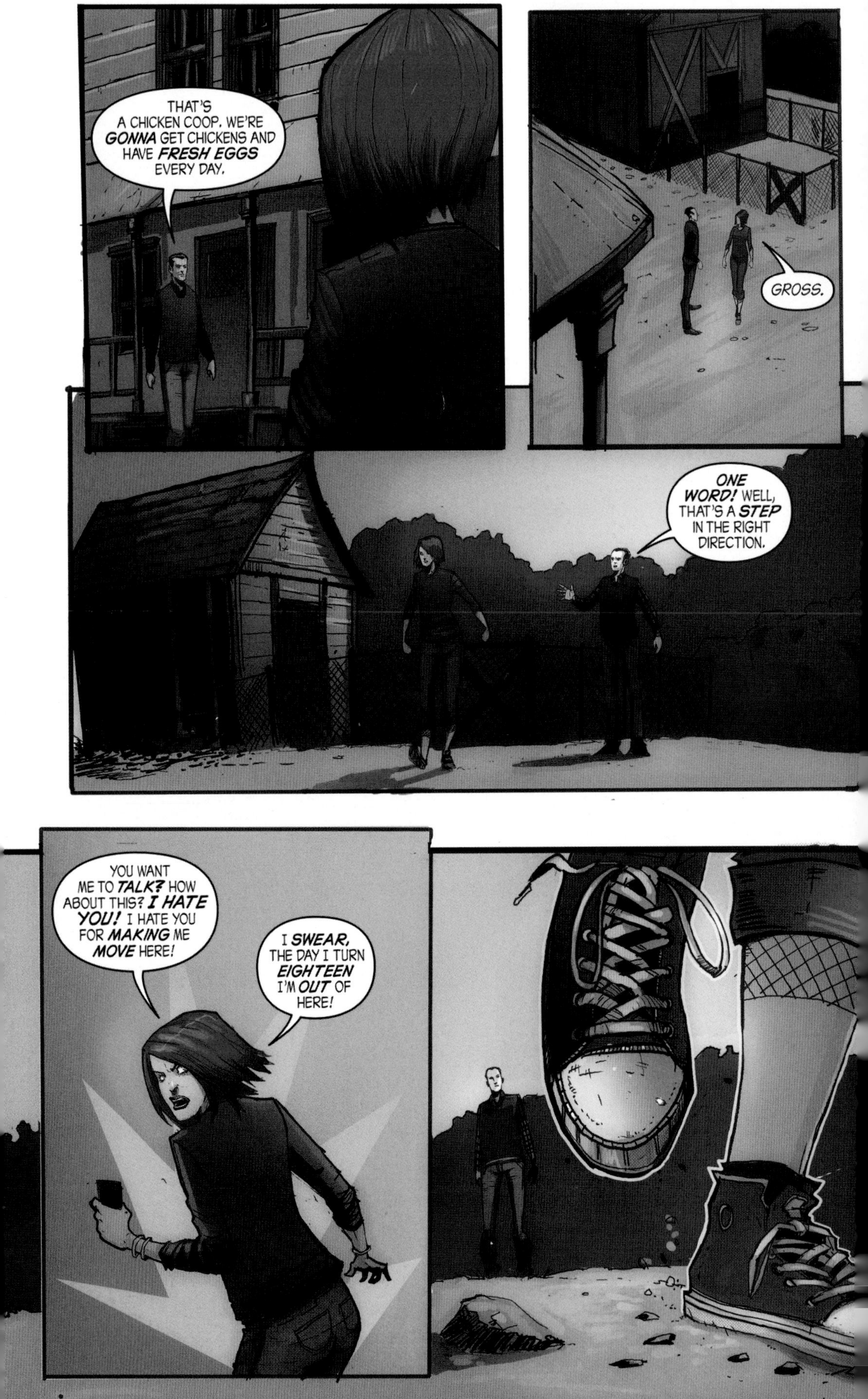
THAT'S A CHICKEN COOP. WE'RE GONNA GET CHICKENS AND HAVE FRESH EGGS EVERY DAY.
GROSS.
ONE WORD! WELL, THAT'S A STEP IN THE RIGHT DIRECTION.
YOU WANT ME TO TALK? HOW ABOUT THIS? I HATE YOU! I HATE YOU FOR MAKING ME MOVE HERE!
I SWEAR, THE DAY I TURN EIGHTEEN I'M OUT OF HERE!

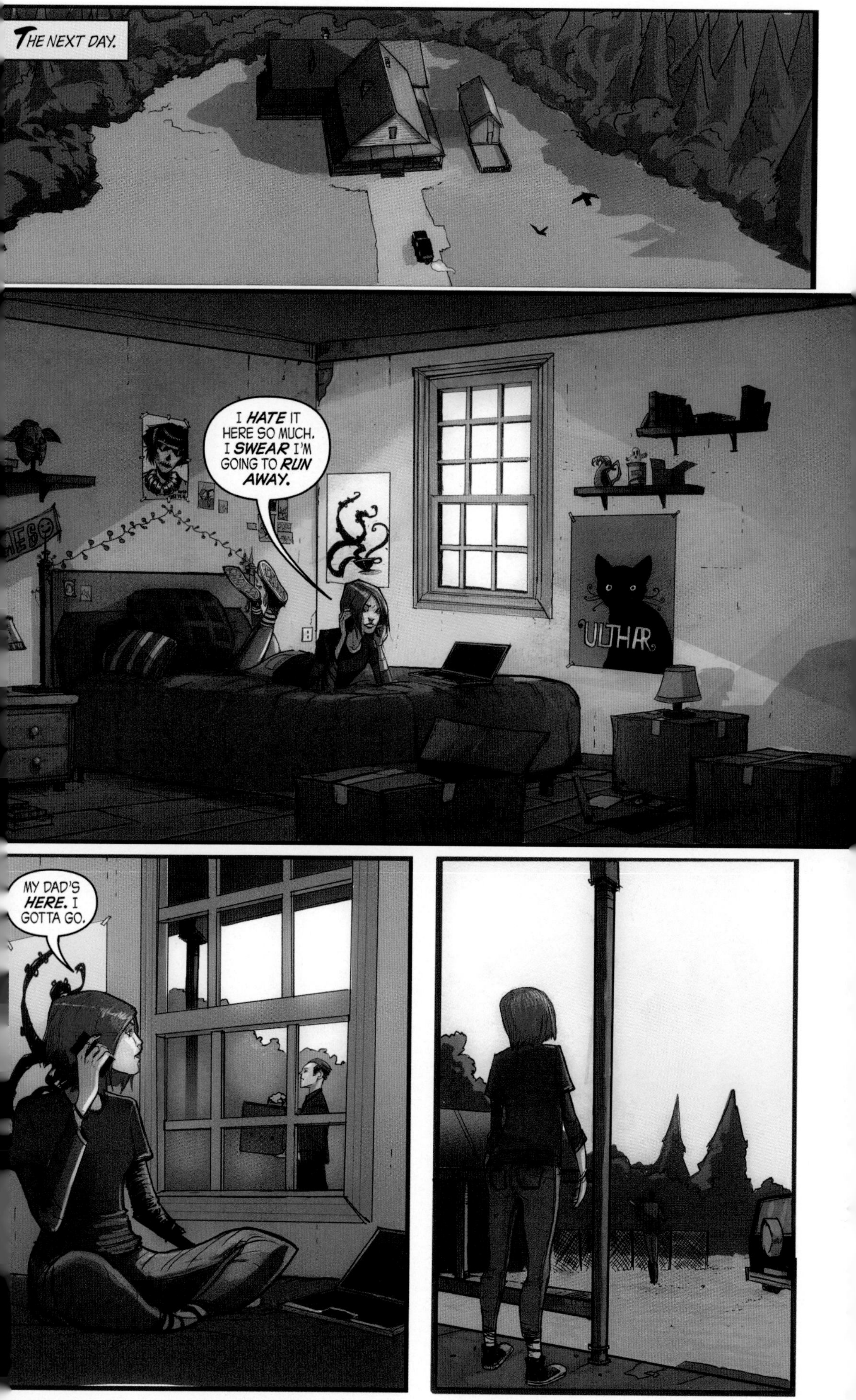
THE NEXT DAY.
I HATE IT HERE SO MUCH. I SWEAR I'M GOING TO RUN AWAY.
ULTHAR
MY DAD'S HERE. I GOTTA GO.

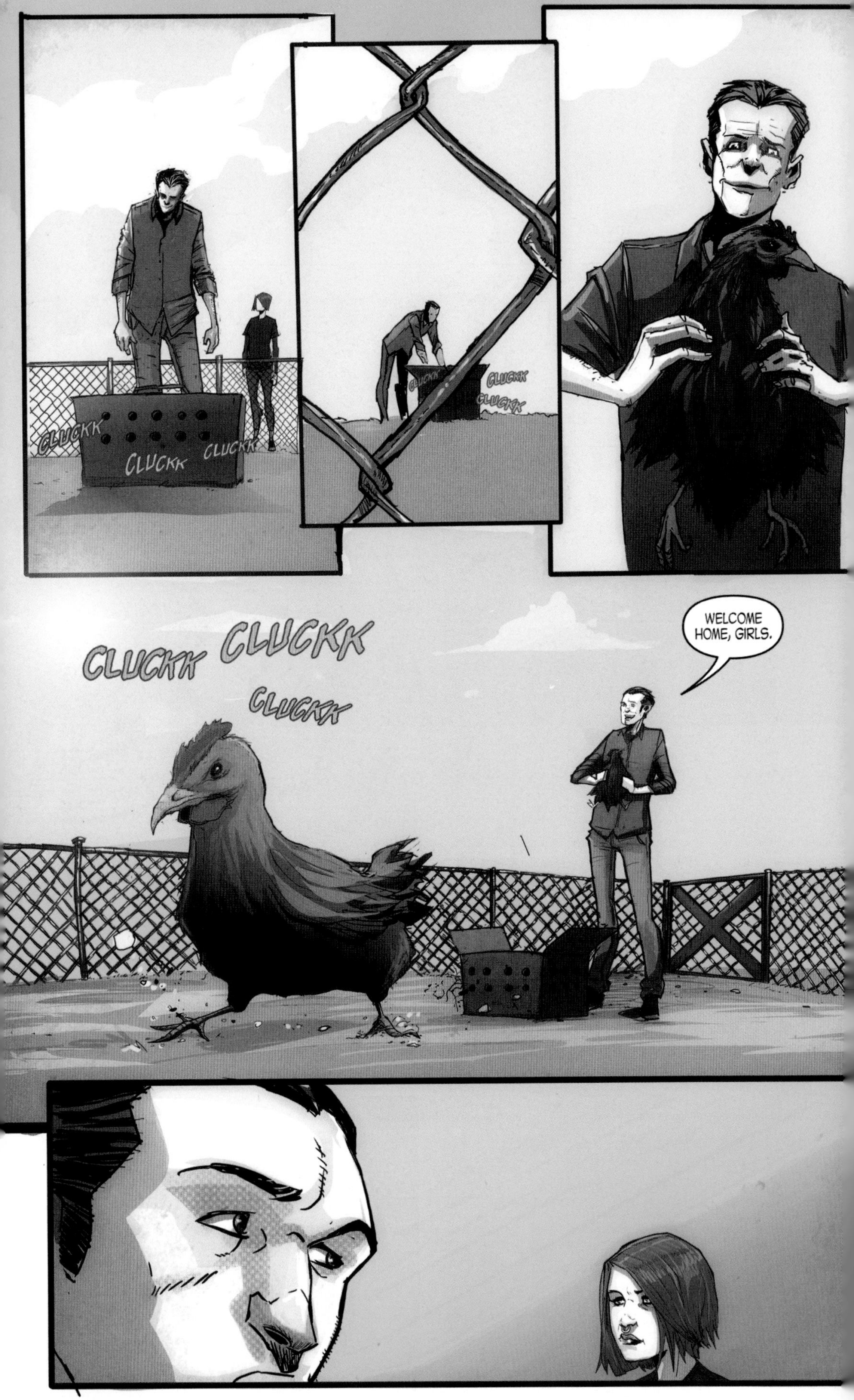
CLUCKK
CLUCKK
CLUCKK
CLUCKK
CLUCKK
CLUCKK CLUCKK
CLUCKK
WELCOME HOME, GIRLS.

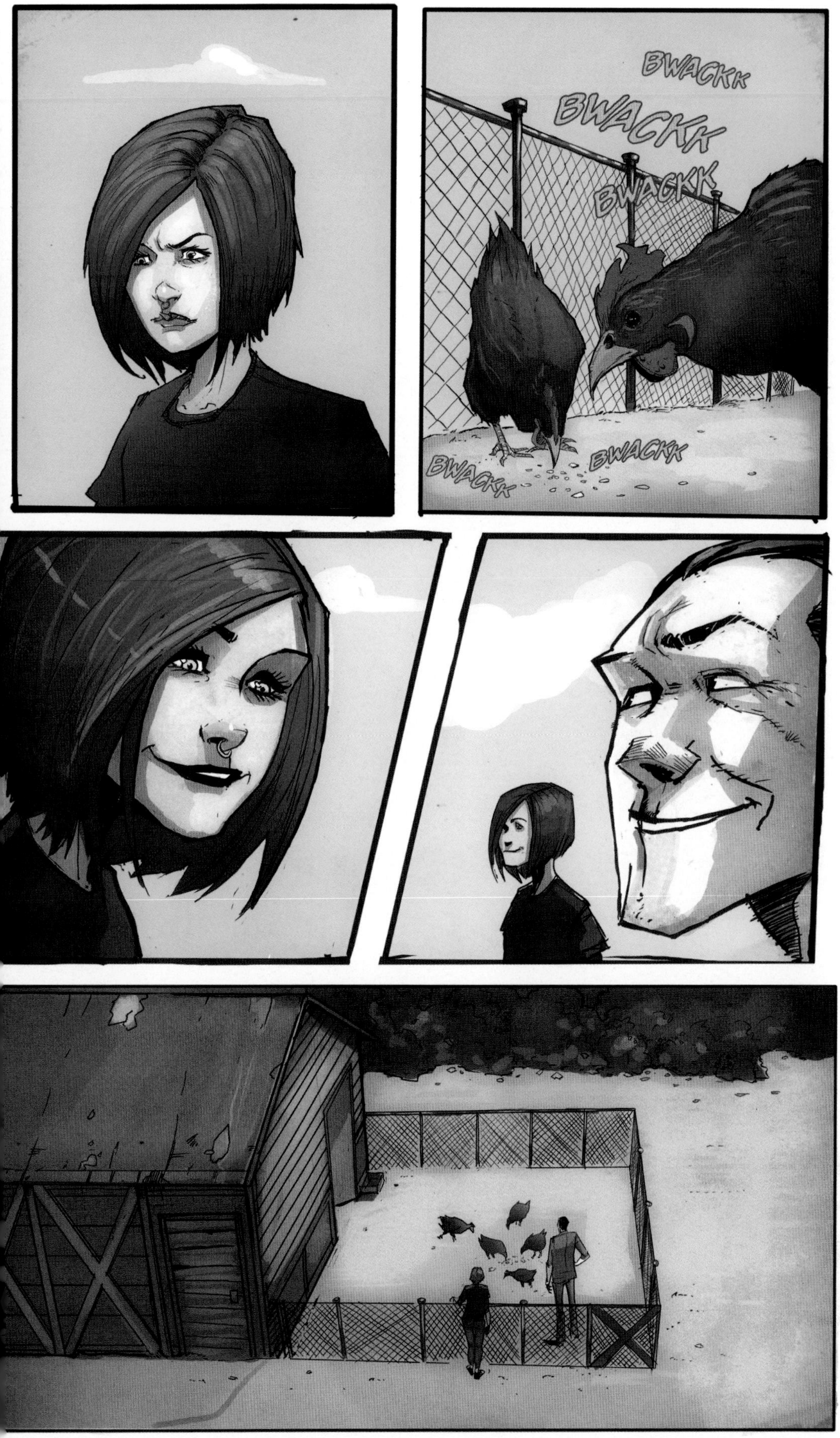
BWACKK
BWACKK
BWACKK
BWACKK
BWACKK

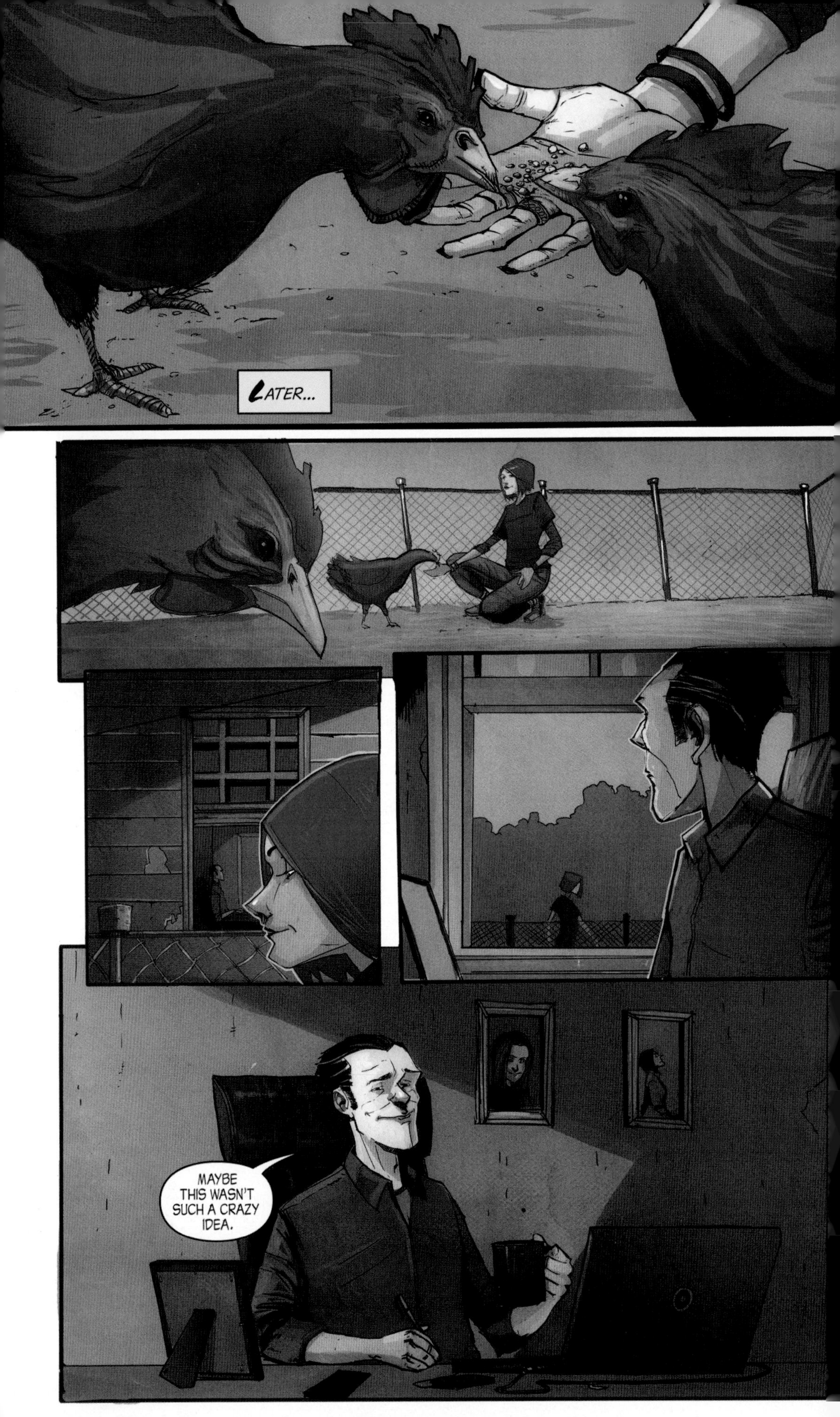
LATER...
MAYBE THIS WASN'T SUCH A CRAZY IDEA.

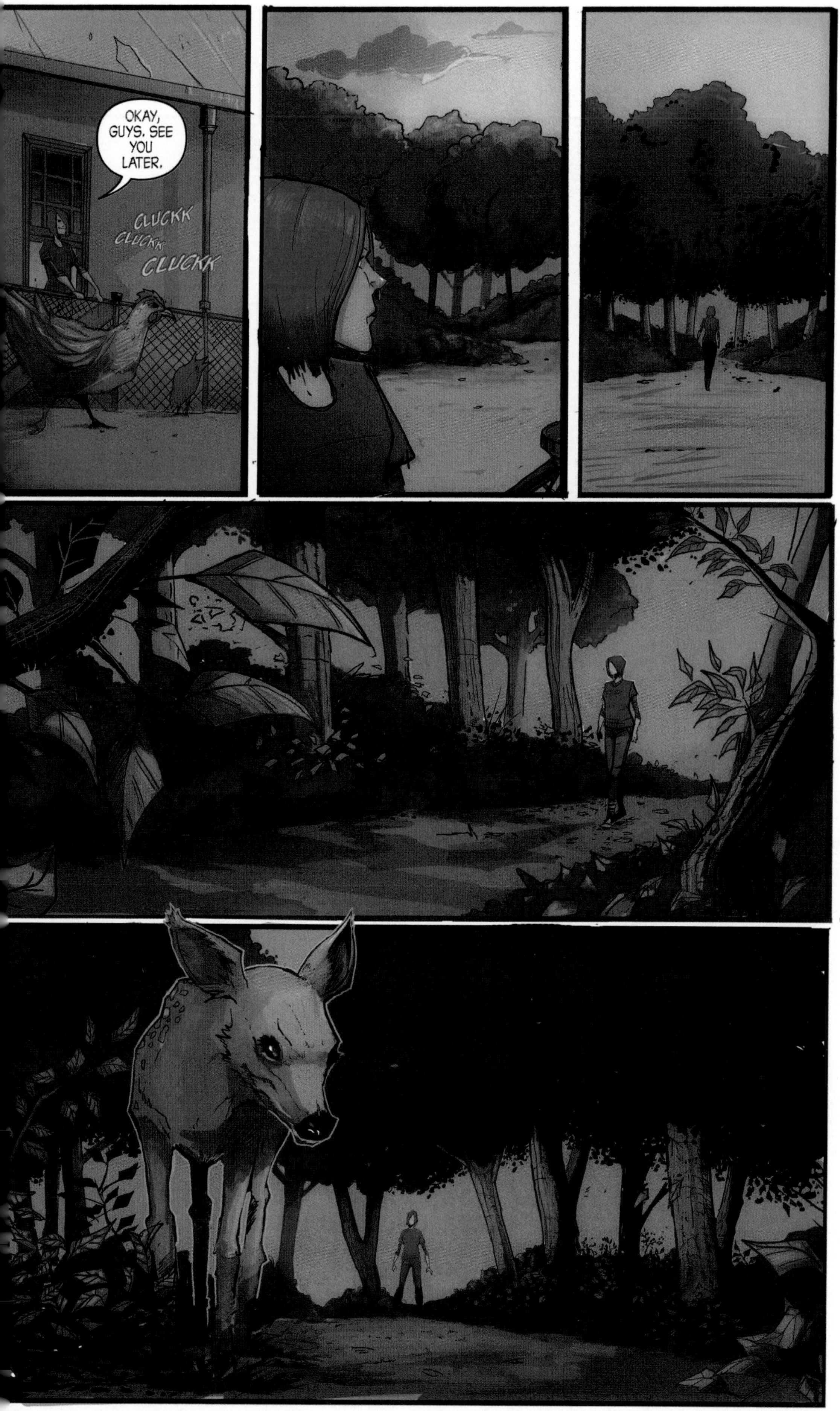
OKAY, GUYS. SEE YOU LATER.
CLUCKK
CLUCKK
CLUCKK

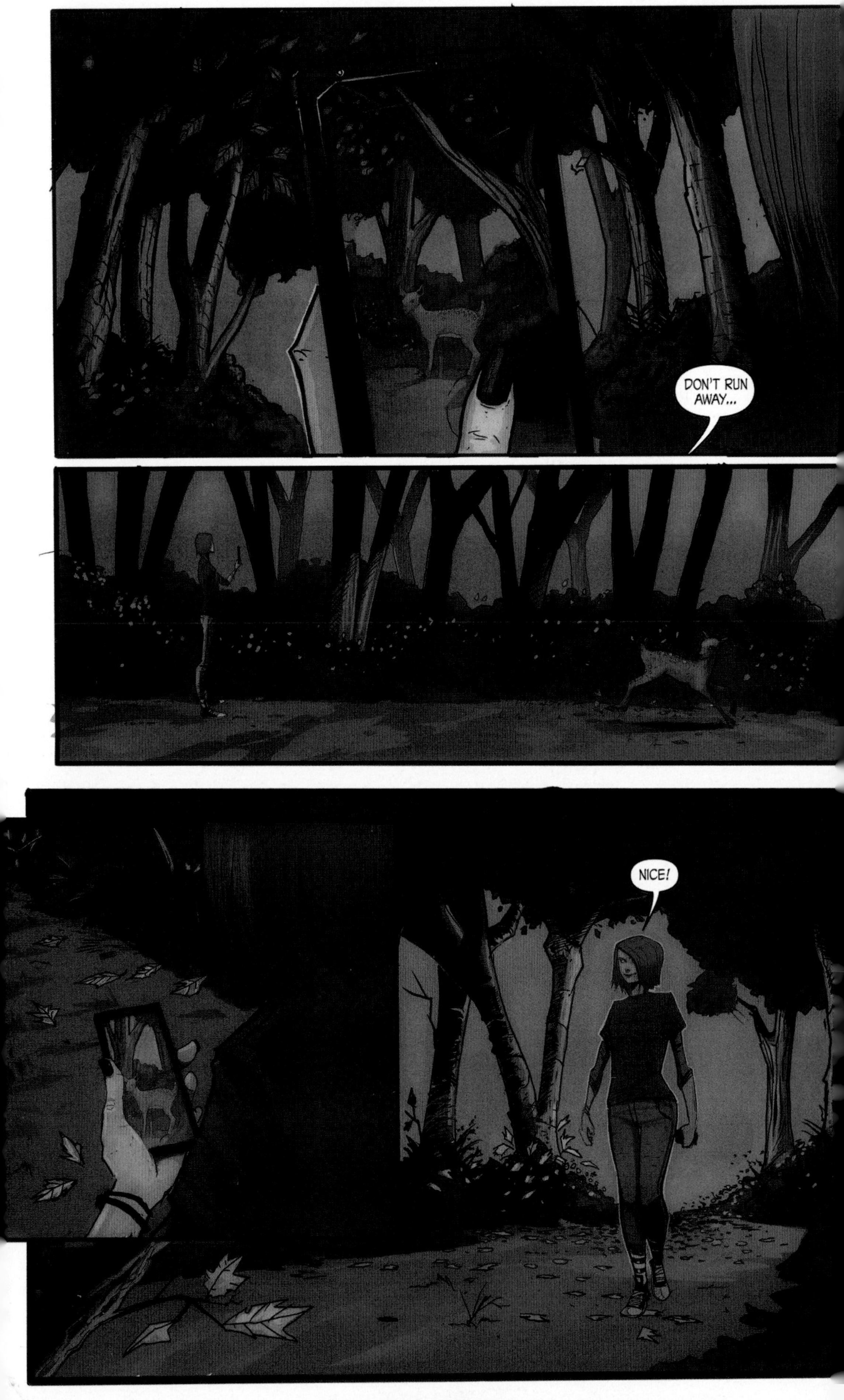
DON'T RUN AWAY...
NICE!

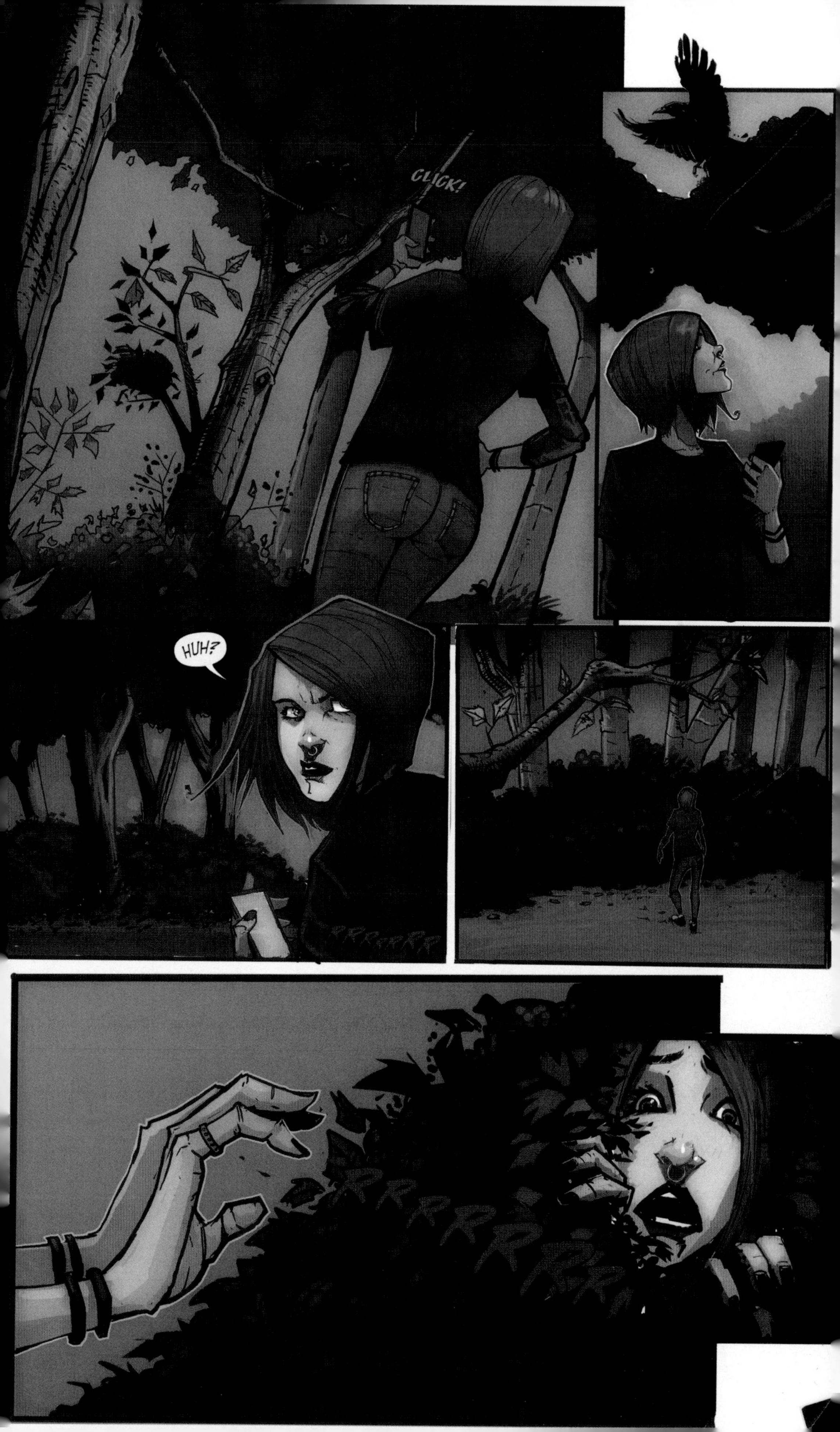
CLICK!
HUH?
RRRRRRR
RRRRRRR

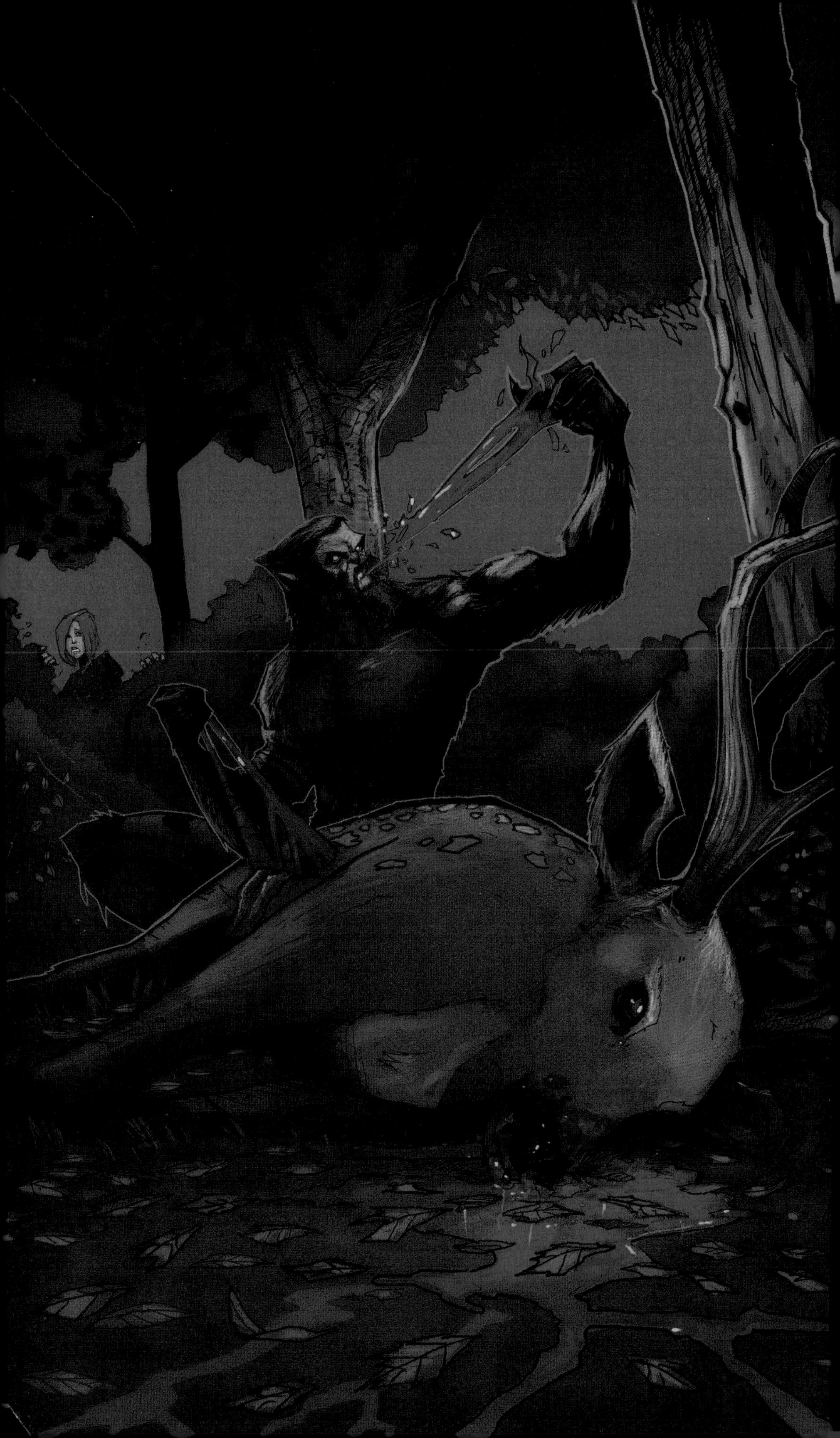

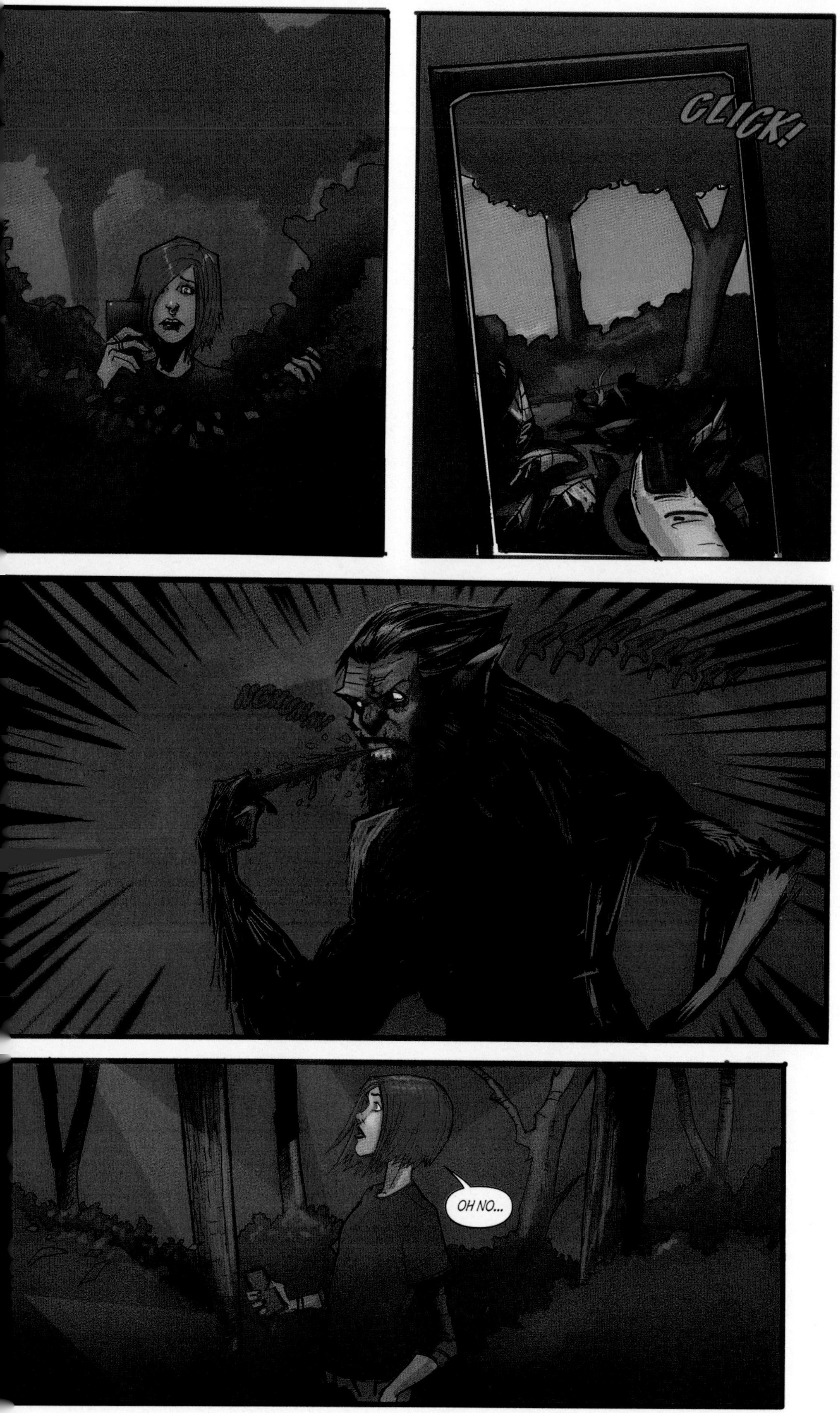
CLICK!
OH NO...

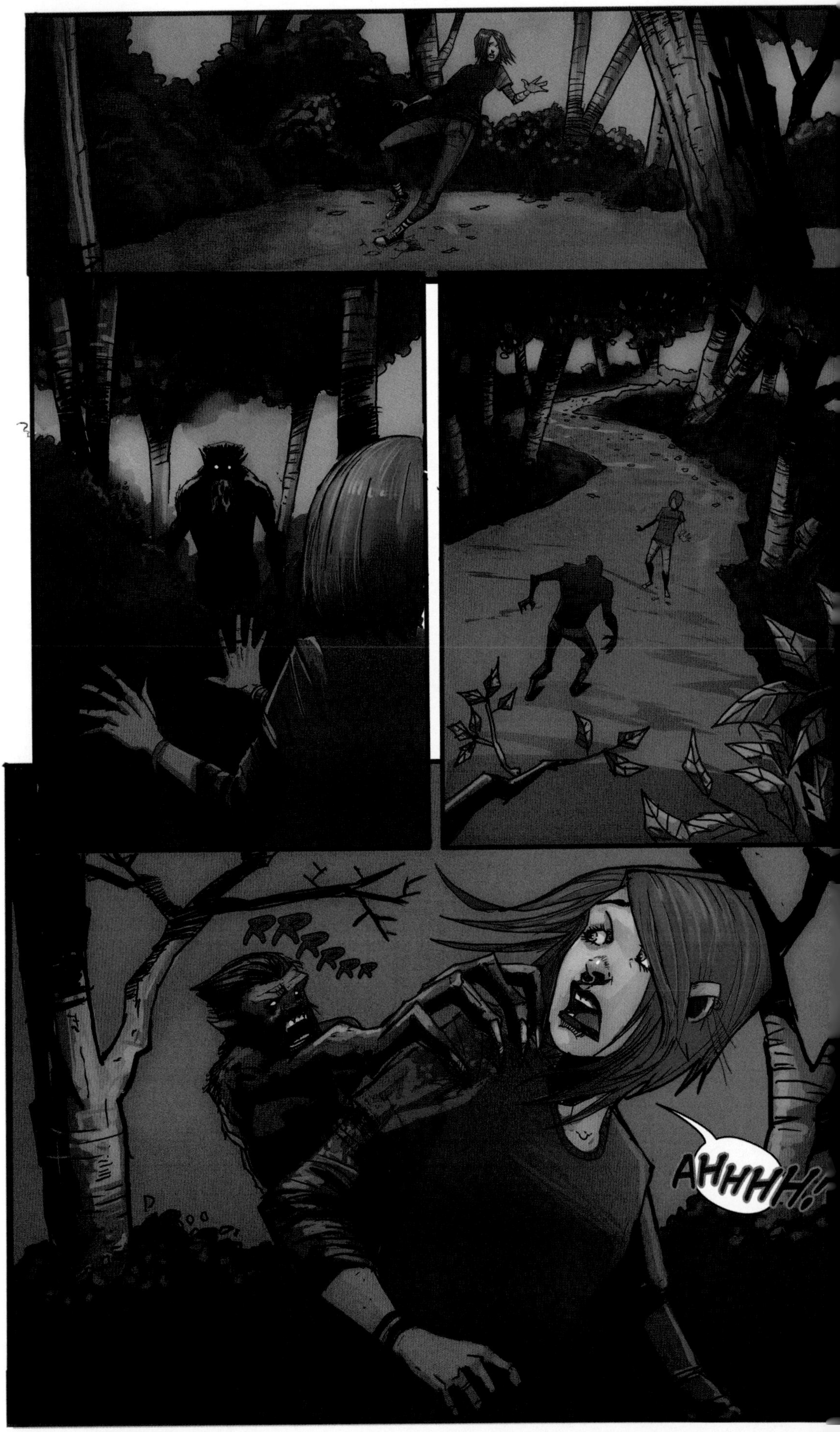
RRRRRR
AHHHH!

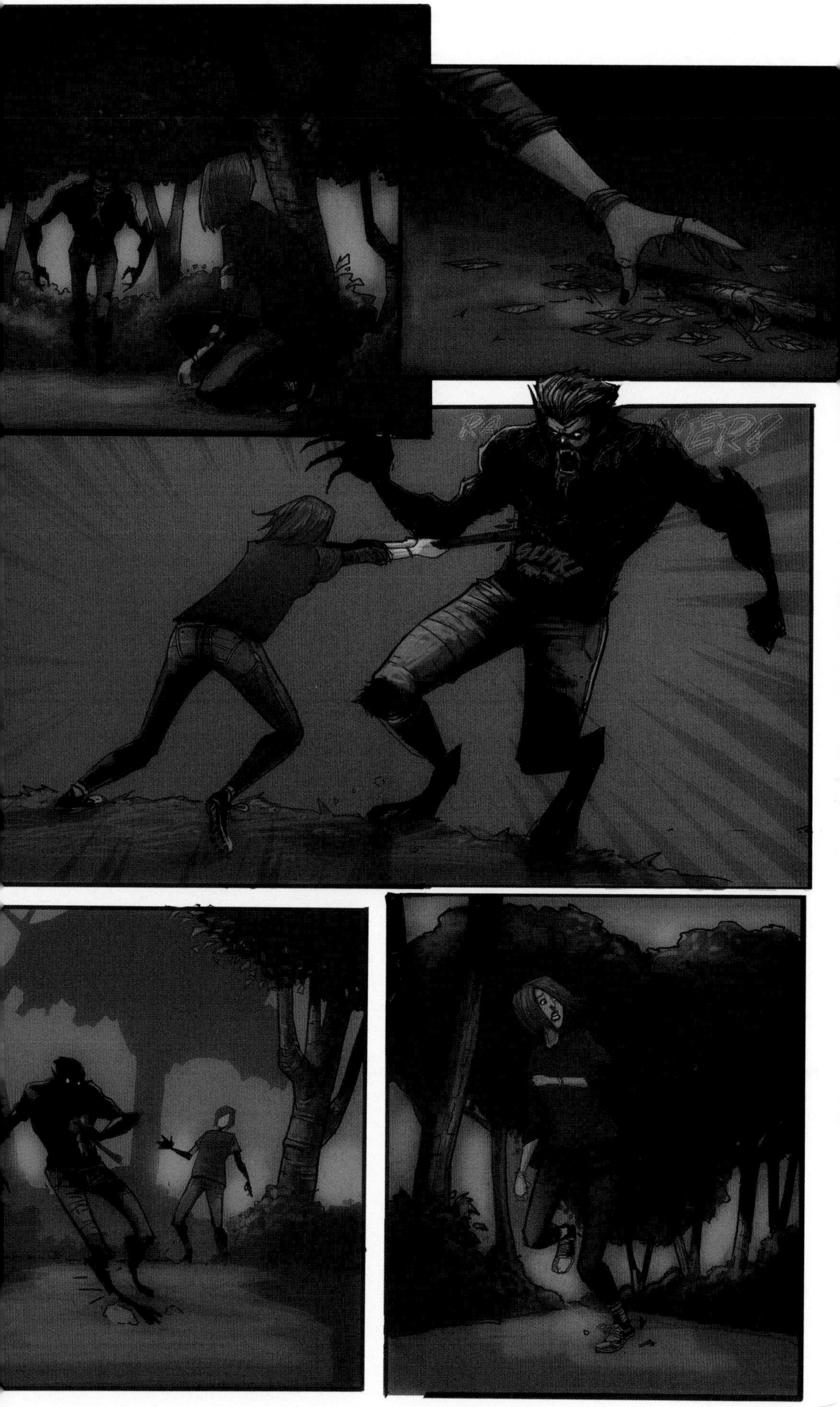

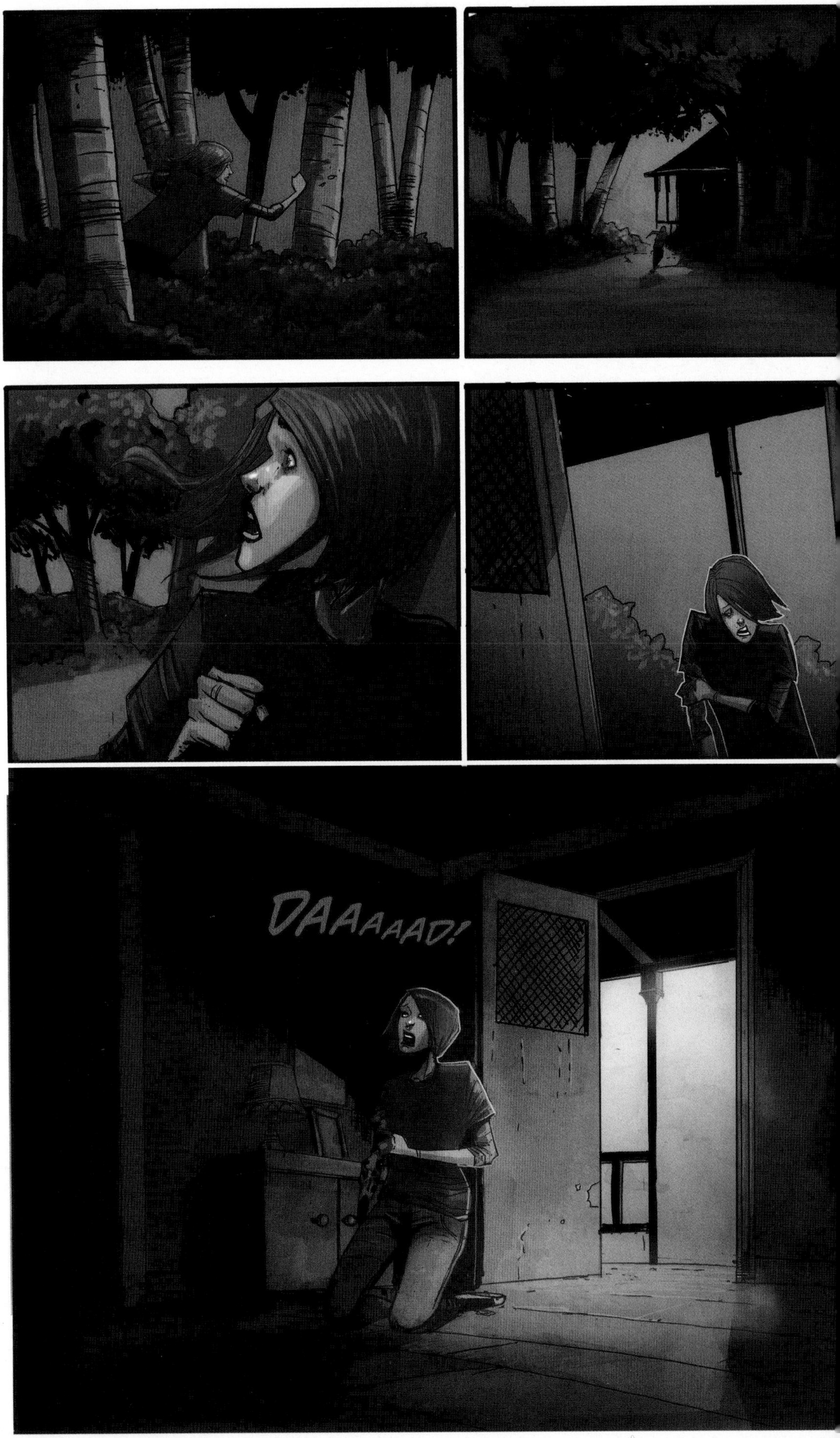
DAAAAAD!

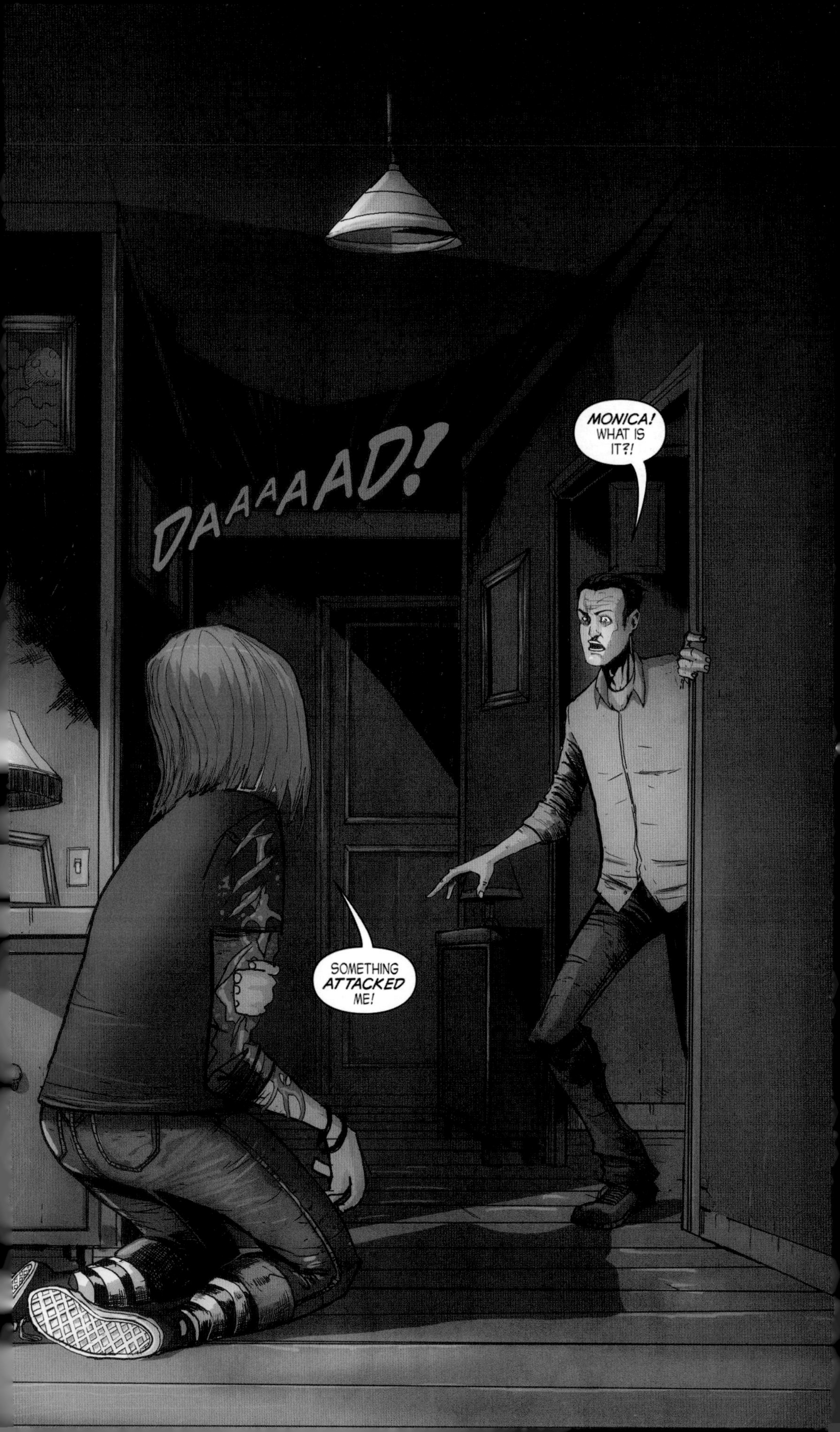
DAAAAAD!
MONICA! WHAT IS IT?!
SOMETHING ATTACKED ME!

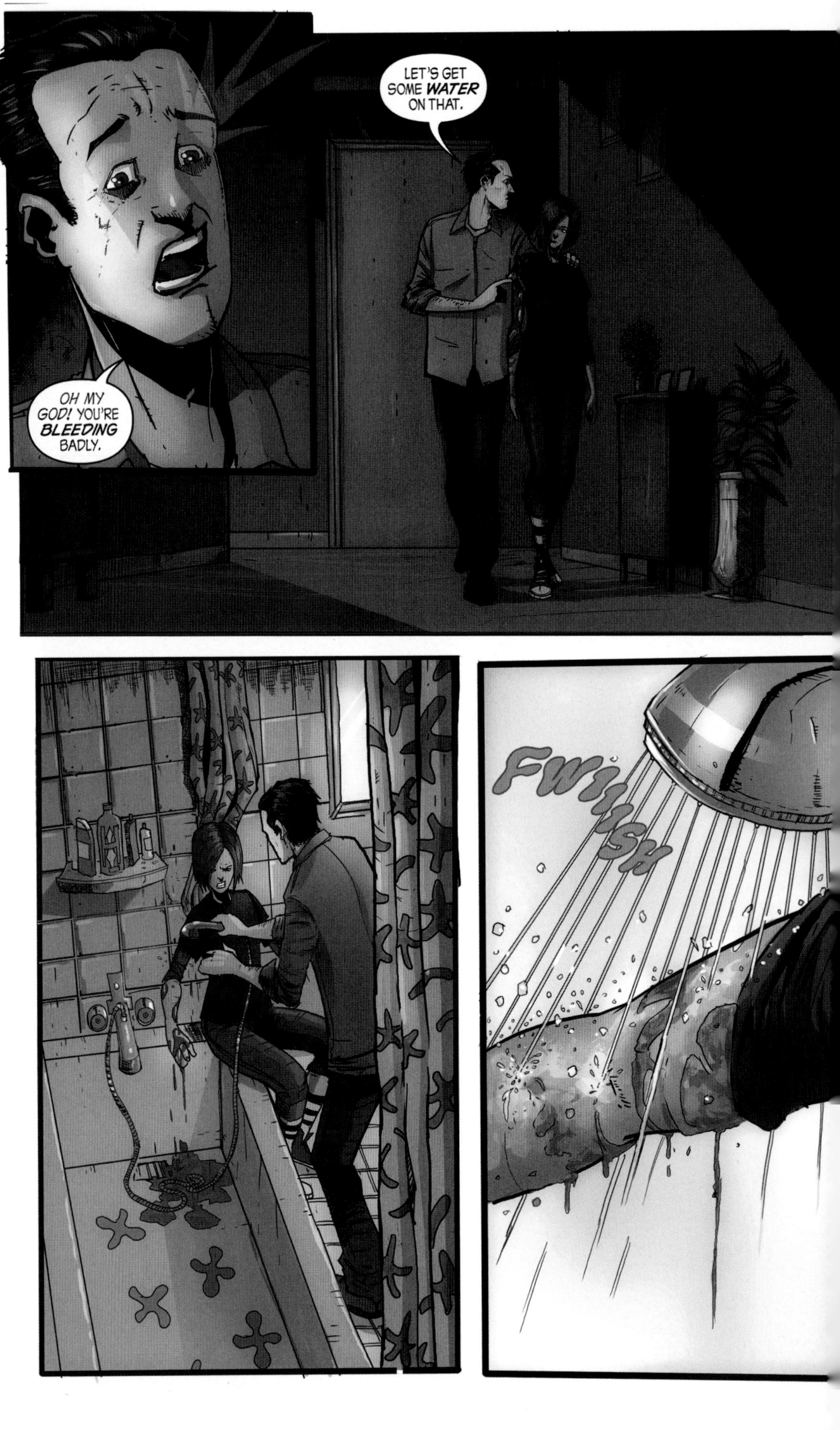
OH MY GOD! YOU'RE BLEEDING BADLY.
LET'S GET SOME WATER ON THAT.
FWIIISH

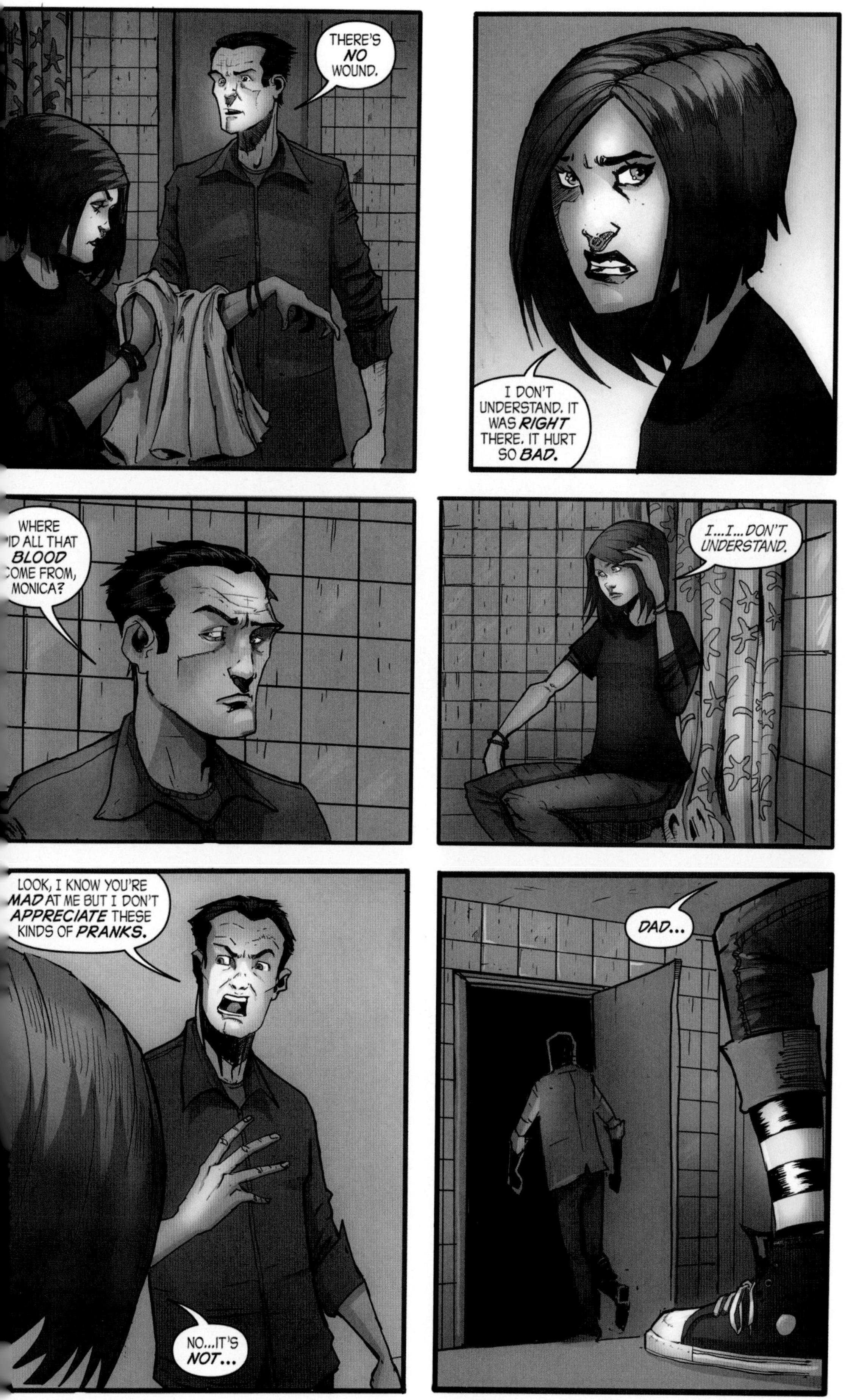
THERE'S NO WOUND.
I DON'T UNDERSTAND. IT WAS RIGHT THERE. IT HURT SO BAD.
WHERE ID ALL THAT BLOOD COME FROM, MONICA?
I...I...DON'T UNDERSTAND.
LOOK, I KNOW YOU'RE MAD AT ME BUT I DON'T APPRECIATE THESE KINDS OF PRANKS.
NO...IT'S NOT...
DAD...

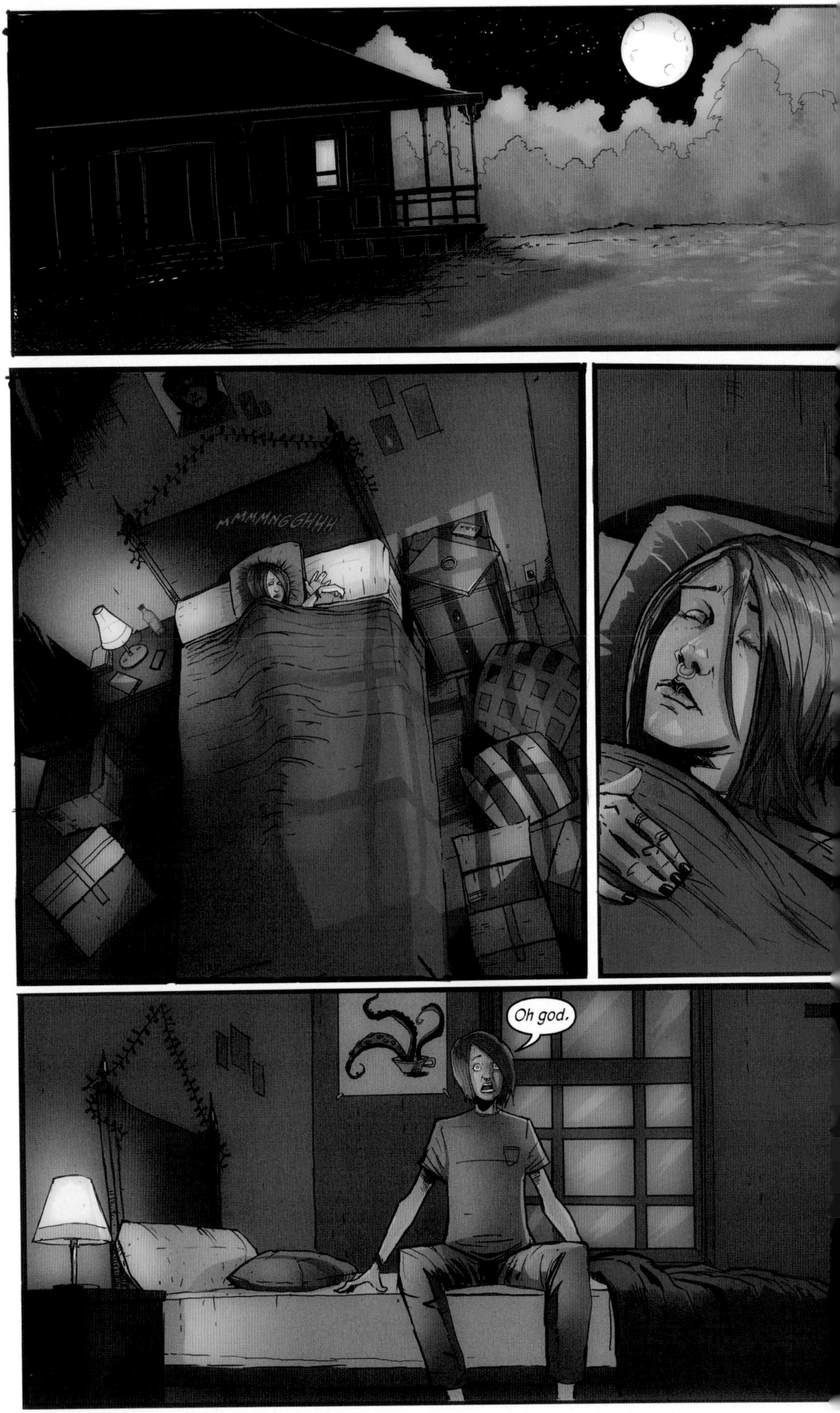
MMMMNGGHHH
Oh god.

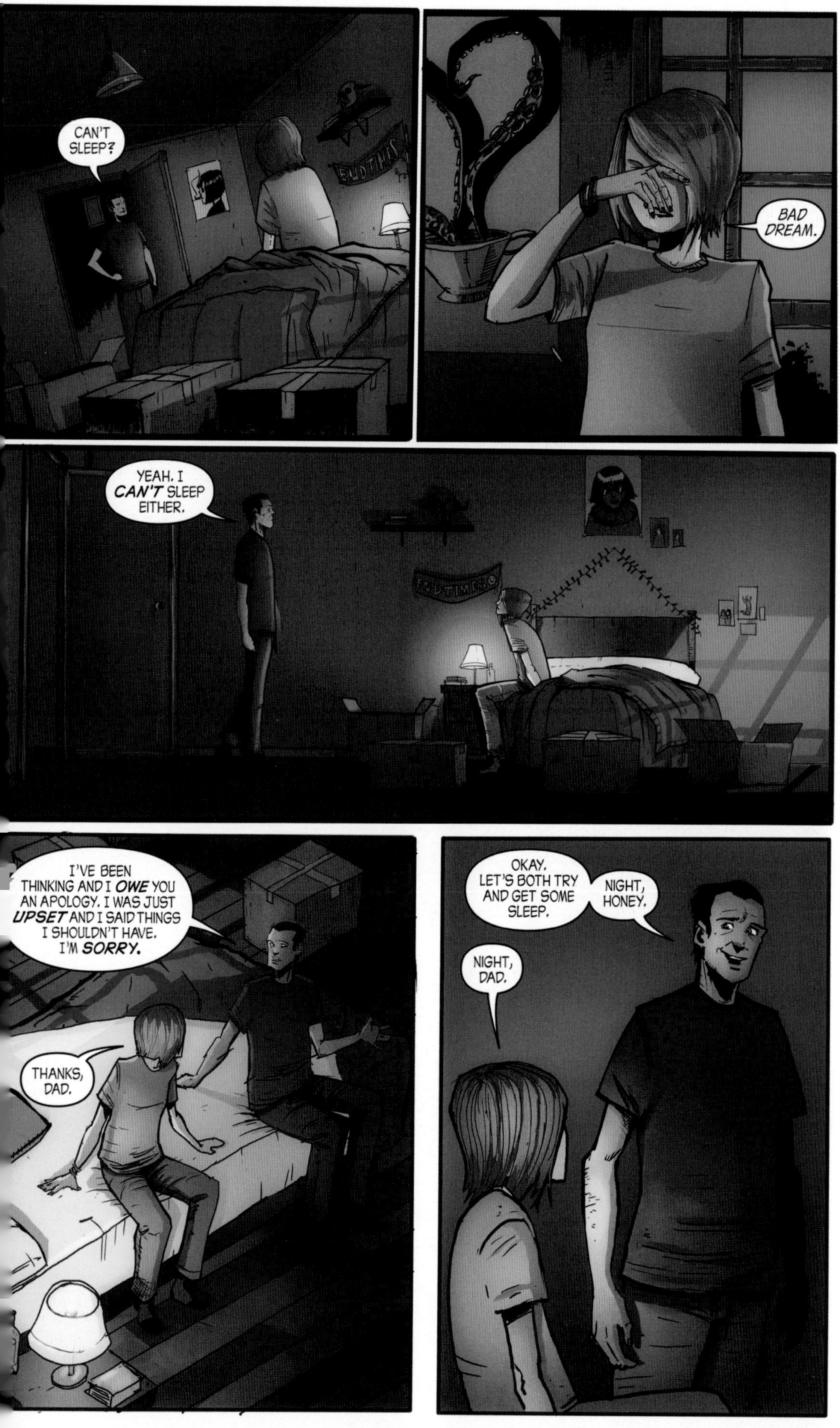
CAN'T SLEEP?
BAD DREAM.
YEAH. I CAN'T SLEEP EITHER.
I'VE BEEN THINKING AND I OWE YOU AN APOLOGY. I WAS JUST UPSET AND I SAID THINGS I SHOULDN'T HAVE. I'M SORRY.
THANKS, DAD.
OKAY. LET'S BOTH TRY AND GET SOME SLEEP.
NIGHT, HONEY.
NIGHT, DAD.

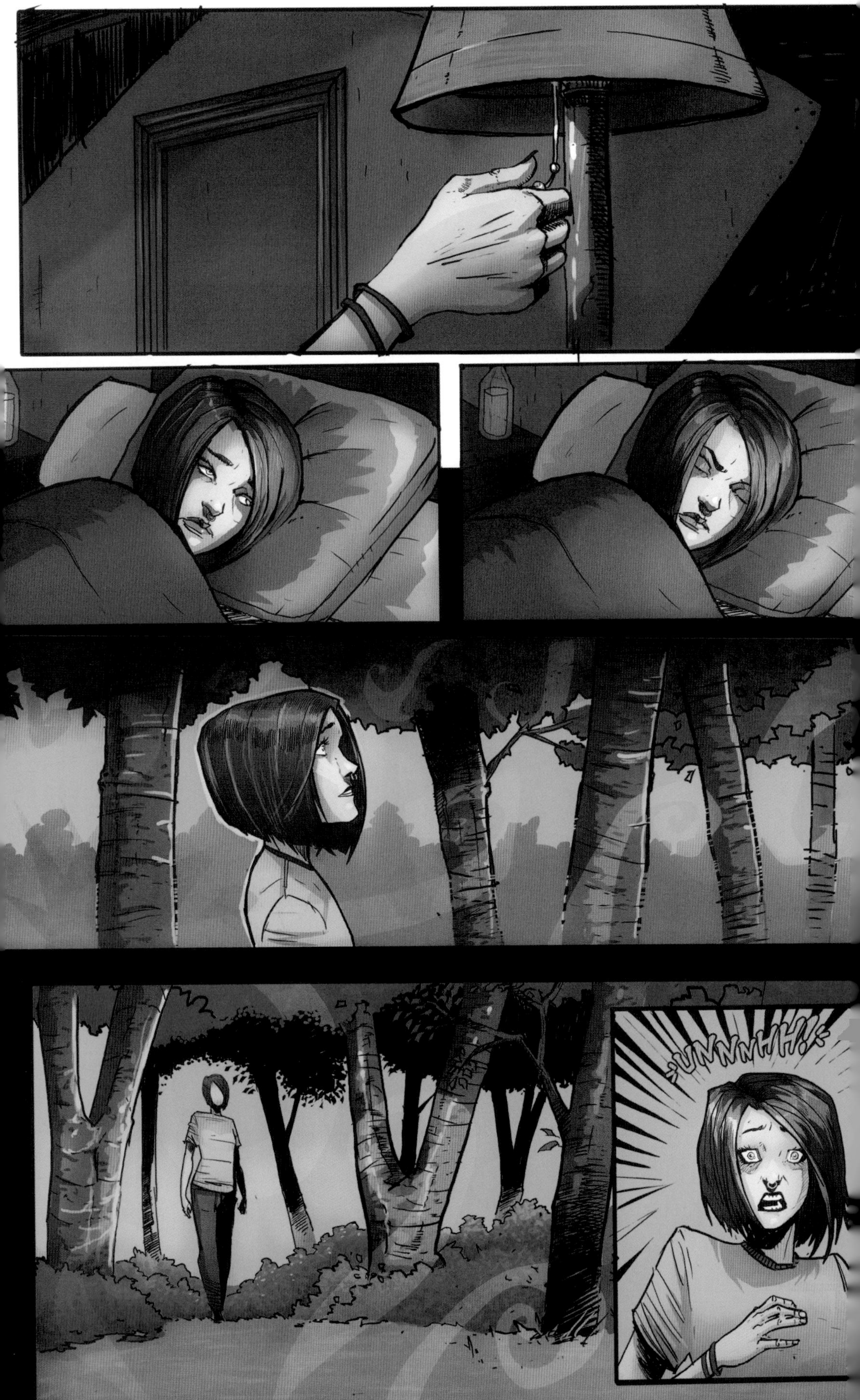
UNNNHH!

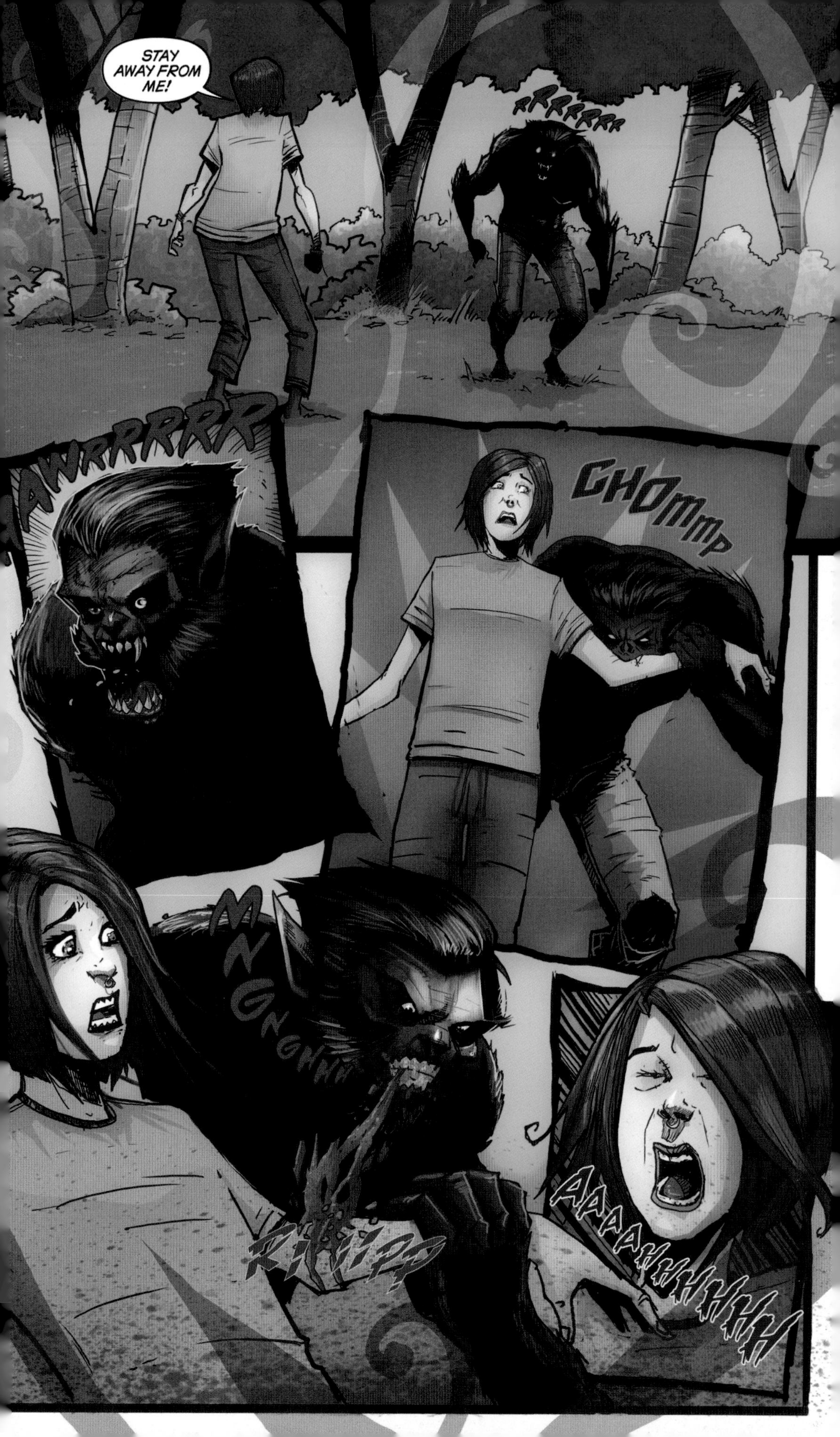
STAY AWAY FROM ME!
RRRRRRRR
AWRRRRRR
CHOMMP
MNGNGNHH
RIIIPP
AAAAHHHHHH

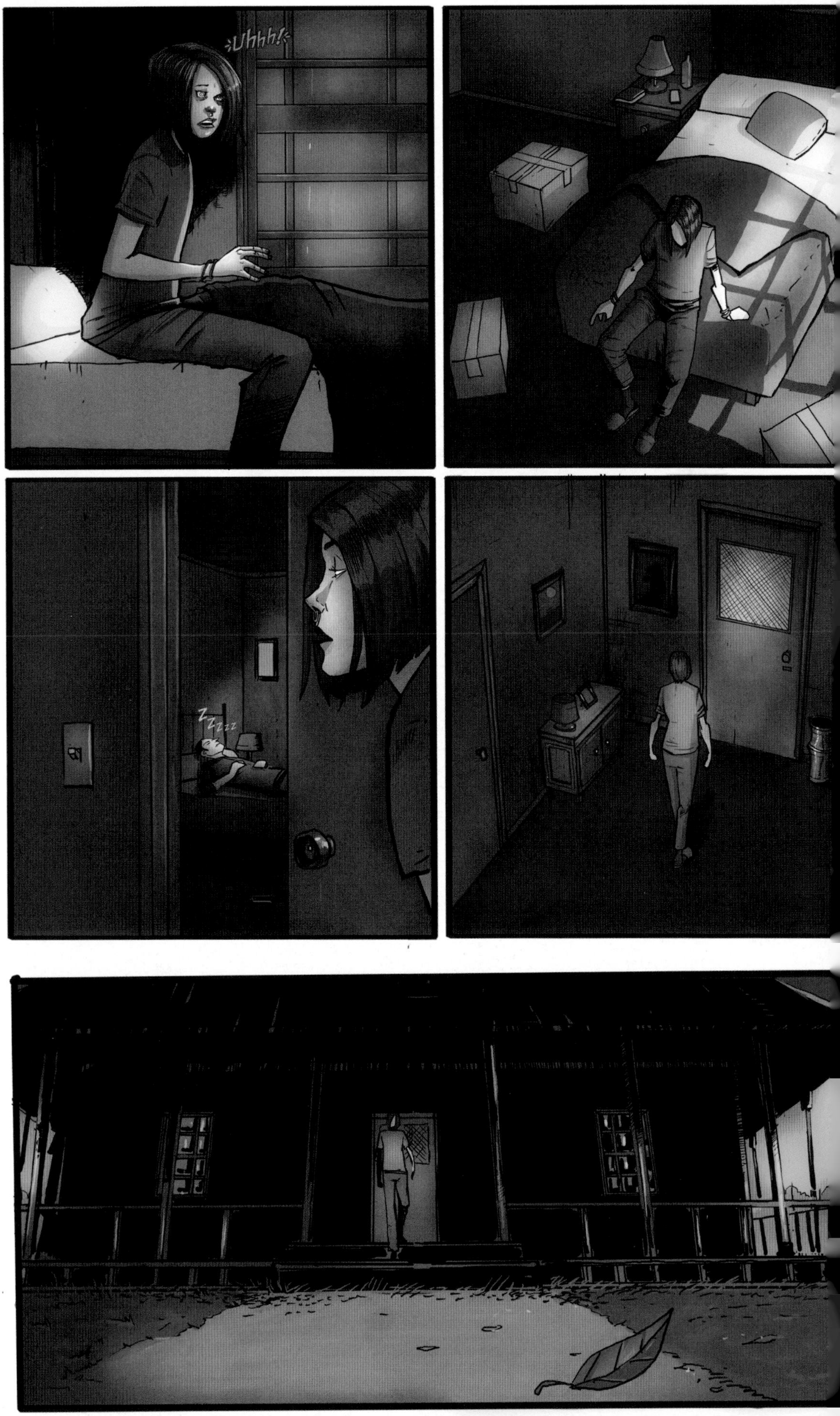
Uhhh!
Z Z z z z

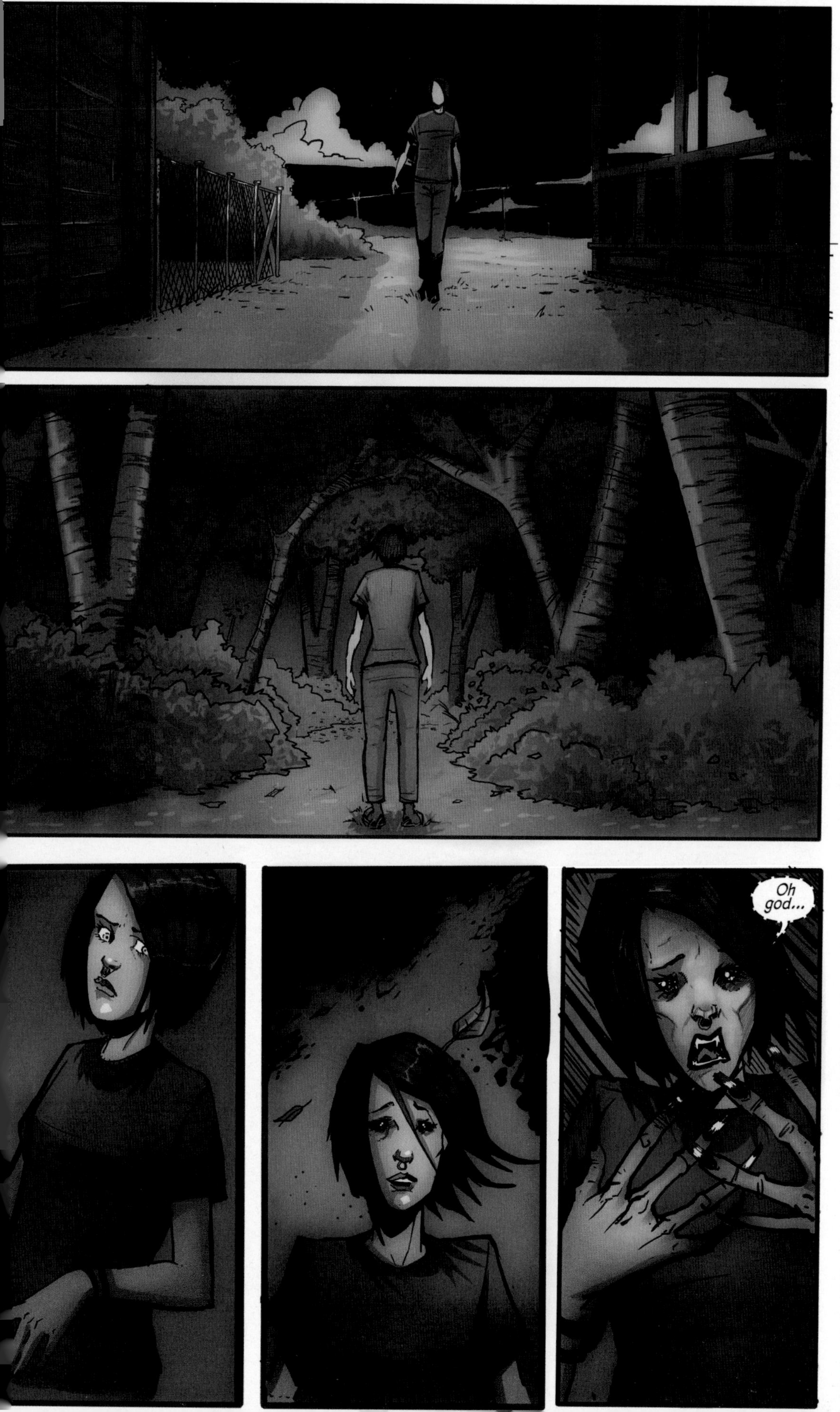
Oh god...

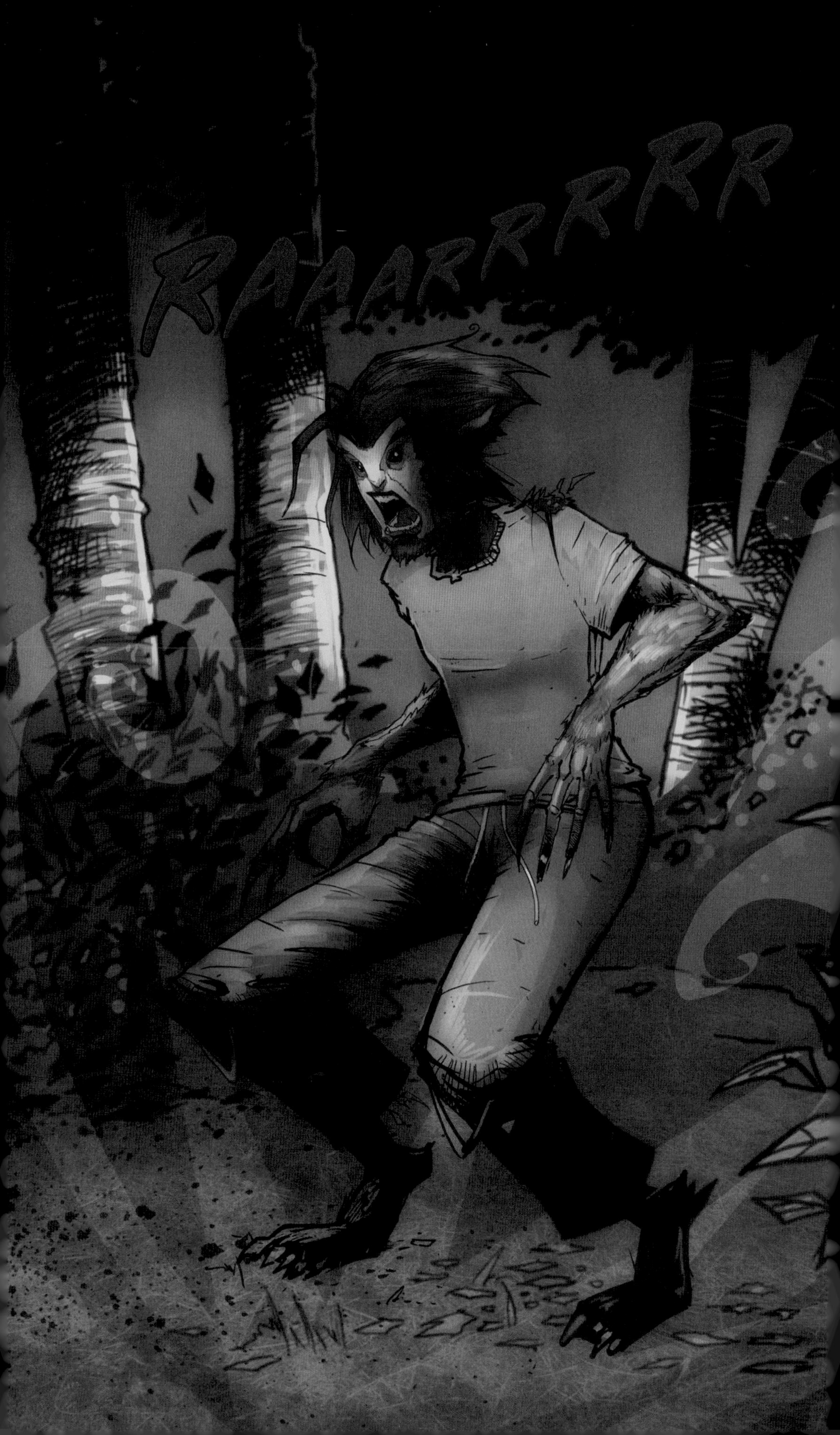
RAAARRRRRRR

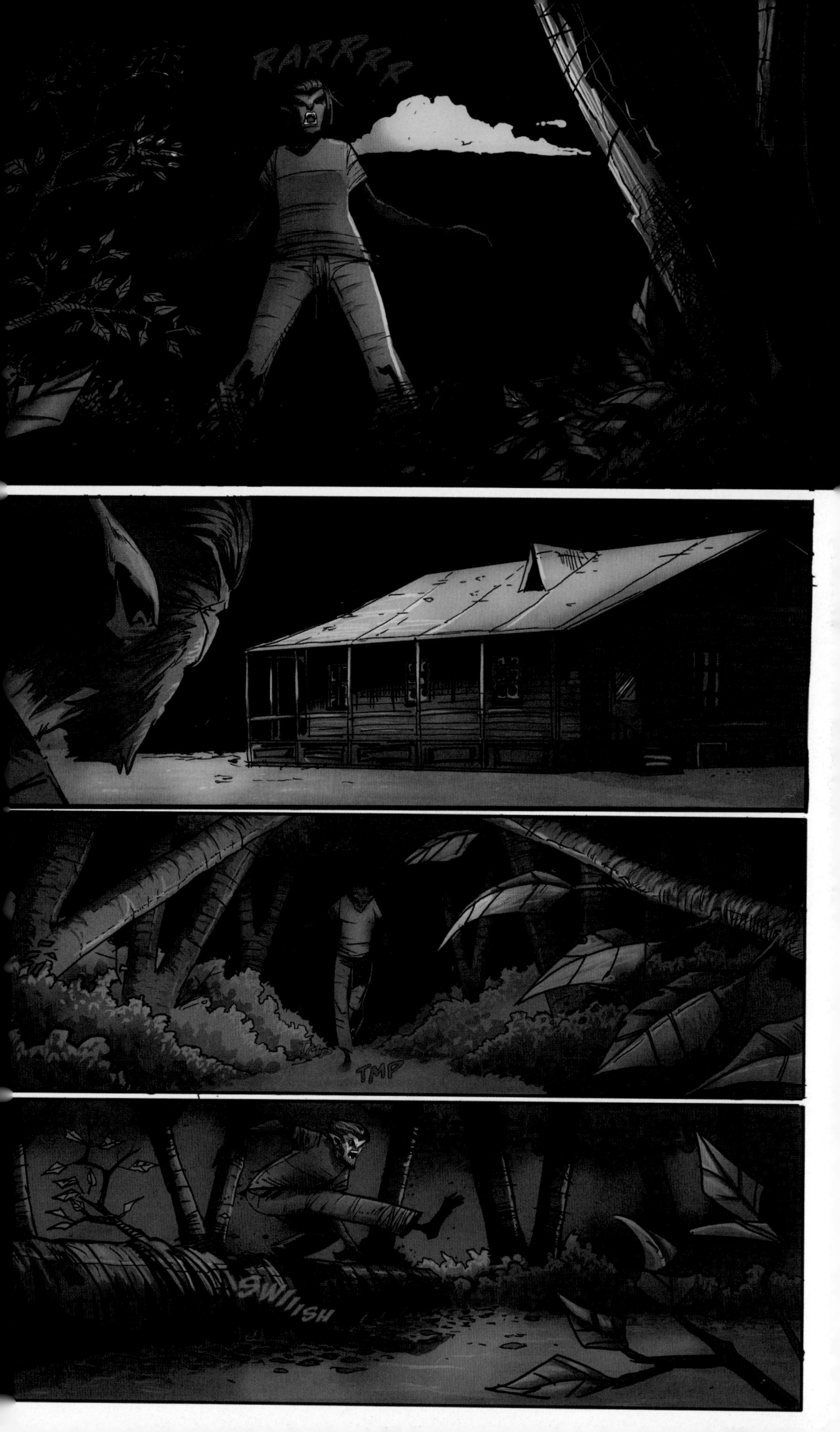
RARRRRR
TMP
SWIISH

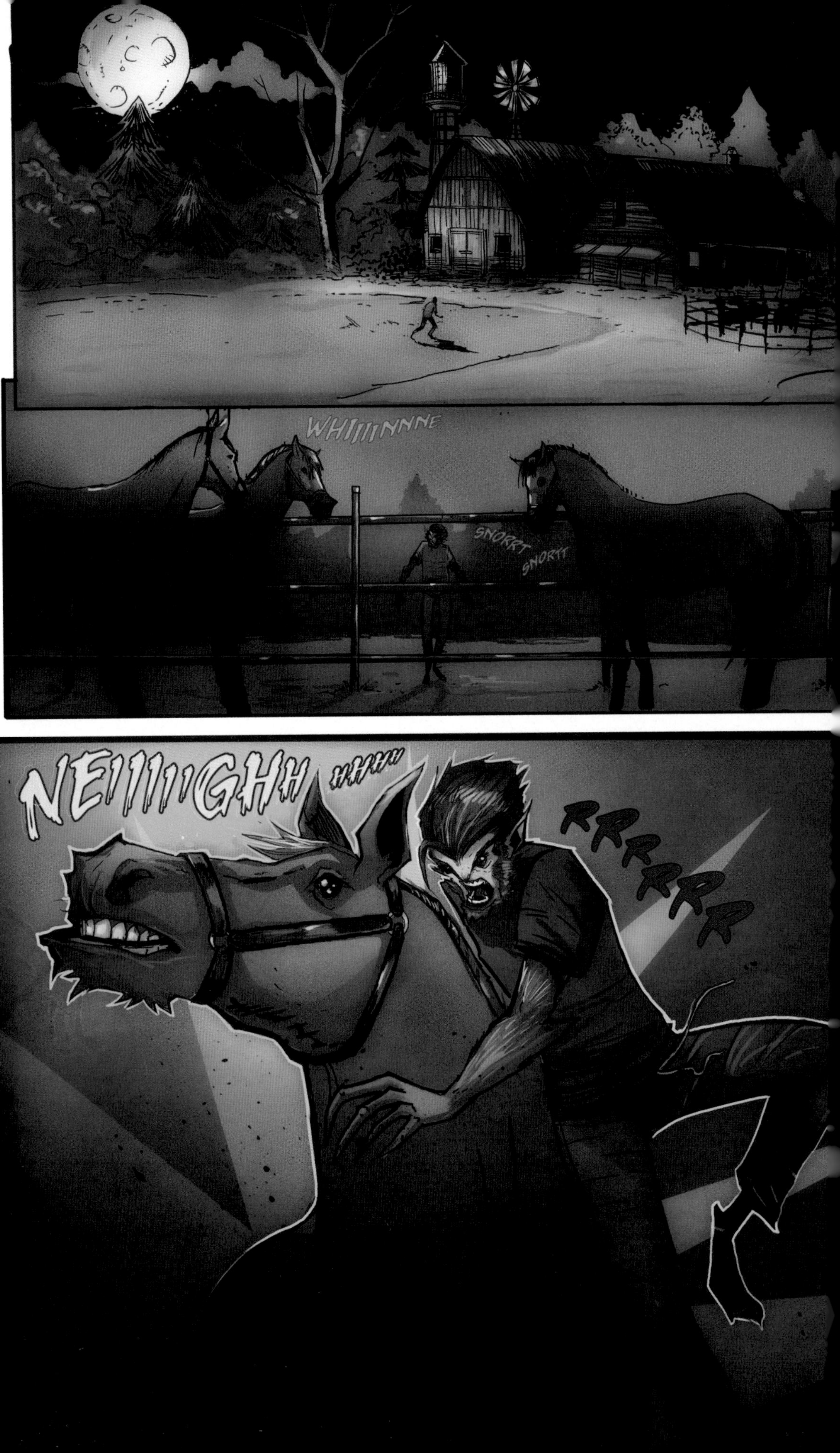
WHIIIINNNE
SNORRT
SNORTT
NEIIIIIGHH HHHH
RRRRRRR

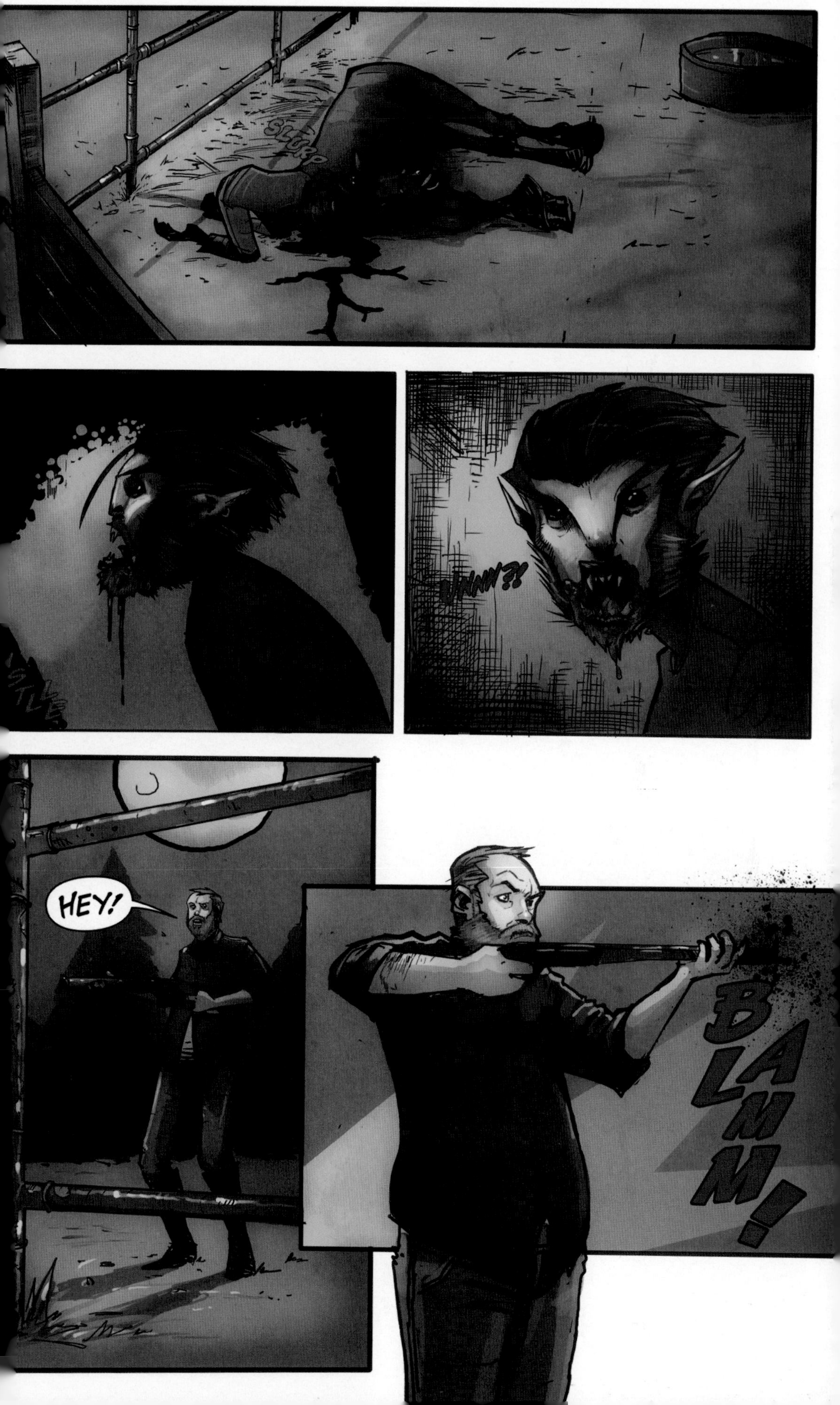
SLURP
UNNN?!
HEY!
BALMM!

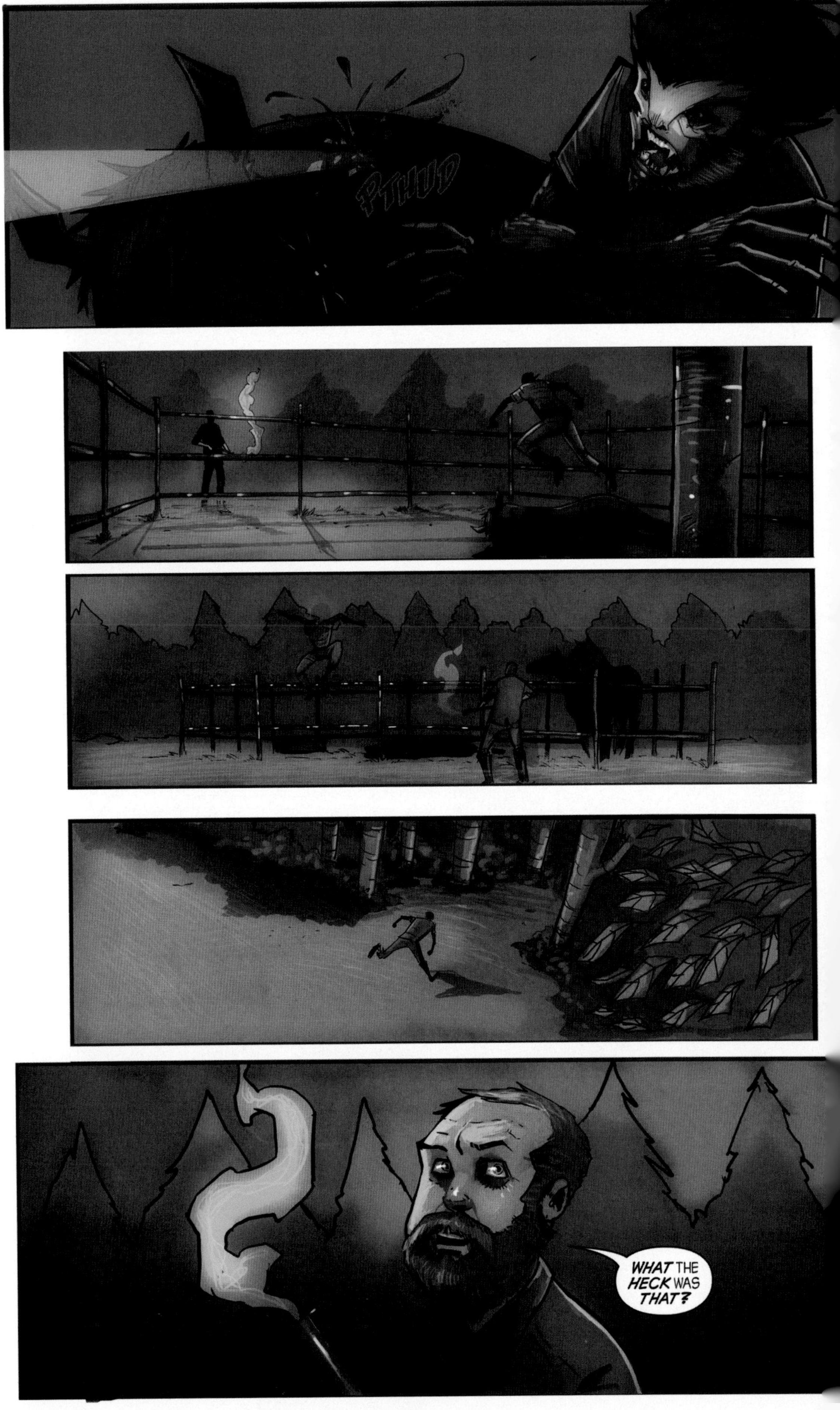
PTHUD
WHAT THE HECK WAS THAT?

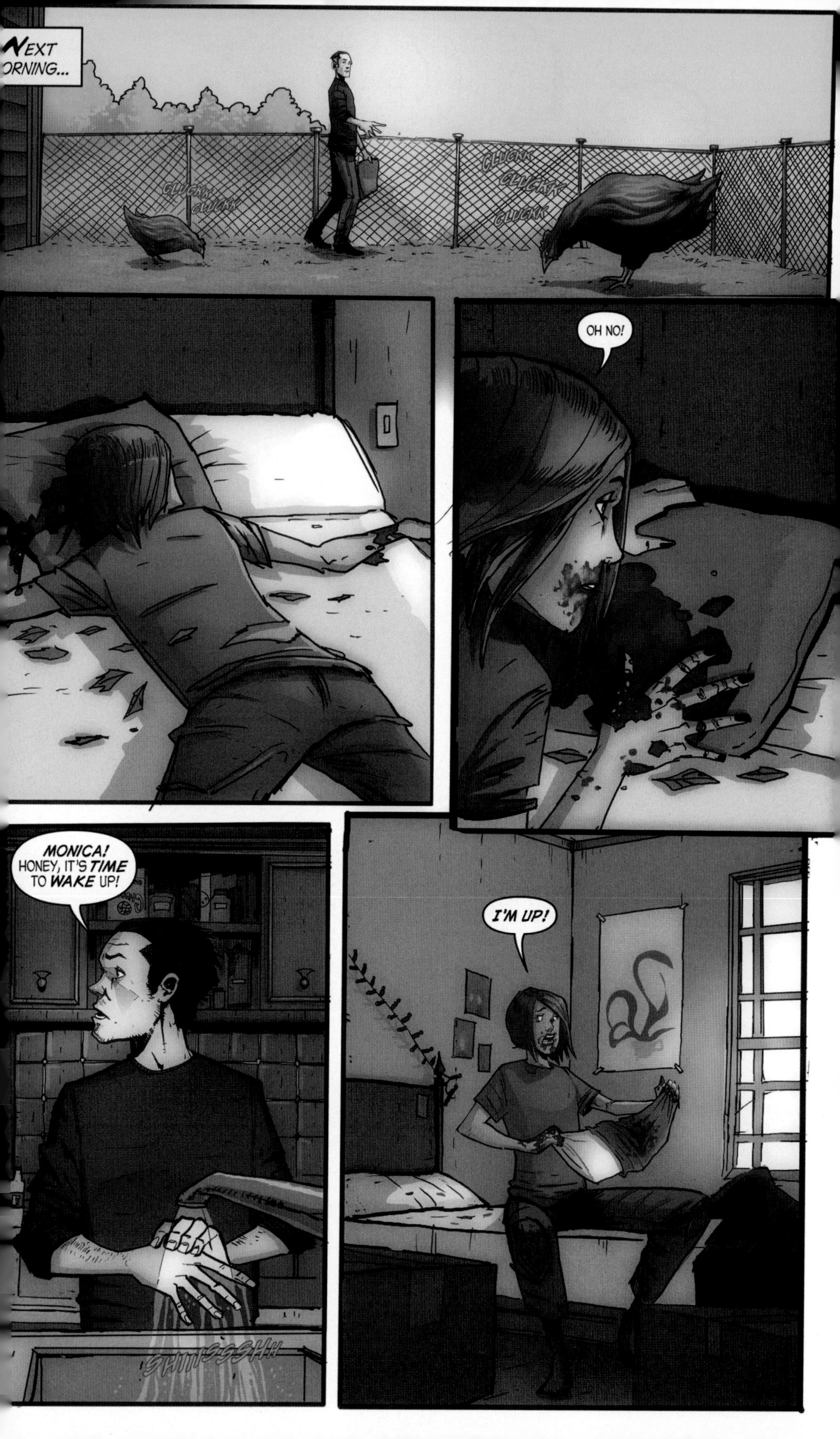
NEXT
ORNING...
CLUCKK
CLUCKK
CLUCKK
CLUCKK
CLUCKK
OH NO!
MONICA!
HONEY, IT'S TIME
TO WAKE UP!
I'M UP!
SHHHSSSHH

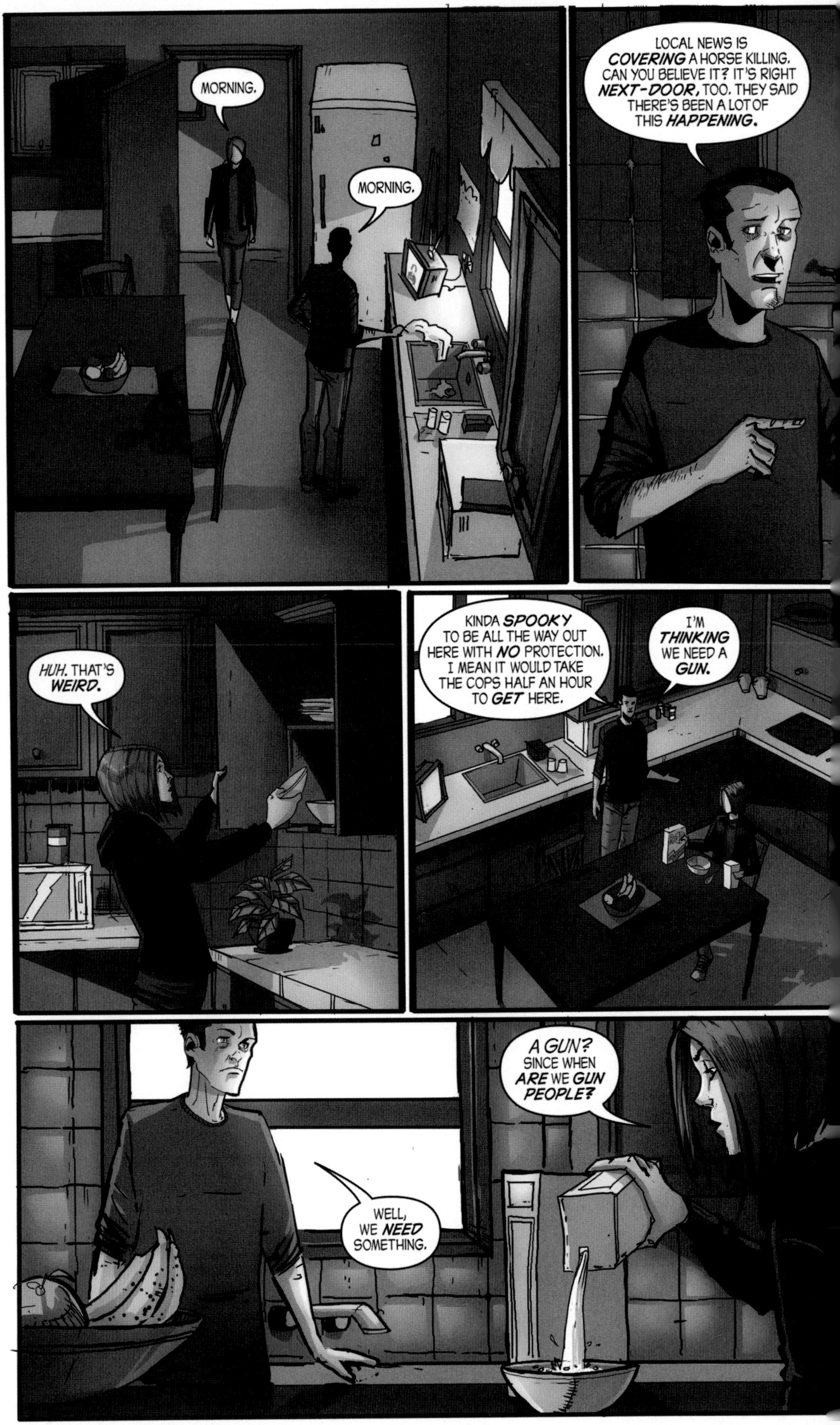
MORNING.
MORNING.
LOCAL NEWS IS *COVERING* A HORSE KILLING. CAN YOU BELIEVE IT? IT'S RIGHT *NEXT-DOOR,* TOO. THEY SAID THERE'S BEEN A LOT OF THIS *HAPPENING.*
HUH. THAT'S *WEIRD.*
KINDA *SPOOKY* TO BE ALL THE WAY OUT HERE WITH *NO* PROTECTION. I MEAN IT WOULD TAKE THE COPS HALF AN HOUR TO *GET* HERE.
I'M *THINKING* WE NEED A *GUN.*
A GUN? SINCE WHEN *ARE* WE *GUN PEOPLE?*
WELL, WE *NEED* SOMETHING.

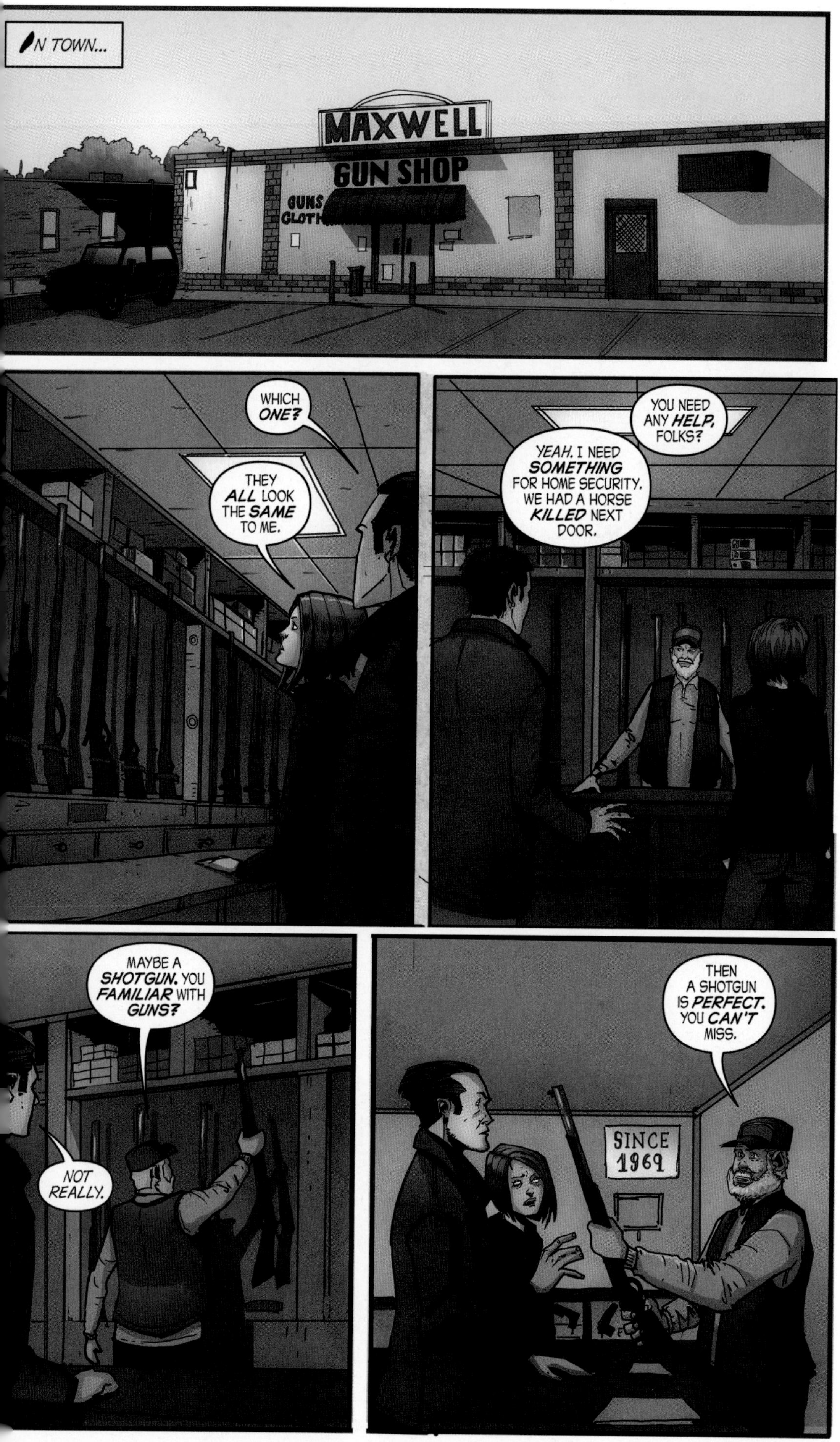
IN TOWN...
MAXWELL
GUN SHOP
GUNS
CLOTH
WHICH ONE?
THEY ALL LOOK THE SAME TO ME.
YOU NEED ANY HELP, FOLKS?
YEAH. I NEED SOMETHING FOR HOME SECURITY. WE HAD A HORSE KILLED NEXT DOOR.
MAYBE A SHOTGUN. YOU FAMILIAR WITH GUNS?
NOT REALLY.
THEN A SHOTGUN IS PERFECT. YOU CAN'T MISS.
SINCE 1969

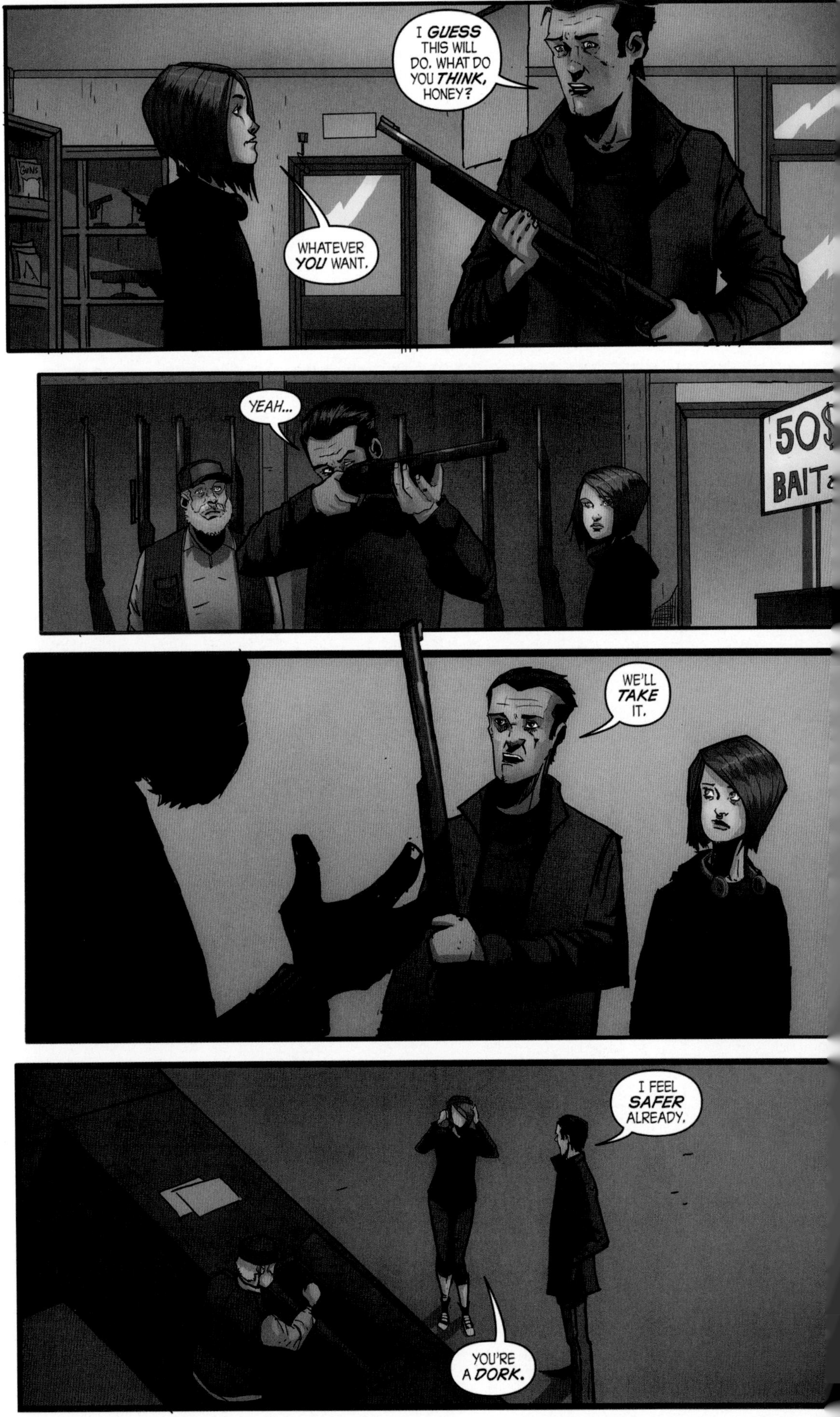
GUNS
I GUESS THIS WILL DO. WHAT DO YOU THINK, HONEY?
WHATEVER YOU WANT.
YEAH...
50$
BAIT
WE'LL TAKE IT.
I FEEL SAFER ALREADY.
YOU'RE A DORK.

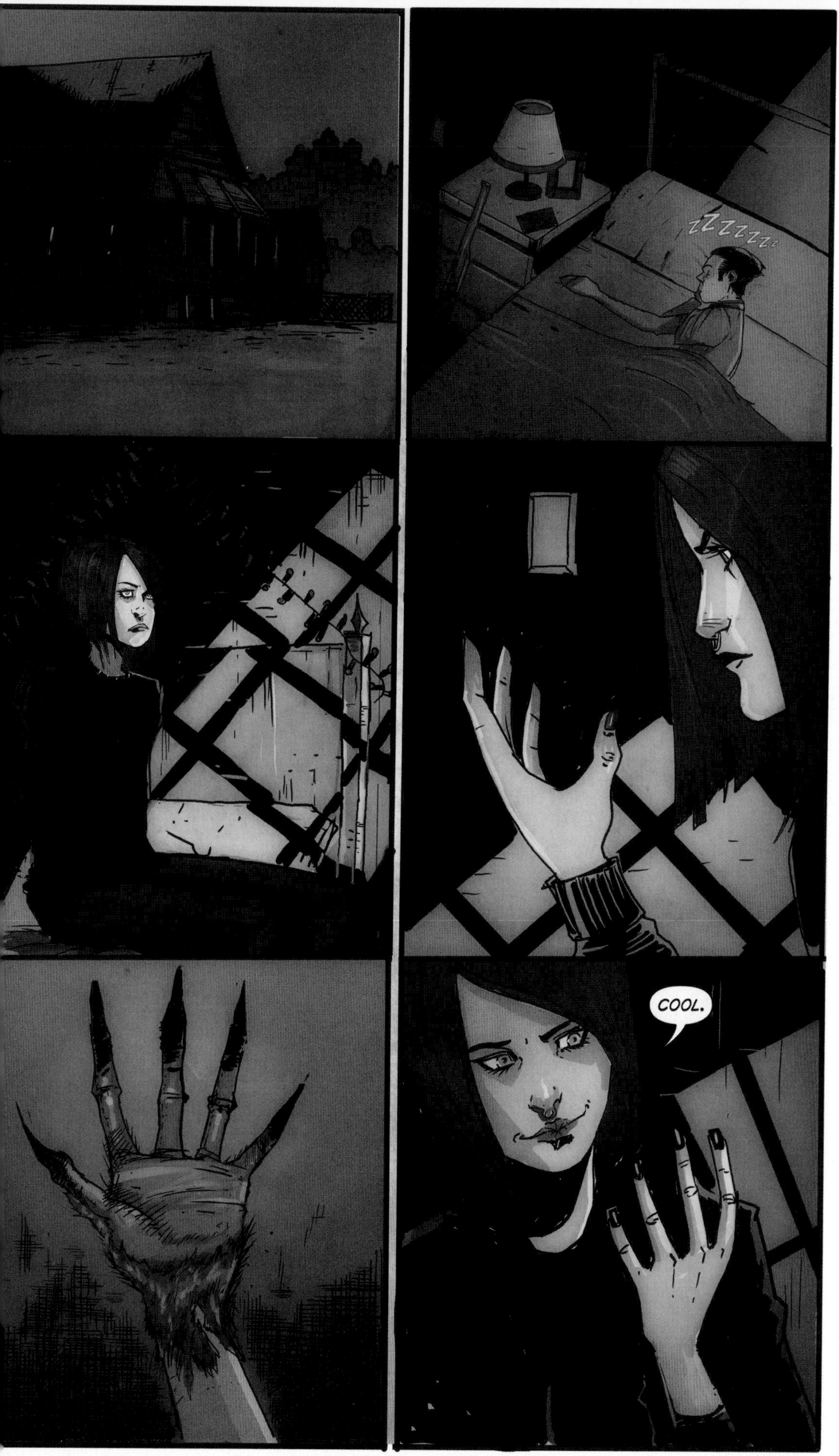
ZZZZZZZ
COOL.

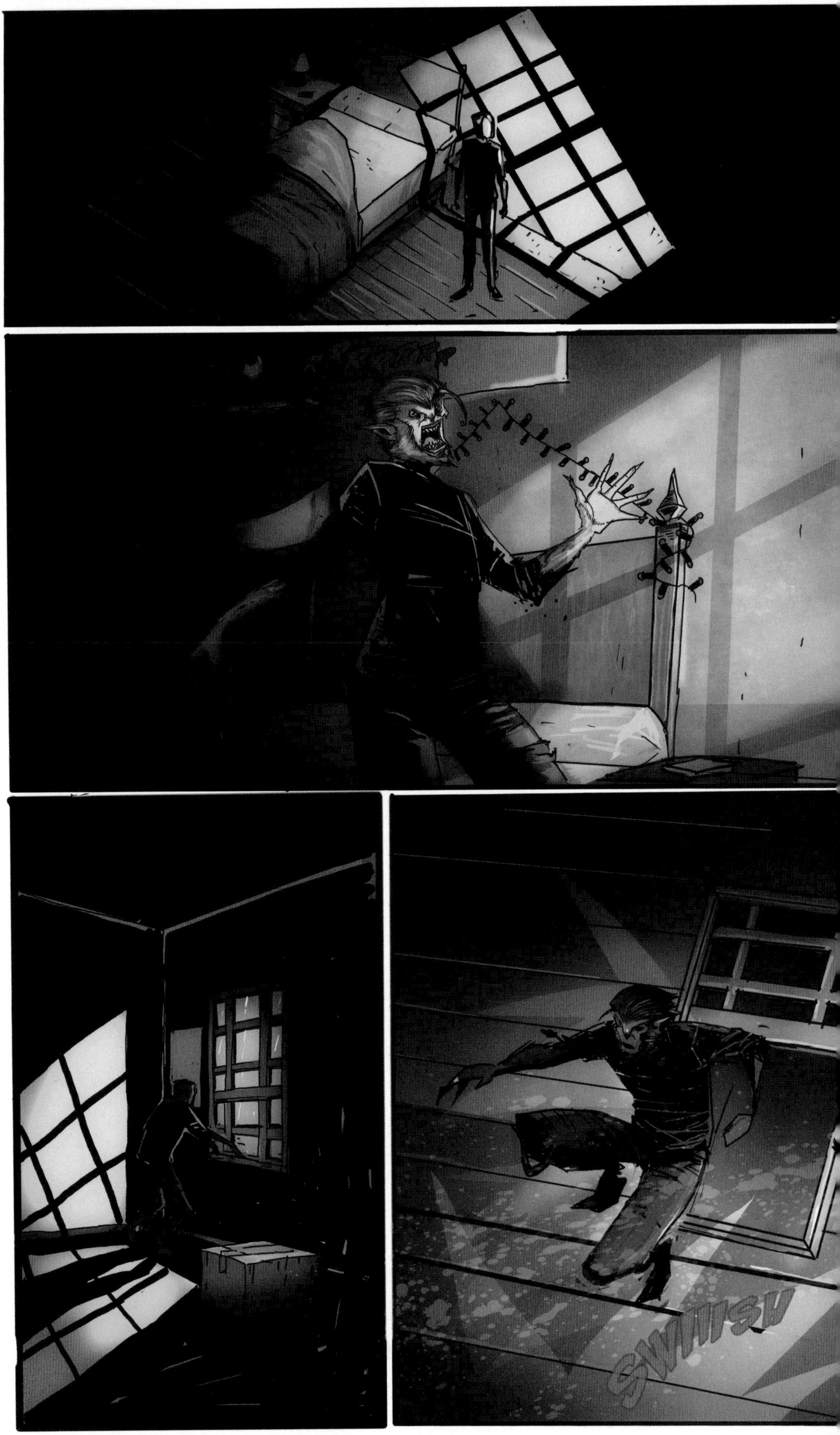
SWIIISH

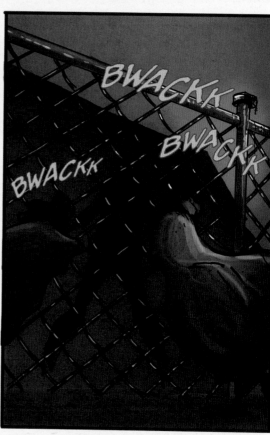

BWACKK

BWACKK

BWACKK

RRRRRR

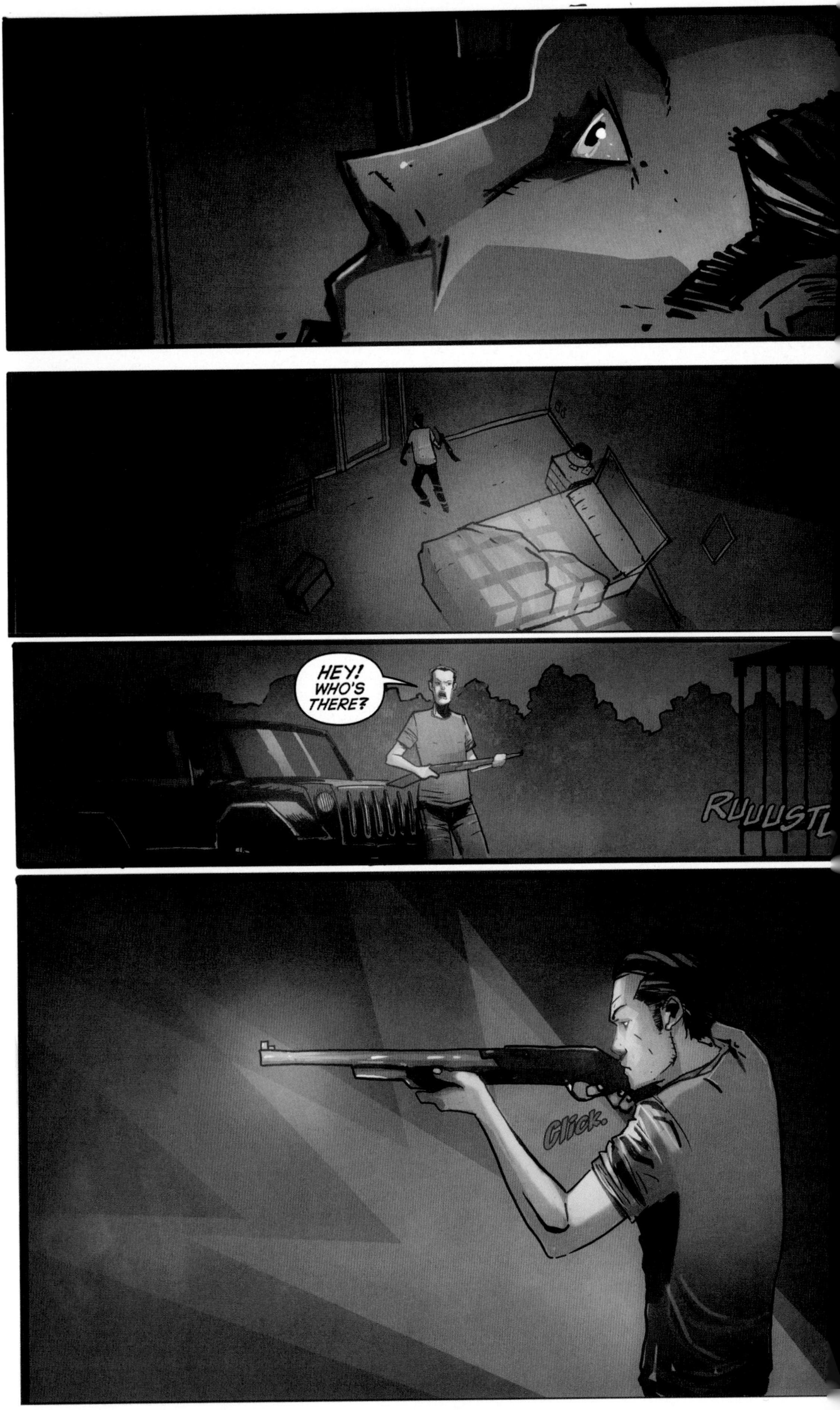
HEY! WHO'S THERE?
RUUUSTL
Click.

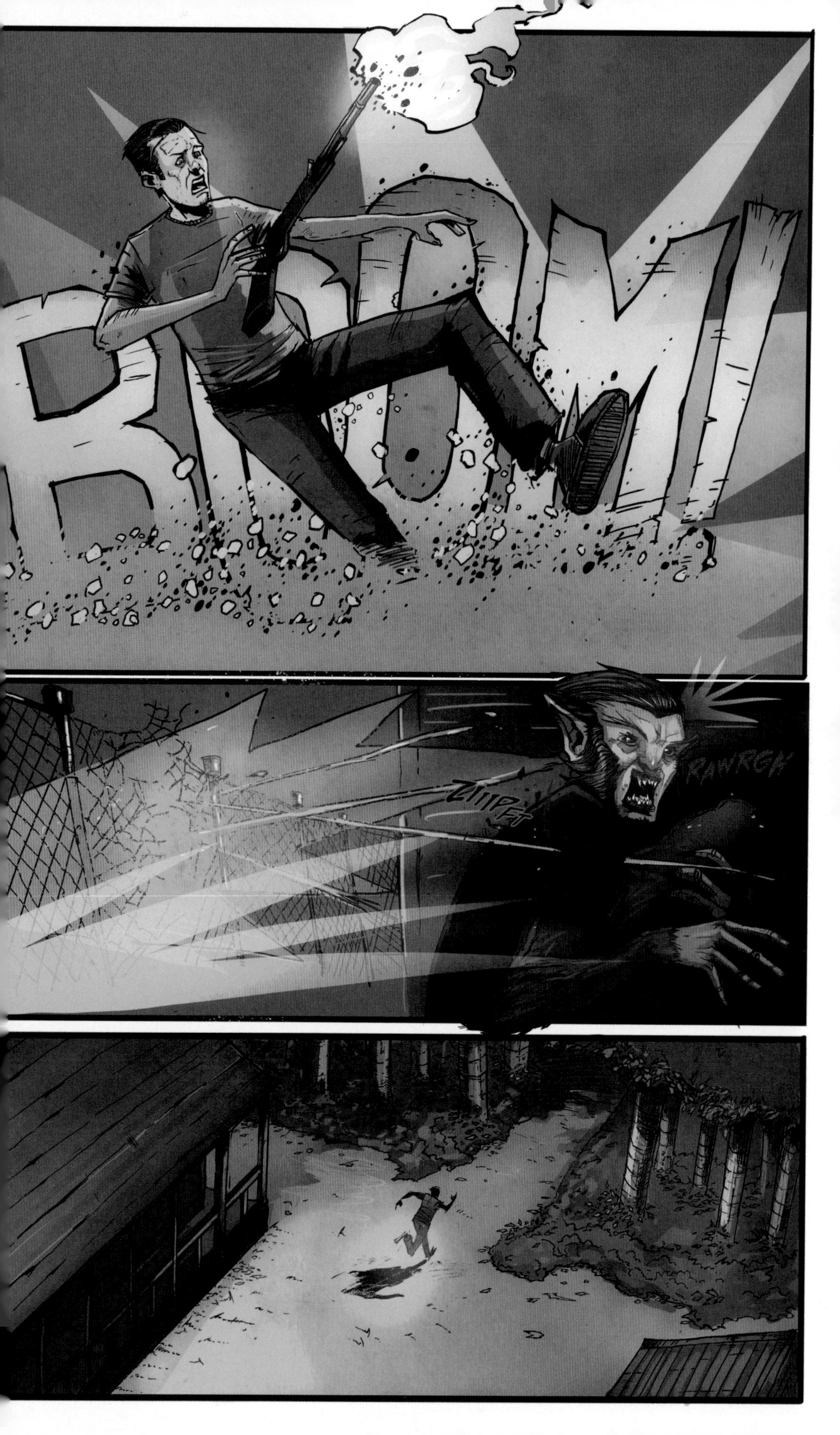
ZIIIPFT
RAWRGH

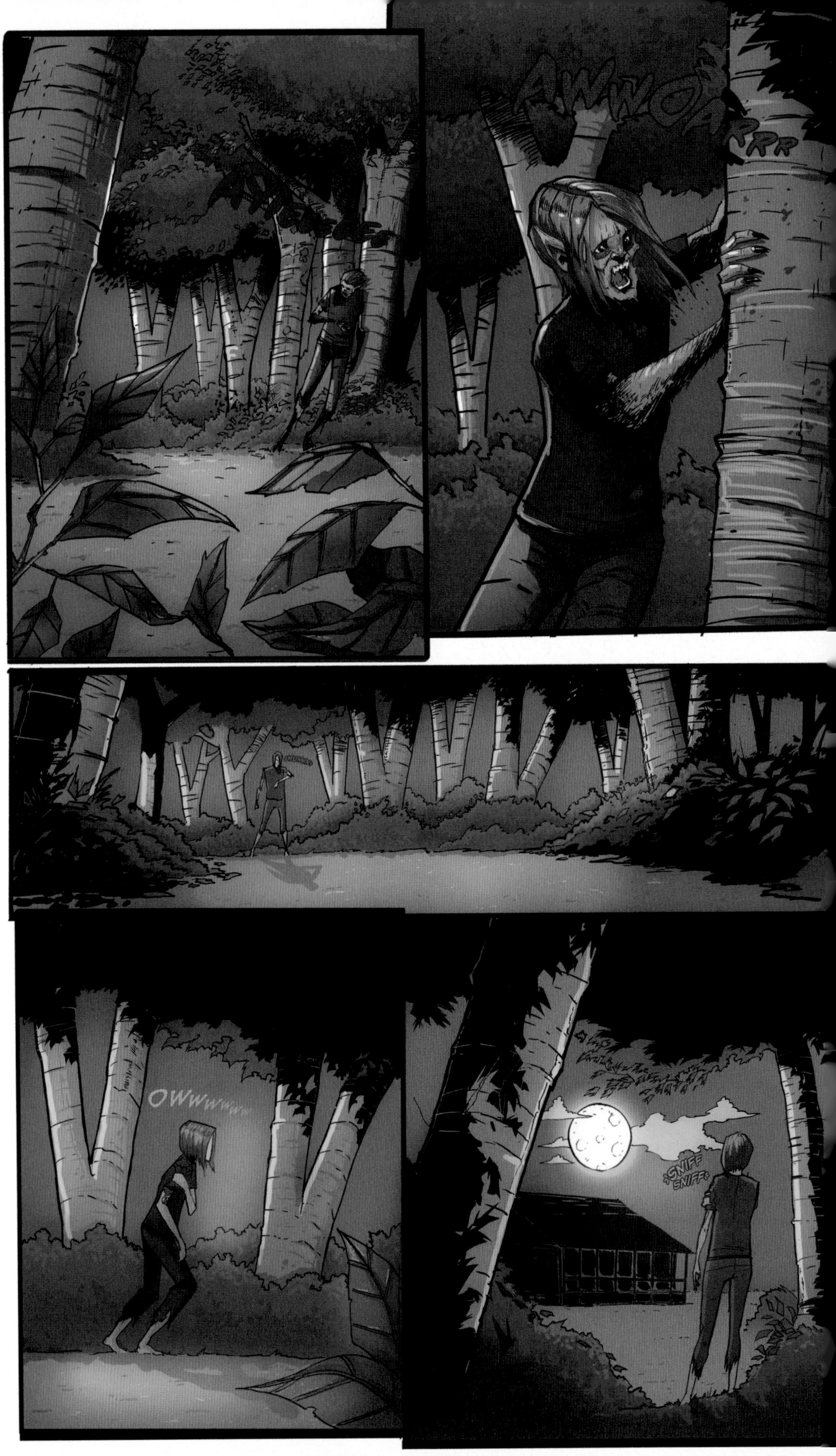
AWWOARRRR
OWWWWWW
SNIFF
SNIFF

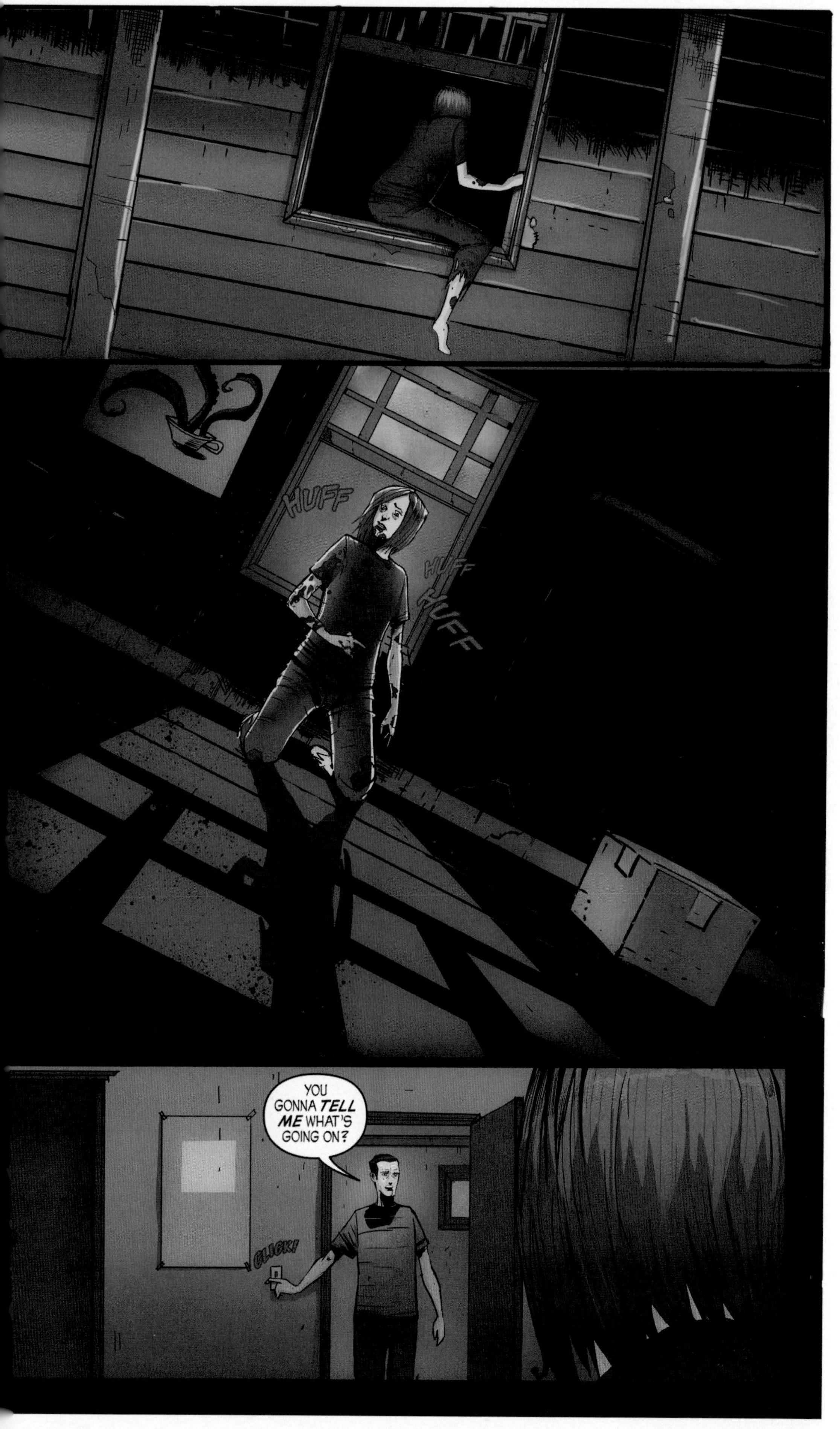
HUFF
HUFF
HUFF
YOU GONNA TELL ME WHAT'S GOING ON?
CLICK!

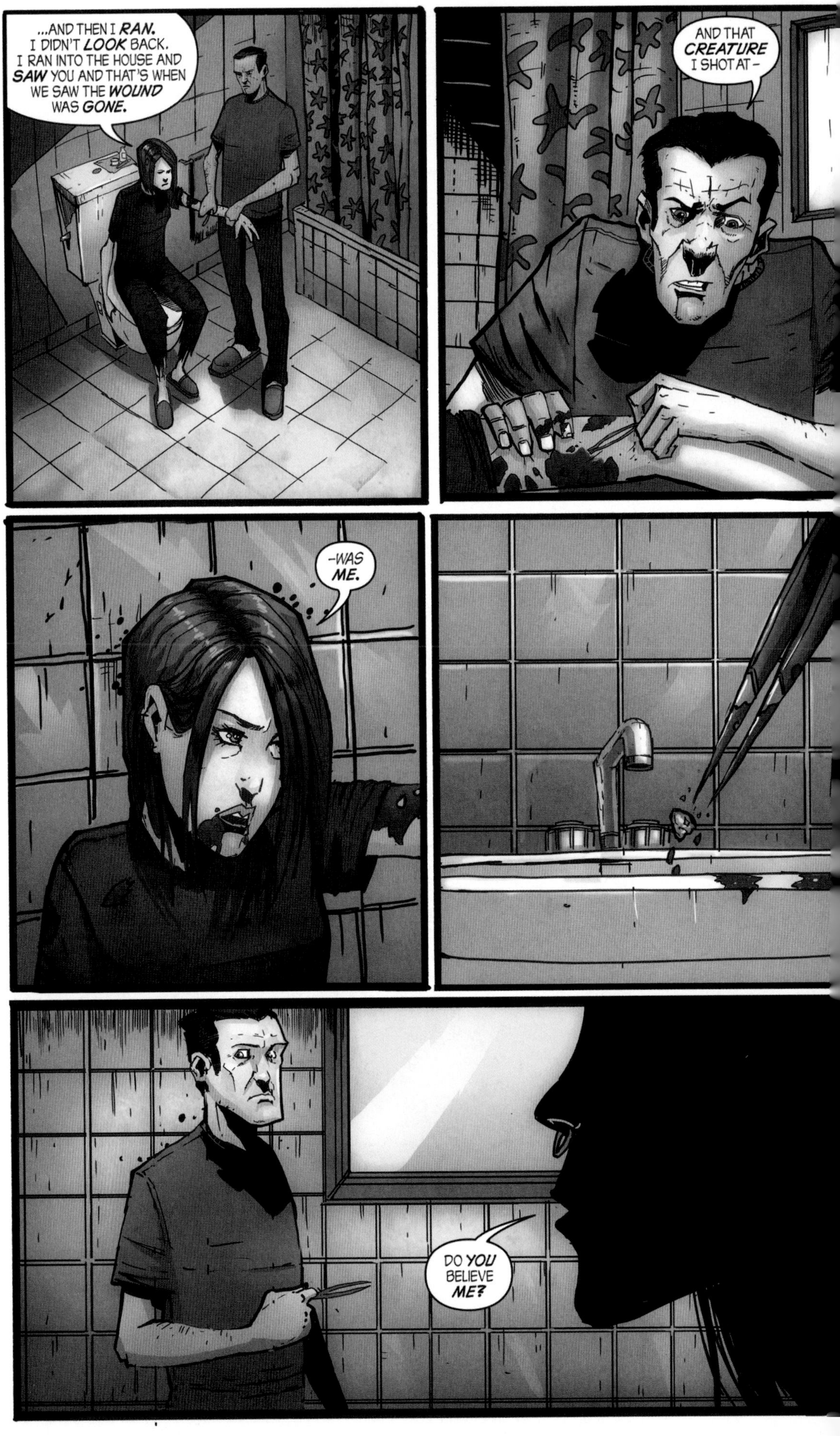
...AND THEN I RAN. I DIDN'T LOOK BACK. I RAN INTO THE HOUSE AND SAW YOU AND THAT'S WHEN WE SAW THE WOUND WAS GONE.
AND THAT CREATURE I SHOT AT -
-WAS ME.
DO YOU BELIEVE ME?

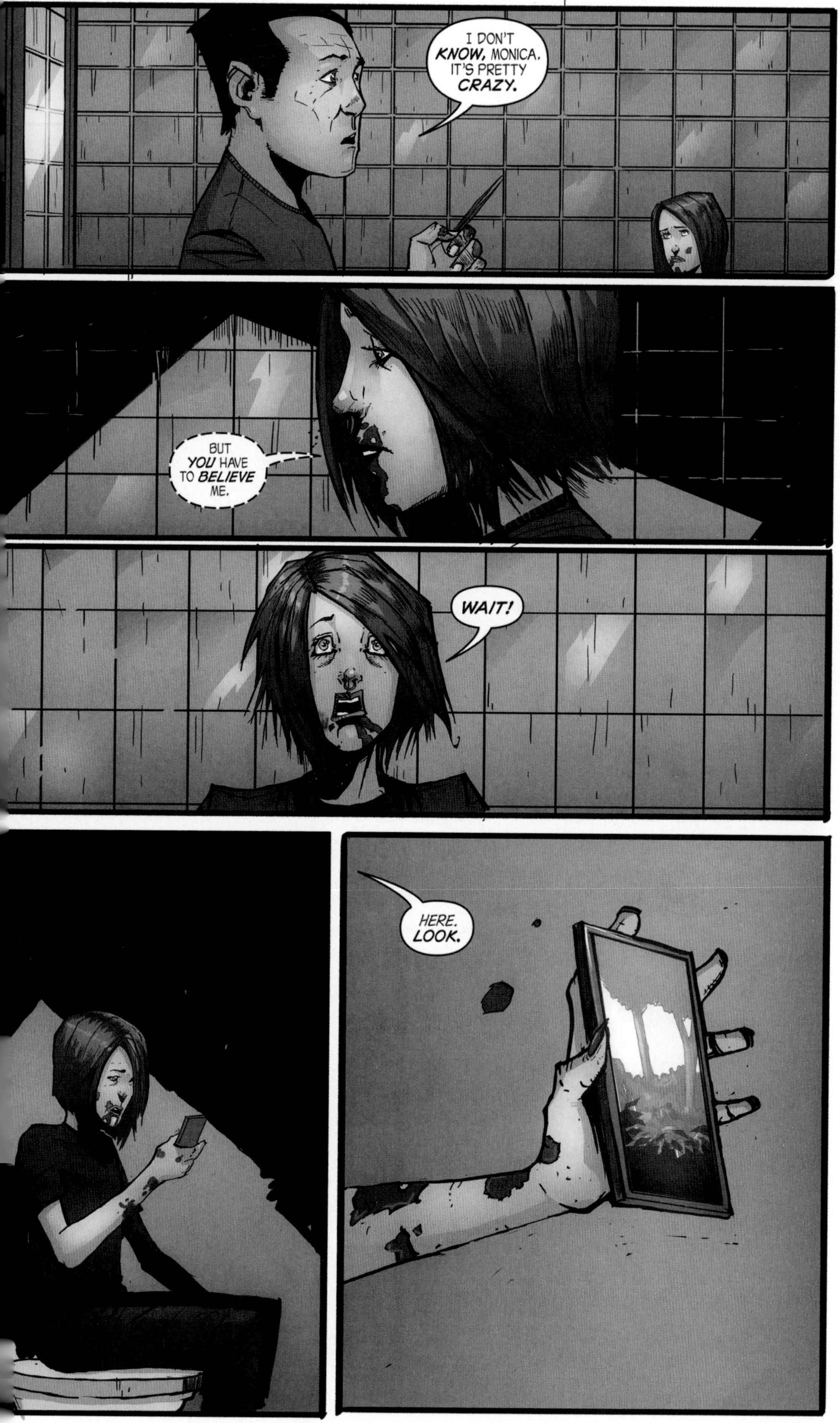
I DON'T KNOW, MONICA. IT'S PRETTY CRAZY.
BUT YOU HAVE TO BELIEVE ME.
WAIT!
HERE. LOOK.

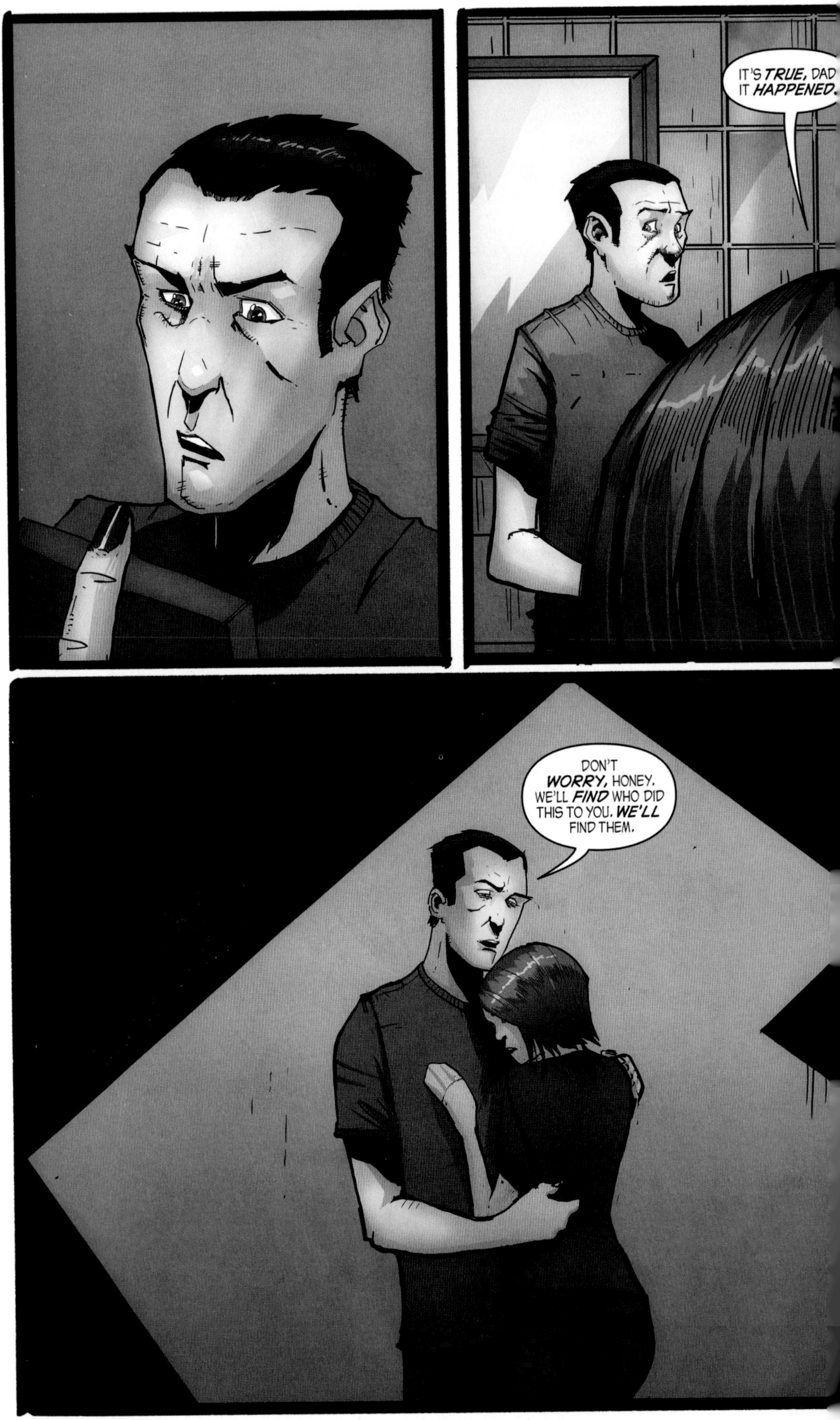
IT'S TRUE, DAD. IT HAPPENED.
DON'T WORRY, HONEY. WE'LL FIND WHO DID THIS TO YOU. WE'LL FIND THEM.

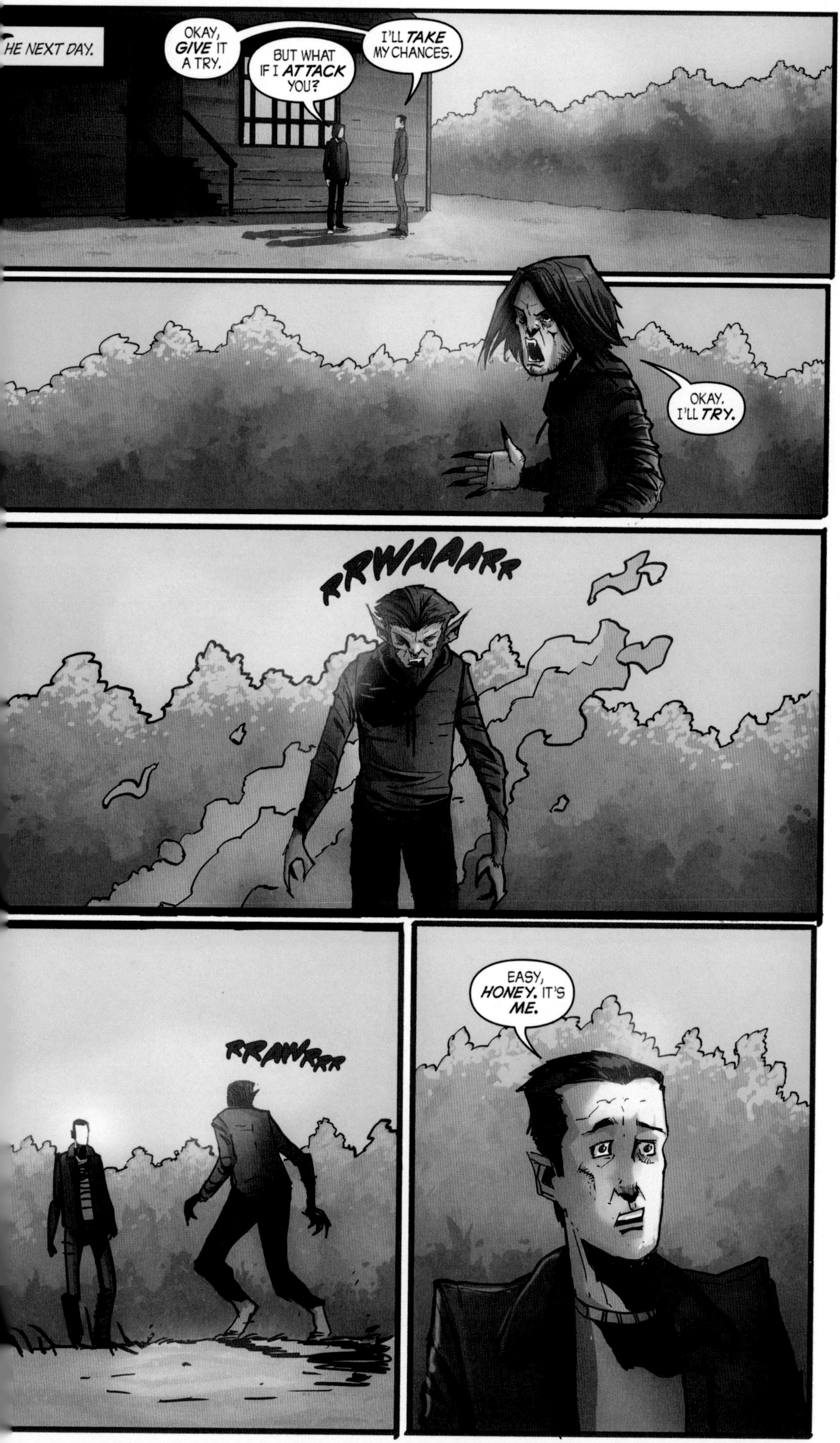

HE NEXT DAY.
OKAY, GIVE IT A TRY.
BUT WHAT IF I ATTACK YOU?
I'LL TAKE MY CHANCES.
OKAY. I'LL TRY.
RRWAAARR
RRAWRRR
EASY, HONEY. IT'S ME.

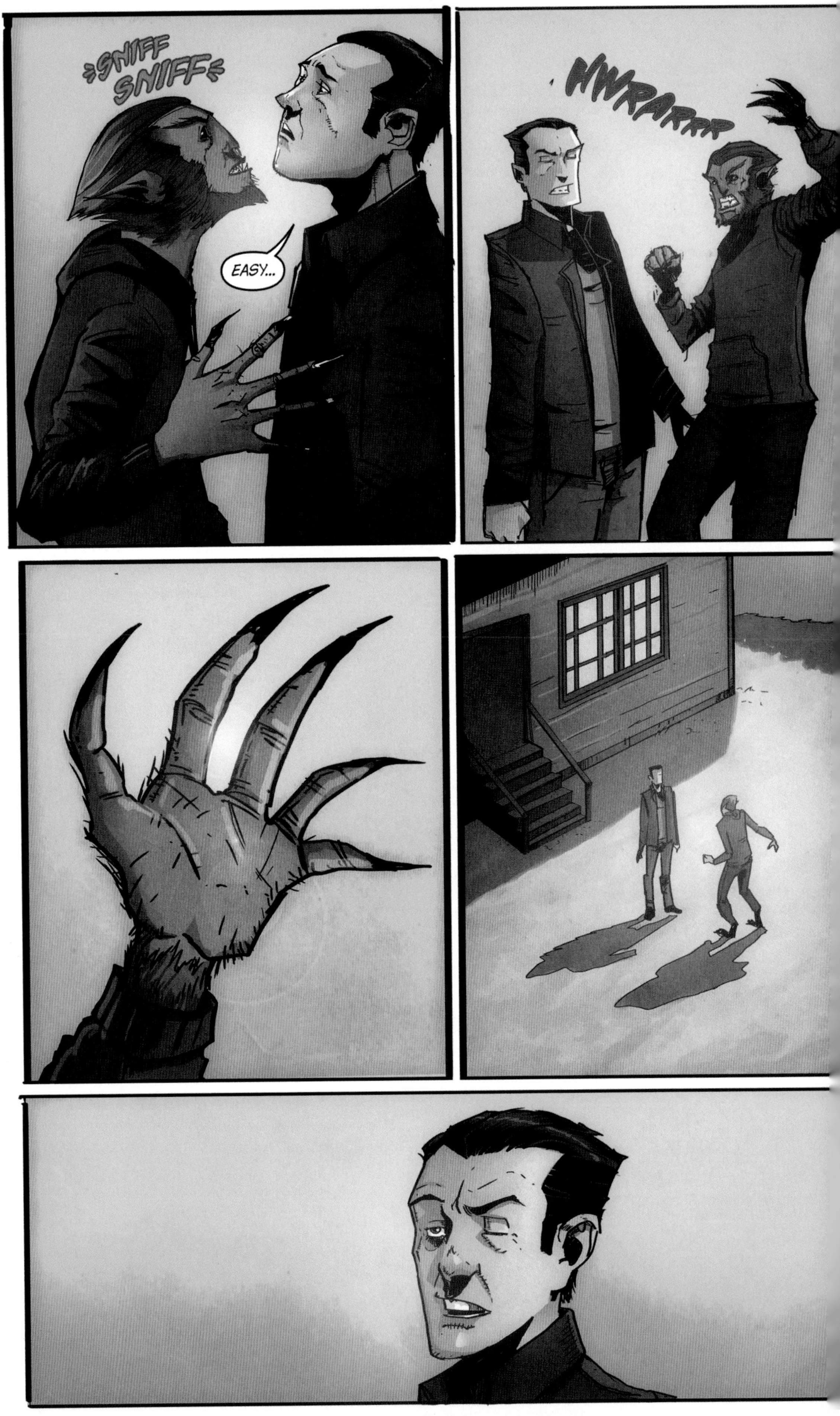
SNIFF SNIFF
EASY...
HWRARRRR

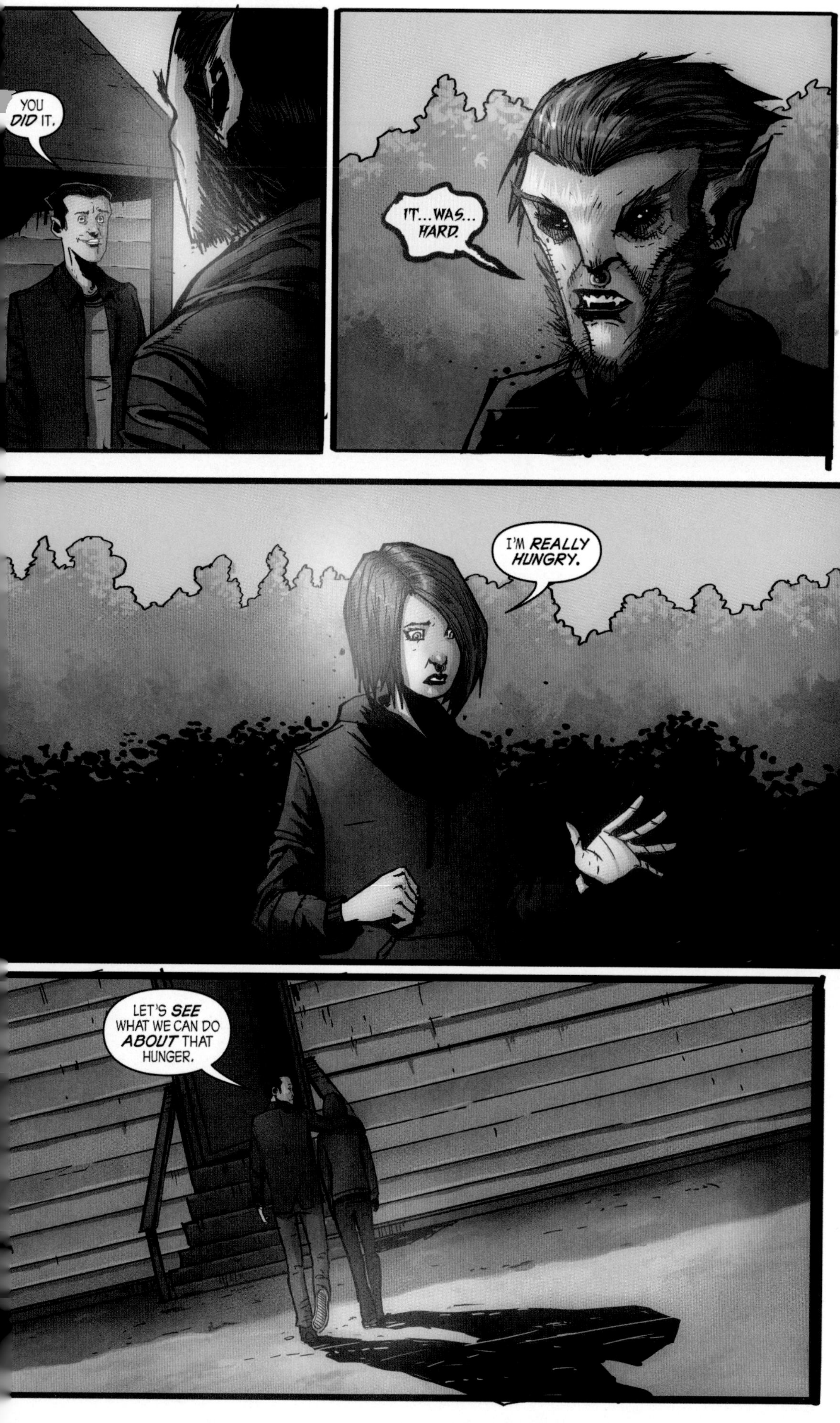
YOU *DID* IT.
IT...WAS... HARD.
I'M *REALLY HUNGRY.*
LET'S *SEE* WHAT WE CAN DO *ABOUT* THAT HUNGER.

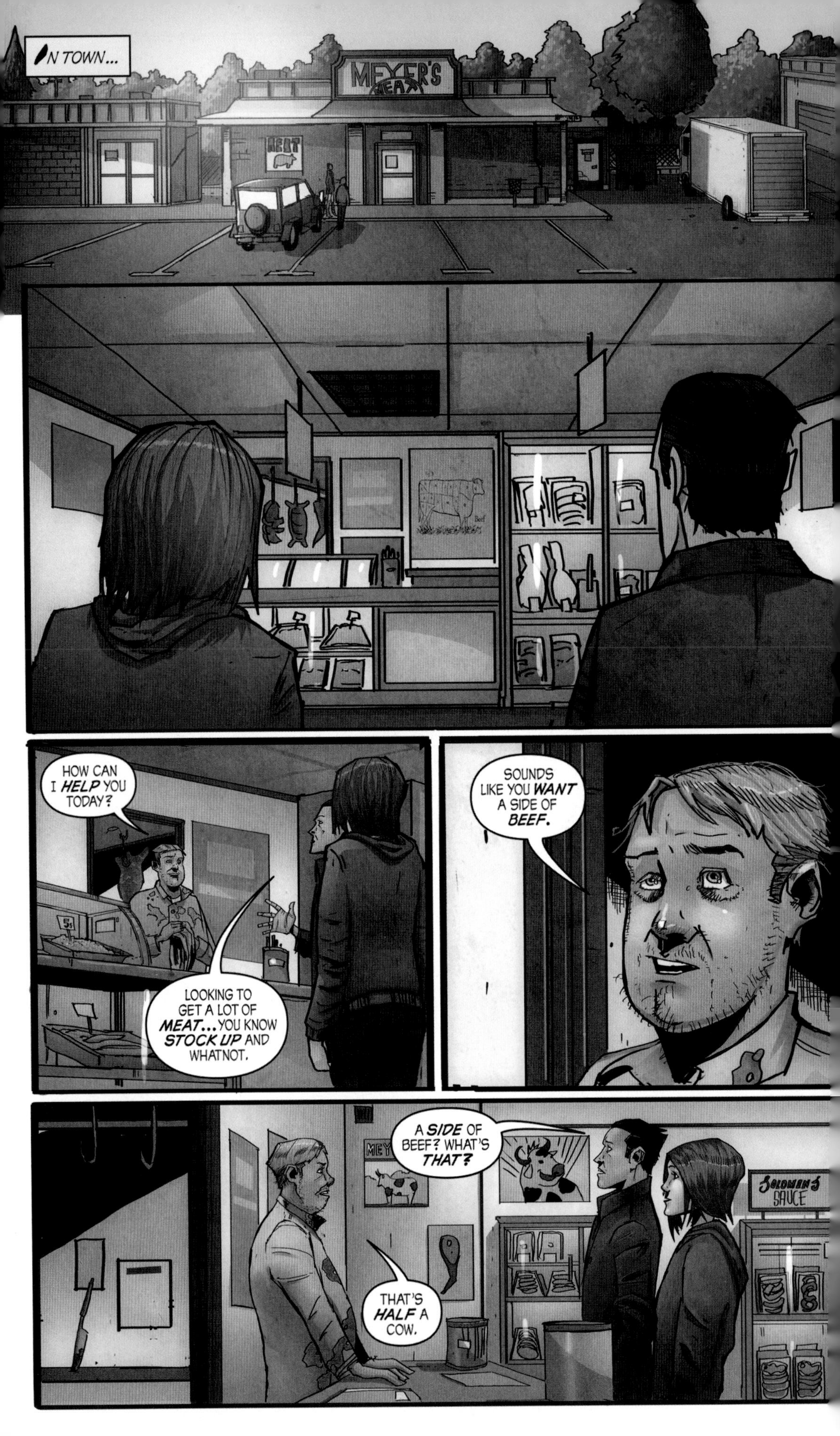
IN TOWN...
MEYER'S MEAT
MEAT
HOW CAN I HELP YOU TODAY?
LOOKING TO GET A LOT OF MEAT... YOU KNOW STOCK UP AND WHATNOT.
SOUNDS LIKE YOU WANT A SIDE OF BEEF.
A SIDE OF BEEF? WHAT'S THAT?
THAT'S HALF A COW.

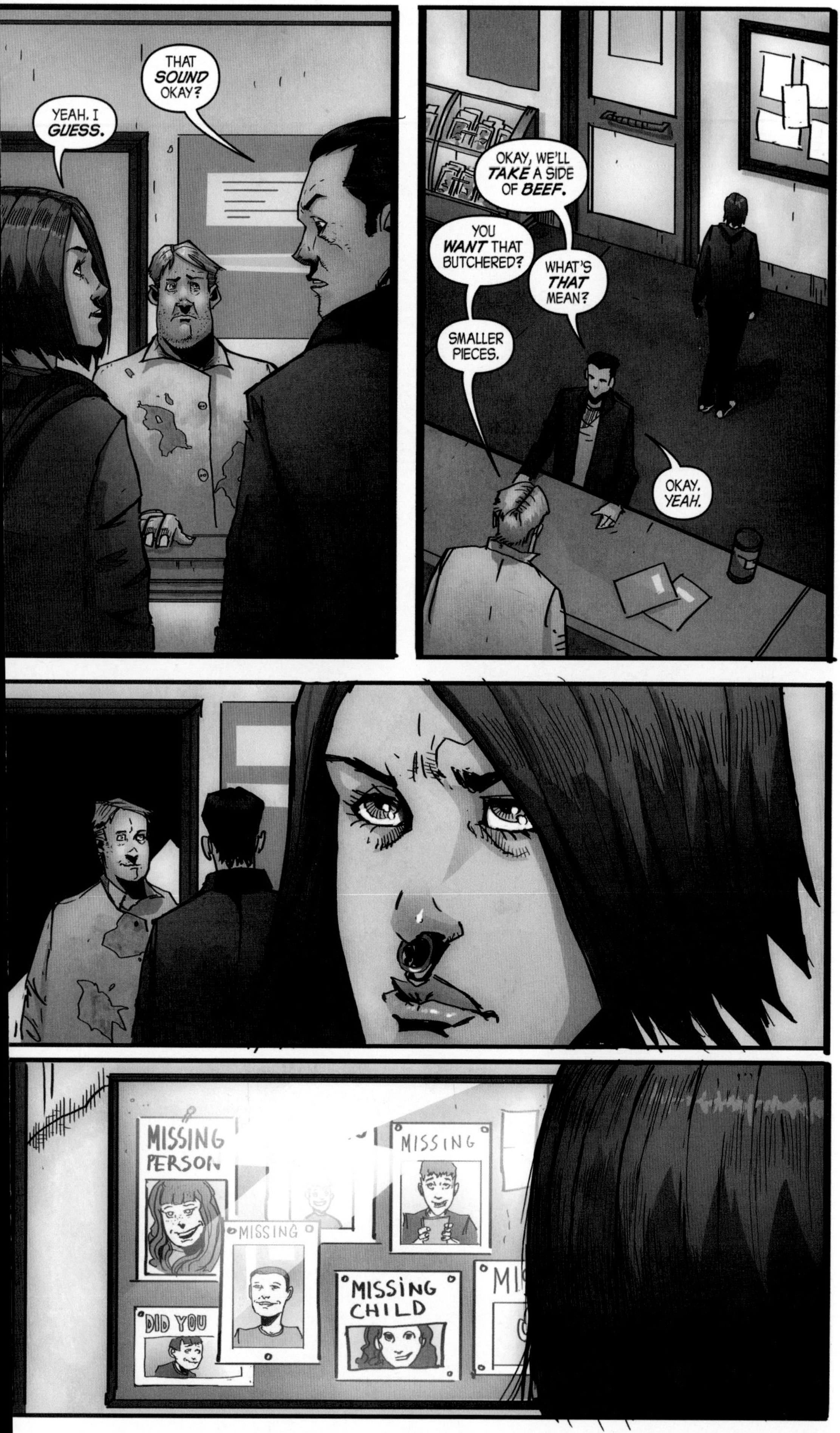
THAT SOUND OKAY?
YEAH. I GUESS.
OKAY, WE'LL TAKE A SIDE OF BEEF.
YOU WANT THAT BUTCHERED?
WHAT'S THAT MEAN?
SMALLER PIECES.
OKAY. YEAH.
MISSING PERSON
MISSING
MISSING
MISSING CHILD
DID YOU

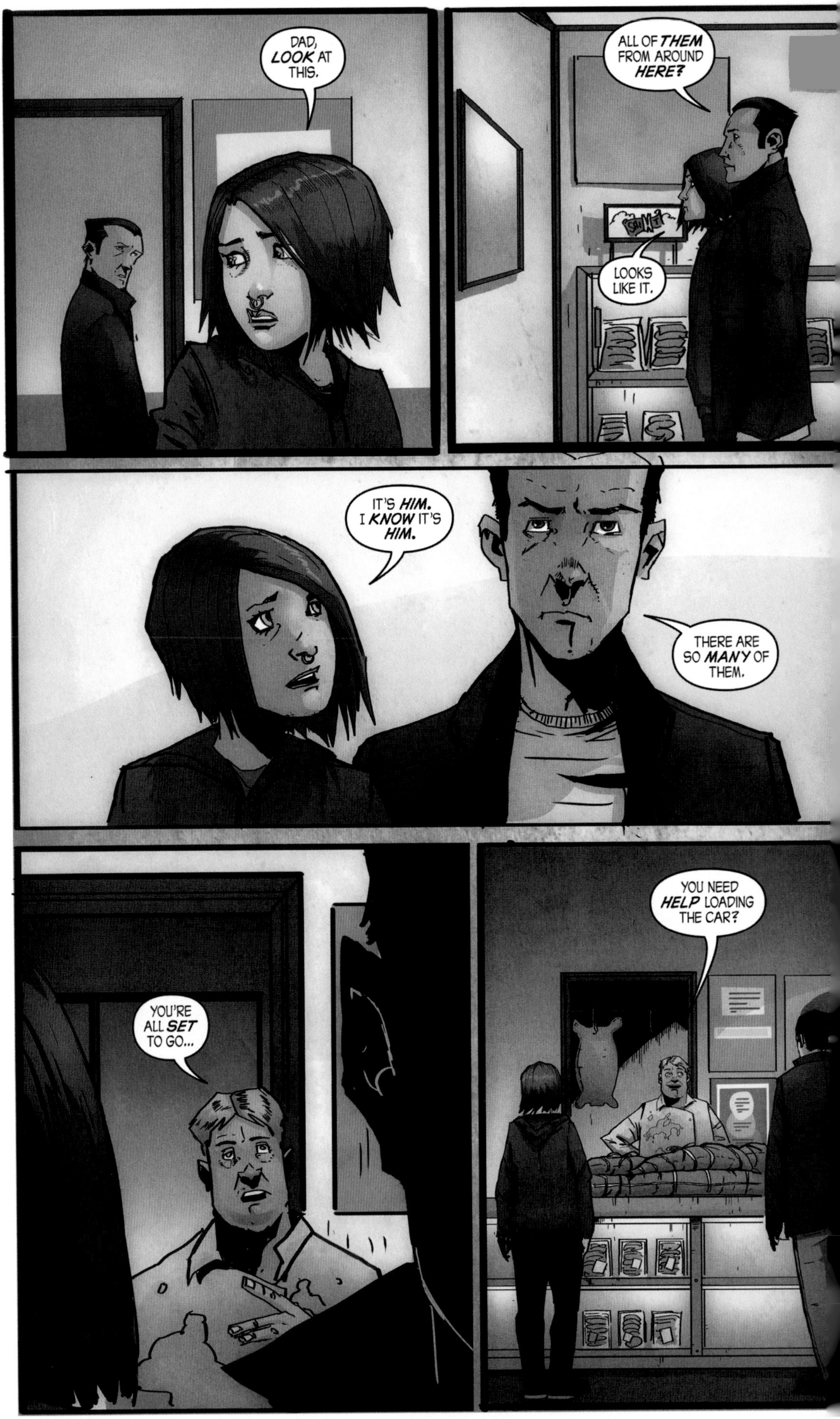
DAD, LOOK AT THIS.
ALL OF THEM FROM AROUND HERE?
LOOKS LIKE IT.
IT'S HIM. I KNOW IT'S HIM.
THERE ARE SO MANY OF THEM.
YOU'RE ALL SET TO GO...
YOU NEED HELP LOADING THE CAR?

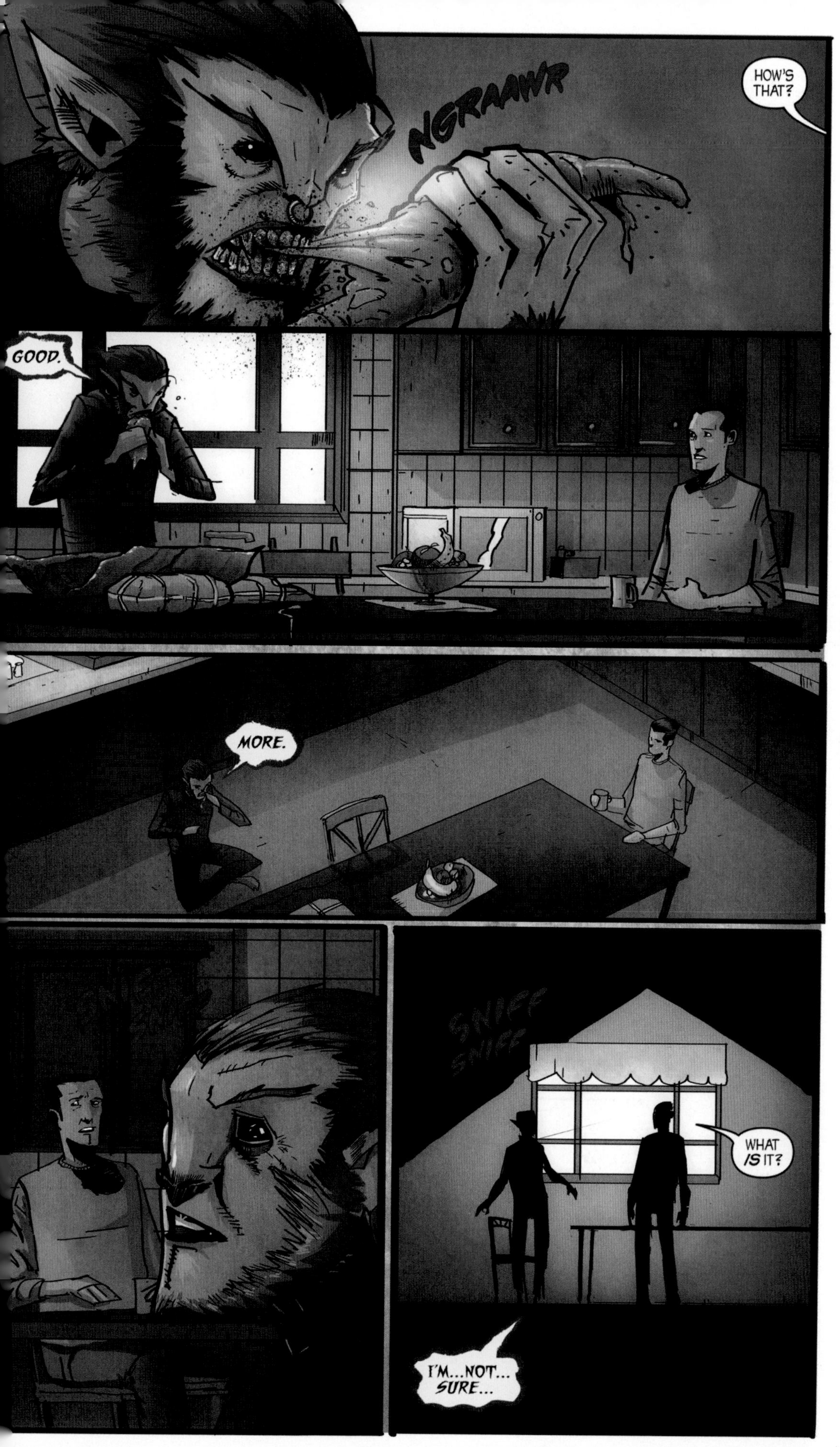
NGRAAWR
HOW'S THAT?
GOOD.
MORE.
SNIFF
SNIFF
WHAT IS IT?
I'M...NOT...
SURE...

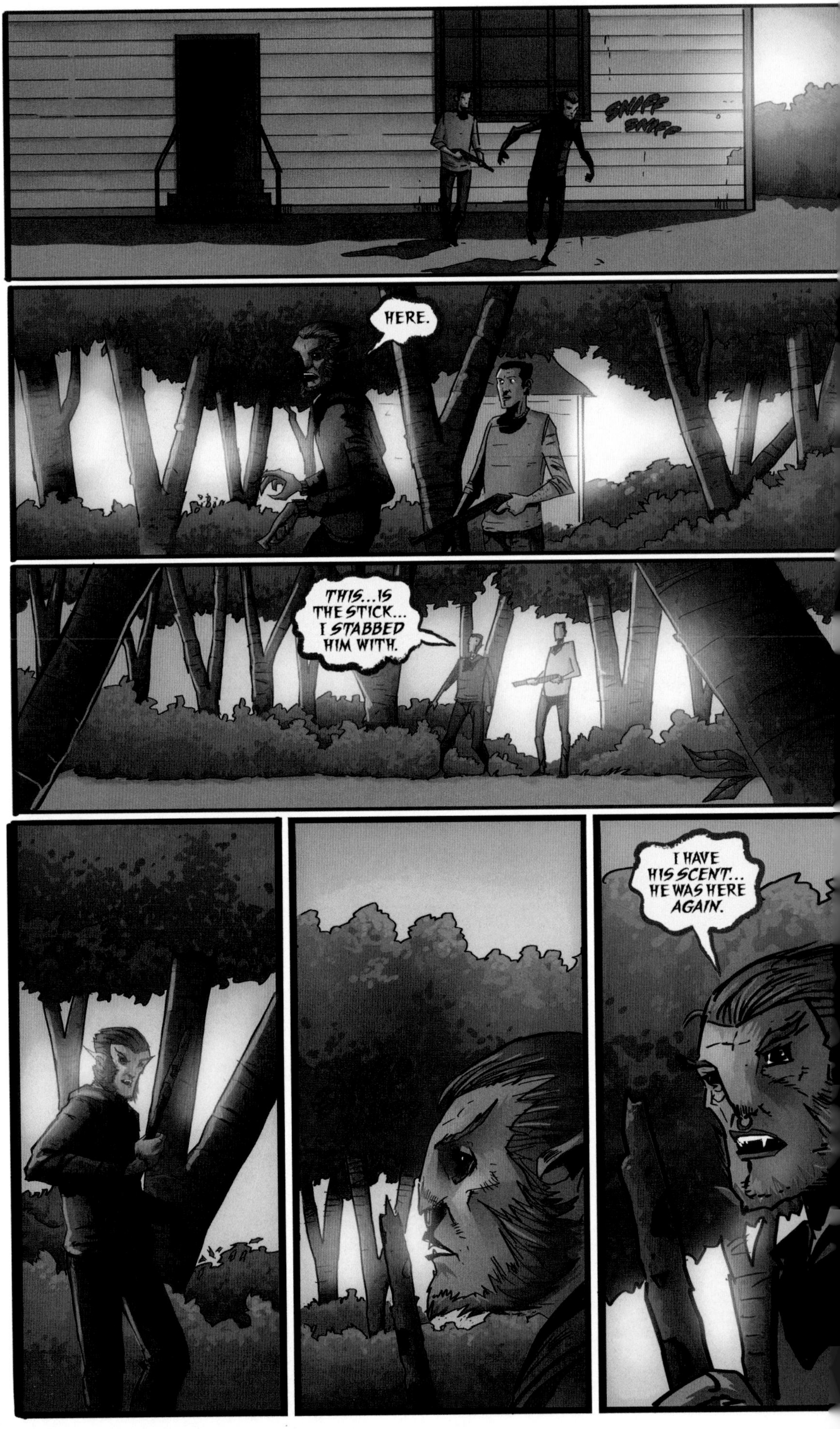
SNIFF SNIFF
HERE.
THIS...IS THE STICK... I STABBED HIM WITH.
I HAVE HIS SCENT... HE WAS HERE AGAIN.

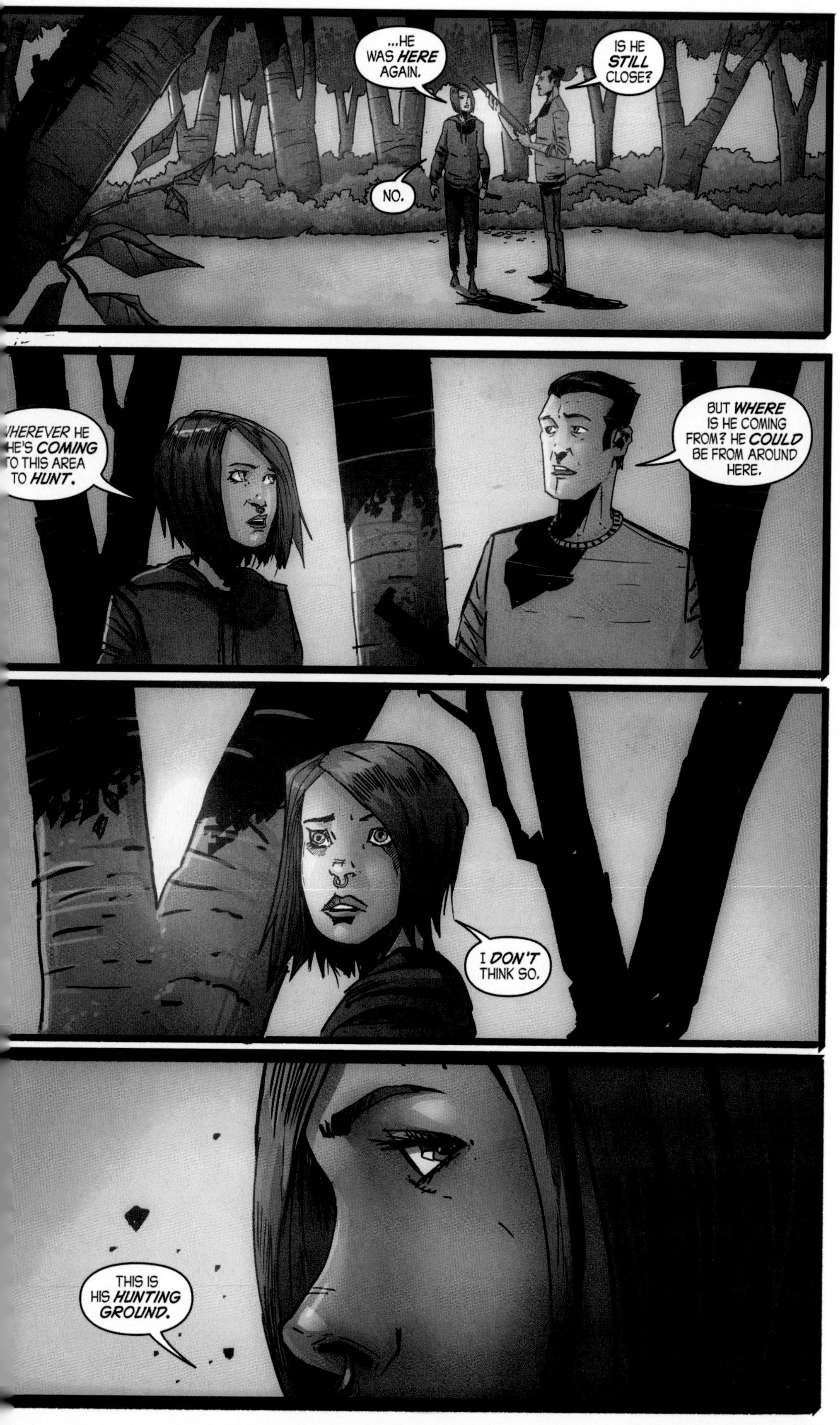
...HE WAS HERE AGAIN.
IS HE STILL CLOSE?
NO.
WHEREVER HE HE'S COMING TO THIS AREA TO HUNT.
BUT WHERE IS HE COMING FROM? HE COULD BE FROM AROUND HERE.
I DON'T THINK SO.
THIS IS HIS HUNTING GROUND.

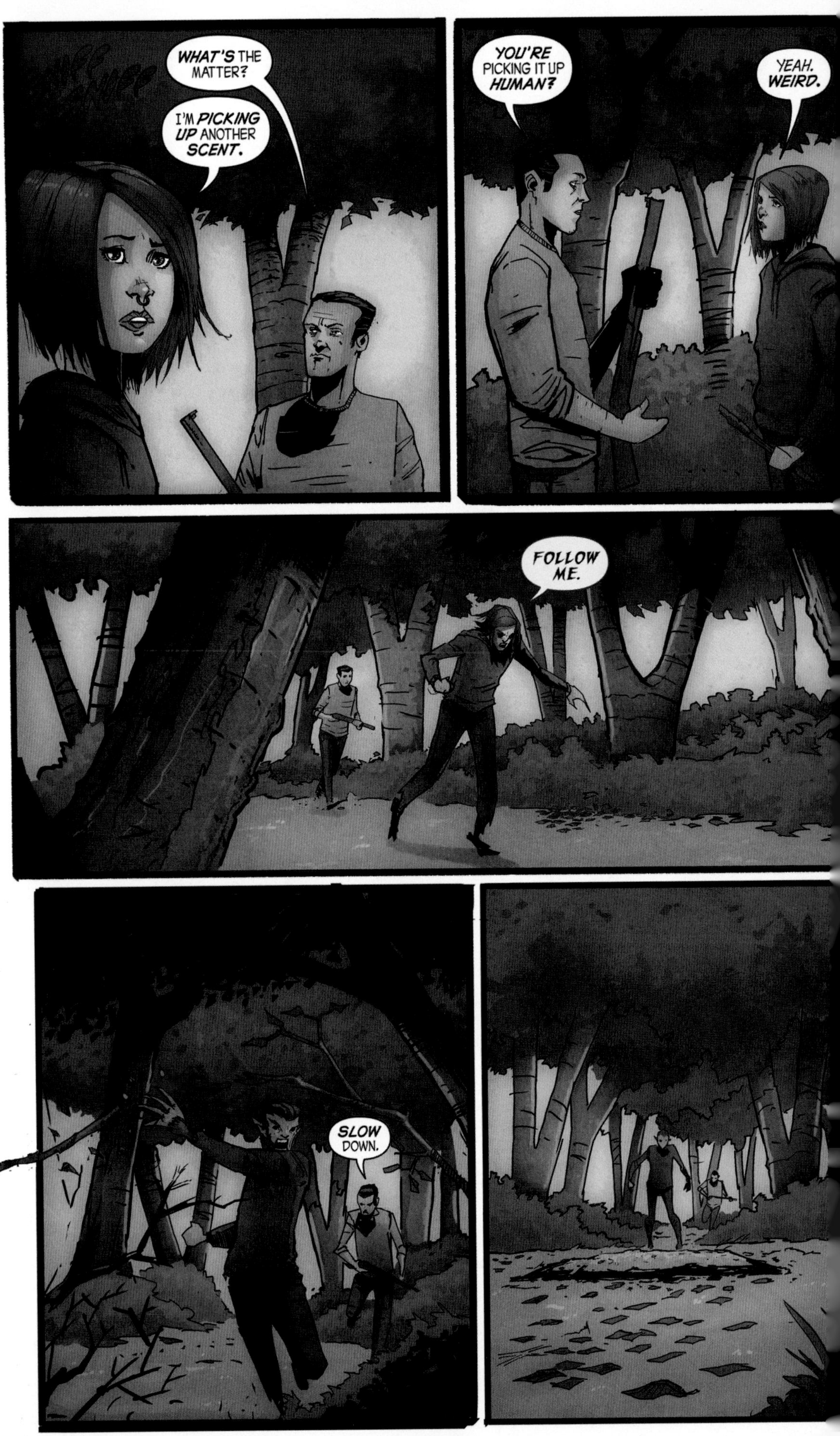
WHAT'S THE MATTER?
I'M PICKING UP ANOTHER SCENT.
YOU'RE PICKING IT UP HUMAN?
YEAH. WEIRD.
FOLLOW ME.
SLOW DOWN.

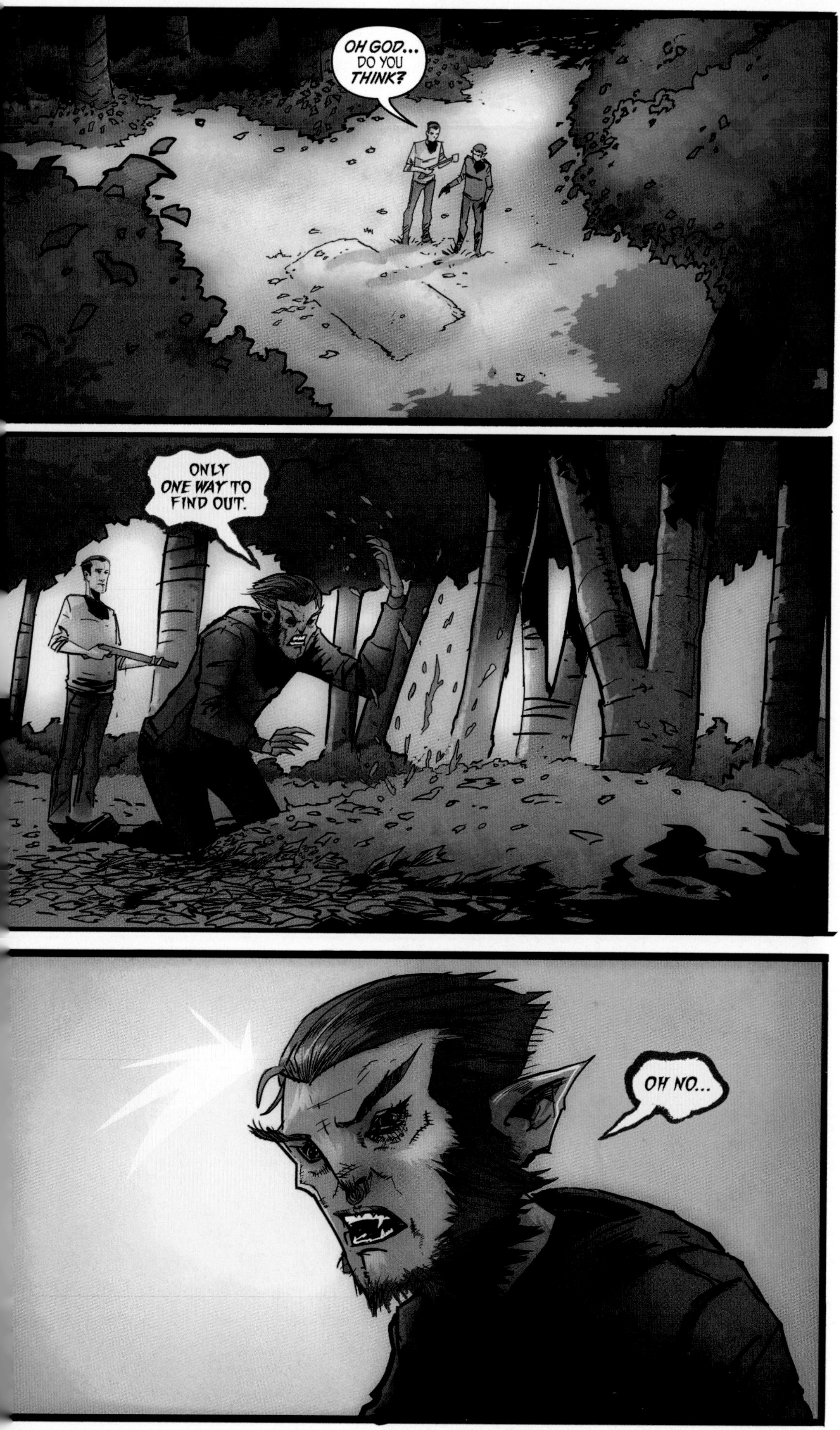
OH GOD... DO YOU THINK?
ONLY ONE WAY TO FIND OUT.
OH NO...

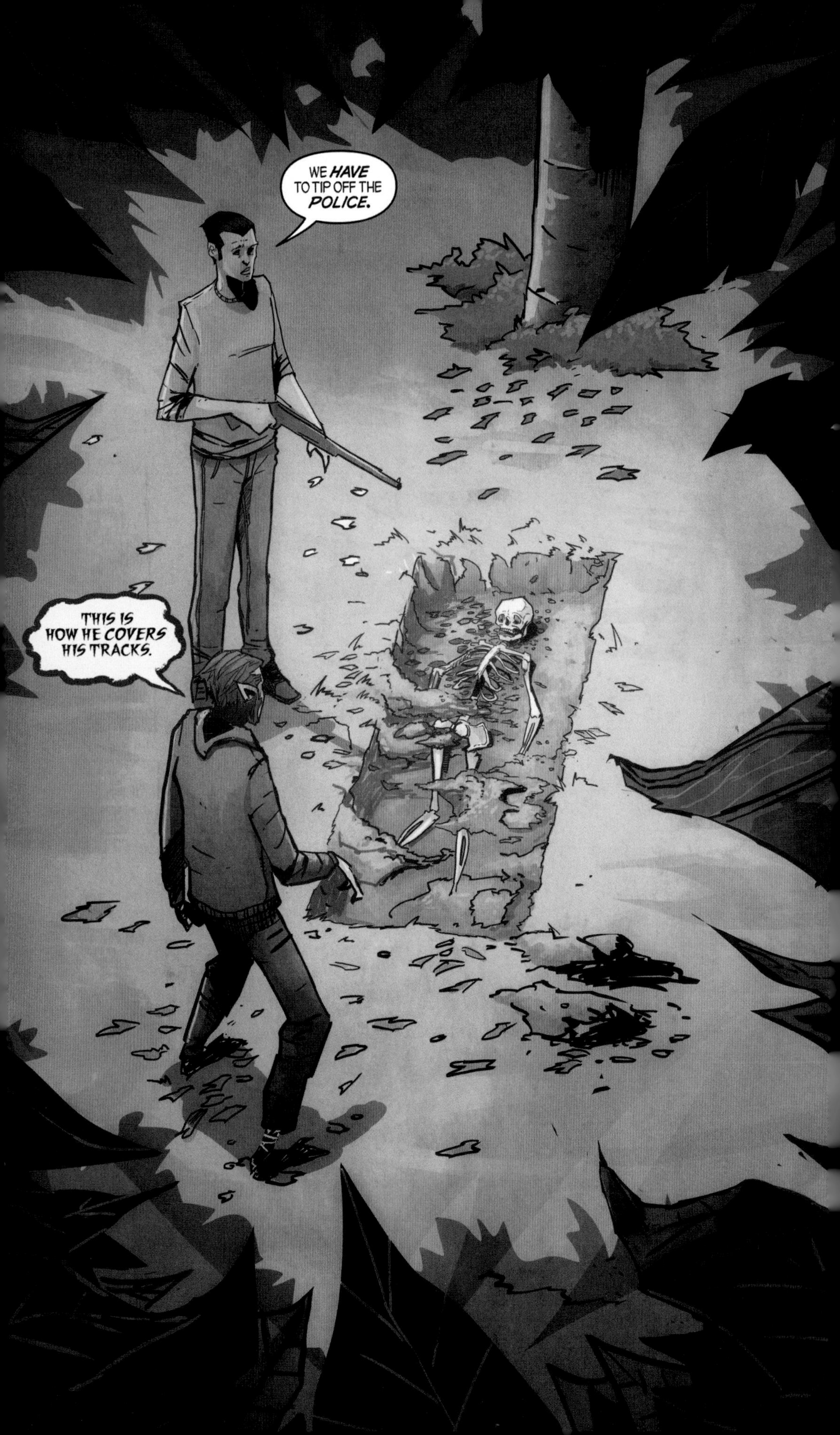
WE HAVE TO TIP OFF THE POLICE.
THIS IS HOW HE COVERS HIS TRACKS.

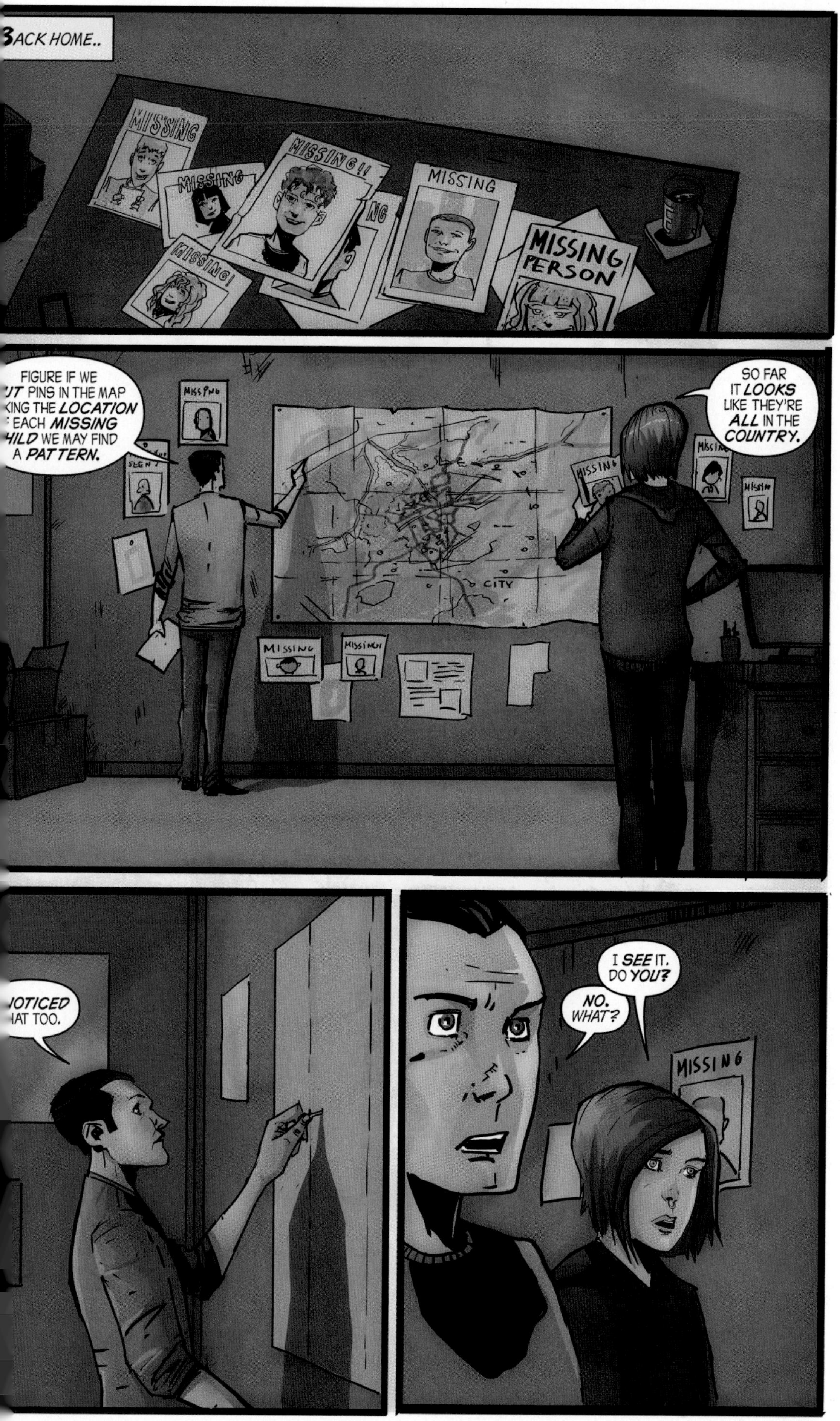
BACK HOME..
MISSING
MISSING
MISSING!!
MISSING
NG
MISSING!
MISSING PERSON
FIGURE IF WE UT PINS IN THE MAP KING THE LOCATION EACH MISSING HILD WE MAY FIND A PATTERN.
SO FAR IT LOOKS LIKE THEY'RE ALL IN THE COUNTRY.
MISSING
CITY
MISSING
NOTICED HAT TOO.
I SEE IT. DO YOU?
NO. WHAT?
MISSING

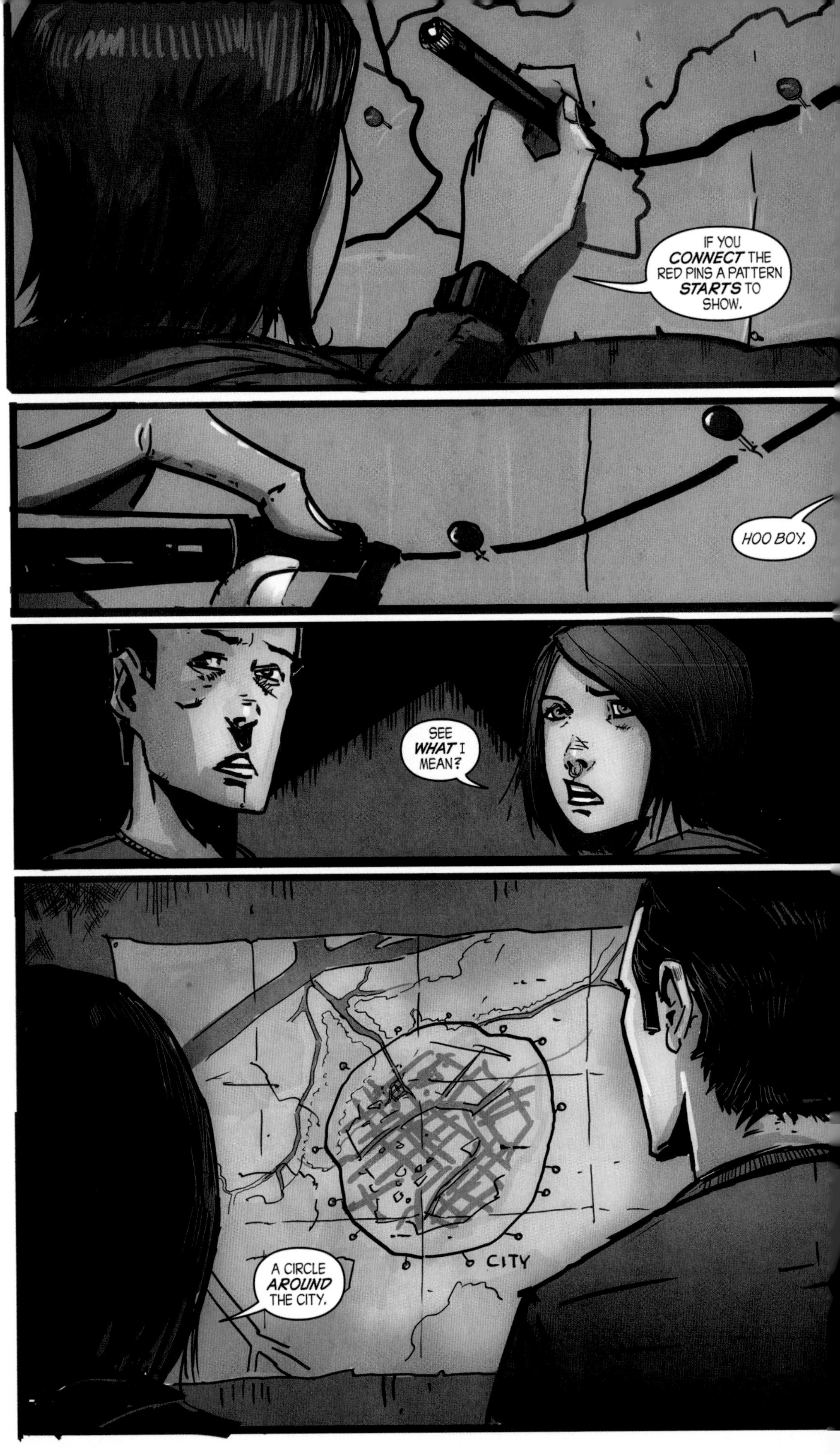
IF YOU CONNECT THE RED PINS A PATTERN STARTS TO SHOW.
HOO BOY.
SEE WHAT I MEAN?
A CIRCLE AROUND THE CITY.
CITY

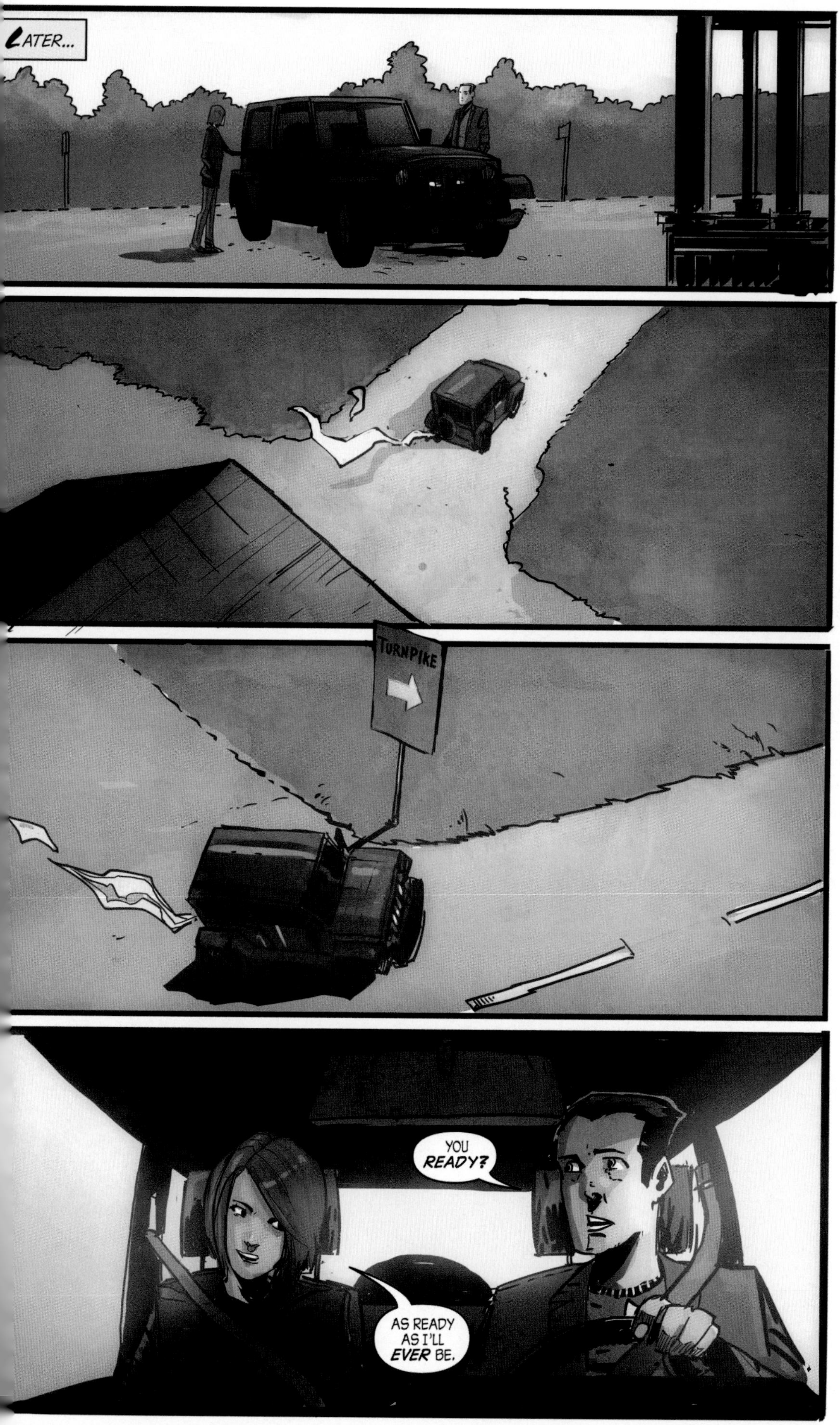
LATER...
TURNPIKE
YOU READY?
AS READY AS I'LL EVER BE.

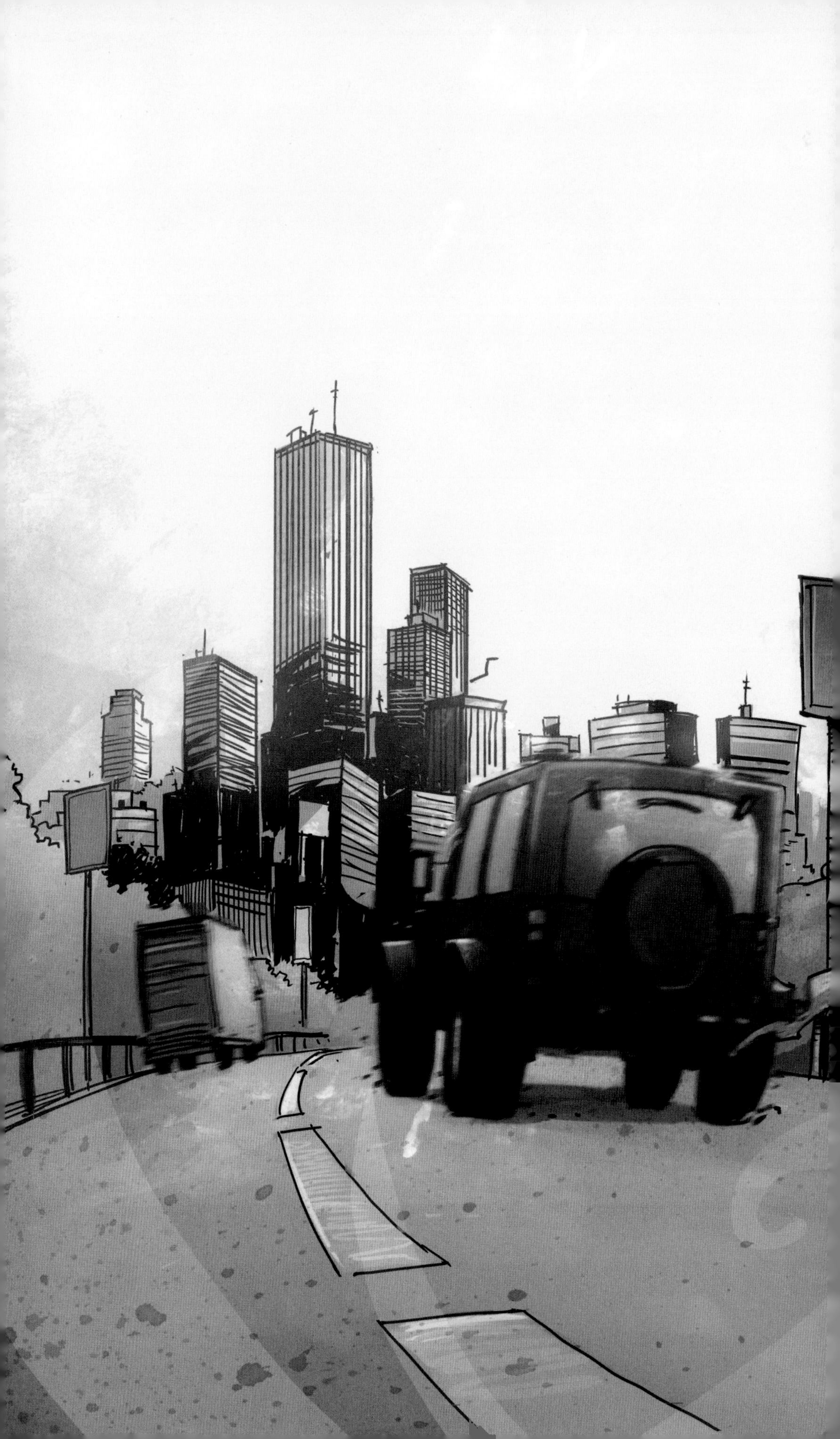

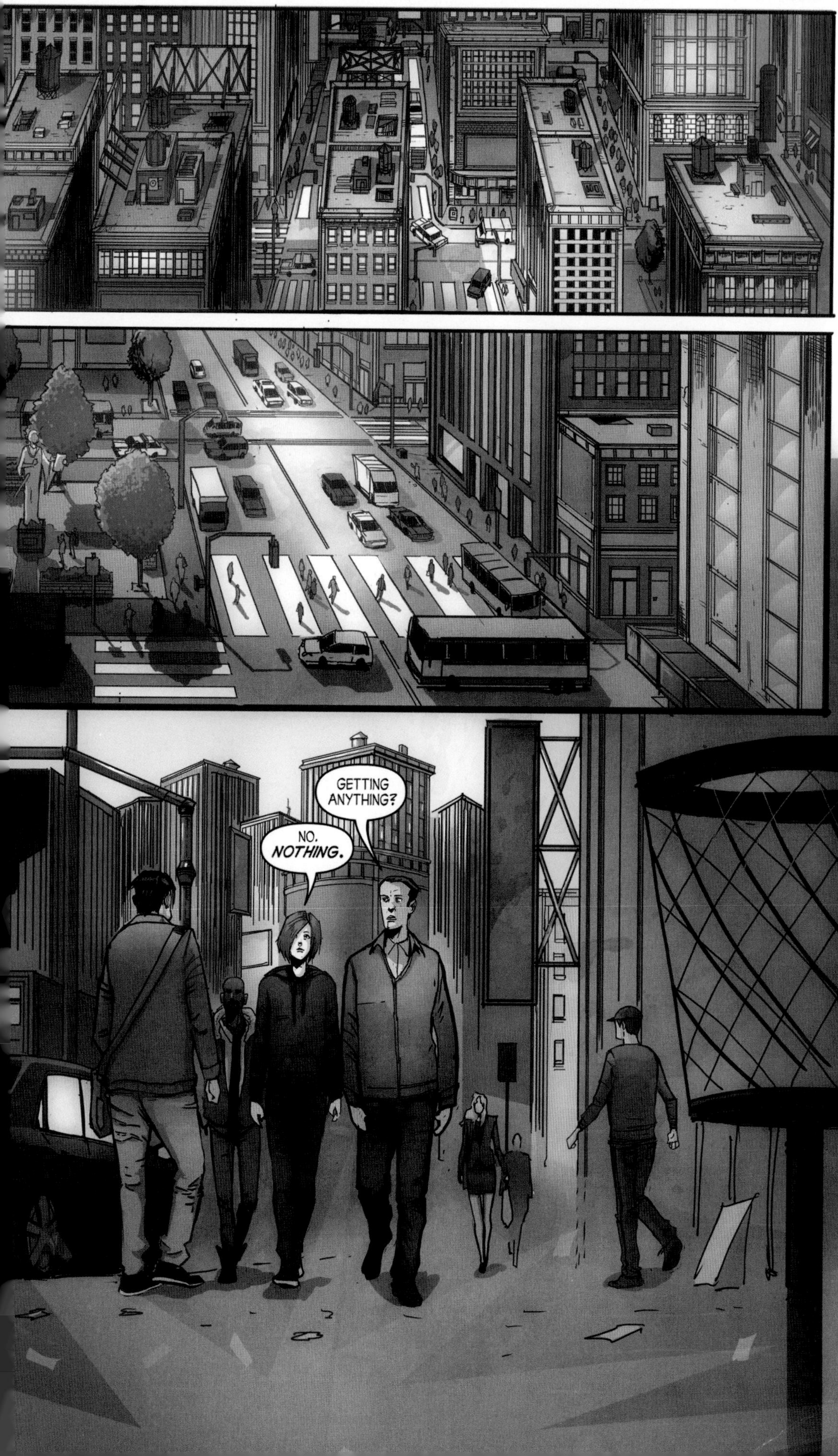
GETTING ANYTHING?
NO. *NOTHING.*

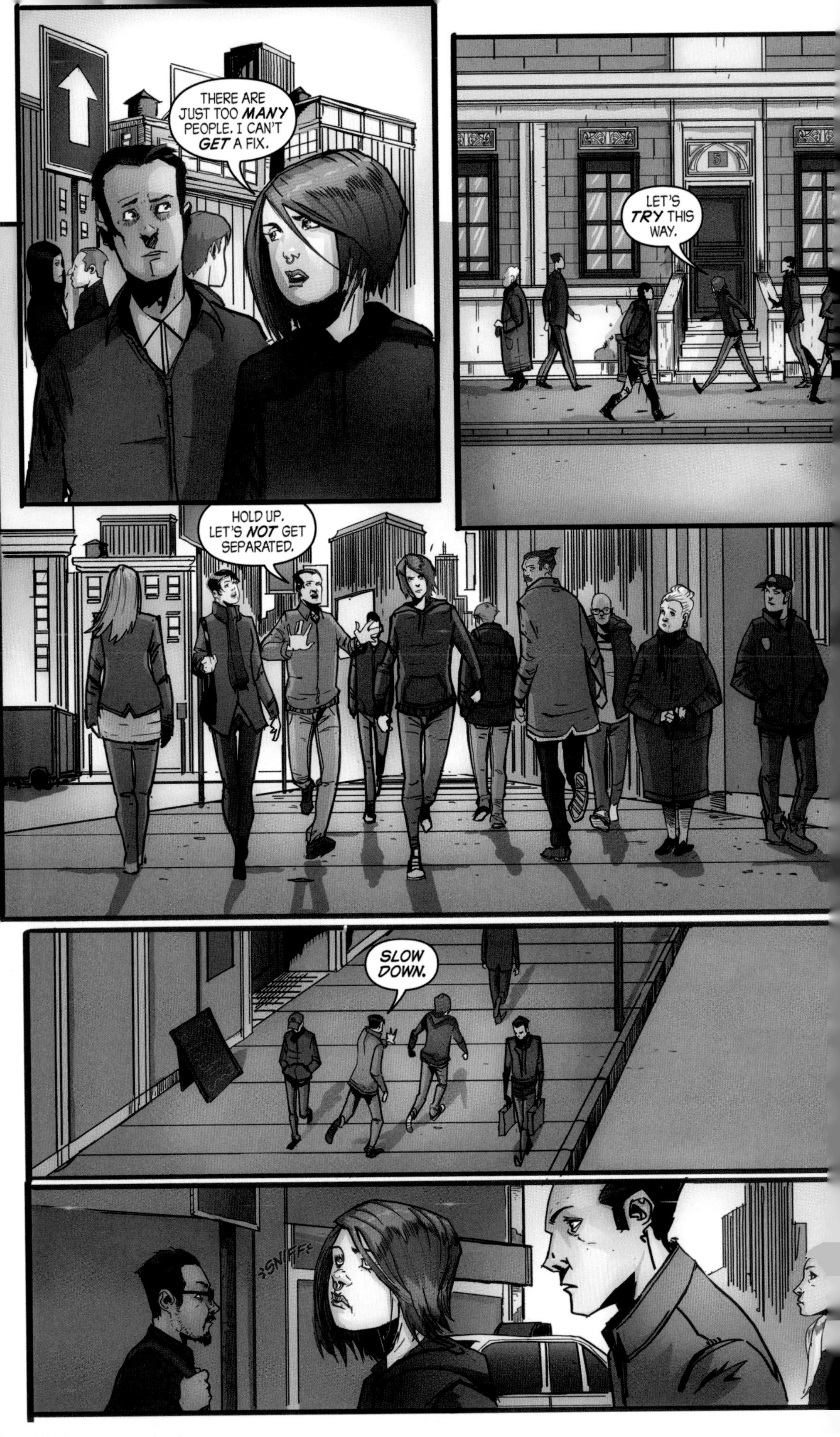
THERE ARE JUST TOO MANY PEOPLE. I CAN'T GET A FIX.
LET'S TRY THIS WAY.
HOLD UP. LET'S NOT GET SEPARATED.
SLOW DOWN.
SNIFF

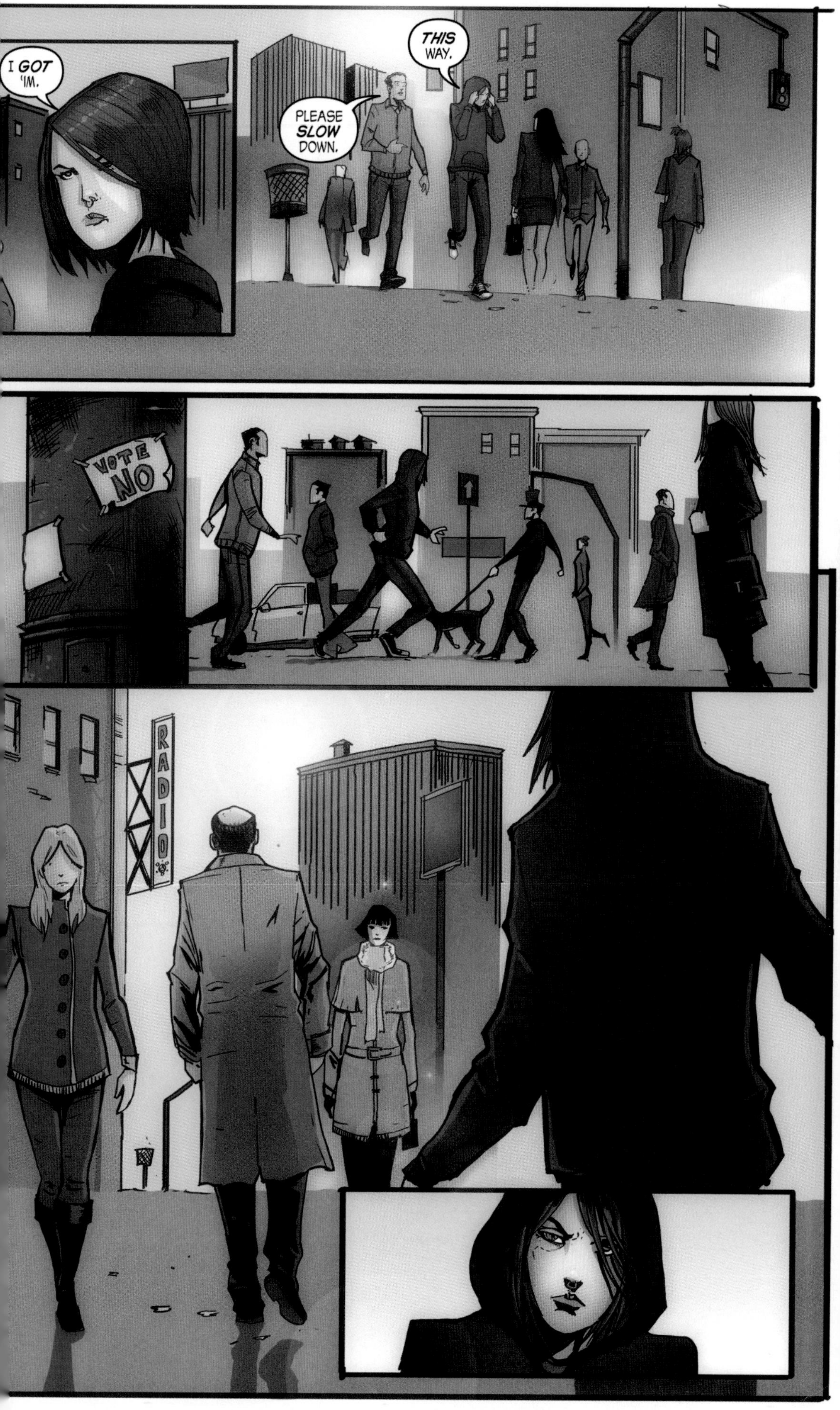
I GOT 'IM.
PLEASE SLOW DOWN.
THIS WAY.
VOTE NO
RADIO

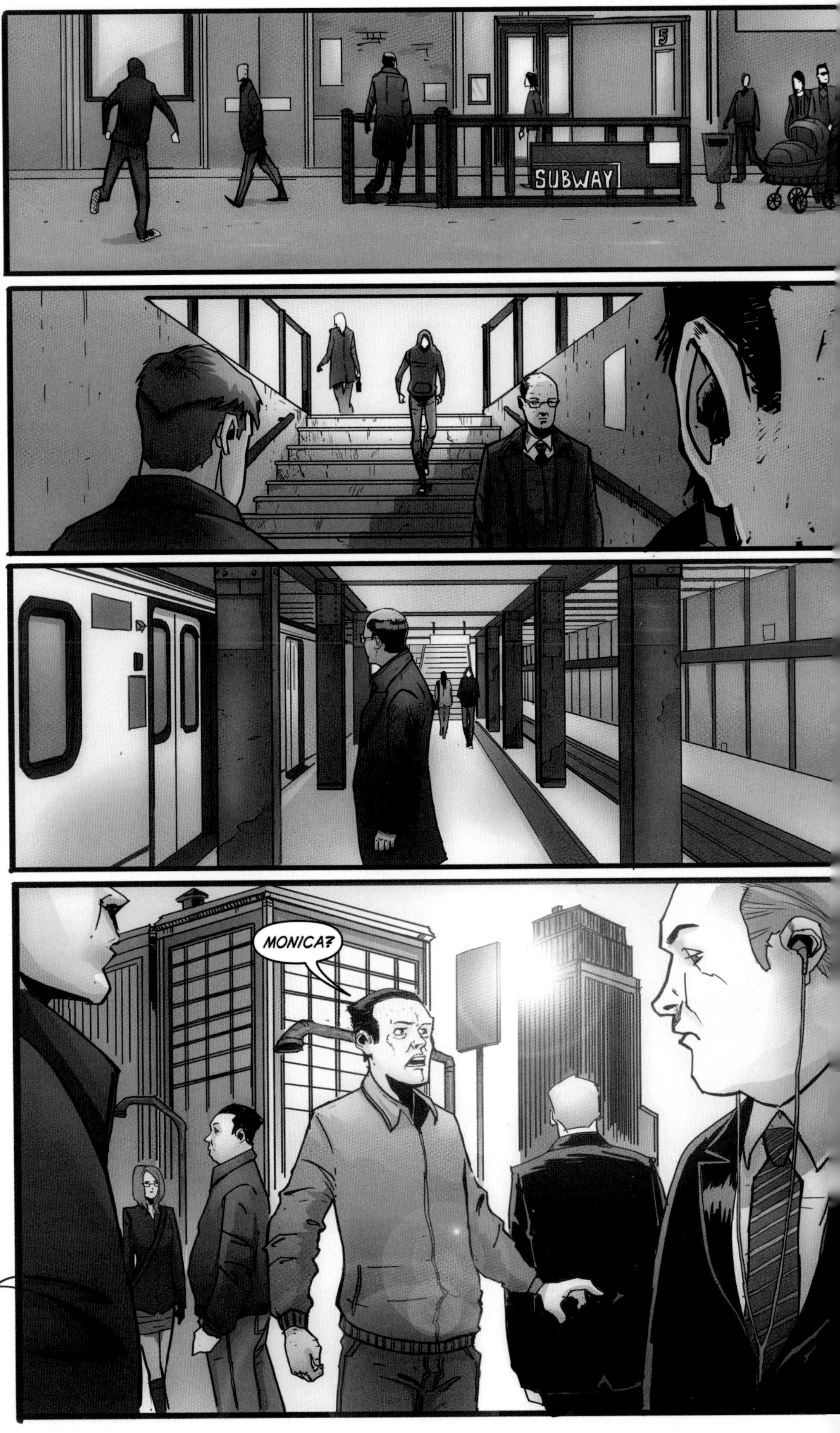
5
SUBWAY
MONICA?

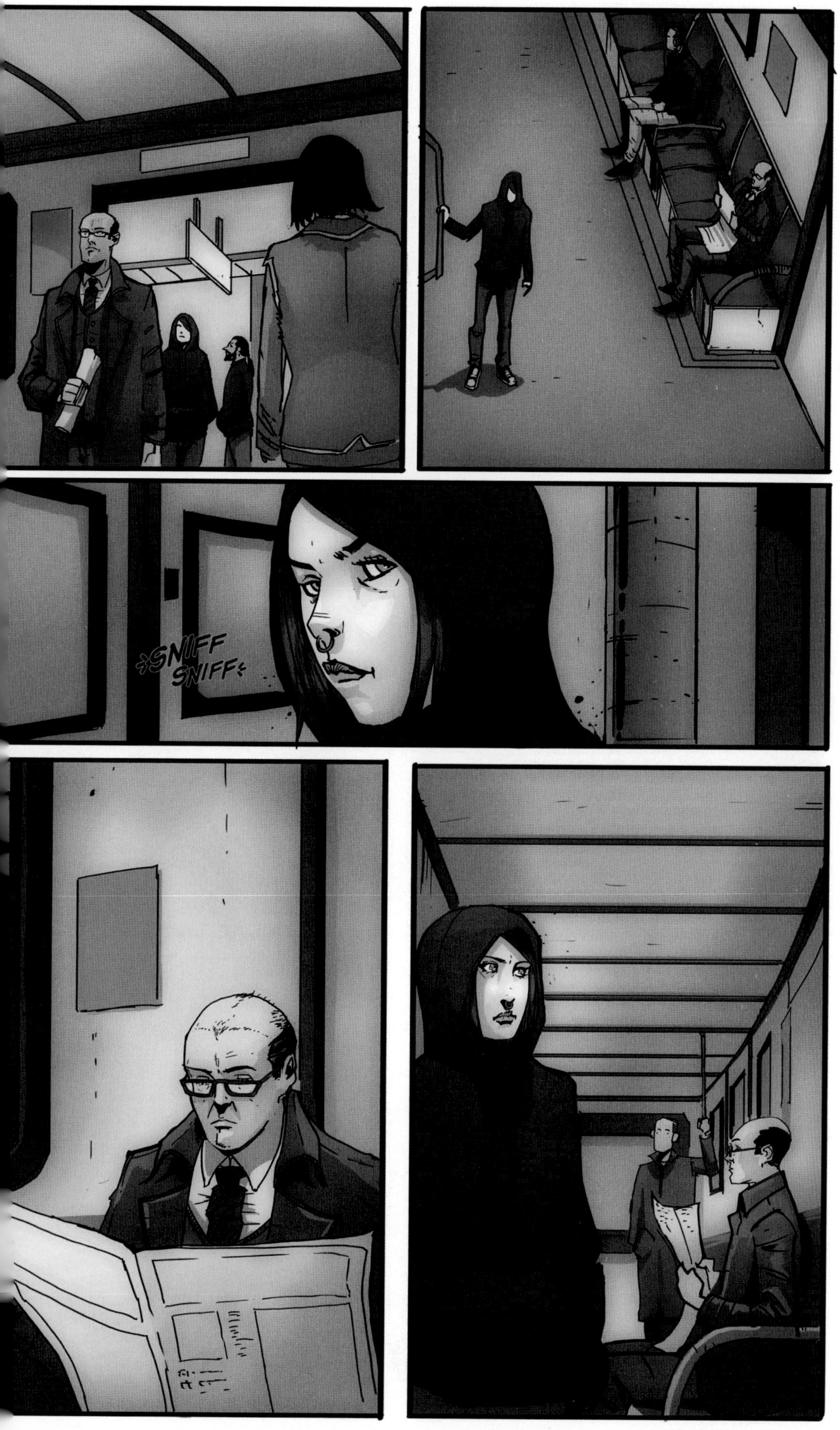
SNIFF SNIFF

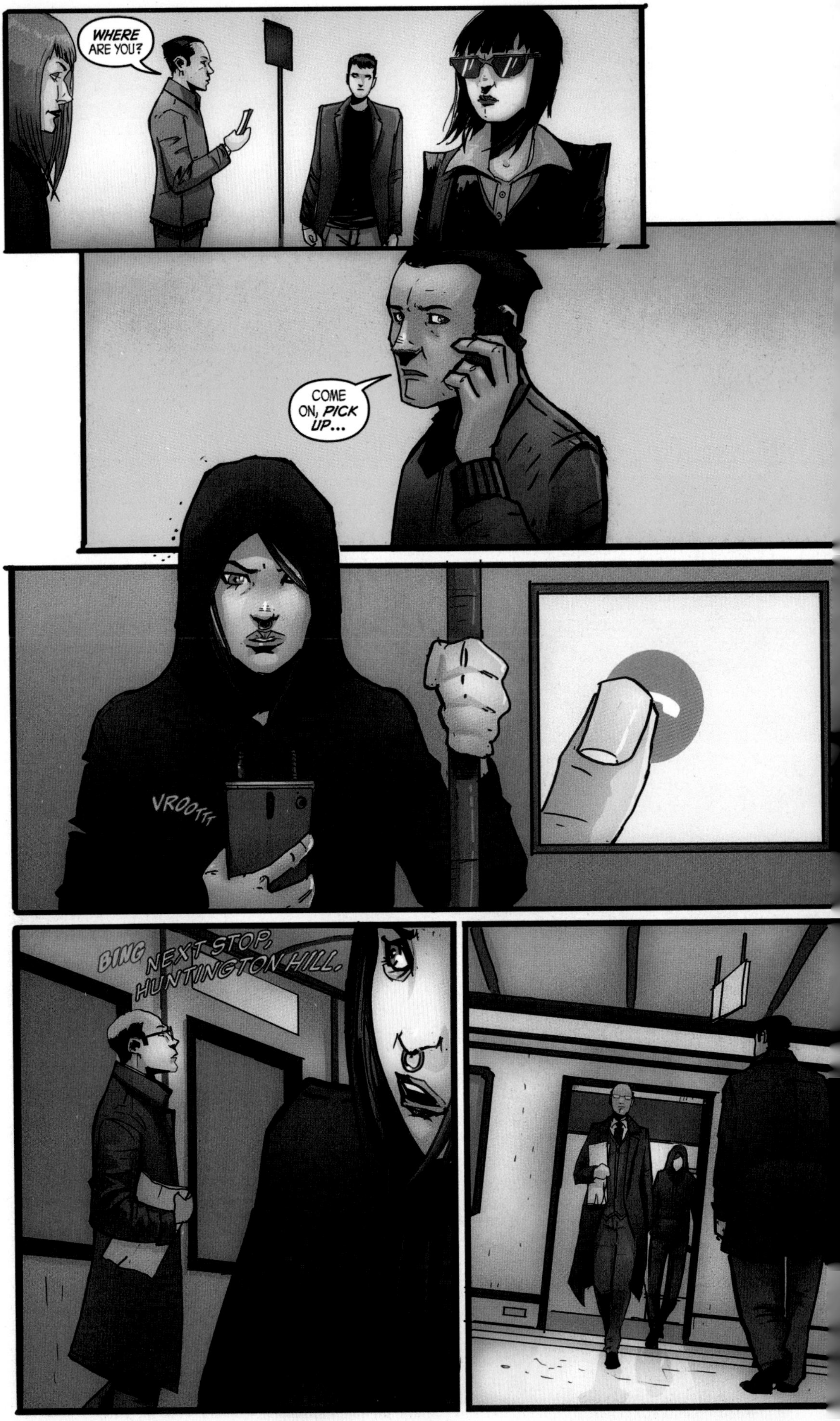
WHERE ARE YOU?
COME ON, PICK UP...
VROOTTT
BING
NEXT STOP, HUNTINGTON HILL.

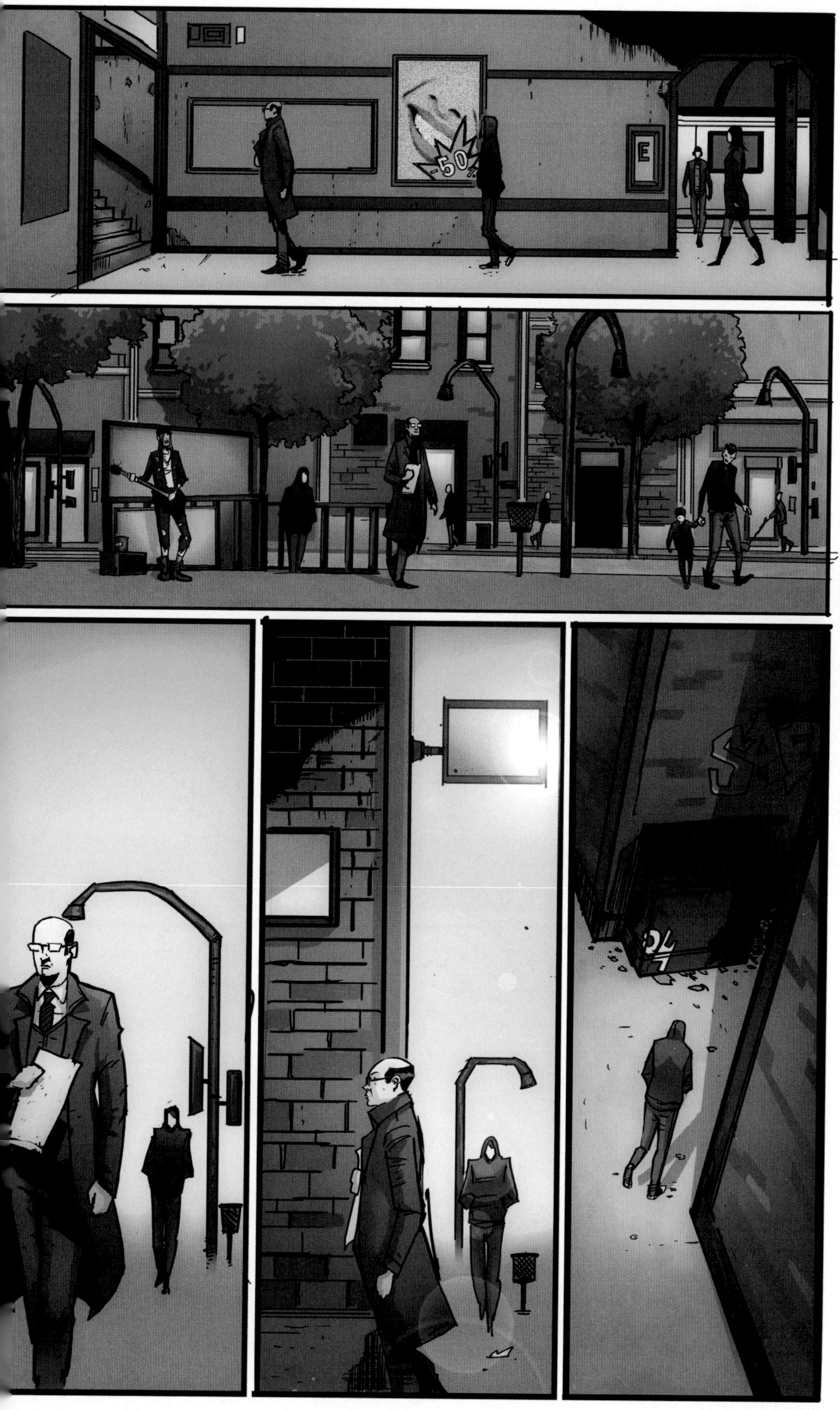
-50%
E

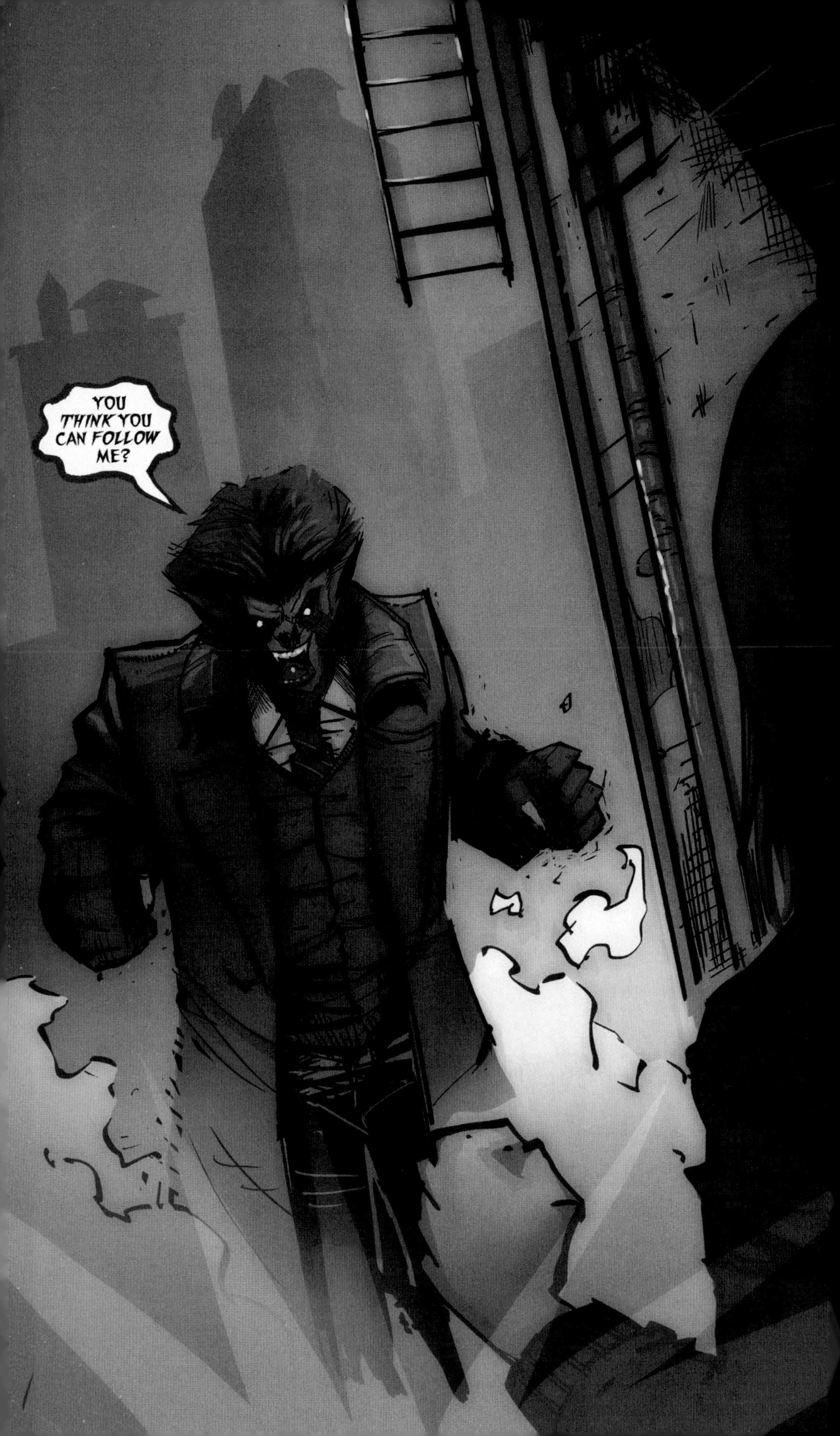
YOU *THINK* YOU CAN *FOLLOW* ME?

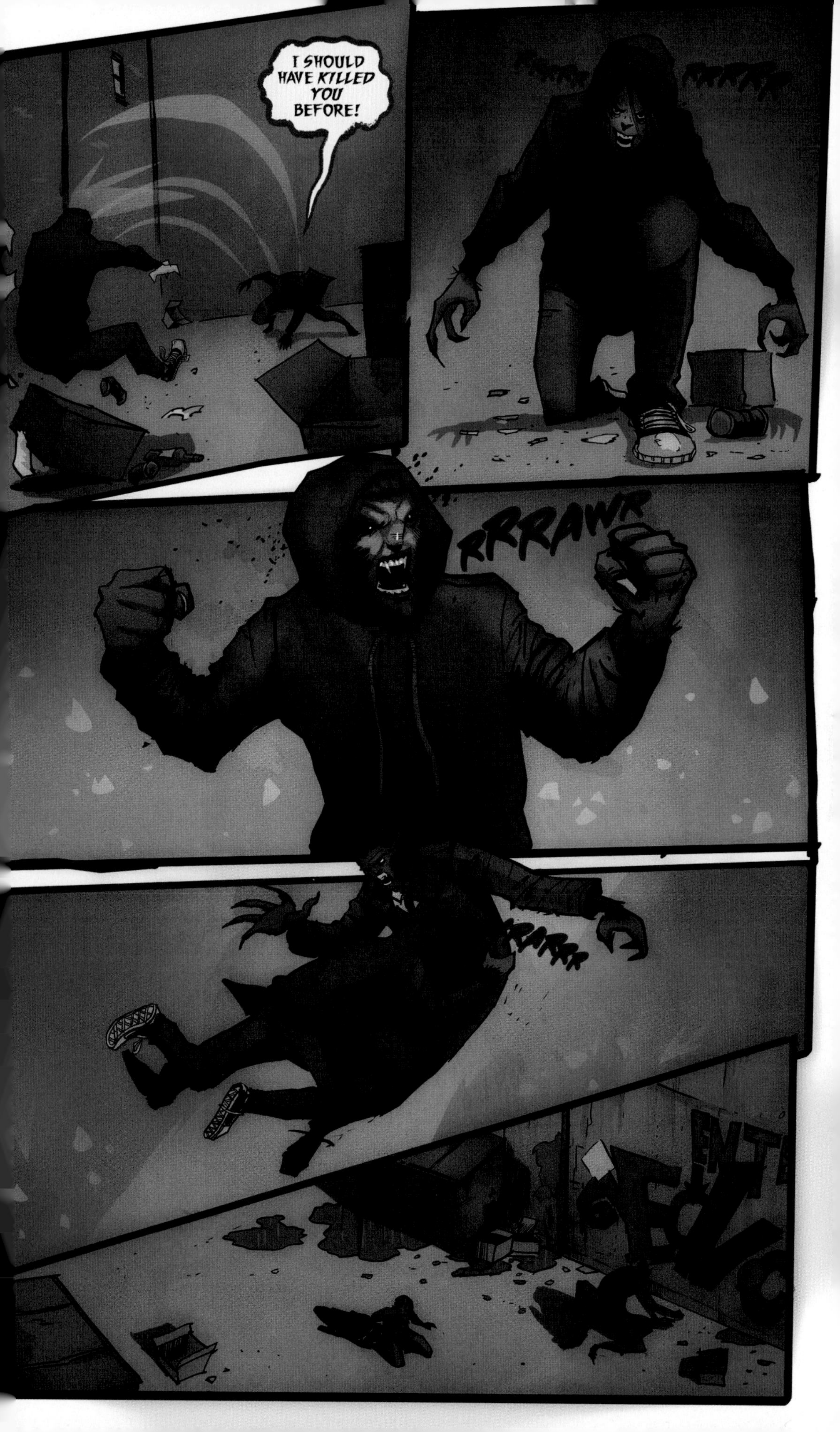
I SHOULD HAVE KILLED YOU BEFORE!
RRRRR
RRRRR
RRRAWR
RRRRRR

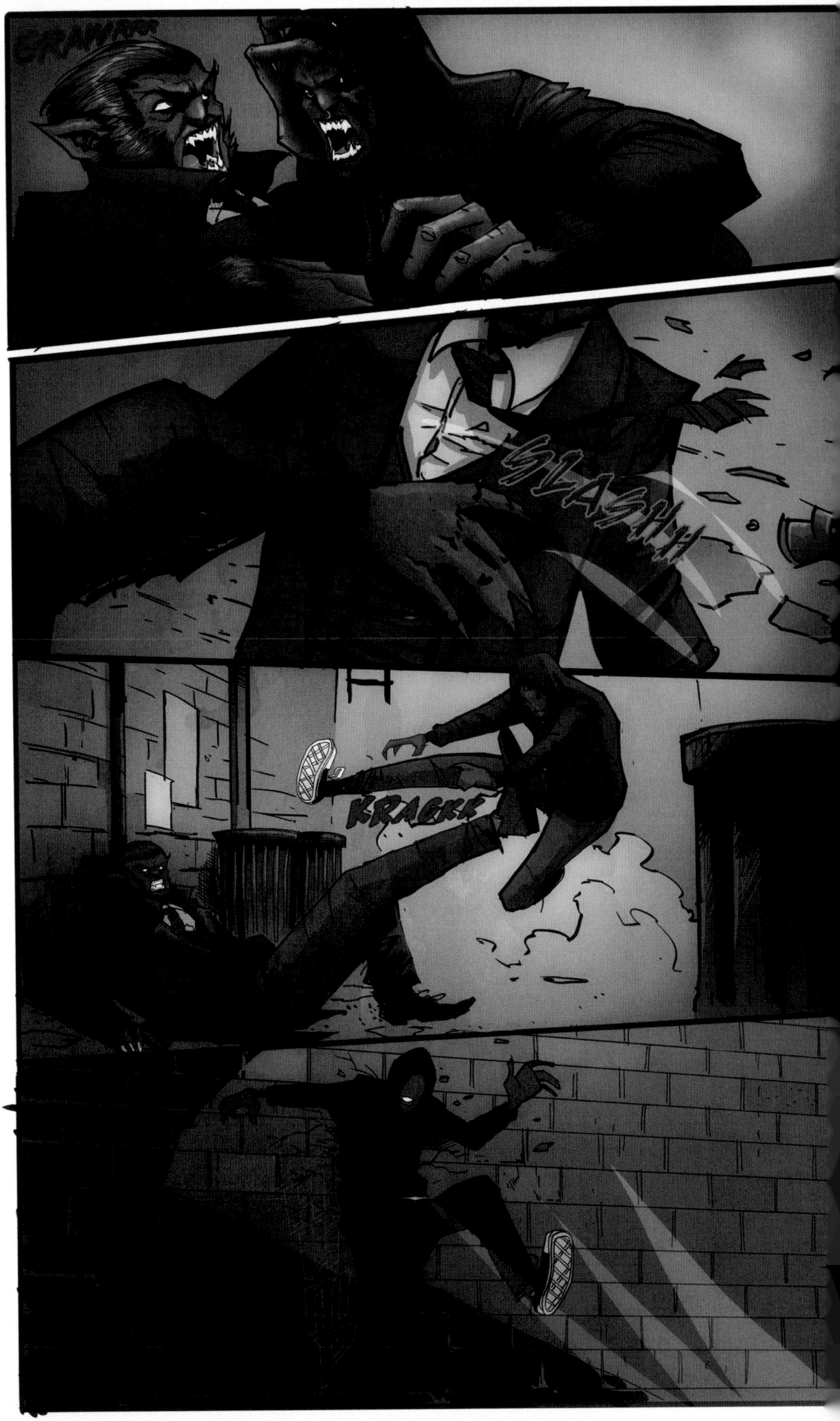
GRAWRRR
SLASHH
KRACKK

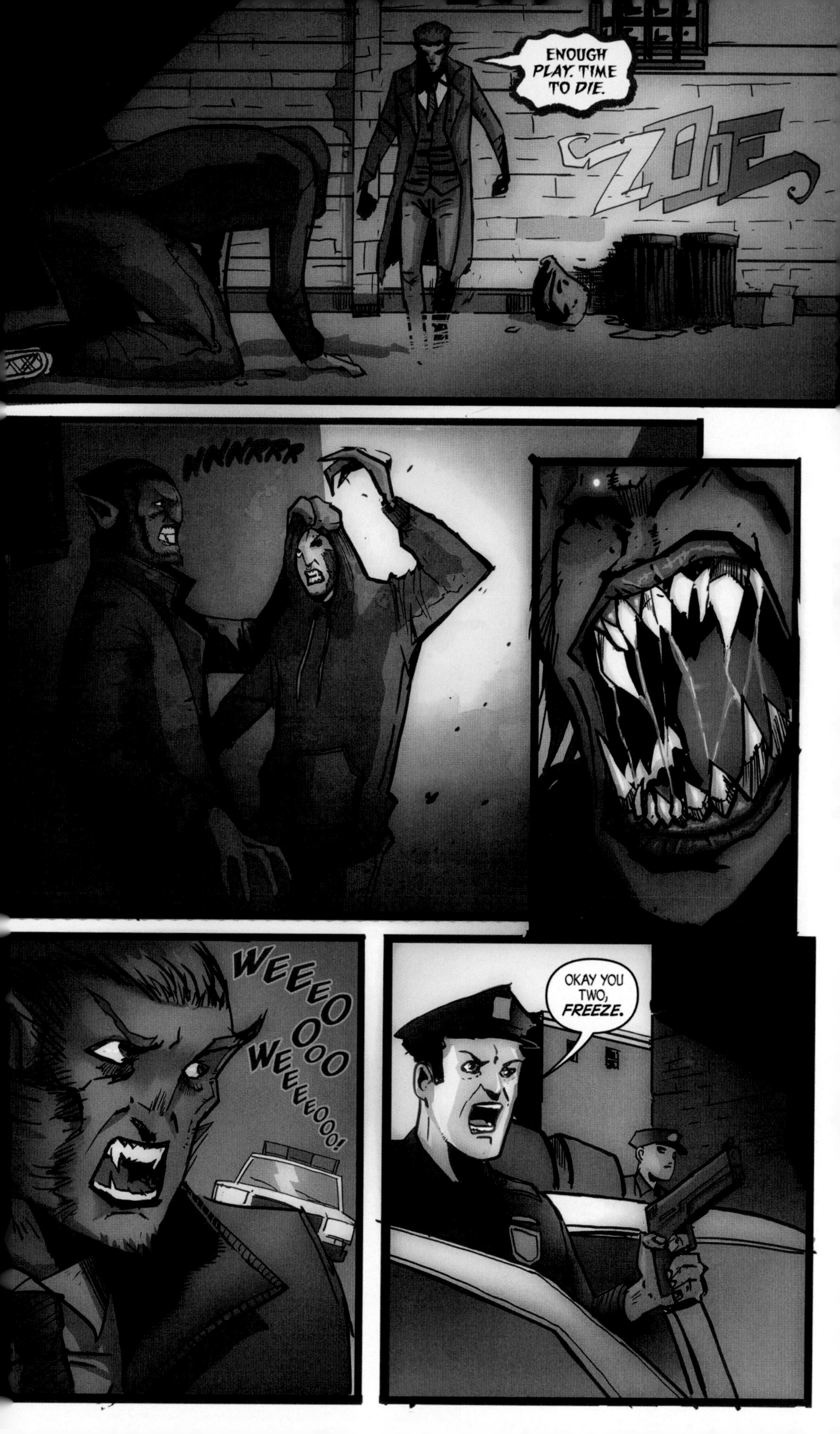

ENOUGH PLAY. TIME TO DIE.
ZOOE
HNNRRR
WEEEOOOO WEEEEOOO!
OKAY YOU TWO, *FREEZE.*

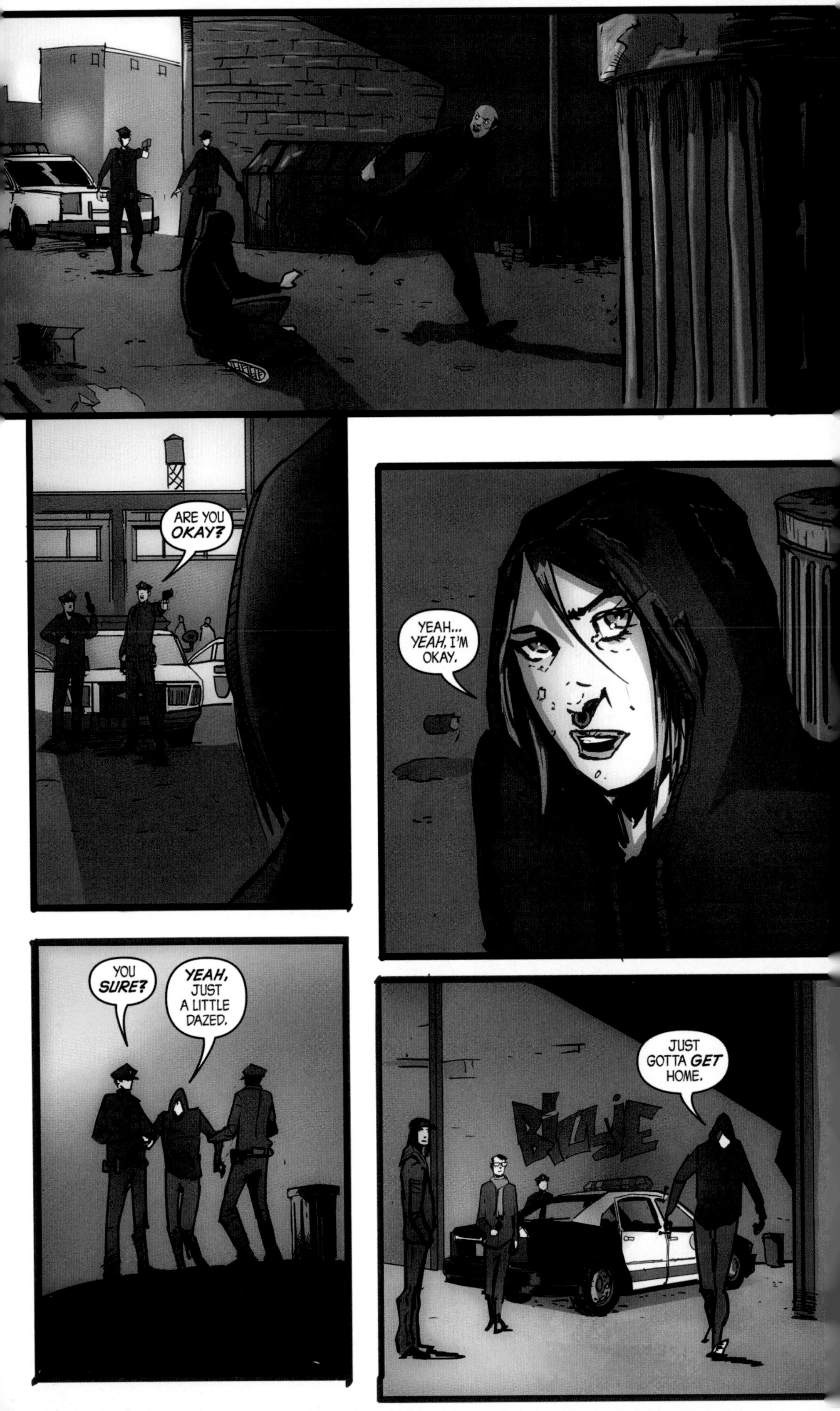
ARE YOU OKAY?
YEAH... YEAH, I'M OKAY.
YOU SURE?
YEAH, JUST A LITTLE DAZED.
JUST GOTTA GET HOME.

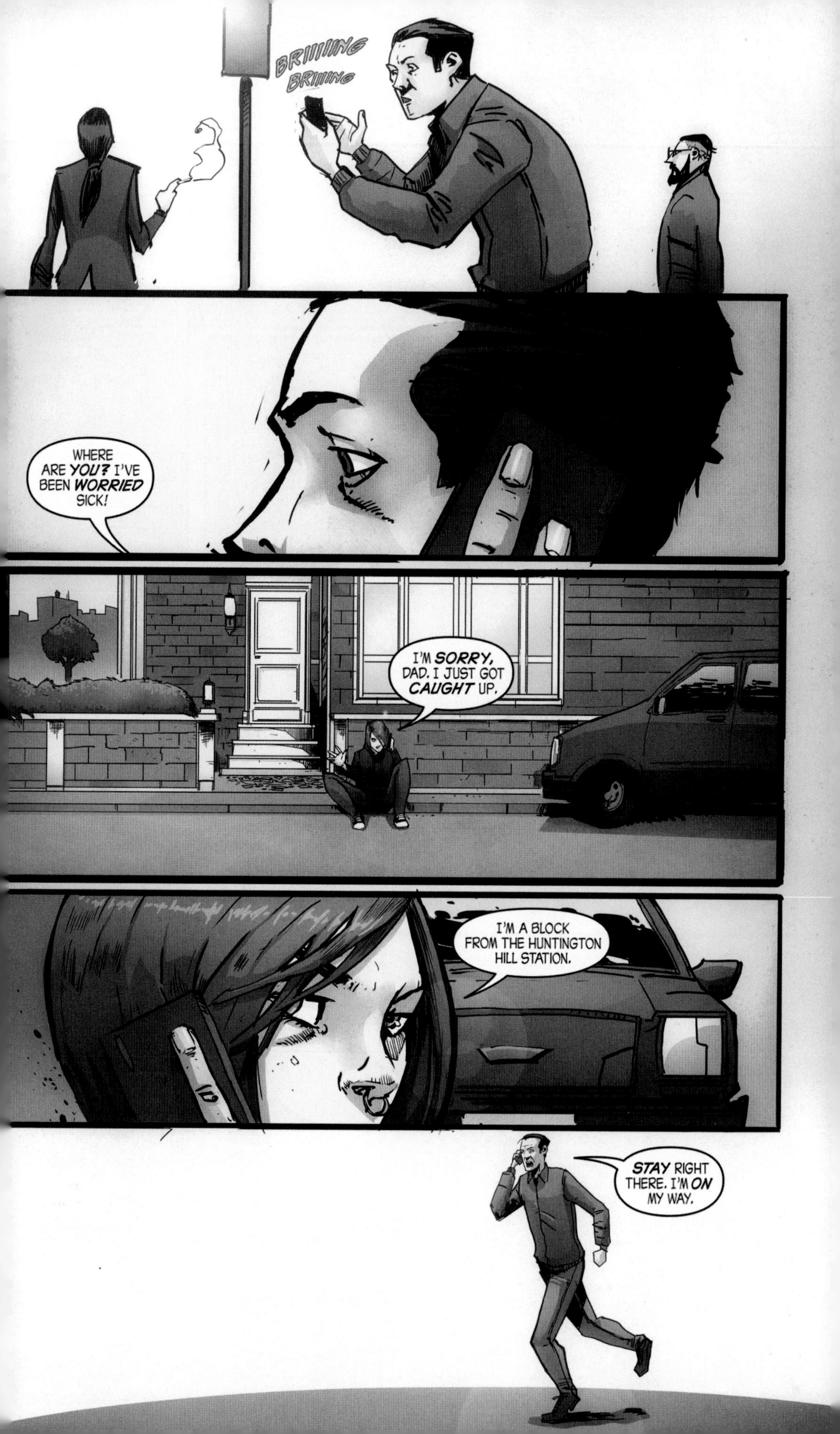
BRIIIIING BRIIIING
WHERE ARE YOU? I'VE BEEN WORRIED SICK!
I'M SORRY, DAD. I JUST GOT CAUGHT UP.
I'M A BLOCK FROM THE HUNTINGTON HILL STATION.
STAY RIGHT THERE. I'M ON MY WAY.

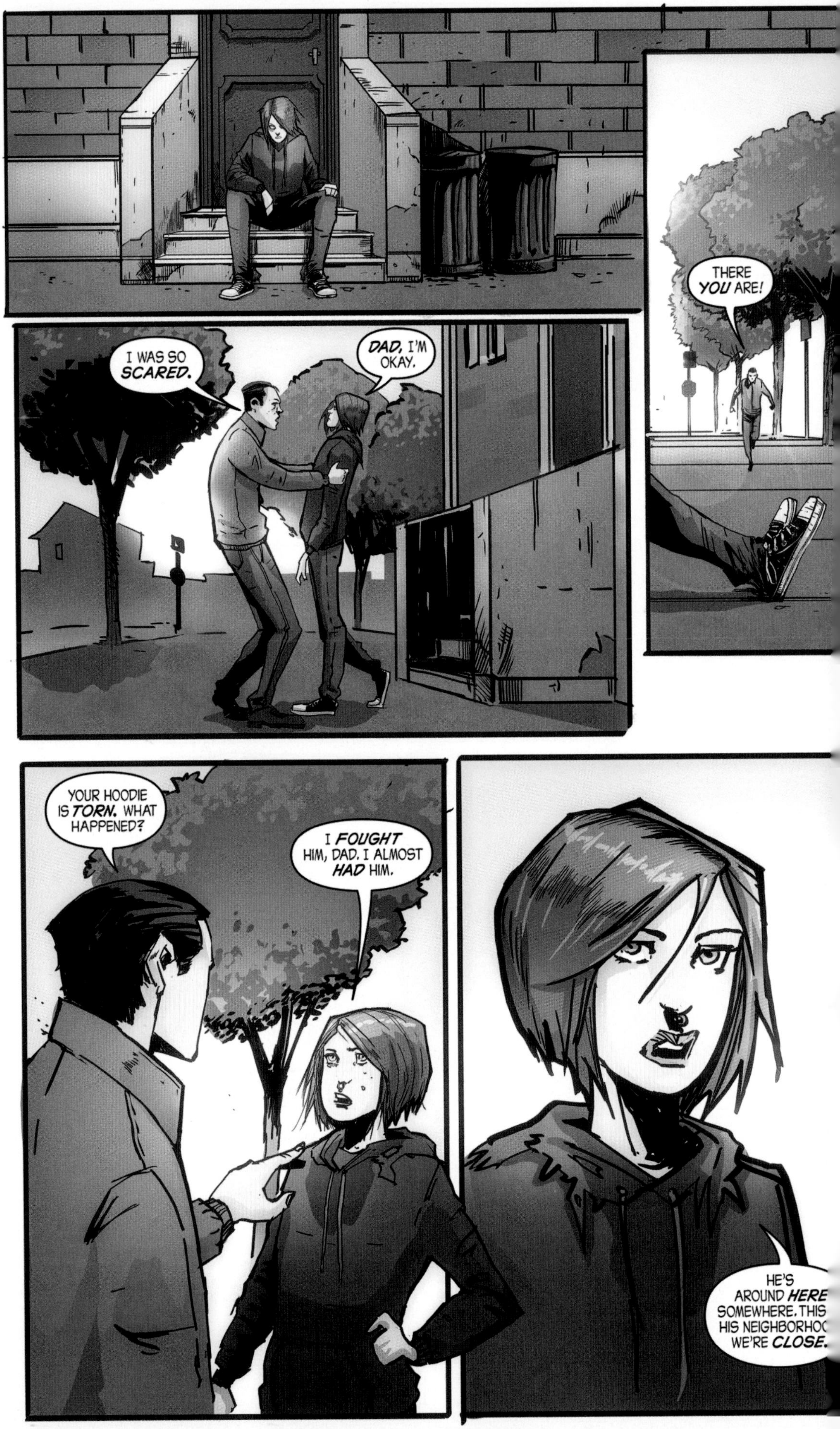
THERE YOU ARE!
I WAS SO SCARED.
DAD, I'M OKAY.
YOUR HOODIE IS TORN. WHAT HAPPENED?
I FOUGHT HIM, DAD. I ALMOST HAD HIM.
HE'S AROUND HERE SOMEWHERE. THIS HIS NEIGHBORHOO WE'RE CLOSE.

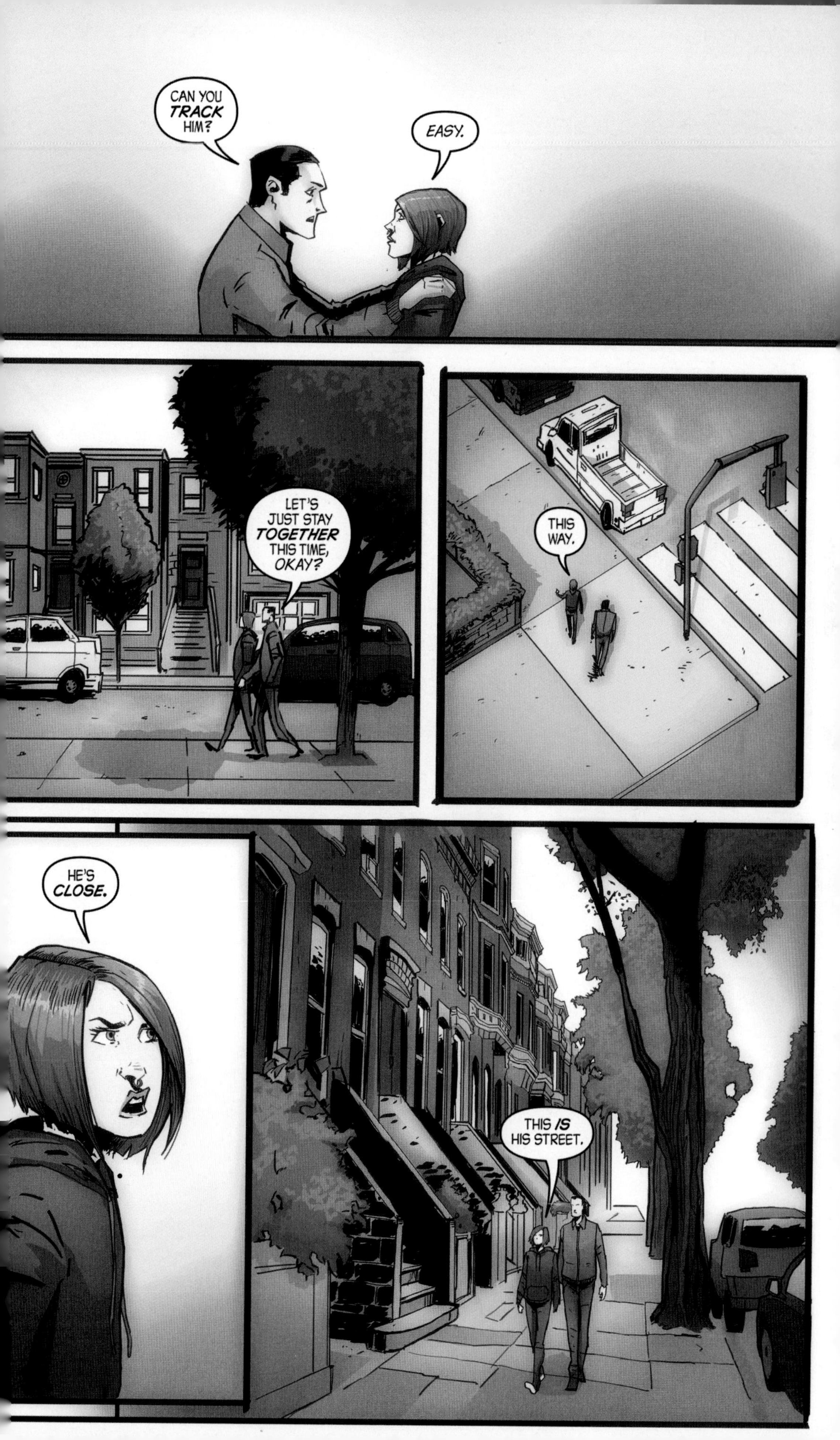
CAN YOU **TRACK** HIM?
EASY.
LET'S JUST STAY **TOGETHER** THIS TIME, *OKAY?*
THIS WAY.
HE'S **CLOSE.**
THIS ***IS*** HIS STREET.

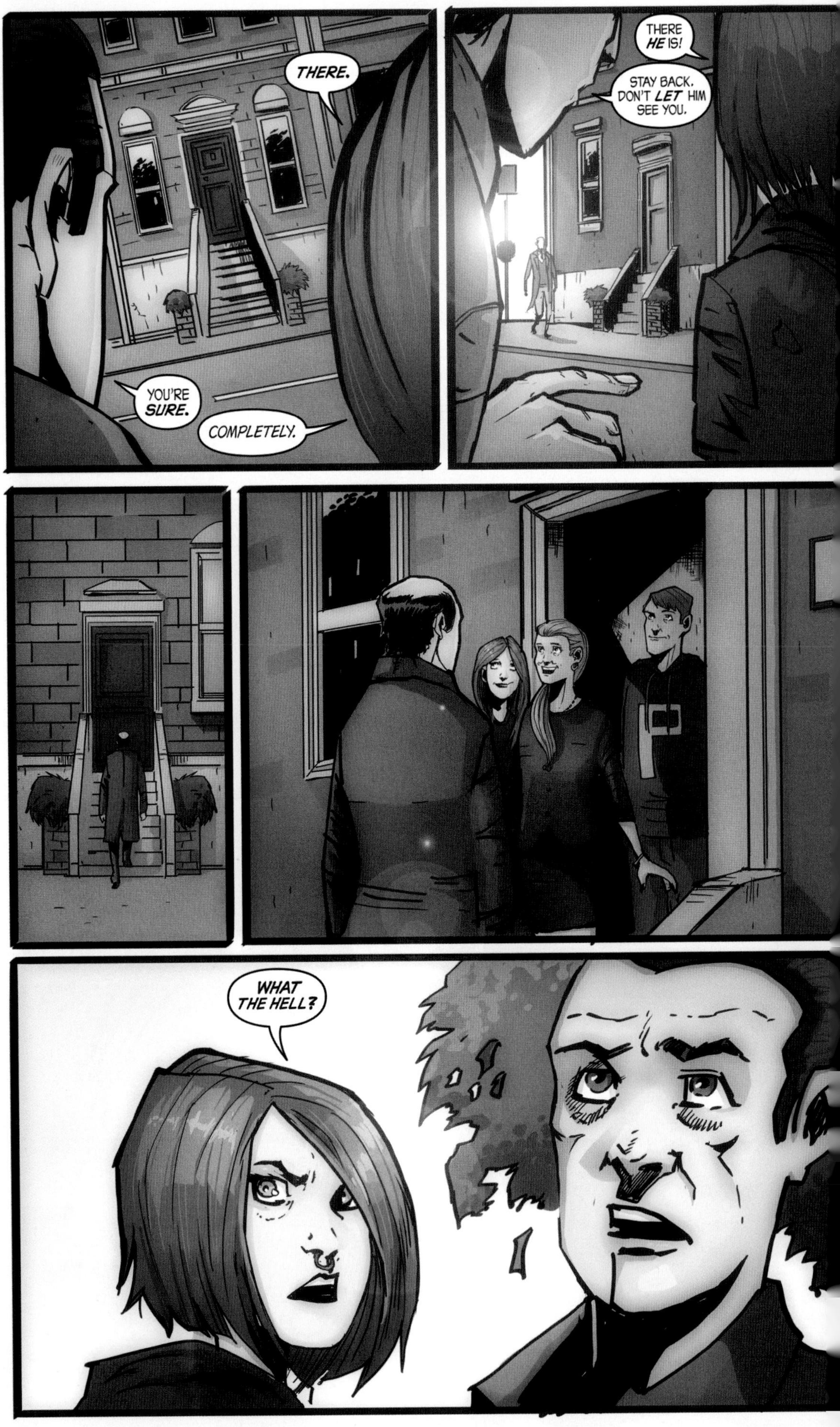
THERE.
YOU'RE SURE.
COMPLETELY.
THERE HE IS!
STAY BACK. DON'T LET HIM SEE YOU.
WHAT THE HELL?

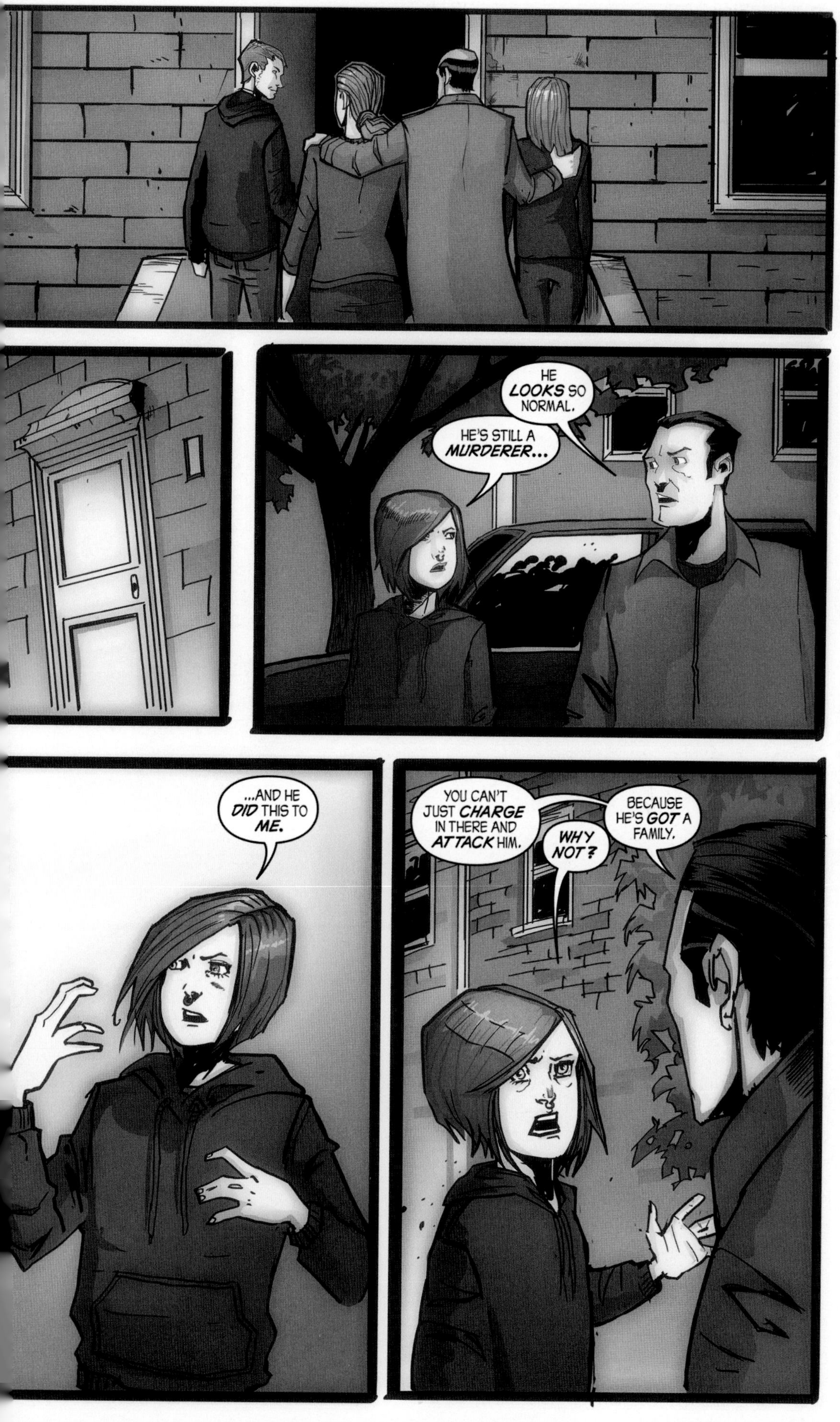
HE LOOKS SO NORMAL.
HE'S STILL A MURDERER...
...AND HE DID THIS TO ME.
YOU CAN'T JUST CHARGE IN THERE AND ATTACK HIM.
WHY NOT?
BECAUSE HE'S GOT A FAMILY.

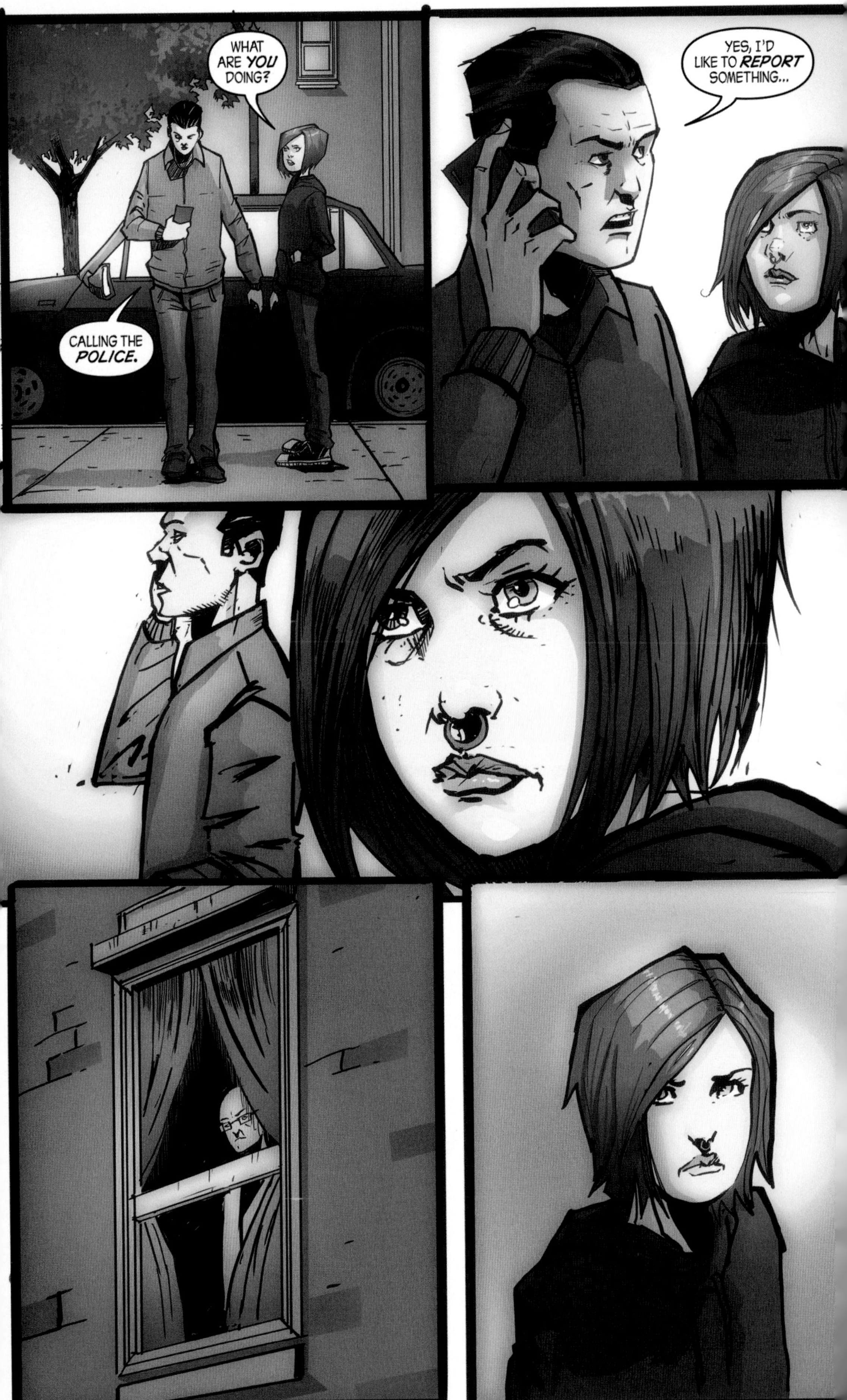
WHAT ARE YOU DOING?
CALLING THE POLICE.
YES, I'D LIKE TO REPORT SOMETHING...

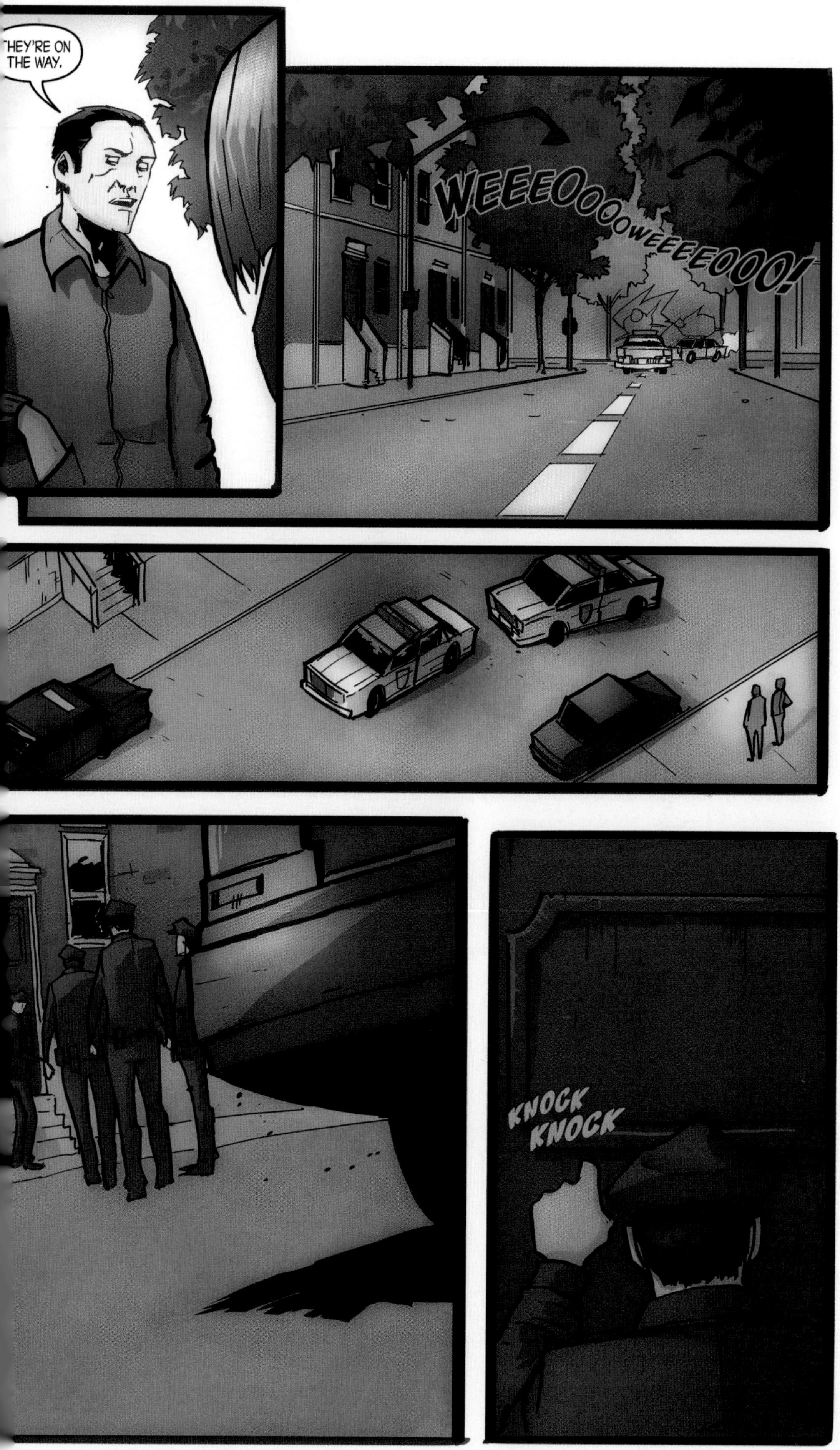
THEY'RE ON THE WAY.
WEEEOOOOWEEEEOOO!
KNOCK KNOCK

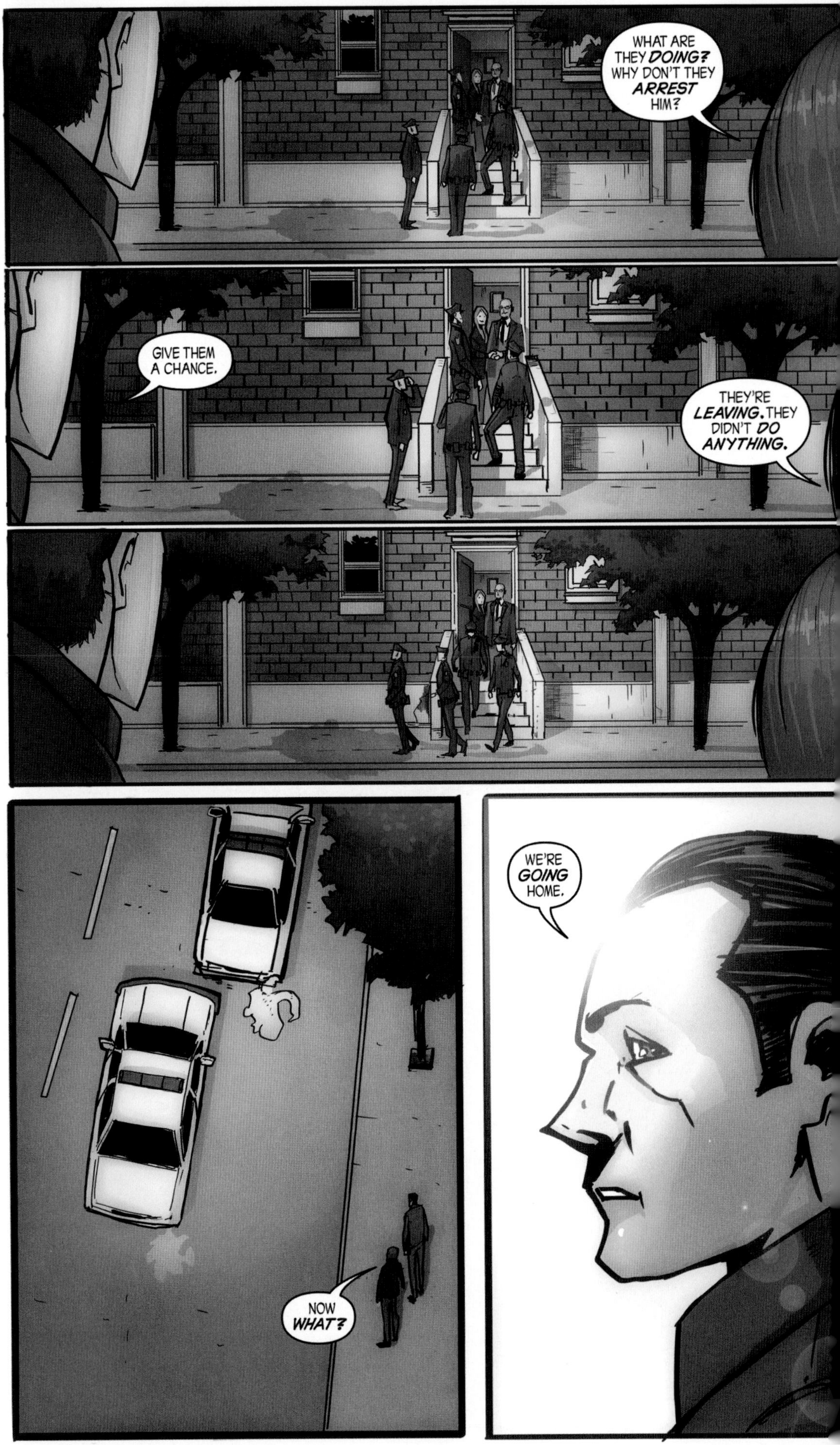
WHAT ARE THEY DOING? WHY DON'T THEY ARREST HIM?
GIVE THEM A CHANCE.
THEY'RE LEAVING. THEY DIDN'T DO ANYTHING.
NOW WHAT?
WE'RE GOING HOME.

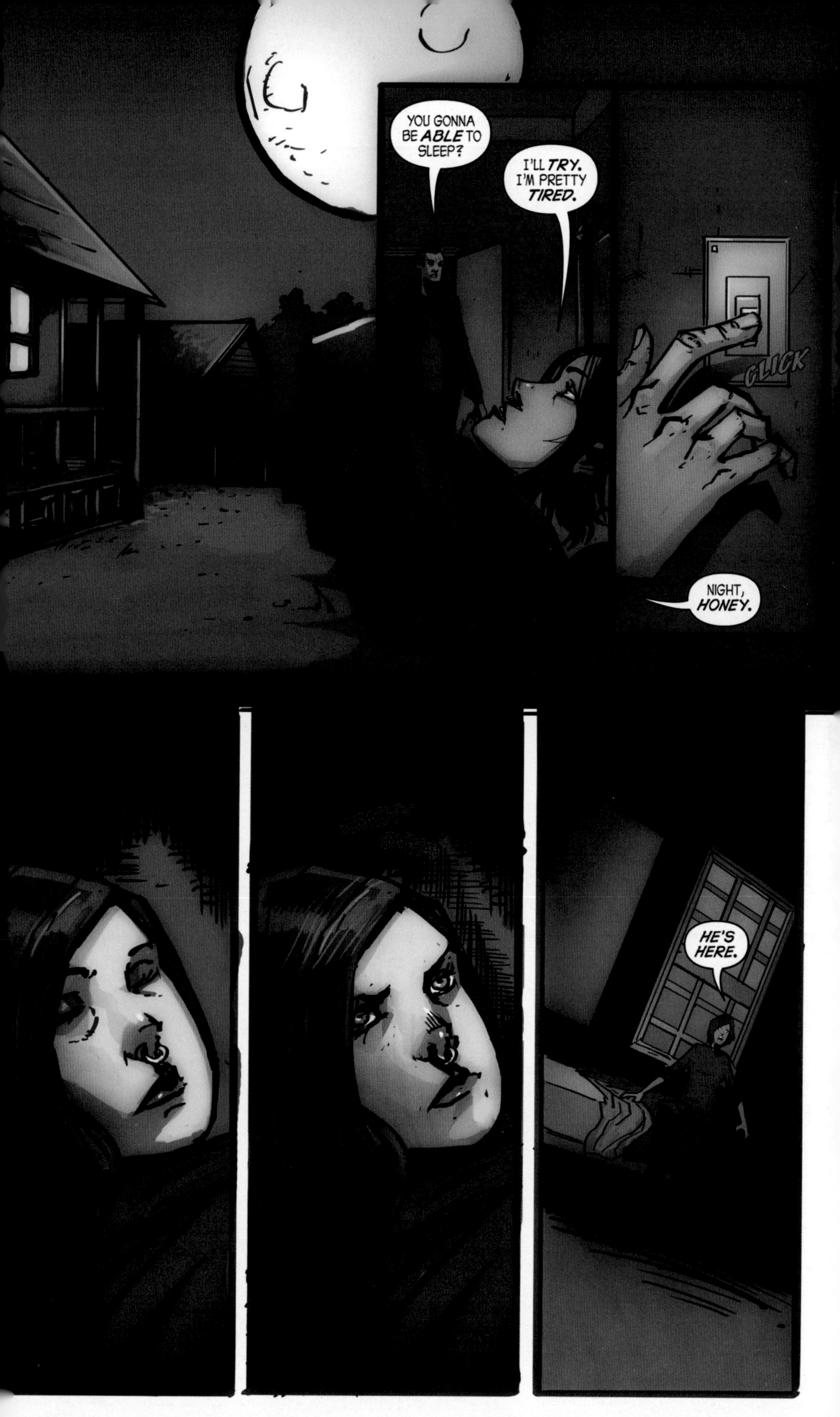
YOU GONNA BE ABLE TO SLEEP?
I'LL TRY. I'M PRETTY TIRED.
CLICK
NIGHT, HONEY.
HE'S HERE.

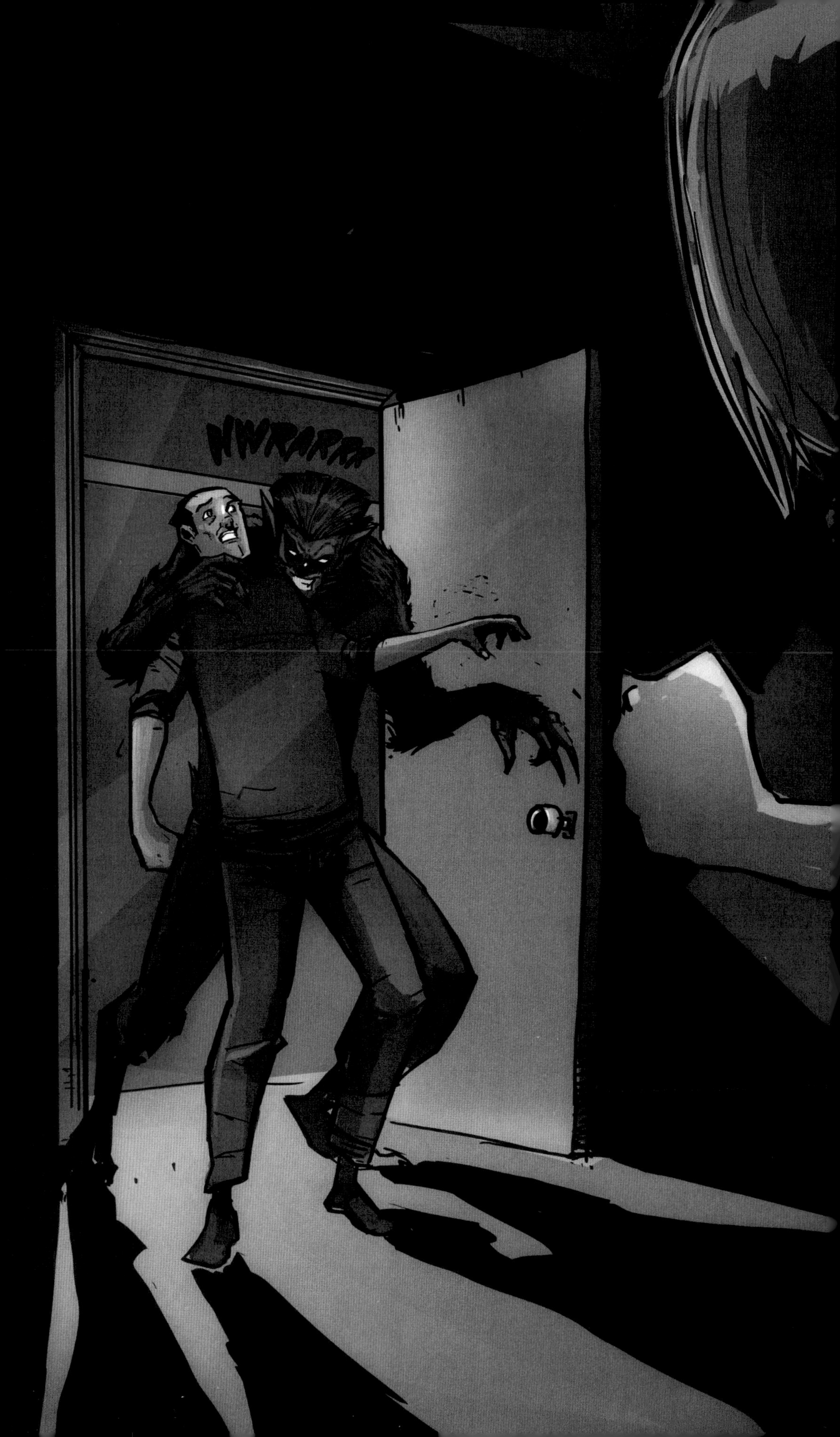
HWRARRR

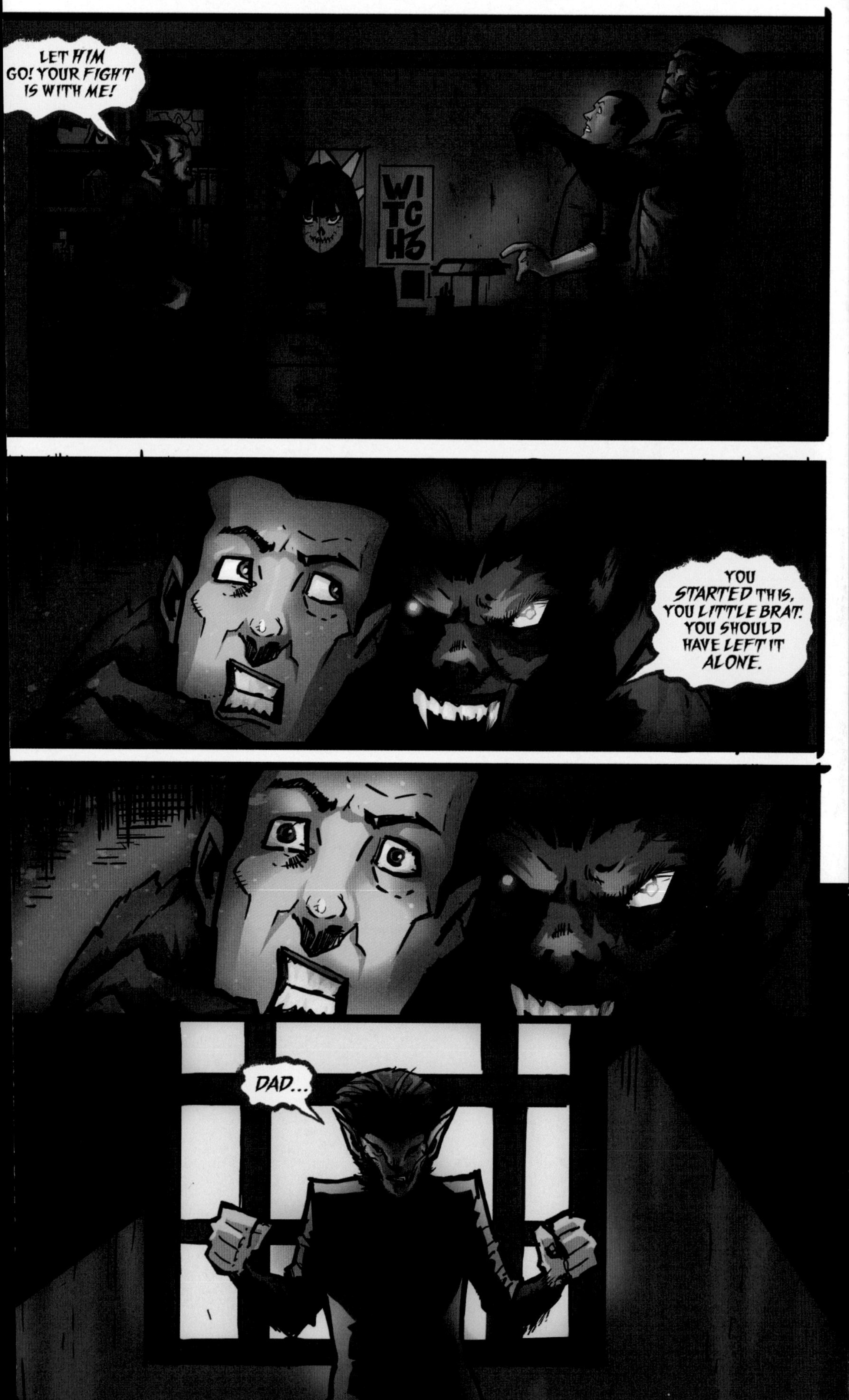
LET HIM GO! YOUR FIGHT IS WITH ME!
YOU STARTED THIS, YOU LITTLE BRAT. YOU SHOULD HAVE LEFT IT ALONE.
DAD...

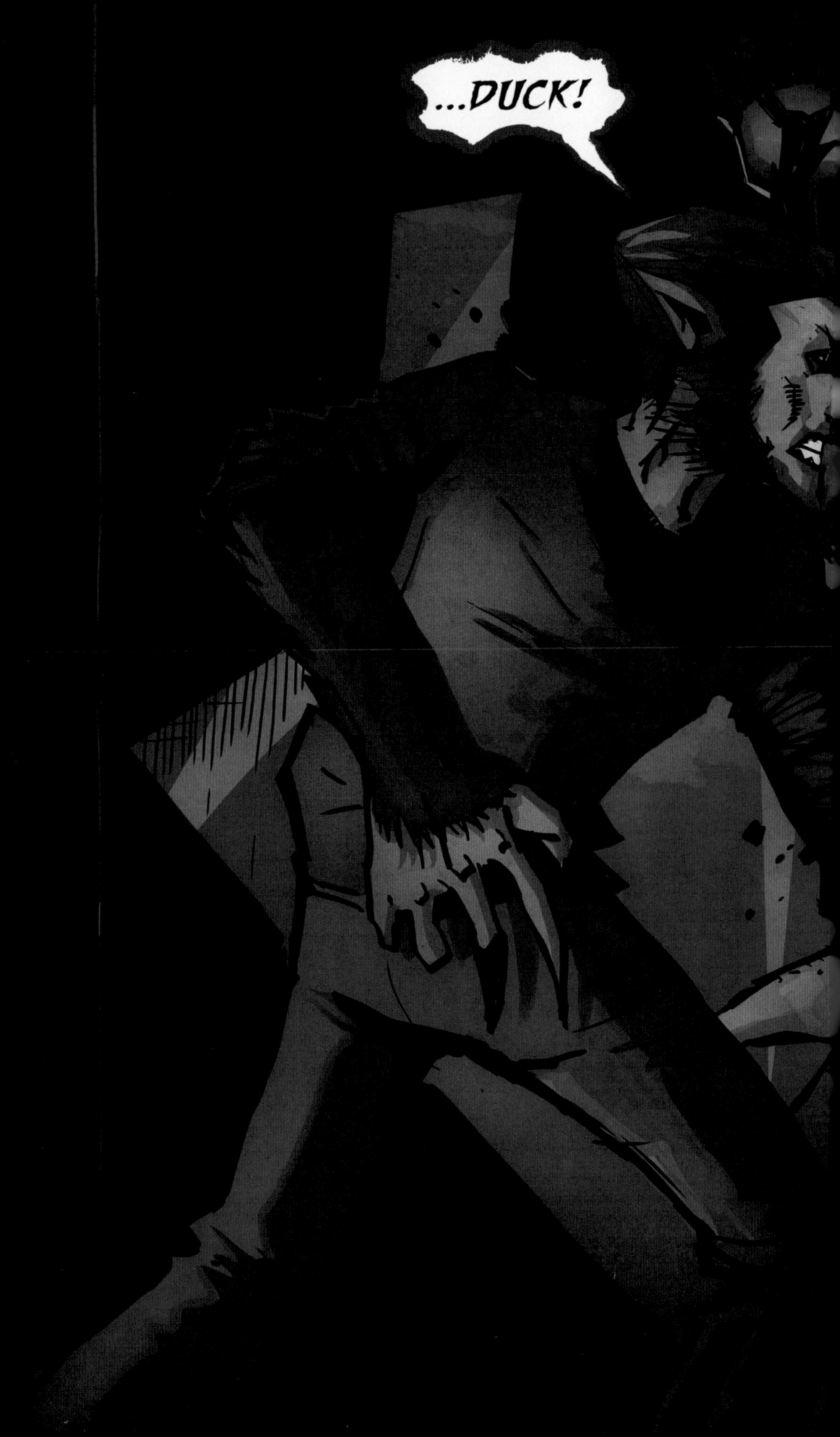
...DUCK!

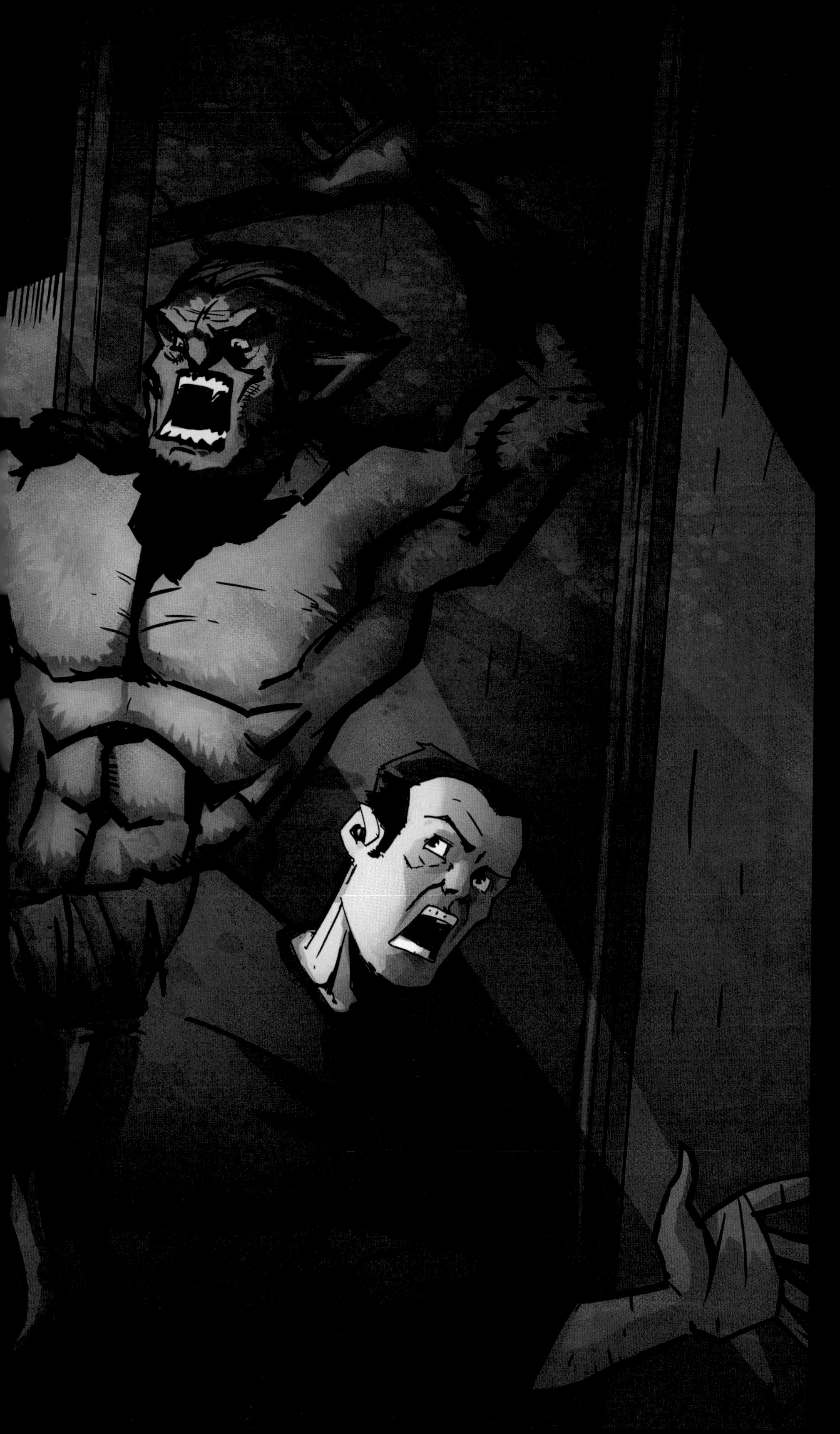

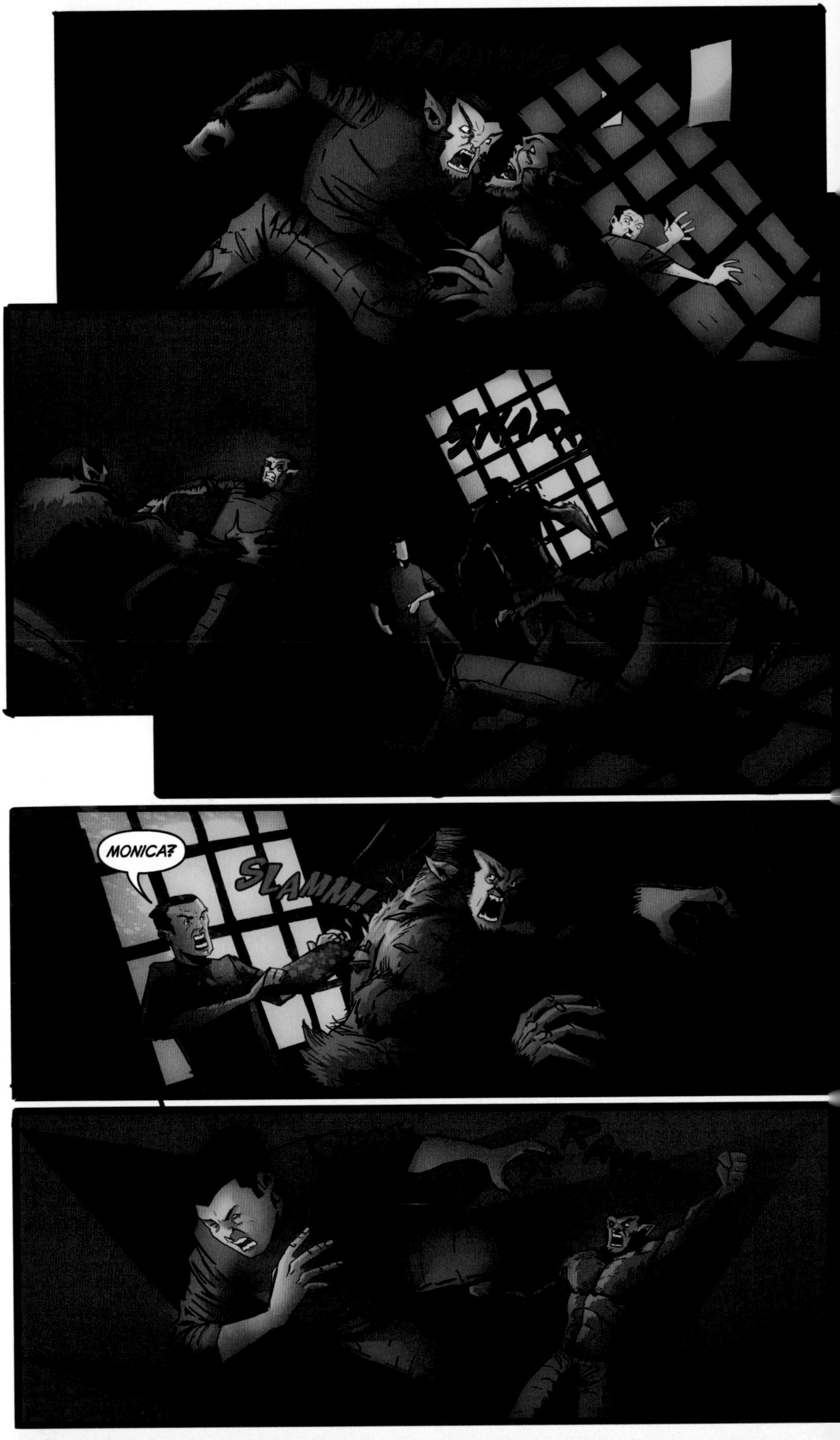
MONICA?
SLAMM!

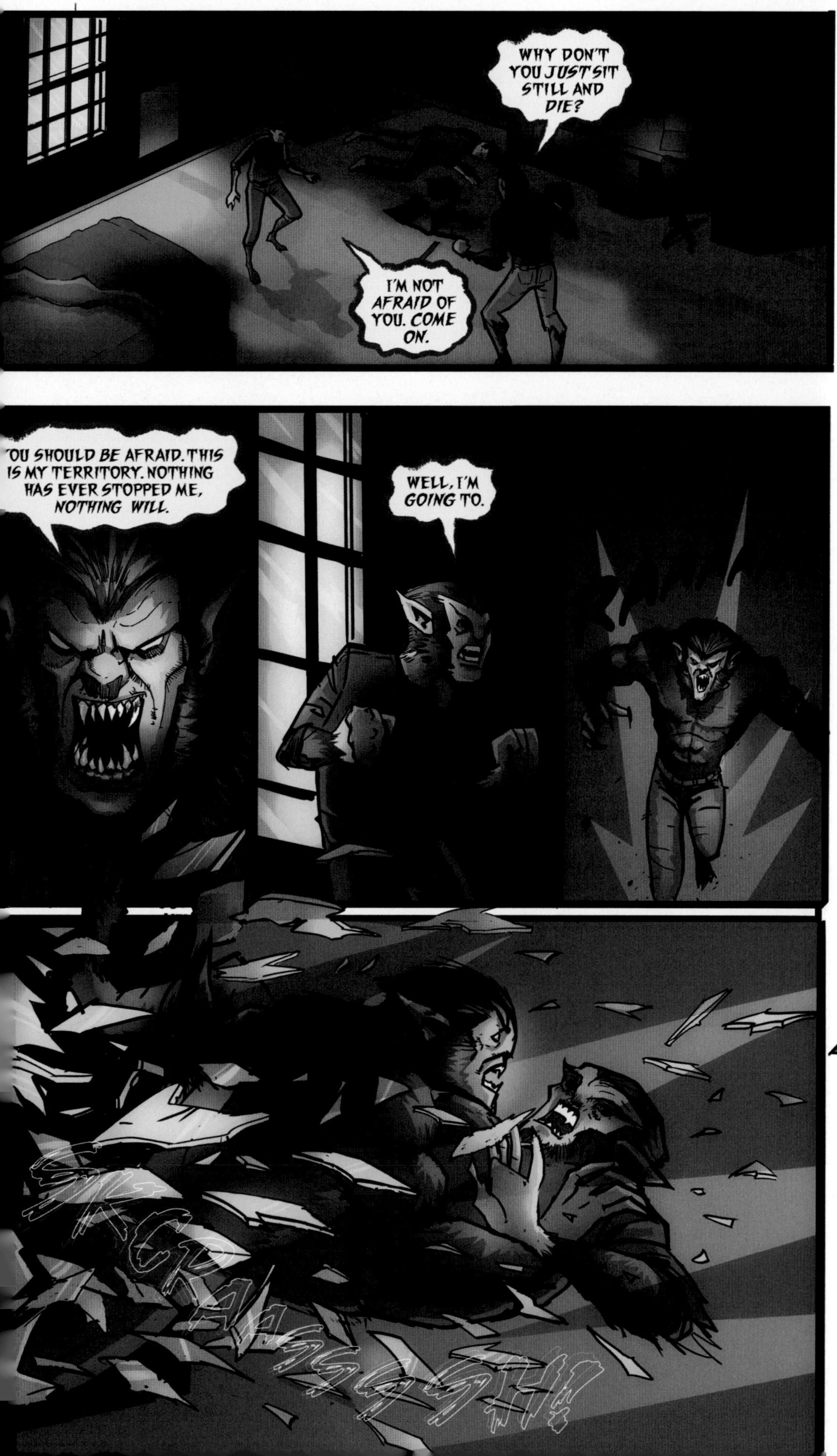
WHY DON'T YOU JUST SIT STILL AND DIE?
I'M NOT AFRAID OF YOU. COME ON.
YOU SHOULD BE AFRAID. THIS IS MY TERRITORY. NOTHING HAS EVER STOPPED ME, NOTHING WILL.
WELL, I'M GOING TO.
SKGRAASSSSH!

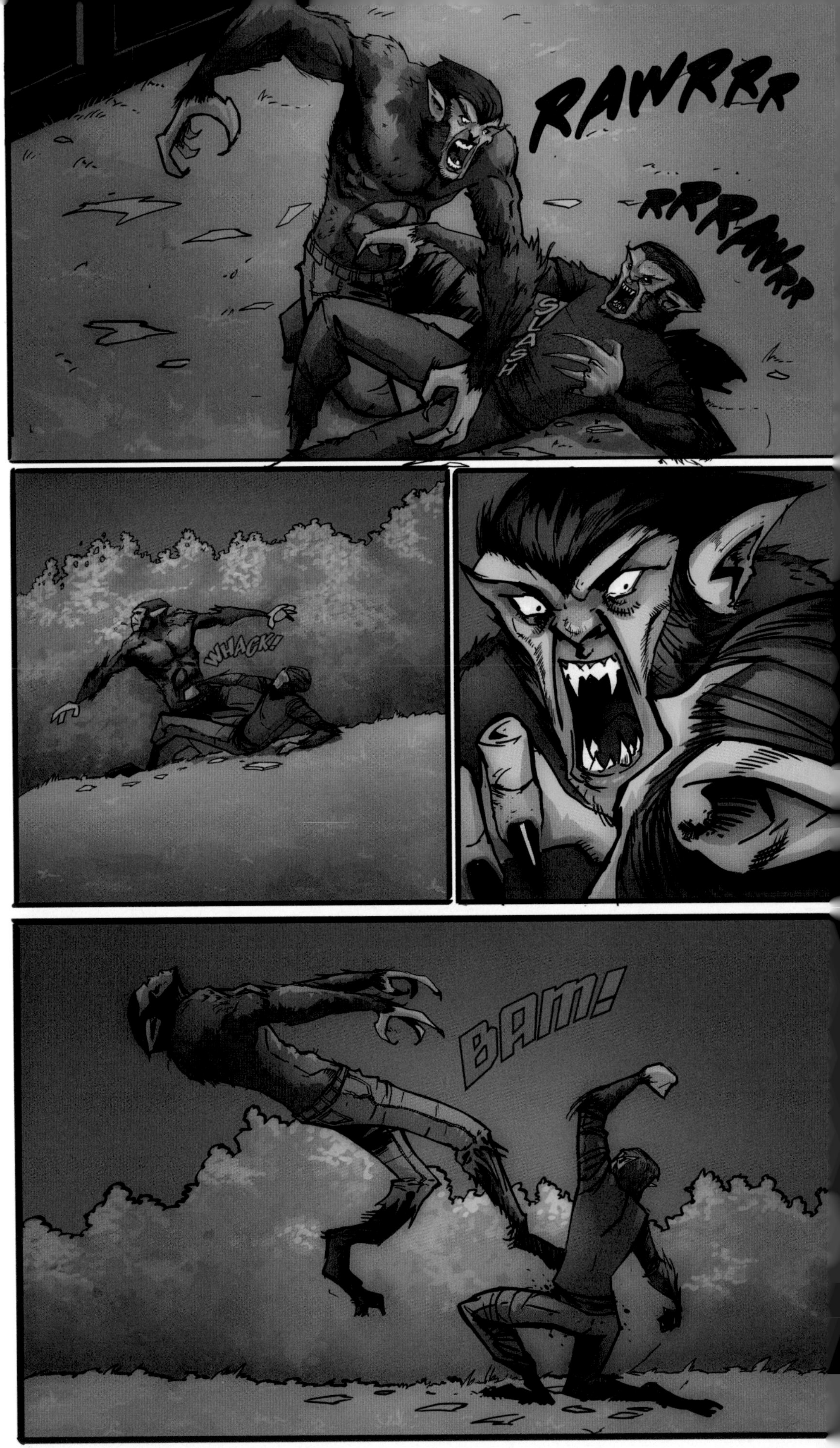
RAWRRR
RRRAWRR
SLASH
WHACK!
BAM!

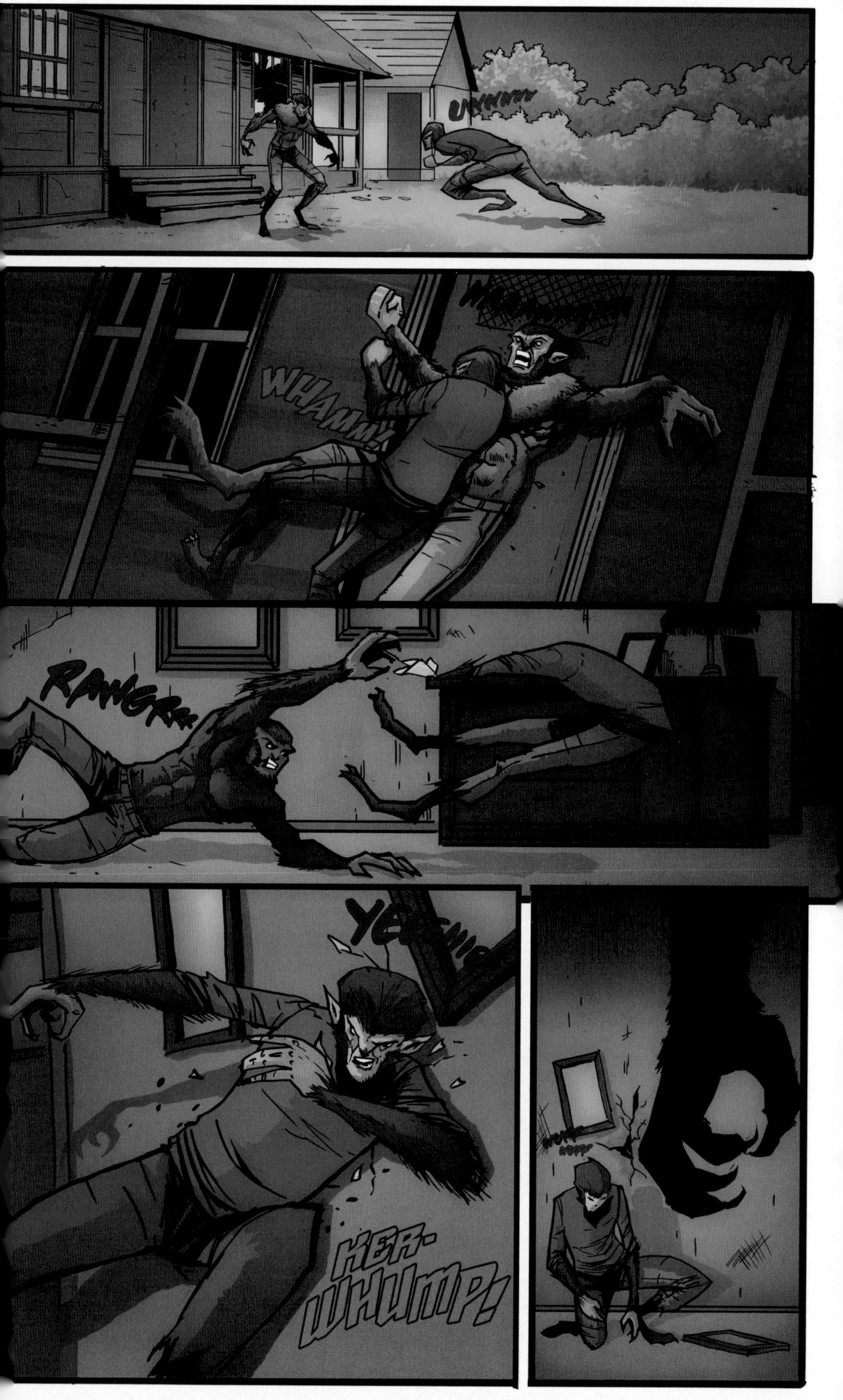
WHAMM
RANGRR
KER-
WHUMP!

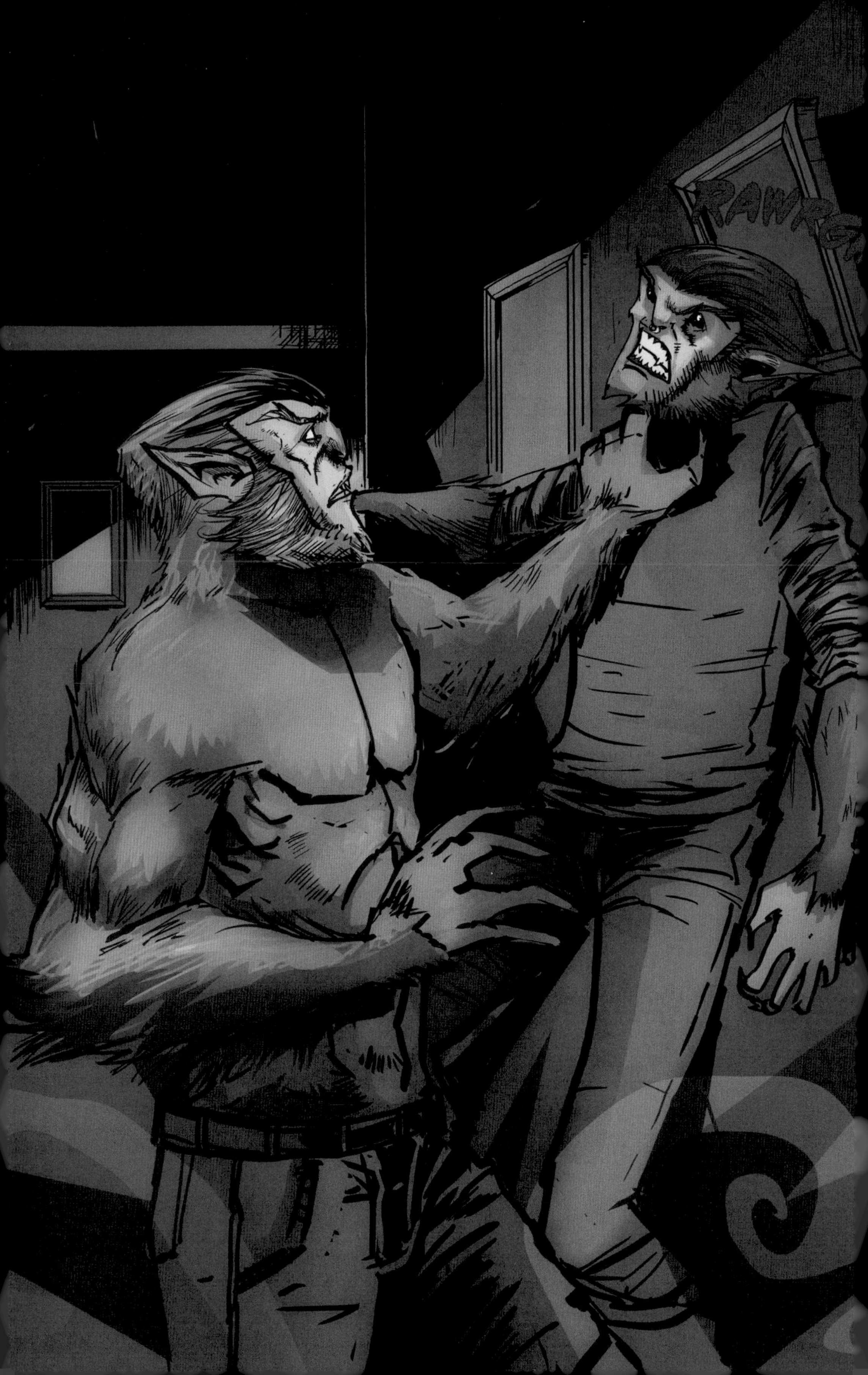
RAWRG

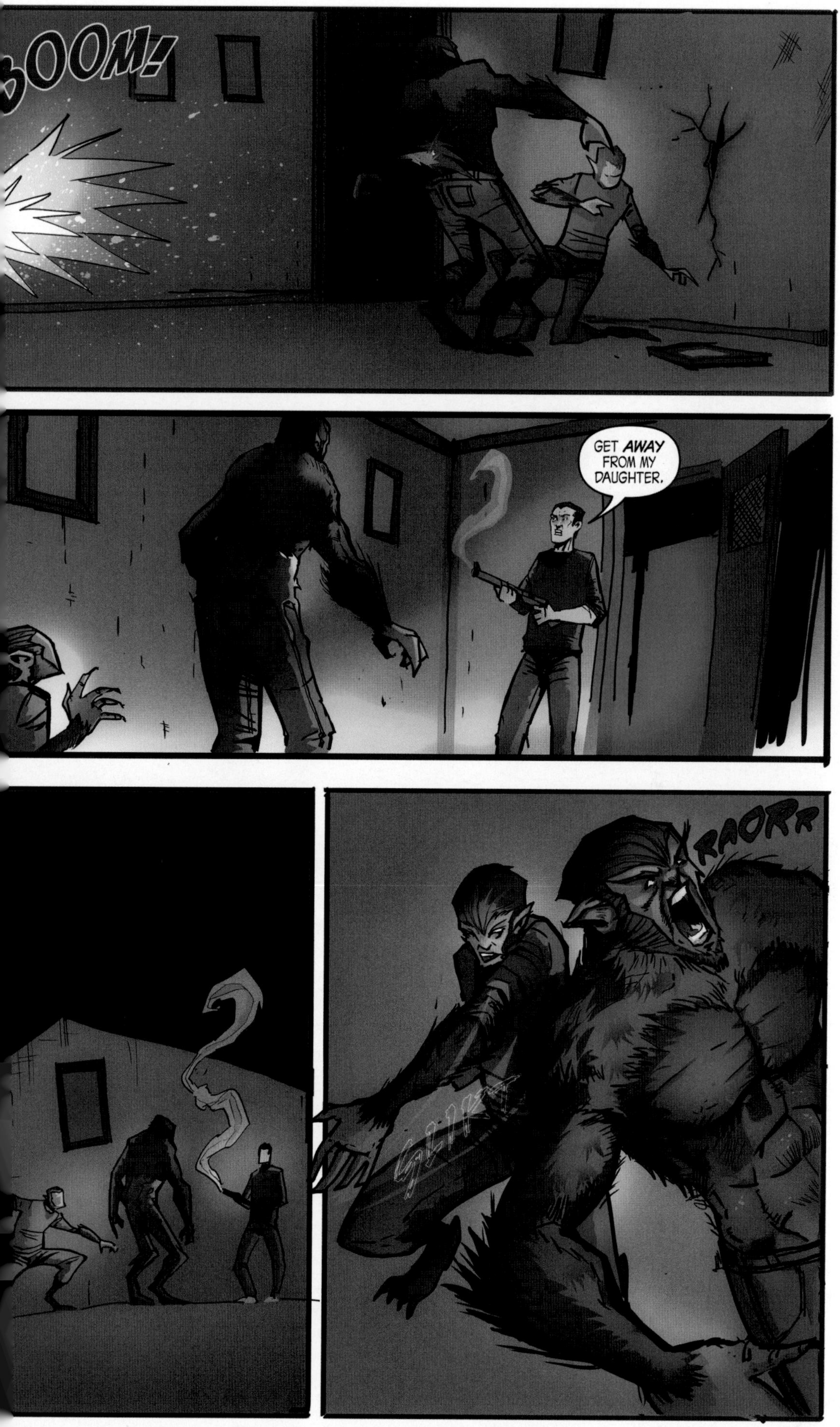
BOOM!
GET AWAY FROM MY DAUGHTER.
RAORR

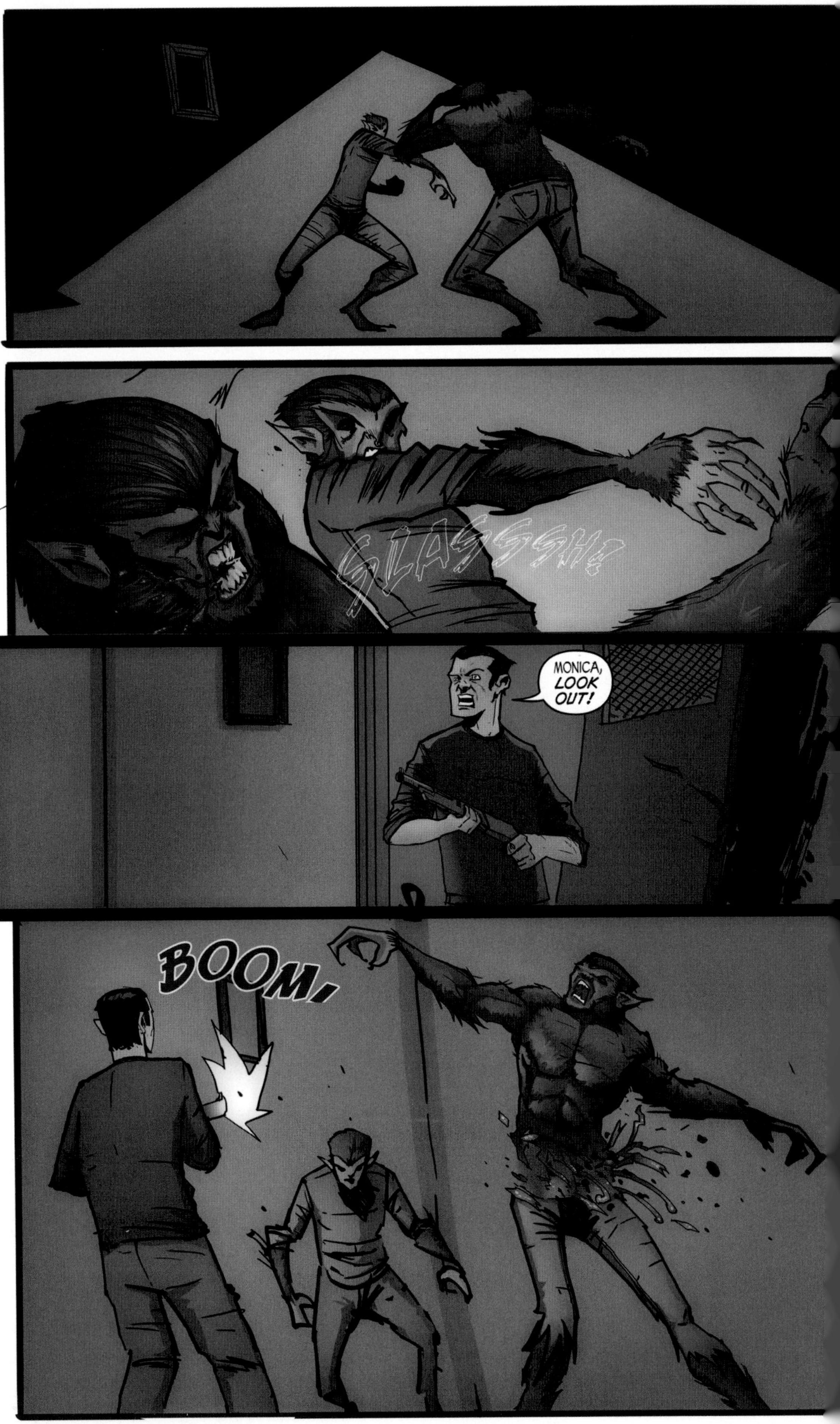
SLASSSH!
MONICA, LOOK OUT!
BOOM!

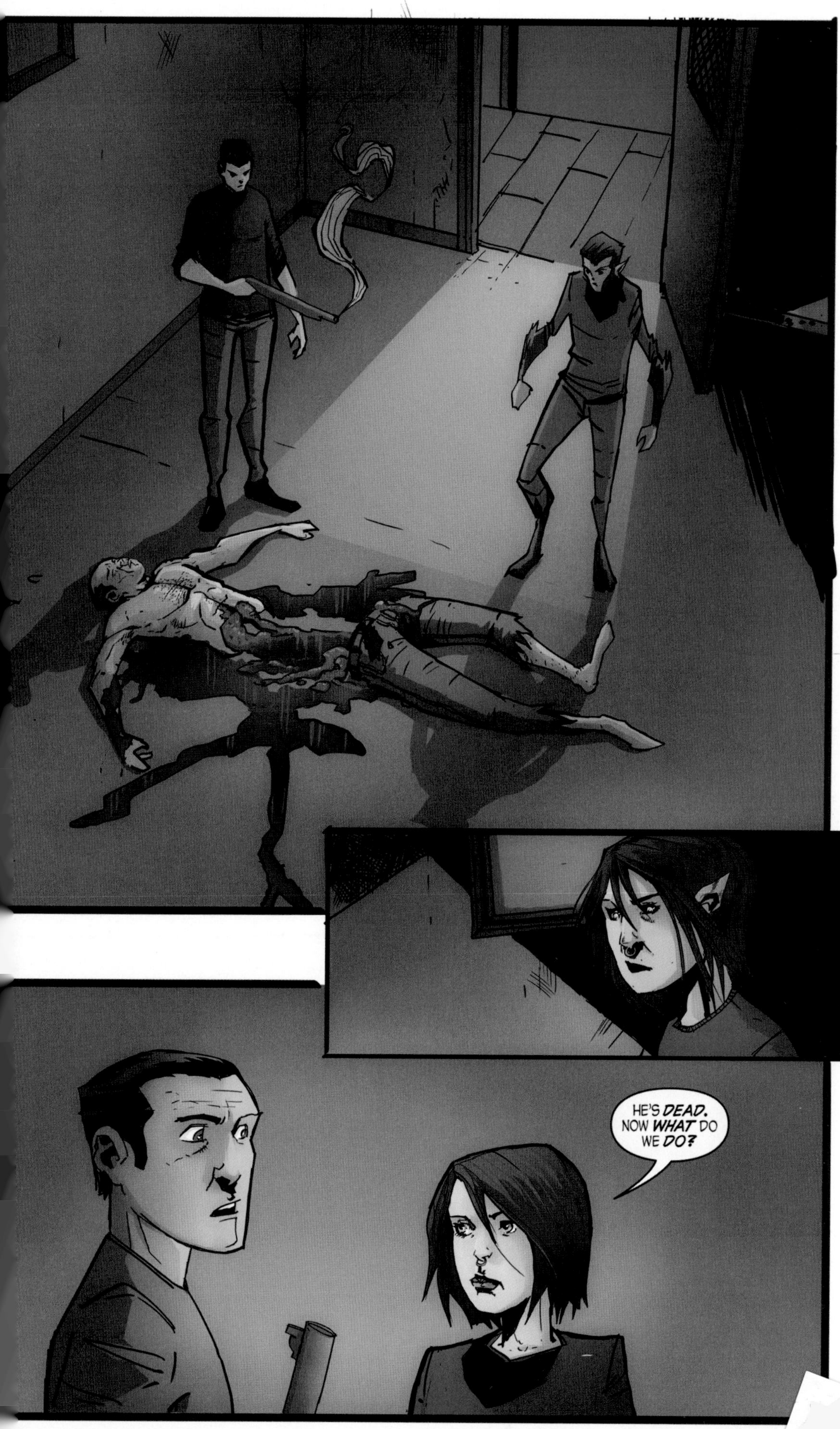
HE'S **DEAD.** NOW **WHAT** DO WE **DO?**

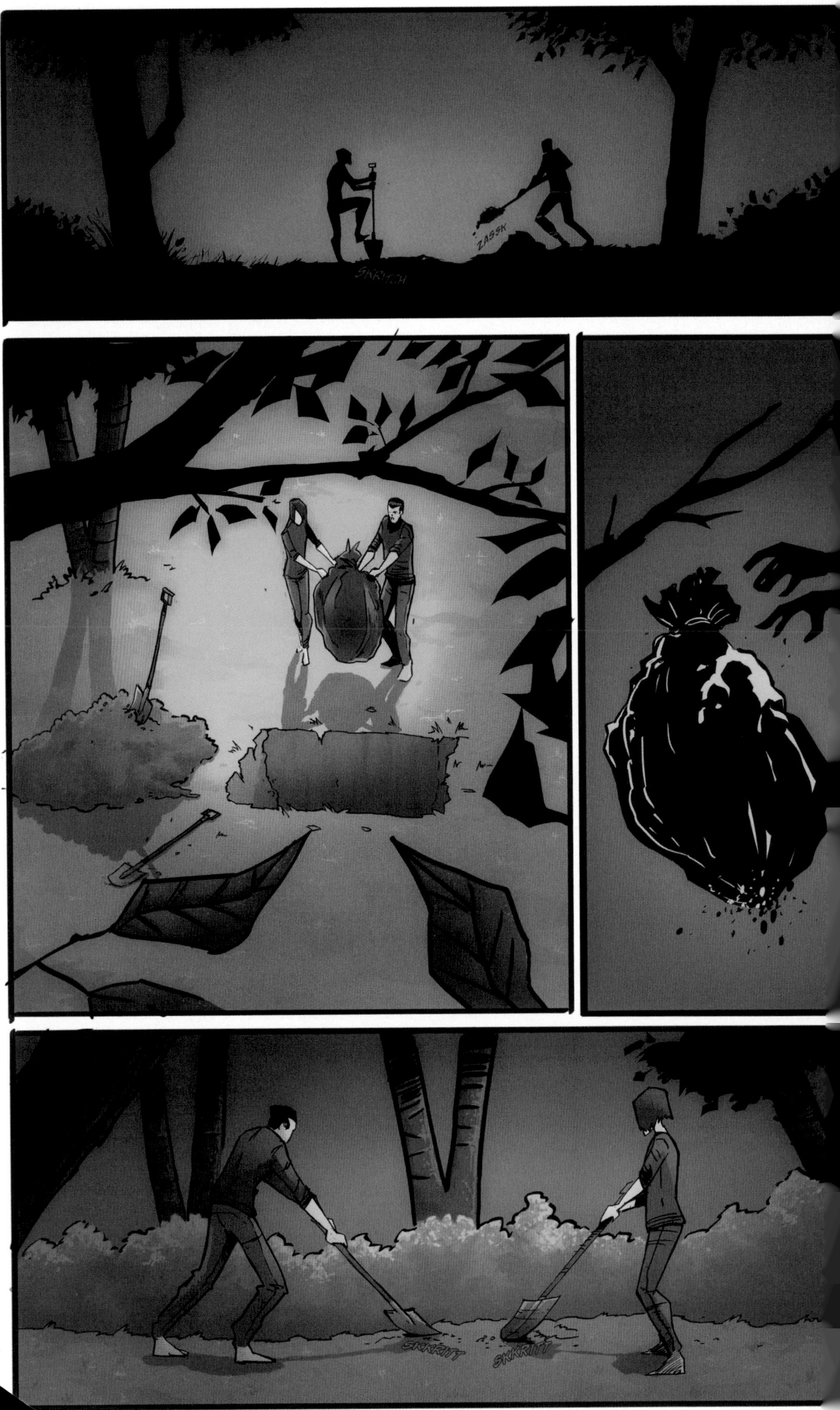
ZASSK
SKRITCH
SKKRITT
SKKRITT

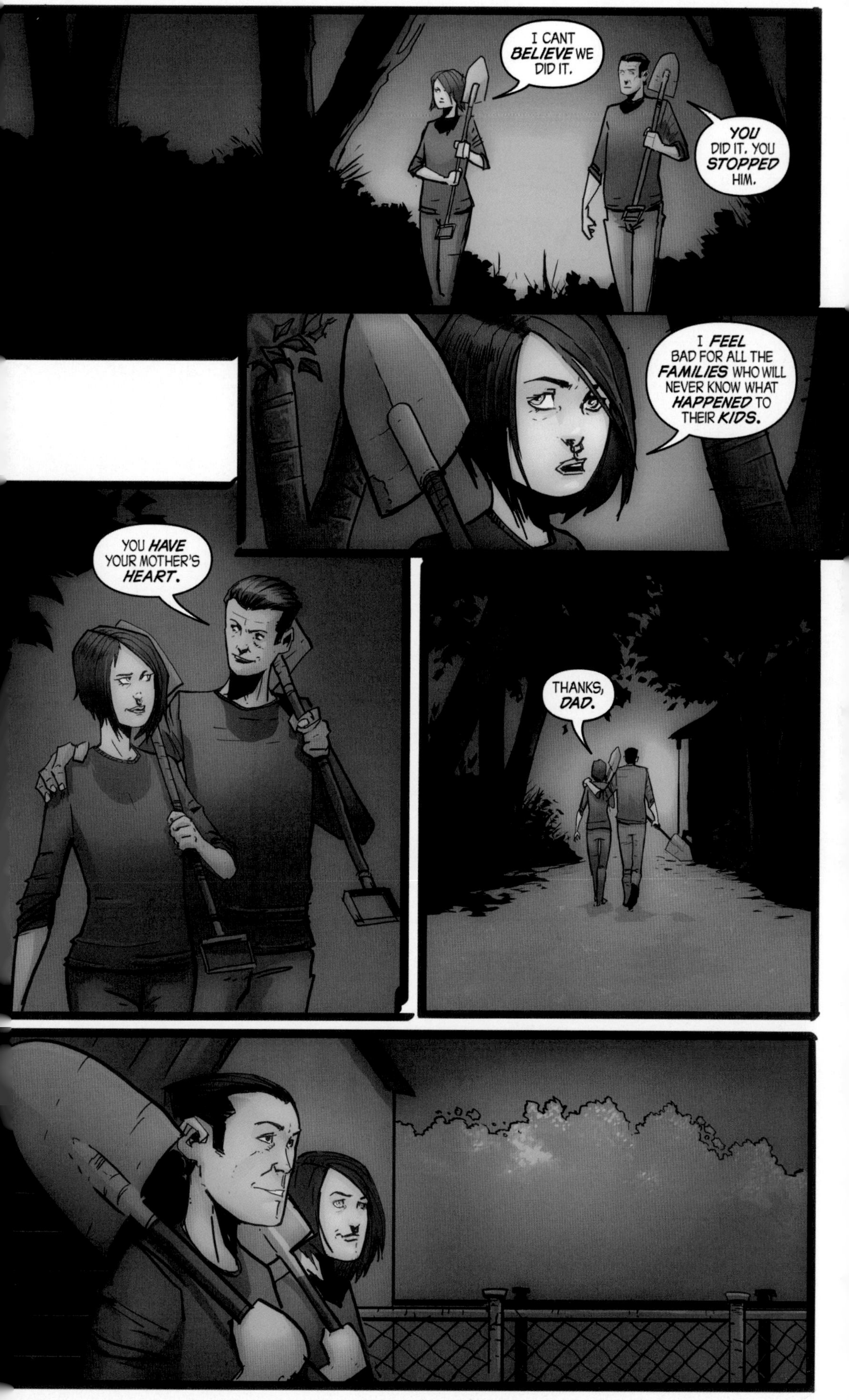
I CANT BELIEVE WE DID IT.
YOU DID IT. YOU STOPPED HIM.
I FEEL BAD FOR ALL THE FAMILIES WHO WILL NEVER KNOW WHAT HAPPENED TO THEIR KIDS.
YOU HAVE YOUR MOTHER'S HEART.
THANKS, DAD.

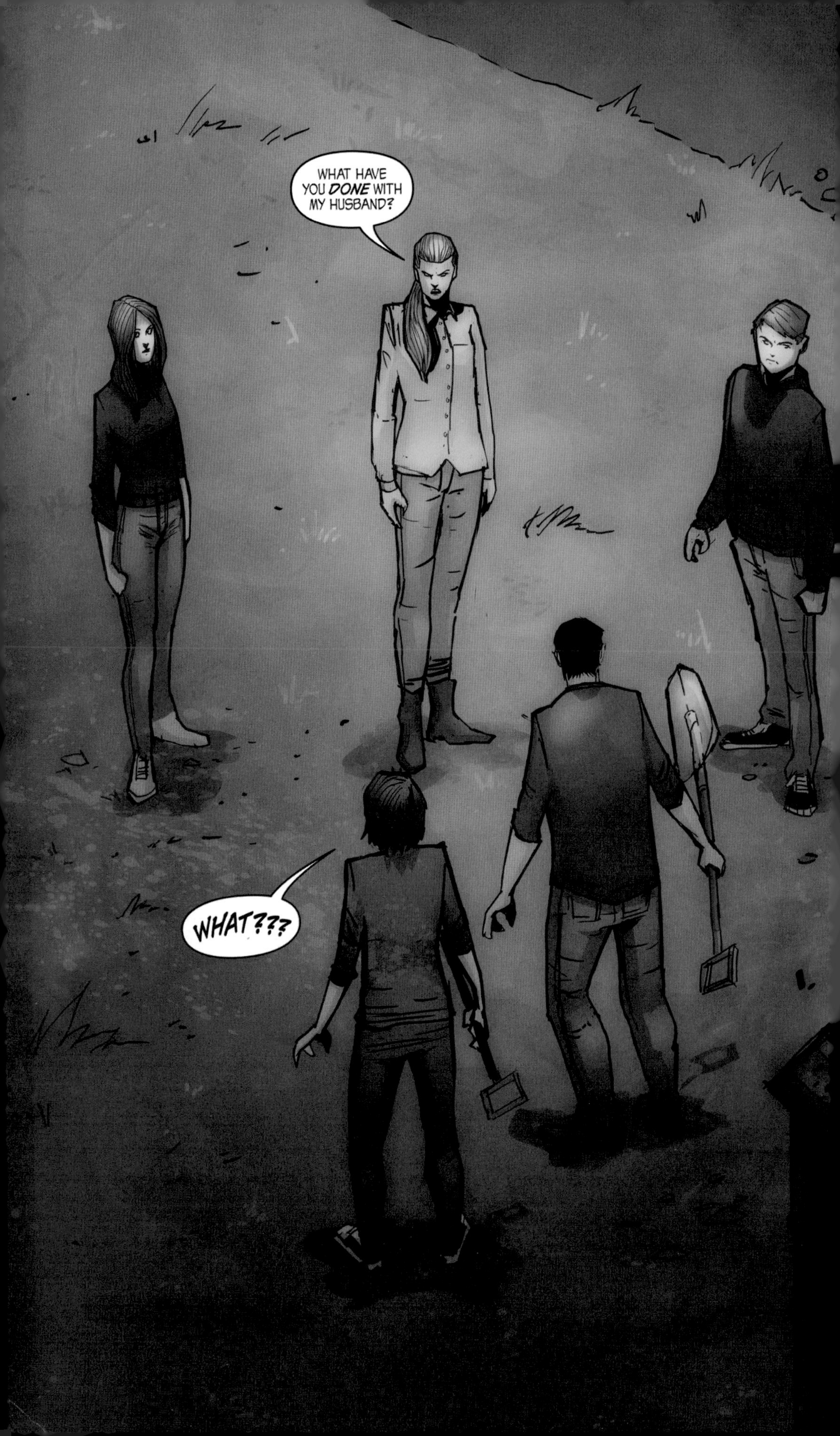
WHAT HAVE YOU DONE WITH MY HUSBAND?
WHAT???

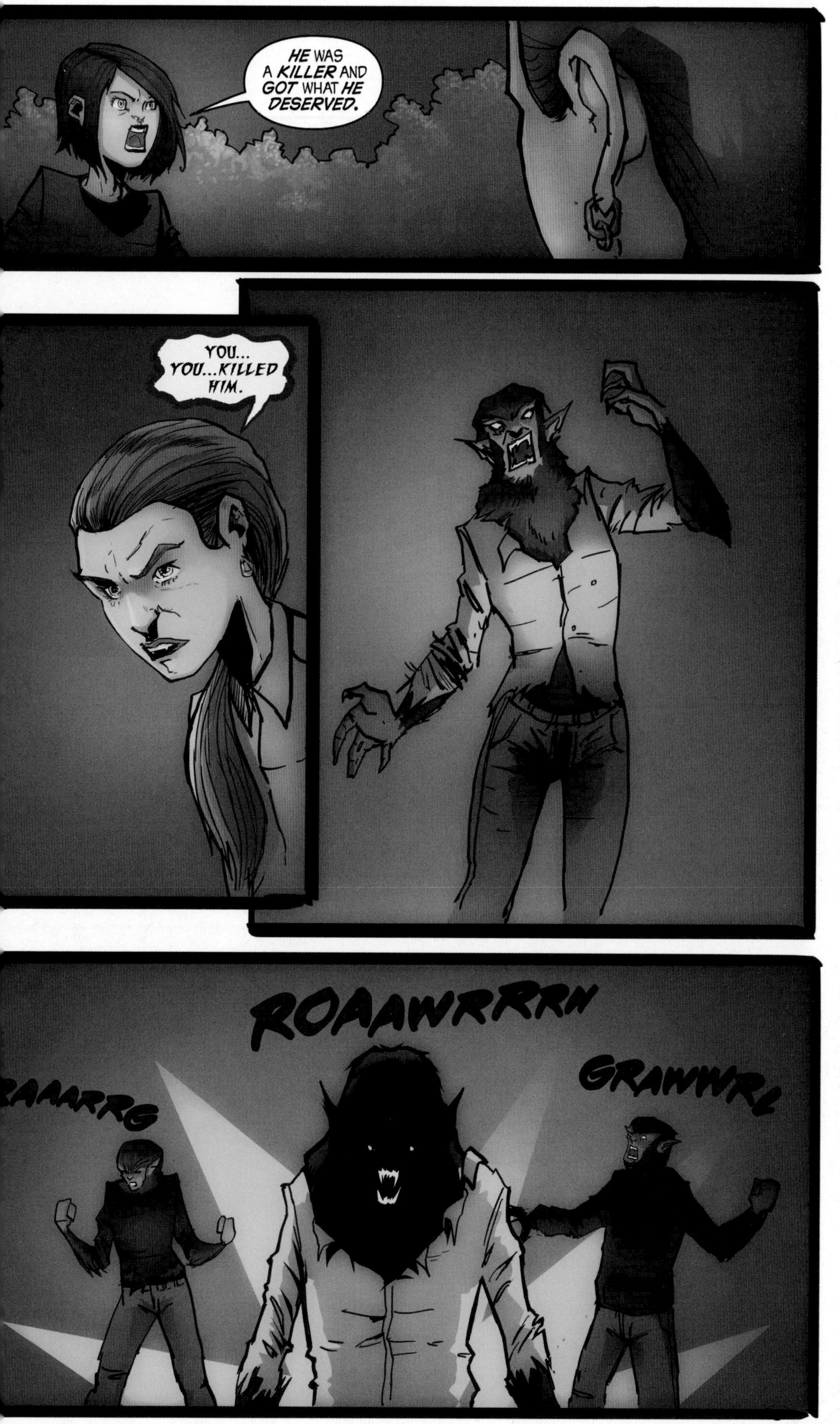
HE WAS A KILLER AND GOT WHAT HE DESERVED.
YOU... YOU...KILLED HIM.
ROAAWRRRN
RAAARRG
GRAWWRL

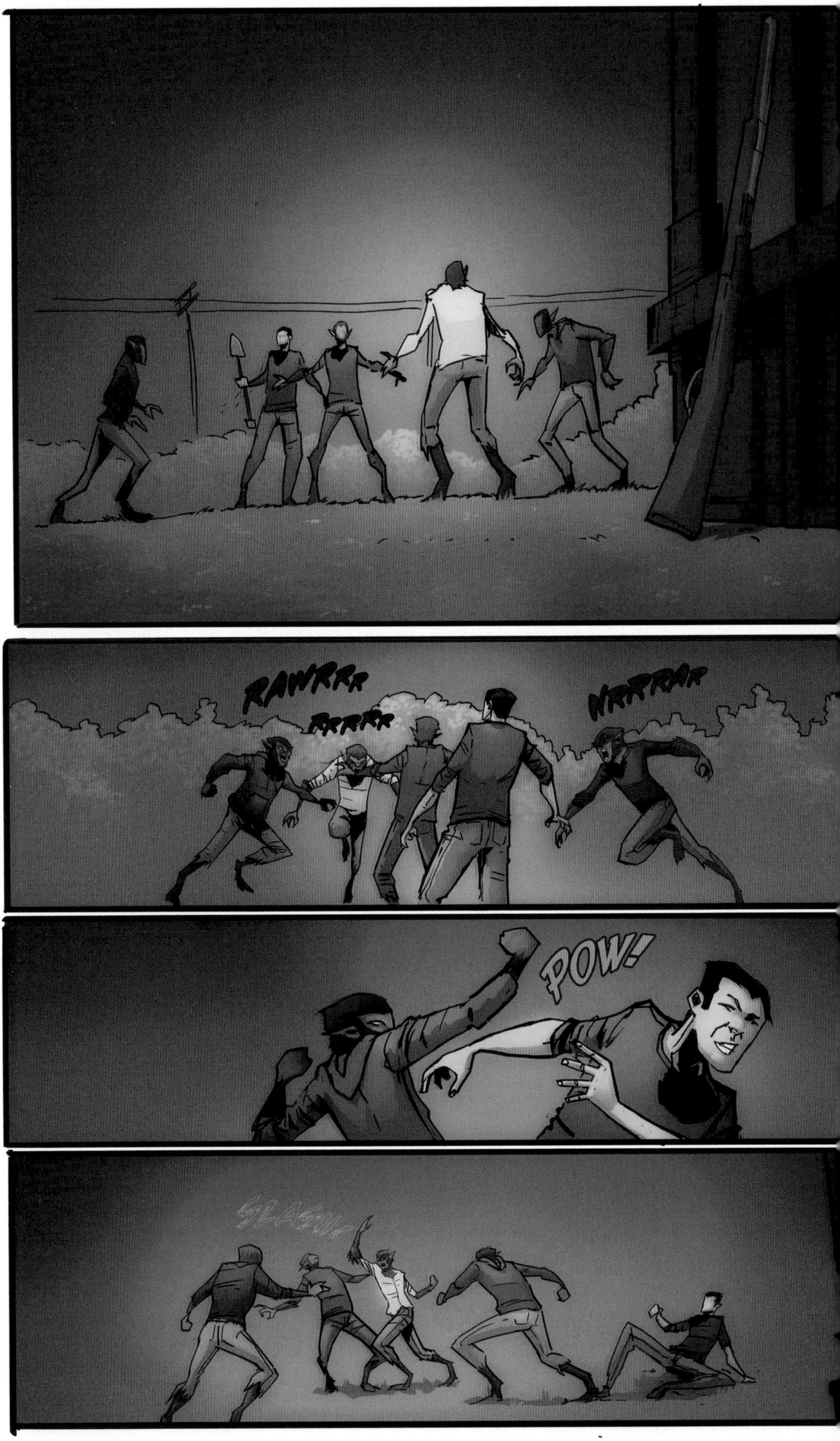
RAWRRR
RRRRR
HRRRAR
POW!
SLASH!

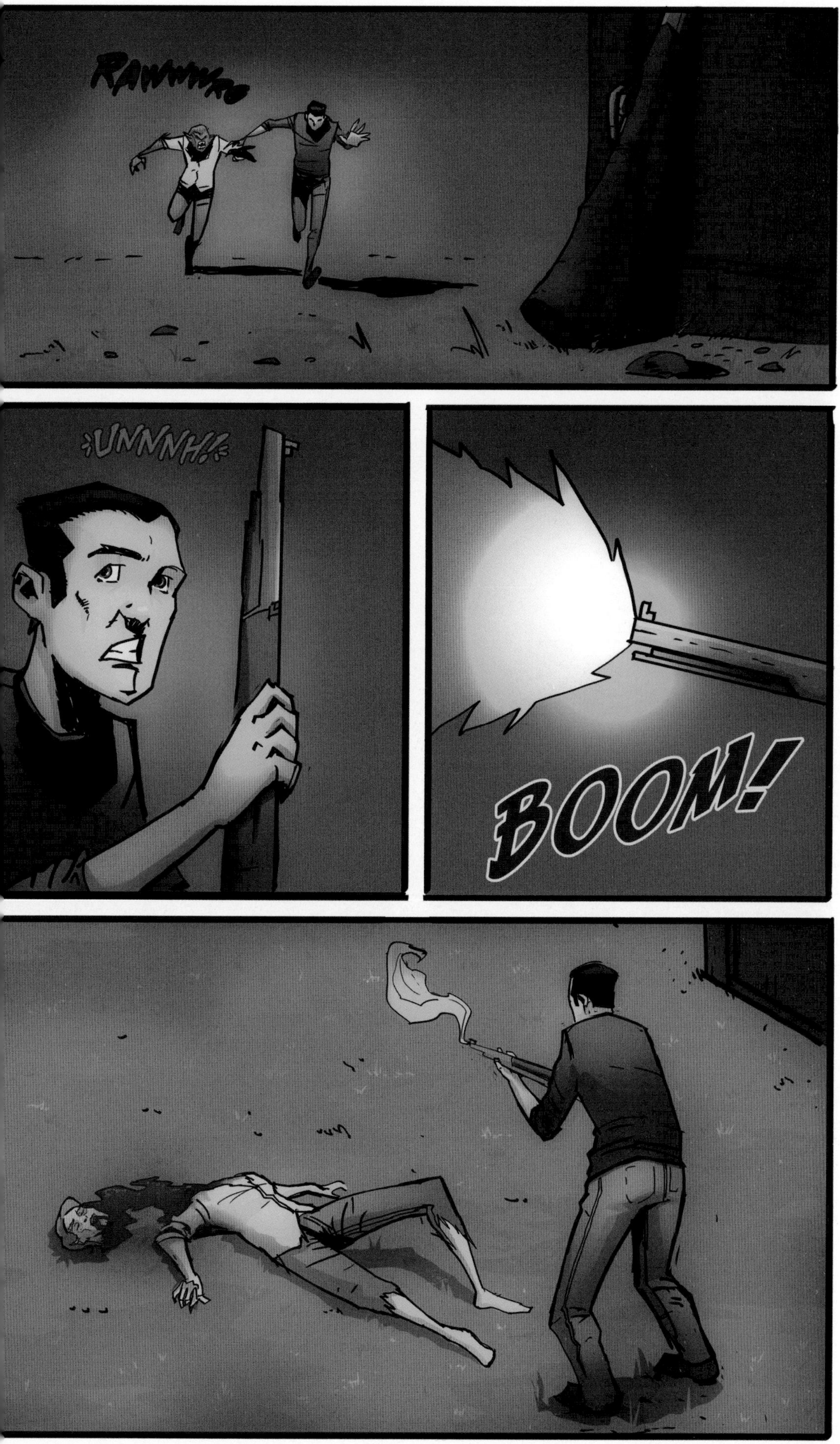
UNNNH!
BOOM!

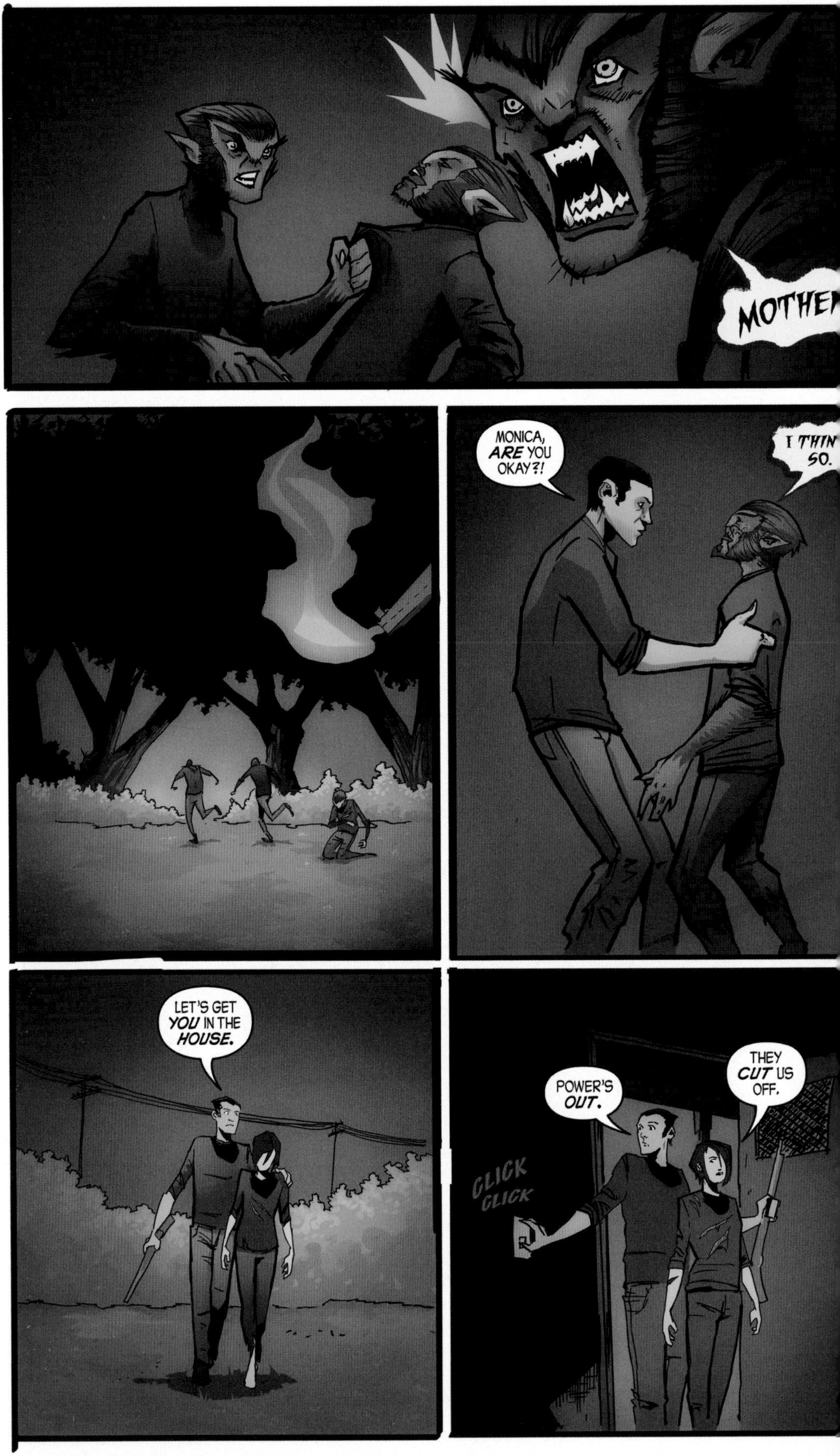
MOTHE
MONICA, ARE YOU OKAY?!
I THIN SO.
LET'S GET YOU IN THE HOUSE.
CLICK CLICK
POWER'S OUT.
THEY CUT US OFF.

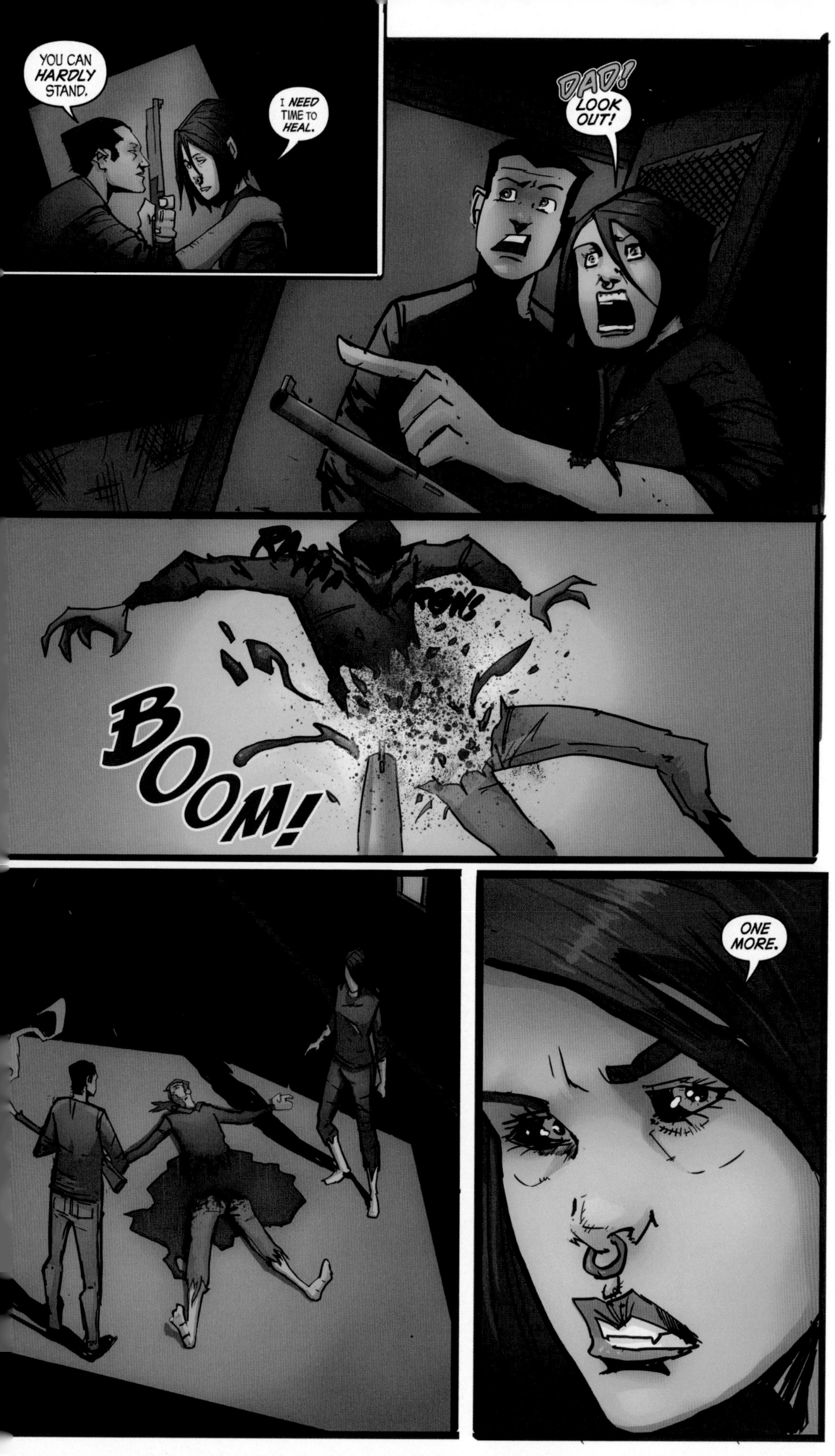
YOU CAN HARDLY STAND.
I NEED TIME TO HEAL.
DAD! LOOK OUT!
BOOM!
ONE MORE.

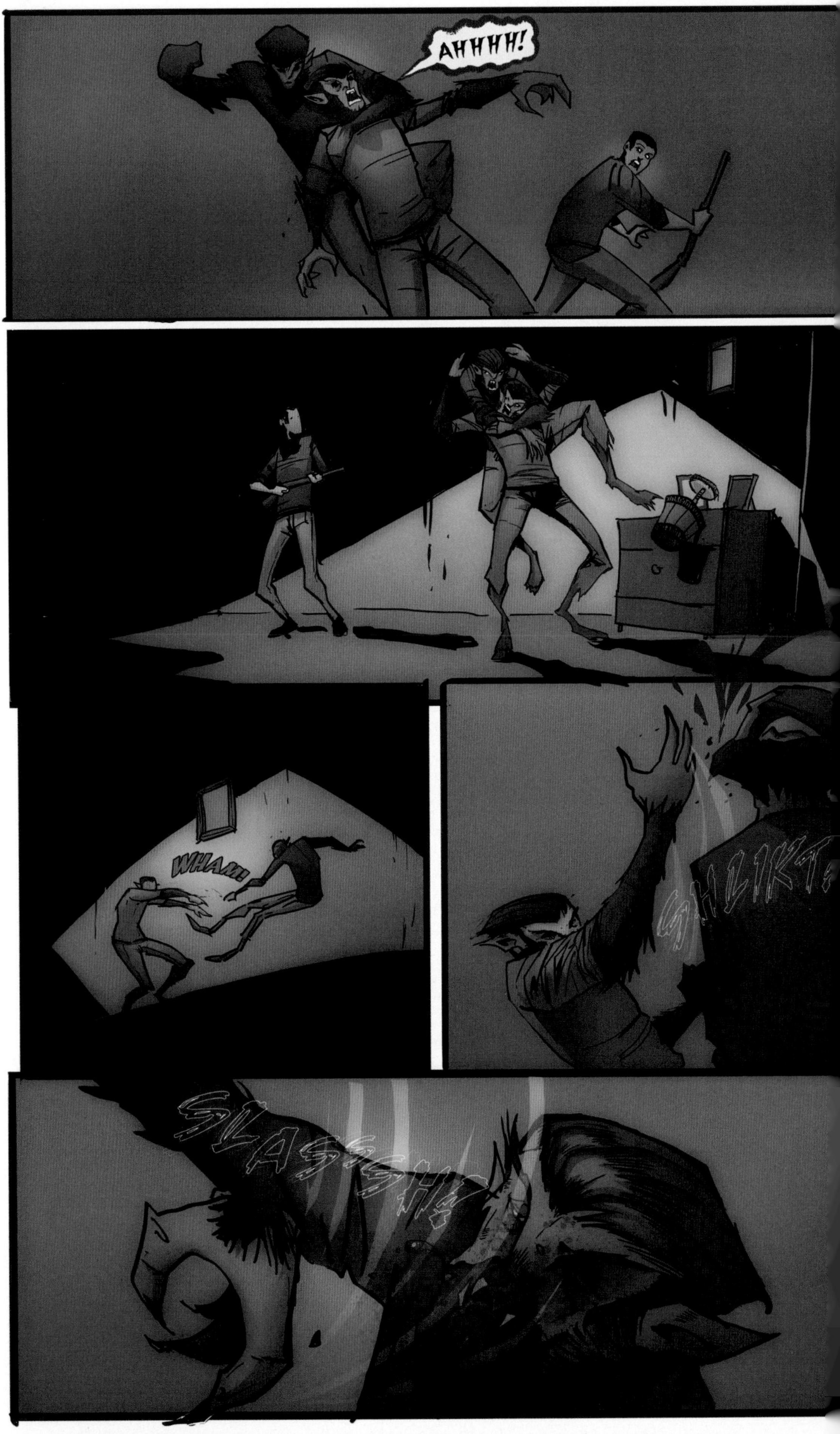
AHHHH!
WHAM!
SHLIKT!
SLASSSHH

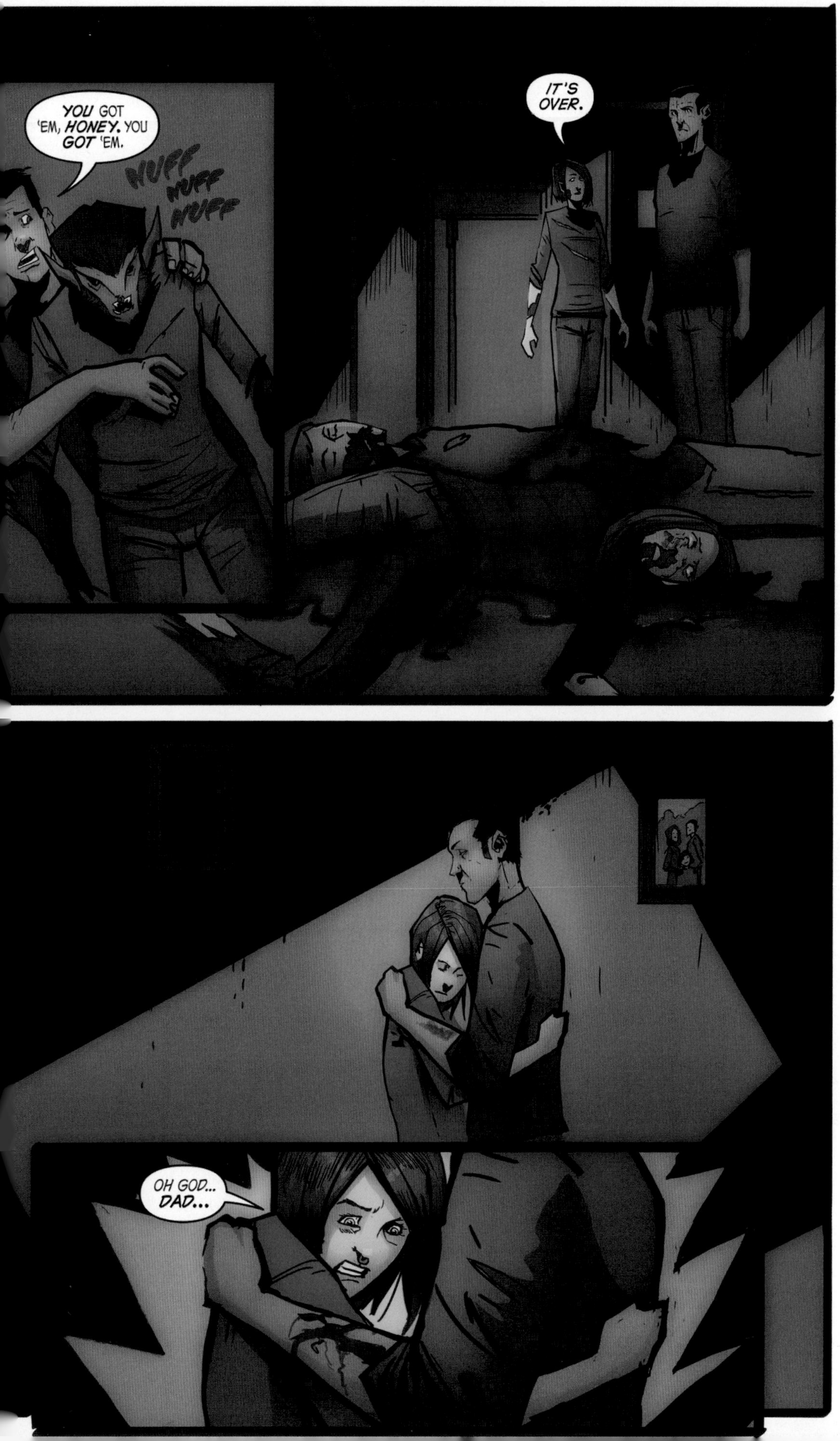
YOU GOT 'EM, HONEY. YOU GOT 'EM.
HUFF HUFF HUFF
IT'S OVER.
OH GOD... DAD...

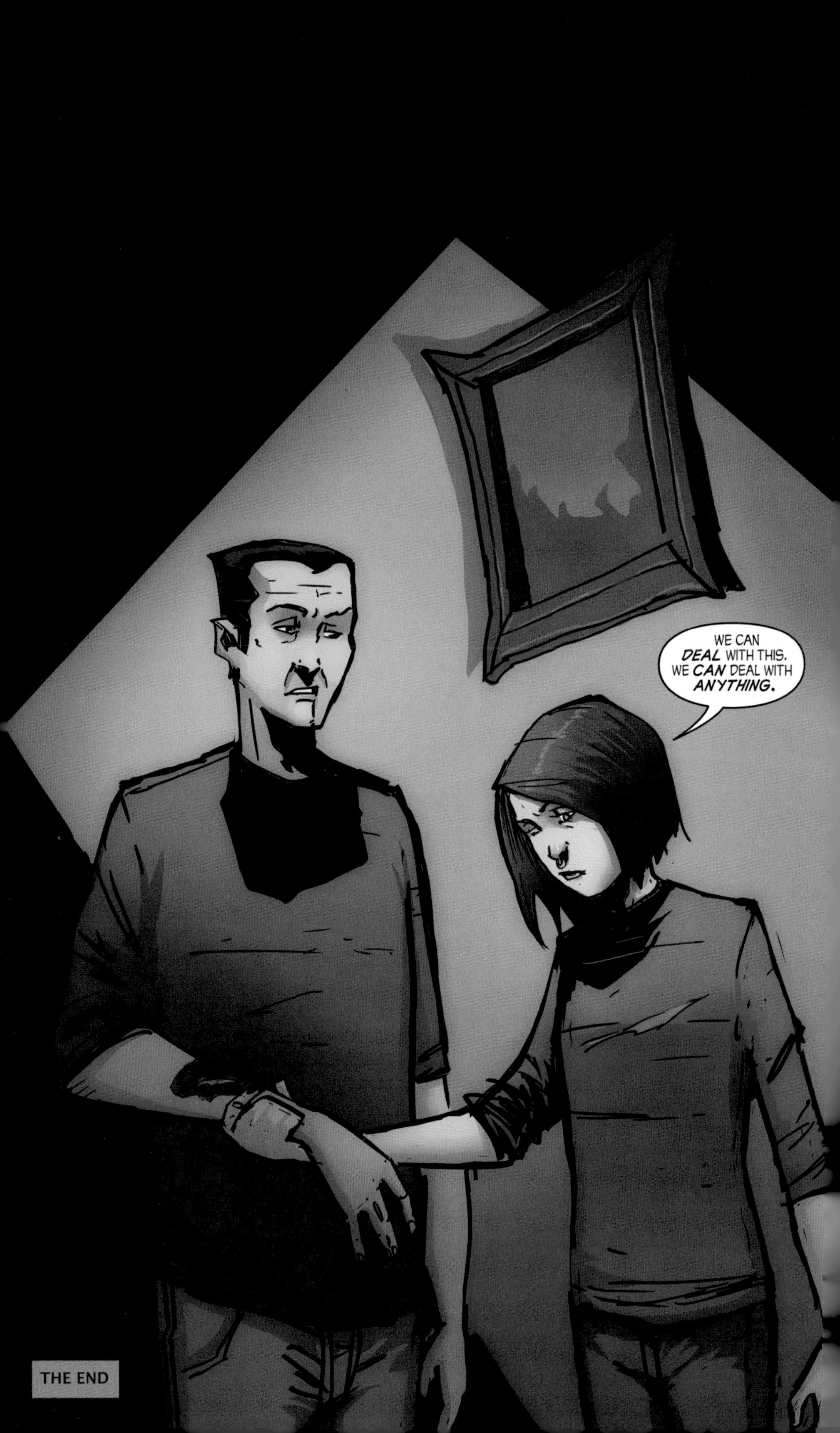
WE CAN DEAL WITH THIS. WE CAN DEAL WITH ANYTHING.
THE END

CHARACTER SKETCHES

BY DAMIEN WORM

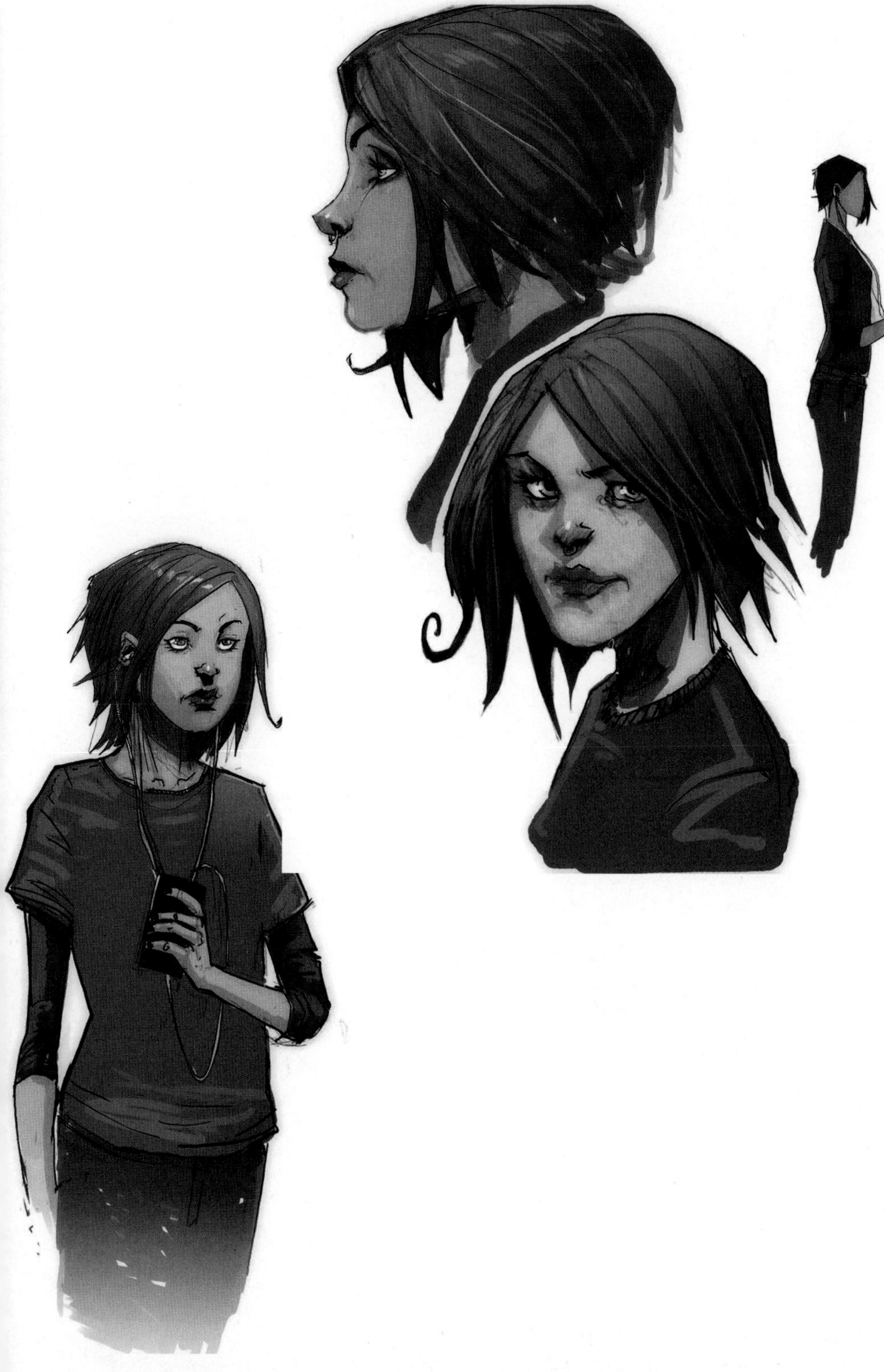

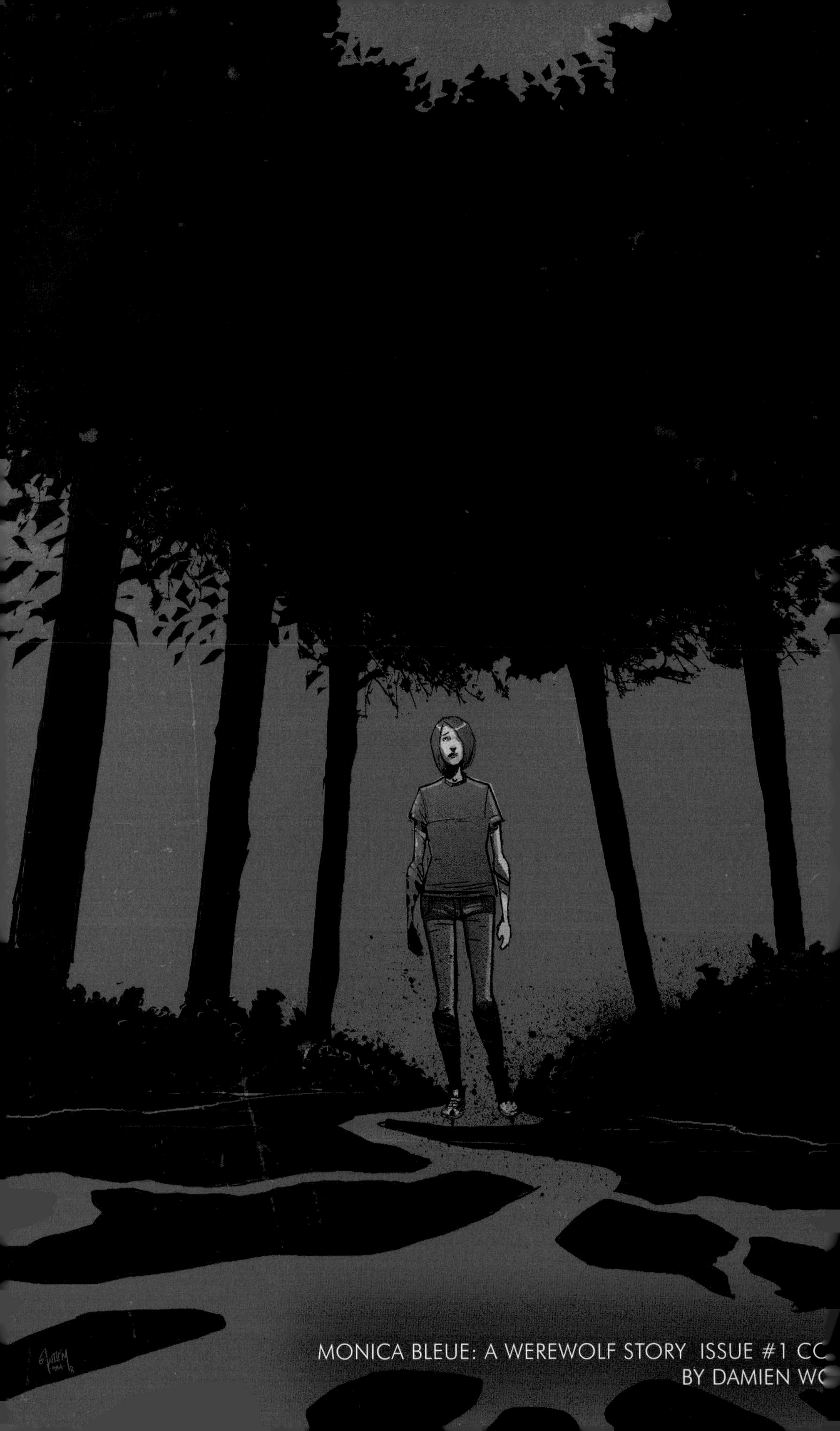
MONICA BLEUE: A WEREWOLF STORY ISSUE #1
BY DAMIEN

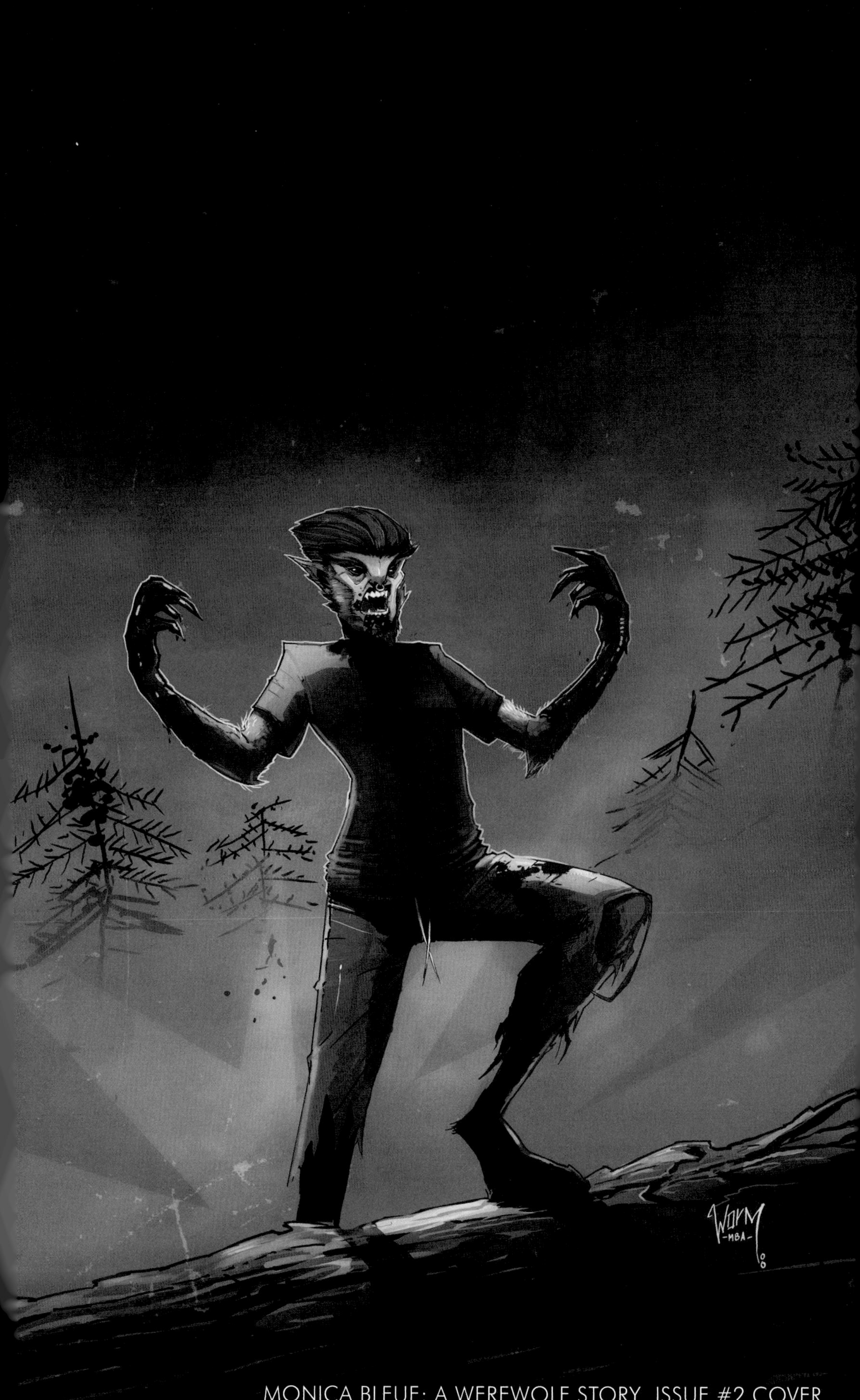
WORM
-MBA-

MONICA BLEUE: A WEREWOLF STORY ISSUE #2 COVER
BY DAMIEN WORM

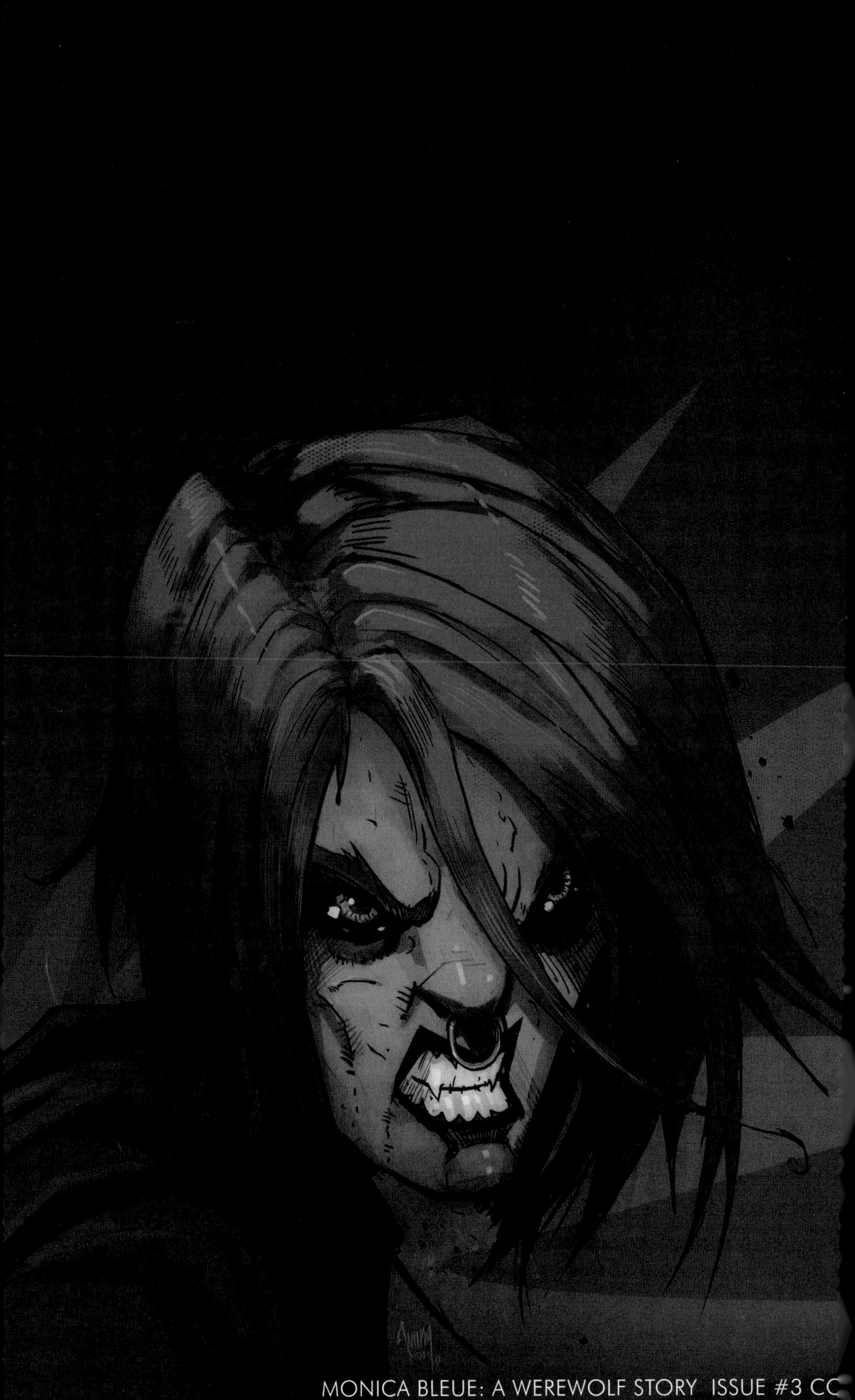

MONICA BLEUE: A WEREWOLF STORY ISSUE #3 CO
BY DAMIEN WO

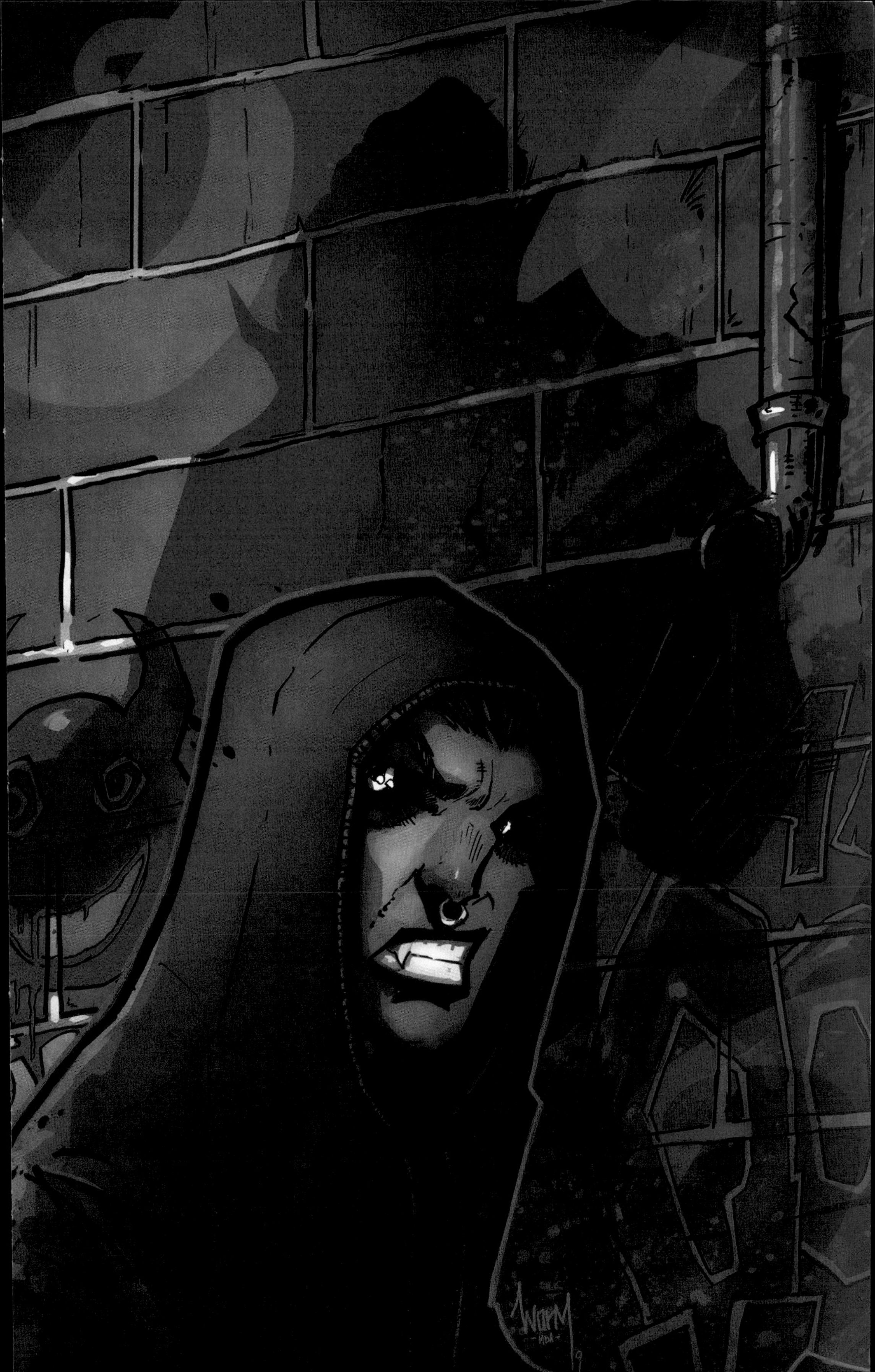

MONICA BLEUE: A WEREWOLF STORY ISSUE #4 COVER
BY DAMIEN WORM

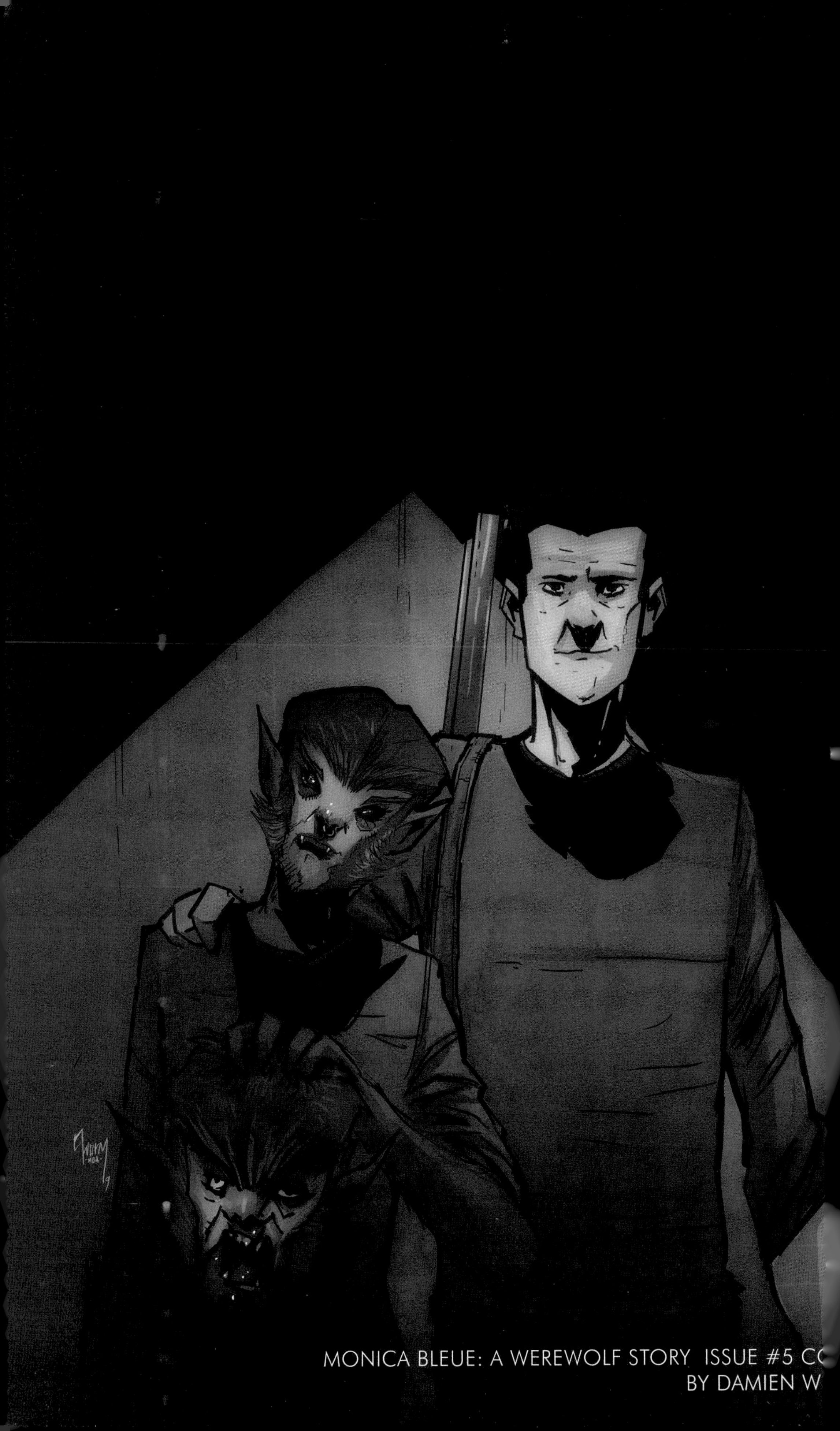
MONICA BLEUE: A WEREWOLF STORY ISSUE #5 C
BY DAMIEN W

CREATOR BIOS

PHOTO BY KYLE CASSIDY

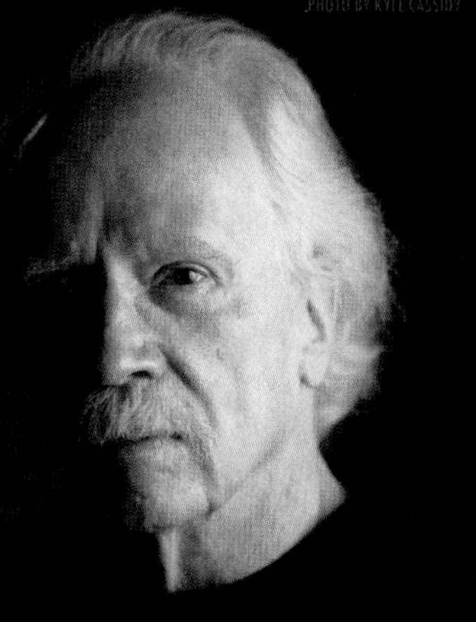

PHOTO BY DAN SANTONI

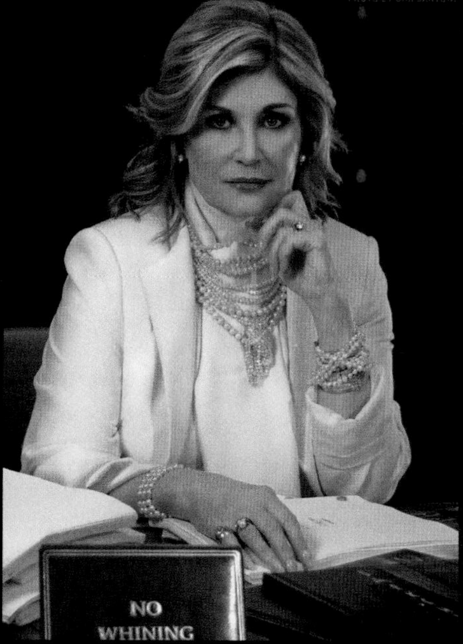
NO
WHINING

JOHN CARPENTER

ohn Carpenter's films are legendary: from the breakthrough ***Halloween*** (1978) to classics like ***Escape From New York, The Thing, Big Trouble in Little China*** and ***They Live***. His sci-fi love story, ***Starman***, earned Jeff Bridges a Best Actor Oscar nomination.

or the small screen, Carpenter directed the thriller ***Someone's Watching Me***, the acclaimed biographical nini-series, ***Elvis***, and the Showtime horror trilogy ***John Carpenter Presents Body Bags***. He also directed two episodes of Showtime's ***Masters Of Horror*** series.

e won the Cable Ace Award for writing the HBO novie, ***El Diablo***.

n the gaming world, he co-wrote the video game ***Fear*** for Warner Bros. Interactive.

the world of comics, Carpenter co-wrote the BOOM! ooks ***Big Trouble in Little China*** with Eric Powell nd the ***Old Man Jack*** series with Anthony Burch. He so co-wrote DC's ***Joker: Year Of The Villain*** with urch. At Storm King Comics he is the co-creator of the ward-winning series, ***John Carpenter's Asylum*** nd the acclaimed annual anthology collection, ***John arpenter's Tales for a HalloweeNight,*** as well as ***ohn Carpenter's Tales of Science Fiction, John arpenter Presents Storm Kids,*** and the upcoming ***ohn Carpenter's Night Terrors***.

SANDY KING

Artist, writer, film and television producer and CEO of Storm King Productions.

With a background in art, photography and animation, Sandy King's filmmaking career has included working with John Cassavetes, Francis Ford Coppola, Michael Mann, Walter Hill, John Hughs and John Carpenter.

She has produced films ranging from public service announcements on Hunger Awareness to a documentary on astronaut/teacher Christa McAuliffe, and major theatrical hits like ***They Live*** and ***John Carpenter's Vampires***. From working underwater with sharks in the Bahamas to converting 55 acres of New Mexican desert into the vast red planet of Mars, new challenges interest and excite her.

The world of comic books is no exception. It allows her to bring her art and story telling experience to a new discipline with an expanded group of collaborators. Through Storm King Comics, she has created and written the award-winning ***Asylum*** series, the multiple award winning ***Tales for a HalloweeNight*** anthologies, and both created and edits the monthly series, ***John Carpenter's Tales of Science Fiction***, the newest series, ***John Carpenter Presents Storm Kids***, and the upcoming ***John Carpenter's Night Terrors***.

STEVE NILES is best known for *30 Days Of Night, Crimin Macabre, Simon Dark, Mystery Society,* and *Frankenst Alive Alive*.

Niles currently works for comic publishers, including Black Mc IDW, Image and Dark Horse. He wrote *The October Faction* IDW, which is now a Netflix series.

30 Days Of Night was released in 2007 as a major mot picture. Other comics by Niles, including *Remains, Aleis Arcane* and *Freaks Of The Heartland,* have been optio for film.

Steve lives in the desert near Los Angeles with his wife Mor and a bunch of animals.

DAMIEN WORM is a comic artist and illustrator base Spain. He is co-creator of *October Faction* and *Mon & Madman* with Steve Niles. He also worked in s videogame related comics, like *Dark Souls, Bloodbo* and *Evil Within*.

JANICE CHIANG is a comic pioneer as one of the female letterers in the industry. From hand-lettering to dig she has forged the way for countless female comic ar Janice works with publishers old (Marvel) and new (I Ringo Award winning *Supergirls*). Comics Alliance hon Chiang as Outstanding Letterer of 2016 and ComicBook gave her the 2017 Golden Issue Award for Lettering. In 2017, Chiang was featured as one of 13 women who been making comics since before the internet on the Women Write About Comics. With her kind and forth nature, Janice has built a loyal family within the c community.